"One of the most readable espionage novels since *The Hunt for Red October*."

—*The Atlanta Journal-Constitution*

Sifting through reams of seemingly unrelated intelligence, CIA analyst Katharine Rule discovers a chilling pattern: a rash of Russian submarine sightings in the Baltic Sea . . . a crafty Soviet spymaster in command . . . a carefully planned invasion about to be launched.

Her suspicions, however, are dismissed by those higher up. They say her theory is too crazy to be true. But to Katharine, it's just crazy enough to succeed, unless she can stop it. If she's right, an attack sub has already penetrated friendly waters. Worse yet, the enemy has penetrated deep into her own life, so deep she can touch him. And in this game, one wrong touch can mean a new world war.

"Vibrating with tension and nonstop action."

—*Publishers Weekly*

"In the tradition of *The Hunt for Red October* . . . *Deep Lie* is as chilling and original as any novel I have read about the Cold War confrontation between Russia and the United States."

—Edward L. Beach, bestselling author
of *Run Silent, Run Deep*

"The action begins at full throttle and doesn't let up until the very end. Enthusiastically recommended for every popular fiction collection." —*Library Journal*

continued . . .

BOOKS BY STUART WOODS

FICTION

Mounting Fears‡
Hot Mahogany†
Beverly Hills Dead
Shoot Him If He Runs†
Fresh Disasters†
Short Straw§
Dark Harbor†
Iron Orchid*
Two Dollar Bill†
The Prince of Beverly Hills
Reckless Abandon†
Capital Crimes‡
Dirty Work†
Blood Orchid*
The Short Forever†
Orchid Blues*
Cold Paradise†
L.A. Dead†
The Run‡

Worst Fears Realized†
Orchid Beach*
Swimming to Catalina†
Dead in the Water†
Dirt†
Choke
Imperfect Strangers
Heat
Dead Eyes
L.A. Times
Santa Fe Rules§
New York Dead†
Palindrome
Grass Roots‡
White Cargo
Under the Lake
Run Before the Wind‡
Chiefs‡

TRAVEL

A Romantic's Guide to the Country Inns
of Britain and Ireland (1979)

MEMOIR

Blue Water, Green Skipper (1977)

*A Holly Barker Novel   †A Stone Barrington Novel
‡A Will Lee Novel   §An Ed Eagle Novel

DEEP LIE

Stuart Woods

A SIGNET BOOK

SIGNET
Published by New American Library, a division of
Penguin Group (USA) Inc., 375 Hudson Street,
New York, New York 10014, USA
Penguin Group (Canada), 90 Eglinton Avenue East, Suite 700, Toronto,
Ontario M4P 2Y3, Canada (a division of Pearson Penguin Canada Inc.)
Penguin Books Ltd., 80 Strand, London WC2R 0RL, England
Penguin Ireland, 25 St. Stephen's Green, Dublin 2,
Ireland (a division of Penguin Books Ltd.)
Penguin Group (Australia), 250 Camberwell Road, Camberwell, Victoria 3124,
Australia (a division of Pearson Australia Group Pty. Ltd.)
Penguin Books India Pvt. Ltd., 11 Community Centre, Panchsheel Park,
New Delhi - 110 017, India
Penguin Group (NZ), 67 Apollo Drive, Rosedale, North Shore 0632,
New Zealand (a division of Pearson New Zealand Ltd.)
Penguin Books (South Africa) (Pty.) Ltd., 24 Sturdee Avenue,
Rosebank, Johannesburg 2196, South Africa

Penguin Books Ltd., Registered Offices:
80 Strand, London WC2R 0RL, England

Published by Signet, an imprint of New American Library, a division of Penguin
Group (USA) Inc. Previously published in W. W. Norton & Company, Inc.,
Avon, and HarperCollins editions.

First Signet Printing, August 2009
10 9 8 7 6 5 4 3 2 1

This book is for Ebbe Carlsson

1

Oskar Oskarsson squinted into the brightly lit mist and looked for a bird. Somewhere above his boat was sunshine, but down on the water, where he was, there was fog. It was like being inside a fluorescent tube, surrounded by gases radiating light. He sighted a petrel off to starboard and from its presence estimated there were, perhaps, five hundred meters of visibility, no more. For Oskarsson, for what he was doing at this moment, conditions were perfect.

He throttled back to 1000 rpm, turned, and nodded at Ebbe. The boy smiled faintly, released the brake on the main winch, and began feeding out the trawl, a long sock of steel mesh that would drag the bottom, twenty meters down. Oskarsson watched with satisfaction as his grandson performed the work; not expertly, just yet, but competently. The boy was wearing only jeans and a T-shirt. These youngsters never felt the chill. Oskarsson marveled at the beauty of the boy's body, the well-muscled, perfectly proportioned physique. All young

Swedish men looked like that when he was a boy, he thought, the result of hard work and hard play. Now they were skinny hippies and fat accountants. Ebbe was the exception, not the rule. The boy skied in winter, hiked in summer and rowed for his school. If he was no academic, he performed physical tasks with joy and little apparent effort.

The boy's father, Oskarsson's son, ran a discotheque in Stockholm. A discotheque—imagine! Oskarsson had visited his son, once, and had been taken there. God in heaven, what a place! The noise—they called it music, these days; the flashing lights; the heat; the smells! It was no way for a grown man to make his living. Ebbe would not do such work; he had told his grandfather that. He knew he was not bright enough for university, and he did not mind. He would come to his grandfather when he was finished with school—only another year—and, together, they would fish. They would make money, too. The light trawler was easily handled by two good men—no crew to split the catch with. The boy would have a good life with his grandfather, and in a few years, when he knew all the places, he could take a partner, and Oskarsson would retire and take a share for the gift of the boat. The boat was good, and Oskarsson was glad he had spent so much of his profits on maintenance. If the boy took care of it, it would last him for many more years. Ebbe's father would be furious when the boy came to his grandfather to fish. All the money he had made at the discotheque, and his son a common fisherman! Oskarsson smiled at the thought of it.

When the trawl was fully played out, Oskarsson

waved the boy to the wheelhouse and unfolded the chart. "Here." He pointed with a thick, gnarled finger. His were a fisherman's hands, permanently swollen from years of cold-water work, fingers scarred, twisted from badly healed broken bones, the daily hazard of working bare-handed with unforgiving tools and powerful machinery. "Here we will fill the trawl to bursting."

The boy's brow furrowed, and he pointed. "But what about this, Grandfather?" he asked, running a finger along a ragged magenta line. "This says we are in a restricted area. Why restricted? Can we get into trouble?"

"It's the naval base at Karlskrona," the old man replied, pointing off into the fog. "They don't want the Russian trawlers sneaking in here and taking pictures of them." He jabbed his thumb into his own chest. "But I'm not Russian, and neither are you, eh?" He winked at the boy. "And the navy won't miss the fish."

The boy laughed. "If you say so, it's all right with me."

"The fish know it's restricted, too, you see. They think nobody will catch them here, but on foggy mornings like this, you and I can pop in early, trawl for a couple of hours, and be away before the mist burns off."

"Don't they have radar? The fog doesn't affect that, does it?"

"Sure, sure, they have radar, but I've taken down our reflector, and a wooden boat like ours doesn't show up so well, I think. At least, they've never caught me. I think if they see us on the radar when it's foggy, they don't pay much attention, because the Russian boats would only come when it's fine, so they can take their pictures. And even if they do catch me, they'll just say, 'Go and fish someplace else, old fellow.' It's not a big thing."

Oskarsson wasn't worried about getting caught. He knew these waters better than any navigator in the Swedish navy. He had been born on the island of Utlangen, not far away, and he had fished here under sail in the old days. He could dart among the islands and away from a patrol boat. He would maintain a proprietary interest in these waters, no matter how many sailor boys the Swedish navy sent here in their fast boats.

They motored along slowly for a quarter of an hour, towing the trawl and chatting companionably. Then there was a loud creaking noise and the boat suddenly stopped short, throwing them both against the bulkhead. Oskarsson quickly cut the throttle and put the engine out of gear.

"What's happening, Grandfather?" the boy asked.

The old man did not reply immediately but put the engine into gear again, and eased the throttle forward. They moved for a few seconds; then the trawl cable went bar tight and the boat stopped again. "We're hooked onto some obstruction," Oskarsson finally replied. He consulted the chart. "There's no wreck charted anywhere near here. I hope the sailor boys haven't sunk something for target practice and left it here. Get the trip cable onto the auxiliary winch, and let's see if we can free the trawl that way."

Ebbe went aft and wound the light cable onto the auxiliary power winch. Oskarsson put the engine into gear again and gave the boat some throttle. "Now," he called out, "now give it some winch. The boy threw the switch and tailed the cable as it began to wind onto the winch. It was tripping, Oskarsson thought, it's going to trip, and we'll be free. Then the trip cable went bar tight, too, and the boat stopped again. "Off! Cut the power," he shouted. The boy threw the switch, and the winch stopped. "Cleat it there; I'm going to try something else."

Oskarsson put the engine into gear and the helm hard to port. "We'll make a circle and reverse the trawl," he called to the boy. "That way it should come off whatever it's snagged on." He hoped so. To replace it would cost thousands of kroner, and even though his insurance would pay most of it, it wouldn't pay for the time lost while the steel sock was being made. You didn't buy a trawl off the shelf.

He swung the boat wide to prevent motoring over the cable, then edged to port, in toward the obstruction, to get some slack. He held his course for a moment; then the boat started to swing to starboard. This baffled Oskarsson for a moment, since he now had the helm hard to port; then he realized that, although the boat's bow had swung to starboard, it was not traveling in that direction. The boat, astonishingly, was running *sideways*. Whatever he was hooked onto was *moving*.

Oskarsson let go the helm and started aft, but the wheel spun sharply to starboard, and the resulting lurch of the boat threw him heavily to the deck. He struggled to his feet, holding a bruised shoulder and shouted to the boy. "Quick, we've got to let go the trawl!" The boat swung back in the opposite direction, then settled. They were now being towed backward.

"What is it, Grandfather?" the boy called, holding tightly to the auxiliary winch. "What's happening?"

"Let go the trip cable!" the old man shouted, struggling back toward the boat's controls. The boy quickly did as he was told, uncleating the cable and unwinding it free of the winch. Still the boat moved backward, and with increasing speed. Horrified, Oskarsson threw the engine into reverse and opened the throttle wide. He had to get some slack in the trawl cable. The boy immediately saw what he was trying to do and moved to the main winch. There were still a few meters of the main trawl cable wound around it. Oskarsson tried to steer the boat in reverse and watched as Ebbe struggled with the brake. If he could release it, they would have slack to unhook the cable, and they would be free.

There was too much load on the winch, though, and the brake would not budge. Oskarsson felt pride as the boy, without hesitating for orders, grabbed an ax from the bulkhead and swung it toward the brake handle. A single blow freed it, and the winch drum spun wildly. The boat dug in its broad stern and nearly stopped, throwing them both to the deck. Oskarsson flung himself toward the cable's cleat, knowing he only had seconds to free it before the slack was snatched up again. He got hold of it and was trying to get some purchase with a foot when the cable was snatched taut again. Oskarsson screamed as the cable crushed his hand against the winch drum. Within seconds of heart-stopping pain, the sawing effect of the cable's strands took away his fingers.

Oskarsson fell back onto the deck and looked incredulously at his hand, which now had only a thumb and was gushing blood. He forgot about what was happening to his boat and dived for his "string bag," a canvas hold-all fixed to the bulkhead that held remnants of line. He quickly came up with a piece of light nylon rope, wound it around his wrist and, one end in his teeth, pulled it tight and knotted it, all the while wondering at the fact that it didn't hurt anymore, that a strange warmth was flooding into his mangled hand.

Now he turned his attention to the boat again. Even at full throttle in reverse, it was still being towed backward, he reckoned at eight or nine knots, increasing every moment. Water was flooding over the stern, and in its wash, Ebbe was struggling to his feet, looking stunned from his fall. Oskarsson looked about him helplessly. Nothing in a long life at sea had prepared him for a situation like this, an absolutely, ridiculously implausible situation. He was up to his knees in water, now, and the boat had to be doing an incredible fifteen knots, stern first.

"What is it? What is it?" the boy was calling to him over the roar of rushing water.

He did not know. He only knew that it couldn't last much longer. Then, as if in response to his thought, there was a sound of unbearable straining of timber and metal, and the two forward bolts which held the bottom plate of the main winch to the deck came loose from their moorings.

"Ebbe!" he screamed. "Get out of the way! The winch is going!"

"What?" the boy yelled back. He was still stunned. "What?"

There was a final, explosive tearing, and the whole part of the deck to which the winch was bolted came away. The winch, still cleated to the trawl cable by which they were being towed, flew over the stern, striking the boy full in the face as it went.

Then all was suddenly, impossibly quiet. The boat came immediately to a stop and bobbed in the light sea. A trail of bubbles disappeared astern with the trawl and the winch. The engine, by now flooded, had come to a stop. Oskarsson stood in water to his thighs. He waded quickly aft, to where Ebbe's body floated, spilling red and gray matter into the water around it. Oskarsson gathered the boy in his arms and sat down on a gunwale, now only inches above the water. The boat's inbuilt buoyancy was keeping it afloat, although the decks were awash. Most of the boy's head was gone, and Oskarsson hugged the limp corpse to him, sobbing.

From somewhere out in the fog he could hear a boat's engine closing fast on him, but he didn't care. Now there would be no days with his grandson, telling him, showing him where the fish were and how to catch them. Now there was only old age and loneliness, stretching toward death. He wanted it now. He plucked at the knot at his wrist until it came loose, and the blood flowed from his finger stumps again.

The patrol boat came out of the fog, now, and slowed. A loud, metallic voice came at him from across the water. "You are in a restricted area; you must leave at once. Please follow me. You are in a restricted area . . ." The boat came alongside his swamped craft, and the voice stopped. The tanned face of a young naval lieutenant came from behind the loud-hailer and looked at him from a few yards away. The face turned white.

Oskarsson looked up at the pale boy in the ensign's uniform. "Go fuck yourself, sailor boy," he said.

2

Senior Lieutenant Jan Helder stood in the conning tower of Whiskey class submarine 184 and breathed fresh air. It was frigid. Murmansk, the headquarters of the Soviet Northern Fleet, is above the Arctic Circle and May there is not like May in other, more reasonable places. Helder watched closely as the sub was made fast in its berth, then looked up to see two men striding in step down the dock, toward where his men were readying the gangplank—a captain third grade in a well-cut uniform and a civilian in a bad suit. He didn't know either of them, and he didn't like it. Rewards in the Soviet Navy did not arrive in the company of a captain third grade and a political officer.

Helder's first thoughts were of what he might have done. He had drunk too much in the officer's mess the night before sailing on his just-completed cruise in the North Atlantic, but everybody drank too much. Since he was, normally, the most careful and correct of officers, he could think of no other infraction, except that he was Estonian. That, of course, might be enough.

He got down on deck in time to meet them as they came aboard. Neither man asked permission. "Captain Helder?" the naval captain asked. Who else? Helder thought. The man's tone carried the sort of formality that accompanied an arrest.

"Yes, Comrade Captain," Helder replied, snapping to attention and saluting. He felt somewhat foolish, engaging in military courtesies in his condition; he had not shaved nor bathed properly for five weeks. He could have, of course, since his facilities were somewhat better than those of his crew, but the crew liked it when their captain remained as filthy as they.

"You are to report to the chief administrative officer at staff headquarters in Leningrad at once," the captain said, stiffly, and thrust an envelope at him. "Here is a written order to that effect and a pass to staff headquarters."

Helder took the envelope. He was amused at the "at once." Leningrad was more than six hundred miles to the south. "Thank you, Comrade Captain. If I may be permitted to bathe and change . . ." He was wearing a filthy cotton coverall over a heavy naval sweater that used to be white. Out of the corner of his eye, Helder saw a truck draw to a halt next to the gangplank. A truck, not a car. Bad.

"There is no time for that; you must leave at once."

"Of course, Comrade Captain. If I may have a moment to collect my gear from my cabin."

"Your gear will be forwarded to you," the civilian said, testily.

"You are relieved, Lieutenant," the captain said.

Helder's heart sank. The man was no longer bothering with the honorary "captain" due the commander of a vessel. But then, he had been relieved. He was no longer entitled to that designation.

"Get going, then," said the civilian.

It offended Helder's military sensibilities to leave his ship in this manner, with not even an opportunity to speak to his officers, but he saluted again and walked quickly toward the gangplank. A seaman saluted him, and Helder said, calmly, "Tell the executive officer that I have been relieved, and he is in command pending further instructions."

As he approached the truck there didn't seem to be a guard, so, as a gesture of optimism, he got in beside the driver, instead of climbing into the back. The driver said nothing to him, but executed a quick U-turn and roared off down the dock.

Twenty-five minutes later, he was in an uninsulated transport airplane, the only passenger among a load of unlabeled crates. The noise was horrific, there were no seats, and it was freezing. He curled up on a deflated rubber life raft, stuffed the corners of his filthy handkerchief into his ears, and tried to get some sleep. As he drifted into a half-doze, he wondered why they hadn't just shot him on the dock. Why all this bother?

Now it was all over. Thirteen years of naval college, training, and service at sea, nearly all of it on submarines, bloody hard work, and it was over, finished. He had been due for a more modern sub, maybe of the Tango class, and, maybe, a promotion. He was already too long in grade. The worst that could happen was death, but since they were taking all the trouble to transport him to Leningrad and the staff headquarters, that seemed unlikely. A quick court martial on whatever charge, reduction in rank, and an unpleasant transfer seemed the best he could hope for. Vladivostok, he reckoned, six thousand miles by the slowest possible means of transport, and the remainder of his service as a cargo officer on the docks. He would become the oldest ensign in the history of the Soviet Navy. He dozed off, too exhausted to care.

Helder woke as the aircraft slammed into the runway. Bloody green pilot, he thought. He went immediately back to sleep and refused to wake up again until a blast of even colder air hit him and a voice shouted his name, none too respectfully. A KGB sergeant was beckoning him from the plane's doorway, his voice suddenly too loud as the engines died. Helder climbed stiffly down the steel ladder and followed the soldier toward a huge building. It was dark and raining lightly. Helder looked at his watch: just past midnight. They entered a door and climbed some stairs, and Helder found himself in Leningrad's civilian airport. They walked briskly through the determinedly modern, nearly empty building. Only a group of Western-looking tourists, smiling weakly under the dour gaze of young KGB immigration officers in their neat uniforms and green epaulets, shared the huge terminal with Helder and the sergeant. Helder's eyes briefly met those of a pretty young girl. English? American? He wished he had time to find out. Where he was going he would be lucky to find women at all, let alone pretty Western ones.

Another truck. Helder dozed, undisturbed by the silent sergeant, as they entered the city. He woke again as they passed the old Admiralty, now a naval college. Helder had taken an electronics course there in his training days. They passed into the large square before the Winter Palace, now part of the Hermitage Museum, and rattled over the wet and shiny cobblestones toward the triumphal archway that was the entrance to General Staff Headquarters. The truck passed through the archway, turned right, passed the main entrance, turned another corner and stopped before a door manned by a single guard. Helder tore open the envelope he had been given in Murmansk and fished out his pass. The guard inspected it carefully, then nodded, saluted and motioned him through the doors, turning up his nose slightly at Helder's filthy clothes. Helder had the feeling that if he hadn't been wearing his officer's cap, he wouldn't have made it past the man. Inside, he was met by a young woman in an ensign's uniform. "Captain Helder, please follow me," she said curtly, and started down the long hallway, which was lit only by every third chandelier at this time of night.

At least he was "captain" again. Her mistake, probably. He followed her like a puppy, her leather heels clicking on the czarist marble, the rubber soles of his canvas deck shoes squeaking on the hard surface. They walked at least a kilometer, he reckoned, past shut office doors with departmental designations. They saw no one. The ensign turned down a wider hallway and passed through a door marked "Chief Administrative Officer." Another woman sitting at a desk nodded at her, and she continued through the anteroom without stopping and knocked on the inner door. A voice bade her enter. She opened the door, waited for Helder to enter, followed him into the room, and closed the door gently. A short, fat contra-admiral was sitting behind a large desk, reading a document. The charges, probably.

Helder came to attention and saluted. "Comrade Admiral, Senior Lieutenant Helder reporting as ordered."

The admiral looked at him and winced. "You look like shit," he said.

"I am very sorry, Comrade Admiral, there was no time . . ."

"Of course, of course." The admiral fished an envelope from a desk drawer and handed it to Helder. "You are to report to the commanding officer of"—he hesitated—"a special brigade in Liepaja at once," he said, then seemed to think better of it. "Well, perhaps not at once. An hour or so won't matter." He reached into a drawer, and removed a printed pad and signed it. He ripped off the page and held it out for the woman, who stepped forward to receive it. "Take him to the headquarters depot, wake the sergeant, and get him a decent uniform. Find him a bath and a shave, too." The admiral reached back into the drawer and produced a bottle of vodka and a glass. He poured a stiff drink and offered it to Helder. "Here, you look as though you need this."

Helder knocked back the drink and set the glass down on the desk. "Thank you very much, Comrade Admiral. I wonder if I may ask . . ."

"You may not," the admiral replied. "Get out of here."

Apparently, there would be no court-martial, and there had been no mention of a reduction in rank. Still,

Liepaja. What the hell did they want with him in Latvia? There were no submarines there. The Baltic Fleet was based in Leningrad and in Baltiisk, in Lithuania, down near the Polish border. Dock officer in Liepaja. Not as bad as Vladivostok, anyway. At least he would be almost at home, which was very unusual. Officers from the republics of Estonia, Latvia, and Lithuania were invariably assigned to duty in other parts of the Soviet Union. The Politburo distrusted the independent attitudes of these peoples. They were not Russian enough, and their young men who served in the forces were stationed in places where their Russification could proceed, unimpeded by nationalist sentiment.

Helder saluted the admiral and followed the woman again. An hour and a half later, he was on another plane, shaved, bathed, and newly uniformed. This time there were heating and seats. He grabbed an hour's sleep before they landed in Liepaja, where a car was waiting, another improvement. It was ten in the morning, now, and there was time only to ascertain that they were headed toward the sea before he fell asleep again.

He woke as the car lurched to a stop at a heavily fortified gate. His pass and face and that of the driver were carefully examined before they were permitted inside. They drove down a smoothly paved street which descended a hillside overlooking the Baltic; ahead of them to their left was a sort of tidal lake, joined to the sea by only a narrow passage. They passed buildings which looked newly completed and others still under construction. As they continued down the hill, Helder suddenly realized that what he had thought was the water's edge was really a huge, flat-topped building along the water-front. What had fooled him was that the entire shelter had raised edges and the roof held a foot or two of water. Bloody clever, Helder thought. In a satellite photograph, the building would appear to be part of the bay. Make a lovely skating rink in winter, too.

It now occurred to him that all the buildings he was passing looked civilian and oddly Western. There was a clutch of shops, not just the usual naval store with its tobacco and vodka, and there was a petrol station. Al-though there was more traffic than would normally ap-pear on the streets of a similar-sized Soviet town, he saw no military vehicles, only civilian cars and trucks, and yet he saw no school, no children, no housewives with prams doing the daily shopping. The place seemed to be nei-ther a military base nor an ordinary town. One last thing intrigued him before he reached his destination. His car drove past a sports center that would have been at home in a much larger city. There was a huge building which, no doubt, housed a gymnasium and a swimming pool, and he counted thirty-six tennis courts down near the water. Past these was a small forest of masts, which meant a marina of some size. As the car stopped before what looked like a small office building, it occurred to him that he must be on one of the most privileged installations in the Soviet Union. So was its commander privileged, he saw as he got out of the car. In the reserved parking space closest to the building's door was parked a silver Mercedes 500 SE, brand-new, from the look of it. He had seen one in Moscow, once.

He was met at the door by a small, very pretty blond

army sergeant and conducted into the building. On entering, he felt as if he had arrived in a foreign country. Nothing he saw seemed of Soviet origin. Even the carpeting underfoot, the hardware on the bronzed glass doors, and the standard of construction of the building were markedly different from the shabby Soviet building efforts of recent years. The place had what he imagined was a Scandinavian air about it. They passed through another set of the glass doors and into an open area with a dozen or fifteen desks. The typewriters bore the letters IBM, and he saw half a dozen computer terminals of futuristic design. But what impressed him more than anything was the appearance of the young women, wearing uniforms of various Soviet services, who sat at the desks and moved around the room. They were nearly all blond, all of trim, athletic figure, and there was not a dog in the bunch. Women in the Soviet military were pretty rough-looking sorts, as a rule. Never in the Soviet Union had Helder been in a room which contained so many attractive young women. A surge of randiness involuntarily swelled inside him. A sight like this after five weeks on a submarine was almost too much.

They passed into a small reception area, and Helder hoped he might be asked to wait there a few minutes, so that he might look at the girls some more, but it was not to be. They barely slowed down as they moved into a large, square, sunlit room. A glass-topped desk lay dead ahead of him, and the wall behind it was mostly covered by two very large, backlit maps. He recognized at a glance that one was a nautical chart of the Baltic, and the other, a map of Sweden.

There was no one at the desk, but his attention was directed to his right, to a group of leather furniture. A naval officer wearing the insignia of Admiral of the Fleet sat in one of the chairs. Helder snapped to and saluted. "Senior Lieutenant Helder reporting as ordered, Comrade Admiral."

The admiral leaned forward and snuffed out a cigarette in a large ashtray. "Report to the colonel," he said. Helder looked further to his right where, in another chair, sat a man wearing the uniform of a colonel in the marine infantry.

Helder was not surprised by this deference from the admiral. In the Soviet military any appointment has assigned to it a maximum, not a minimum rank, as in Western services, and an officer's importance is judged not by his rank, but by the appointment he holds. During World War II, Helder knew, it had not been unheard of for a senior lieutenant to command an army division, while the regimental commanders beneath him might be majors or colonels. He saluted again. "Lieutenant Helder reporting, Comrade Colonel."

The admiral rose. "Well, I will leave you to it, Viktor," he said to the colonel, and made his exit.

The colonel waved a hand, but did not rise as the admiral left. When the admiral had gone, the colonel rose and walked toward Helder. The lieutenant chose the moment to steal a look at him. He looked to be in his early forties, quite tall, trim, fit-looking. He had a high forehead and a thick head of salt-and-pepper hair cut considerably better than was usual in the Soviet military. Helder thought he looked like a prosperous Western businessman jn a Soviet uniform. The colonel stuck out his hand.

"My name is Majorov; I am very pleased to meet you, Helder," he said in perfectly accented British English.

Helder was a little jarred. He had never before been greeted by a new commanding officer in this fashion, let alone in English. Rather cautiously, he shook the colonel's hand.

"Please sit down," the colonel said, waving him to a chair.

Everything instilled in Helder by thirteen years of Soviet military training and service resisted this suggestion, and he must have showed it, for the colonel chuckled.

"Please," he said. "You must begin to get used to our informal ways here." He waved Helder toward the chair again.

Helder sat down, but he could not immediately bring himself to lean against the back of the chair.

"Would you like a drink?" the colonel asked. "A gin and tonic, perhaps? Please do have a drink."

"Thank you, Comrade Colonel." The colonel went to a rosewood cabinet, mixed the drink, and handed it to him. Helder sipped the drink tentatively. His opinion of the colonel climbed as he noticed that it contained a wedge of bright green lime. Who was this colonel that he could obtain a lime in Latvia?

The colonel mixed himself a drink and sat down opposite Helder. "Now," he said, smiling slightly, "tell me a little about yourself—your background and upbringing. Please continue to speak English."

This was something else Helder had never been asked

to do before by a commanding officer. It surprised him even more, because there was a thick file on the coffee table between them which he knew must contain every detail of his life since birth. He realized that the colonel probably wanted to hear him speak English. "Comrade colonel, my full name is Jan Helder, no middle name; I was born in Tallinn, on the Estonian coast; I am thirty-one years old. I attended, uh, primary and uh, secondary schools in Tallinn, then university in Moscow, where I studied both English and physics. I also speak Swedish, which is commonly spoken on the coast where I grew up. After graduation I requested and was assigned to the Naval College at Leningrad. Upon graduation I was assigned to the Northern Fleet at Murmansk. After two years of general duties I was accepted for submarine training and upon finishing was assigned to a series of Whiskey and Juliet class boats. I had one year at the Command Academy in Moscow, then returned to the fleet. I served as navigation and executive officer in Juliets, and for the past twenty months I have commanded Whiskey 184, conducting training exercises and reporting on NATO shipping movements in the North Atlantic."

The colonel nodded. "Very good, Helder, your American accent is excellent, though a bit stilted. But that will improve as we go along." The colonel shifted in his seat and sipped his drink. "Of course, I know all you have just told me, and a great deal more. I know that your parents were both physicians, and that your father was decorated for his resistance against the Nazis, that your mother was also a talented painter. I know that you had a place on the 1976 Olympic sailing team in single-handed Finn dinghies but that you suffered a compound fracture of your left thigh when struck by a taxi in Leningrad and were unable to compete. In fact, as you must have surmised, I know just about everything about you, or you would not be here now."

"Thank you for your trust, Comrade Colonel," Helder replied.

The colonel's eyebrows shot up. "Oh, you have not yet won my trust, Helder, merely my interest." He smiled. "Still, it is a serious interest, and having read your record, I have little doubt that you will do well here."

"Thank you, Comrade Colonel."

"Now, Helder, perhaps you would like to know a little about this place and what you will be doing here." The colonel rose and began to walk idly about the room as he talked. "I command here and . . . elsewhere. This is a SPETSNAZ installation, but perhaps you had already realized that."

Helder had not realized it, although there had been clues aplenty, and a dual twinge of excitement and fear jolted him. SPETSNAZ, the naval special forces, was a closely guarded secret, even within the Soviet navy. All Helder knew about it was that it was an elite force, drawn from the finest examples of Soviet youth, scholastically and athletically, both men and women. Rumor had it that they were trained to do all sorts of dirty work, and that, although the service was, in theory, an arm of the navy, control of it was exercised, at least in part, by the KGB.

Majorov went on. "Each of the four fleets, Northern, Pacific, Baltic, and Black Sea, of course, has its own diversionary SPETSNAZ subunits, but here, in Liepaja, we are a special brigade, made up of personnel drawn from sub-units in all the fleets." Majorov leaned forward. "What we are here, one might say, is the *crème de la crème de la crème* of all the SPETSNAZ subunits."

Helder was impressed and tried to look it.

"Your transfer here does not mean that you are now SPETSNAZ," Majorov continued. "You are still carried on the rolls of the northern submarine fleet, although for some hours, now, you have been carried as a captain, third grade. Congratulations."

"Thank you, Comrade Colonel." Helder was nearly overwhelmed. The position of submarine commander carried a maximum rank of captain first grade, and he had already been too long in grade as a senior lieutenant. Now he had skipped a rank; captain third grade was the equivalent of full commander in Western navies. He had caught up and surpassed nearly all of his classmates in a single promotion. Not only that, but he had been given the promotion at the beginning of his assignment, which was unheard of.

"You are also listed as a division commander," Majorov said.

Helder's heart went wild. A division meant nuclear subs. Diesels were grouped in brigades.

"But we will not use rank here, nor will we address each other as 'comrade,'" Majorov said. "You may continue to address me as 'colonel' and as 'sir,' but all others you will address by surname. When you get to know your fellow officers well enough to address them by their first names, you will not employ the patronymic. I hope that is clear; it is very important."

"Yes, Colonel."

"About two-thirds of your colleagues here speak Swedish and English, as you do; the remainder speak only English and, perhaps another European language. You will conduct all your training and personal conversations in English, except in those few cases where our instructors speak only Russian. It is most important that you continue to refine the American character of your English. With that end in mind, you will find a television receiver in your quarters which broadcasts American programs." Majorov smiled wryly. "I know that your training and resolve as a Soviet citizen will prevent you from becoming corrupted by this unaccustomed and entirely decadent influence."

Helder smiled back. "Of course, sir."

"You will be issued naval, army, and marine infantry uniforms. Please alternate your dress among these. This is mostly for the benefit of the locals in Liepaja, who have been told that this is an interservice sports training facility. You will also be issued civilian clothing of Western manufacture. Please wear this when you are off duty. You need to become used to it, and it needs to become worn."

Majorov raised a cautionary finger. "You will not leave this installation under any circumstances during your training. If you wish to sail, you will not leave the saltwater lake adjacent to the base nor land anywhere except at the base marina. You will have no contact whatever with the outside. If you should die, you will be buried here. This is your home until your assignment is completed."

Majorov rose. "Well, that's about it for now. I want

you to take a few days to acclimate yourself; think of it as leave. I trust you will not find your stay here too confining. The officers training here have a nickname for the place: they call it 'Malibu,' after an apparently very attractive place in California." He smiled. "I rather like that. There is much to divert you here, not the least of which is the group of young women who serve as support personnel. One of them will now take you to your quarters and explain the various facilities of the base."

"Thank you, sir," Helder said. "I assure you of my very best performance." It occurred to him that he had not been given the slightest idea what duties he was to perform, and it didn't seem a good idea to ask.

Majorov smiled and put a hand on Helder's shoulder. "I am sure you will do very well, and when the going gets tough in your training, remember that the maximum rank of a division commander is, of course, contra-admiral. If you succeed in the work here, and if the work itself succeeds, I promise you the achievement of maximum rank faster than you ever dreamed possible, and I will not exclude the possibility of flotilla commander." Majorov gazed at him intently. "What I am talking about, Helder, is the classical circumstance that gives an outstanding officer the chance of a lifetime to make his whole career."

Helder blinked. The classical circumstance which created that sort of opportunity was war.

He left the office and followed the same blond sergeant out of the building and across a grassy lawn to a long, low building with many doors. She led him to one, opened it, and stood back for him to enter. Helder had never seen anything like it. The room was about fifteen feet square.

One wall contained a built-in wardrobe, bookcases, and a desk. There was a comfortable-looking leather chair, a reading lamp, and a Bang & Olufson television set with a small black box on top. A door led to a private, tiled bathroom. The curtains and bedcover were of a bright, Scandinavian fabric. On the desk were copies of *Time*, *Newsweek*, and the *International Herald Tribune*, only two days old. But of all the things in the room, Helder was most impressed by the bed. He had never slept in a double bed, except in a hotel or a whorehouse.

"Let me show you how the television works," the girl said, picking up a remote control box from the bedside table. She switched it on and rapidly began changing channels. "You get the same television here as you would in New York," she said, "although there's a seven-hour time difference. It's pirated from an American satellite. There are the three major networks, four movie channels, sports, cartoons, transmissions from the American House of Representatives—altogether, fifty-four channels. There's a *TV Guide* magazine to help you figure it out."

"Fifty-four channels!" Helder was stunned.

"Give me your wristwatch," she said. He handed it to her, and she gave him a massive Rolex Explorer. "Do you have any other personal jewelry or belongings?" He gave her his wallet and a German cigarette lighter he had traded for years before. He didn't smoke, but he loved the lighter and hated to see it go. "Don't worry," she said, reading him. "You'll be given lots of junk like that to keep." She handed him a small folder. "Here's a map of the place. Anything that's too far to walk, just grab any bicycle you see. Meals are in any of the half-dozen restaurants on the installation, whenever you like, or you can pick up the phone and order food in your room. There's a menu in the bedside table drawer."

Helder stood in silence and gazed at the things around him. He was stunned. He had no experience of a Holiday Inn.

She moved to the door. "My name is Ragulin; you can call me Trina, if you like."

"You're a beautiful girl, Trina," Helder said, unable to keep the hunger from his voice.

She laughed. "Oh, all the girls here are beautiful. Those of us in the office are all gymnasts." She gave him a wry smile. "Majorov has a special interest in women's gymnastics." She leaned against the doorjamb. "I get off in a couple of hours. I could come back, if you like."

Helder nodded. "I would be very pleased if you did," he said, shakily. He was going to like Malibu.

She smiled again and closed the door. Helder took a deep breath and went immediately to the TV set. A man called Rather was reading the news as if he had experienced all of it. The President of the United States, looking slightly uncomfortable, answered penetrating questions from journalists with chuckles and shrugs. Helder sat down and switched channels. He watched, transfixed, for an hour as an outrageous policeman called Dirty Harry turned San Francisco into a war zone.

Helder was asleep when Trina came back. She woke him up.

3

Katharine Rule sat quietly through most of the regular Wednesday morning meeting of EXCOM TWO at Central Intelligence Agency Headquarters in Langley, Virginia. She took no notes. Later, she would update her files from memory, and she rarely missed anything.

EXCOM ONE was official stuff, formed of the Director of Central Intelligence (DCI), his deputy (DDCI), the Executive Director, and the four Deputy Directors for Operations, Intelligence, Science and Technology, and Administration. EXCOM TWO was, on the other hand, entirely unofficial. It was formed, more or less, of a shifting group of "office" (department) heads from the two sexier directorates, Operations (OPS), the covert arm, and Intelligence (DI), the overt analysis arm, respectively referred to by insiders as the "Company" and the "Agency."

Any younger officer in either wing would have much preferred, given the choice, to sit on EXCOM TWO. TWO, it was widely acknowledged, ignored domestic politics, didn't worry about what the president should be told, and didn't have to restrain itself for the record, since there were no minutes. TWO was where the dirt was, and everybody loved dirt. A member of TWO could dine out in perpetuity on the international gossip that rose from the muck raked at its meetings and still never compromise national security. TWO had the additional attraction of being just about the only place where officers of the Company and the Agency had much to do with each other; indeed, it was about the only time when the two groups felt they worked for the same organization.

At these meetings each member tossed in tidbits (reports would be too strong a word) from his section which might be of wider interest, either new facts gleaned from the Agency's worldwide network of listeners and watchers, or new questions raised by such facts. Under the informal rules that had evolved, nothing was too small or obscure to be introduced, although, in practice, and in the interest of time, each member condensed his information to what he thought might be significant, or, almost as important, amusing. The plum item this morning was that a high-ranking figure in MI-5, the British counterintelligence service, had been arrested for "immorally assaulting" an undercover policeman in a Soho gay bar.

"It never ceases to amaze me," commented the member who had introduced this information, "how any slightly queer member of the British intelligence establishment can, in a room filled with six hundred raving queens, unerringly place his hand on the crotch of the single vice cop in the place."

"I got an idea," somebody else offered. "Why don't we invite the guy over here for a goodwill tour and run him up and down the hallways as a sniffer? I'll bet your average MI-5 faggot could clean out the whole intelligence community for us in a short day's work." The CIA took a dimmer view of homosexuals in its ranks than did its British counterparts and was forever trying to screen them out.

Rule chuckled along with everybody else, but she was bored. She was the new head of the Office of Soviet Analysis, the youngest office head in the Agency, and she thought she had something more substantive to toss on the table. There was a shuffling and a glancing at watches around the table. "Anybody else?" the moderator for the day asked. She caught his eye. "Rule?"

Everybody resettled. Katharine Rule was the only woman in the room; she had attended TWO meetings as a deputy office head for years; her colleagues sometimes found her tedious and stubborn when it came to her theories, but she was a brilliant analyst, and she usually came to the meetings with good stuff. She was tall and auburn-haired, and most of the men found her attractive, in a businesslike sort of way, but she was divorced from Simon Rule, who had recently become Deputy Director for Operations. That scared off the more timid of her male colleagues, and she turned down the bold ones. Sitter problems was always her excuse. She had a small son and all the usual problems of a single mother, in addition to a demanding job which, apparently, obsessed her.

Rule took a tray of slides to the projector at the end of the table and shoved them into the machine. "I've got something here. I'm not sure just what, but something I'd like you all to keep in mind. I want to review what we know about two Soviet names." She switched on the projector and pressed the ADVANCE button. A color photograph of a dark-haired young man in a well-cut tweed suit filled the screen. He was sitting on a bench in a park and seemed interested in two passing girls in very short skirts.

"London," somebody said. "Sixties. I'd know those skirts anywhere."

"The breadth of your knowledge never ceases to amaze me, Harry," Rule said. "You make him?"

"Uh . . ." another voice interjected. "Yeah, what's his name—Roy something."

"Firsov," somebody else said.

"Very good, gentlemen. Harry, this just goes to illustrate what we've always suspected: when you were in London you were more interested in miniskirts than in the KGB."

"Yeah, that's Firsov," said Harry, defensively. "He wasn't much. We tailed him, off and on. He seemed to be more interested in soaking up London in the swinging sixties than spying on anybody."

"You must have seen a lot of him, then, Harry," Rule came back. "Let me refresh your memories, everybody. Roy Firsov—we never had a patronymic on him—was way down the pecking order at the Soviet Embassy in London in 'sixty-eight and 'sixty-nine. His cover was counselor for culture and sports, mostly to do with sports; he never showed much interest in the opera or ballet. Harry's right; we never tied him to any operation.

He seemed to spend most of his time learning to be an Englishman. He went to the movies all the time; he had suits made—at Huntsman, no less; shoes, Lobb; shirts, Turnbull & Asser. He made it to Ascot, he shot grouse in Scotland, he sailed at Cowes Week. He passed himself off as a Polish aristocrat quite successfully, more English than the English. He went down well. His single known intelligence coup was that he crashed the Carlton Club for lunch nearly every day for the last three months of his tour in London."

"Isn't that the Tory club?"

"Right, and they never nailed him. Everybody thought he was a member. One of our people, though, was asked to lunch there one day and nearly choked on his soup when he spotted old Roy. Firsov actually gave him a broad wink. Our man never told his host."

"That's terrific," somebody said, with genuine admiration.

"After 'sixty-nine we didn't pay him much attention. He turned up at the Munich Olympics in 'seventy-two as the deputy manager—really the political officer—of the women's gymnastics team. He came there directly from the sailing Olympics at Kiel, where he had won a bronze medal in Starboats."

"Gee, why doesn't anybody from the Agency ever win at the Olympics? Why does the KGB get all the medals?"

"Firsov turned up again at the UN for about a year, in 'seventy-three–'seventy-four, where, in contrast to his London service, he kept a low profile. He was in Stockholm for eighteen months in 'seventy-four–'seventy-five,

DEEP LIE / 33

again as cultural officer. In neither New York or Stockholm did we ever tag him with anything." She quickly flipped through other slides taken at these locations. "Then he went home, we reckoned for more training, and dropped out of sight until he was spotted at Andropov's funeral, wearing the uniform of a navy captain first grade, or commodore. He would have gone unnoticed then, except that he was the only person seen at the funeral, aside from Mrs. Andropov, who shed an actual tear, crocodile or otherwise."

"Now *that's* interesting," somebody said. "Anything on him since then?"

Rule ignored the question and switched off the projector. "I don't have a photograph for the other name. None exists." She returned to her seat. "The other name is Viktor Sergeivich Majorov."

There was a stirring in the room. "A deputy director of the KGB," somebody offered.

"Chairman of the First Chief Directorate—foreign operations," Rule said. "Anything else, anybody?"

"He seemed to lose out in the shuffle when Andropov succeeded Brezhnev," somebody said. "I got the impression he was out of favor. Apart from that, we seem to know even less about him than we knew about Andropov."

Rule flushed slightly. Her section had been made to look like idiots in the press when Andropov had come to power. Although Rule had had a good file on Andropov for years, the administration had somehow furthered the notion that nobody knew anything about the man. All those news stories about how he liked American novels and Glen Miller records hadn't helped, either. But today, she figured to make up lost ground. "We know a bit more, now," she said. "A couple of years ago, an Italian computer expert named Emilio Appicella had a visit from a Russian at his workshop in Rome. Appicella had a white Russian grandmother and grew up speaking the language at home. He's more than just an expert in computers—he's a pirate. He specializes in stealing computer software and making it run with previously incompatible hardware, without, of course, paying any royalty to the people who developed it. He comes to the United States, hits a few computer stores for the latest stuff, takes it back to Italy, breaks the entry codes, and turns it to his own uses. He designs and makes a lot of his own circuit boards to make it all hang together."

Rule looked around. She had the undivided attention of everybody present. "Anyway, Appicella had this little visit from a Russian, KGB, of course, but posing as a trade official. He said that his office in Moscow had some substandard word processing equipment that was driving them crazy. They wanted Appicella to come to the Soviet Union and adapt the equipment to run a well-developed and refined WP program, WordStar, then train their personnel to use it."

"Ho!" somebody hooted. "Wait'll they try WordStar. That'll drive 'em even crazier."

"You can buy WordStar off the shelf in hundreds of computer stores," somebody else interjected.

"Yes, but the Soviets couldn't make it work on their hardware. You know what a pinch they're in for up-to-date computer stuff. They didn't even have the MS-DOS operating system up and running, which they needed for IBM compatibility. Our ban on shipments to the East is working, it seems."

"I'm glad to hear *something's* working," was the reply.

Rule continued. "Of course, this sort of thing was right down Emilio's alley, and he saw an opportunity to turn a handsome buck. He made three trips to Moscow during the next four months, staying anywhere from a week to a month at a time. He was taken to a building in Dzerzhinsky Square, diagonally across from the Children's World department store."

"Jesus, you mean he was *inside* Moscow Center?"

"He was, indeed, although he had no idea what it was. He always entered the building from Kirov Street, and he thought he was in some government trade office. He still thinks that, in fact. He was introduced to the head of the office, a Comrade Majorov, and given a large, windowless conference room in which to work. Majorov, who turns out to be something of a technology freak, stopped in to see him often. Emilio trundled back and forth from Rome to Moscow, flying via Vienna, taking just enough hardware with him each time to complete part of the job. No fool, our Emilio, he played his cards very close to the chest. He refused to teach any Soviet anything about what he was doing with the hardware, and, after he had adapted the WordStar software for their use, he set up his own security codes, which he says the Russians couldn't break in a million years, so they couldn't copy it. He developed a special keyboard for the machines that made it easier for an operator to switch from typing Roman to typing Cyrillic characters, and he translated the manuals and instructed the office girls in the use of the software. But if anything breaks, they have to go back to Emilio. I expect he must have driven them crazy."

"What about Majorov? What did the Italian give us?"

"He was very happy to talk about Comrade Majorov, who he reckons is very high up in the Soviet trade mission, because of his ability to get what he wants in a hurry, and because of his lifestyle. He actually spent a weekend as Majorov's guest at a dacha in the Crimea— this, when Majorov apparently held out some hope of persuading Appicella to part with his technical secrets. When Emilio made it plain—after consuming quantities of beluga caviar and not a few of the office girls—that he had no intention of parting with his technology, the relationship became strictly businesslike again."

"So what about Majorov?"

"Quite handsome, likes the ladies, more than one at a time, usually. Always blondes. Dresses well, seems quite smooth and cultivated, has a weakness for anything expensive and Western. He was tooling around in a Porsche 928 at the dacha. Good company, holds his vodka well, has terrific self-confidence."

"That's it? That's all Appicella gave us?"

"That's all Majorov gave Appicella."

Harry spoke up. "There's something else, isn't there, Rule?"

"Yes, there is. The Rome station showed Emilio Appicella some pictures, and Emilio immediately made him."

"You said there were no photographs of Majorov."

"None. But there are lots of photographs of Roy Firsov."

"Ahhhhh . . ."

"Ah, indeed. It seems we underestimated Comrade Firsov. We should have known that anybody who lived like a duke on KGB funds was giving them value for money. It's my best guess now that he was running the London station when he was there, although that would have been remarkable for a man only in his late twenties."

"Sounds as though we'd better all take another look at Firsov/Majorov."

Rule sat back in her chair. "We'll have to find him, first. He's disappeared."

"When?"

"I'm not sure, exactly. I've crawled through everything I could find on Majorov, and there isn't much. There was apparently a Majorov in Lenin's Cheka, under Dzerzhinsky, right after the Revolution, but he seems a bit old to be our boy's father. He was a minor figure, but he progressed under Stalin and Beria."

"How'd he do in the purges?"

"The story is that Stalin shot him, personally."

"Oh."

"We got anything on Firsov before London?"

"Only a rumor that he was personally close to Andropov."

"And nothing else on Majorov?"

"All we know about Majorov is what I've told you—a deputy director at Moscow Center, and what we know about him as Firsov. Of course, now that we know the two are one, we have a better shot at him. I'd like for all sections to turn up what they can on either name, especially personal reminiscences."

There was a murmur of assent around the table.

"What's baffling about him at the moment is that we know he was a deputy of Andropov, and from what we can gather, the heir apparent. The question is, why didn't he inherit? Why isn't he head of the KGB now?"

There was a thoughtful silence in the room. Harry said, "Kate, I expect you have a theory."

She nodded. "I think he got something better."

"When you've been in the KGB probably all your adult life, what's better than head of the KGB?"

Rule shook her head. "I don't know, but I think if we can find out, we might be onto something very interesting indeed. This man is a survivor; he's run rings around us for more than twenty years; indeed, we hardly knew he was alive. I want to know what he's up to now. It can't be anything good, can it?"

"You say he was wearing a navy uniform at Andropov's funeral?"

"Yes, and as far as we know, he's never had anything to do with the navy. He wasn't prominently seated, either, although he was personally very close to Andropov. I think he went to ground for some very good reason after Andropov became chairman and only emerged for the funeral out of respect. Then, poof! He's gone again."

"Well," Harry said, "I guess we'd better put the word out to all sections."

"Yes," Rule replied. "But do it under the name of Firsov, not Majorov. Let's not take any chances on a leak that we've made the connection when we're dealing with other services, especially the British. Since he was at Munich in 'seventy-two, we might drop a casual hint to the Israelis that he had something to do with the terrorists; that would get a rise out of them, and with their dissident network in the Soviet Union, they might get a line on him that much faster. In fact, I think we might even tell the Israelis he's Majorov."

"No Soviet moles in the Israeli service," somebody said.

"One more thing," said Rule. "It's sort of a long shot, and I know I can't ask you to do it officially, but why don't we put out a general query on exotic cars anywhere in the Soviet Union? Any agent claps an eye on a Porsche or a Ferrari or anything out of the ordinary sends in the number plate and the location, pronto."

Another murmur of agreement.

"Anybody else?" the moderator asked. There was no reply. "Okay, let's find Majorov."

4

Rule sat and watched her boss sweat. The huge Senate hearing room was far too large for the dozen or so people involved in the closed hearings, but it had been the only thing available. Alan Nixon looked particularly small in the setting, and Rule was rather enjoying watching him twitch. Nixon, as Deputy Director for Intelligence (DDI), was in charge of a significant portion of the CIA's resources: research and analysis, scientific and weapons research, imagery analysis, central reference, and a great deal more. What was more, he also did most of the talking, especially to Congress, for the directorates of Administration and Science and Technology. He was a decent administrator, good on his feet, and an outstanding politician, but a man with only the most superficial grasp of the techniques practiced under him and the analysis passed up the line to other departments and his superiors. Rule thought of him as a librarian, who could supply a reader with a book on any subject, but hadn't a clue about the meaning of any of the books; whose knowledge of his library ended with the Dewey Decimal System. In these hearings, he would be very good on a question about why the CIA subscribed to every periodical in the world and nearly helpless to explain why it took the *New Yorker*.

Rule watched as Will Lee, an assistant to Senator Carr, Democrat of Georgia, surreptitiously slid a paper across the table to Carr, who was Chairman of the Senate Select Committee on Intelligence. The senator glanced at the paper and nodded. "Mr. Nixon," he said, taking off his glasses and rubbing the bridge of his nose—a certain sign of trouble—"I've got a little computer over in my office, can do just about anything. My people type on it. They do some accounting on it. They send out letters to thousands of people on it. Why, they do just about anything you can think of on it."

Before he had finished his first sentence, Rule had opened a file and begun to search rapidly through it.

"And that thing cost less than three thousand dollars," Senator Carr continued. "Why, every day, you pick up a newspaper and read how computers are getting cheaper, how machines that used to fill up a room can now fit right in your pocket and cost next to nothing."

Rule slid a sheet of paper filled with large typing toward Nixon, who passed a handkerchief over his face, then started speed-reading.

"Now, with all that going on," the senator said, "why does the Central Intelligence Agency want to spend"—he glanced down—"nineteen million dollars on a computer update—not a whole new computer, mind you, but just an *update*."

It was one of Alan Nixon's chief talents that he could read a sheet of paper at a glance, then recite its contents nearly verbatim. He wouldn't remember it for very long, but long enough to recite it. "First of all, Senator," he began, "that figure includes not just hardware, but a complete reworking of the computer's operating system, which is already the most powerful and most secure in existence. That will give us a whole new range of capabilities absolutely essential in the middle of a computer revolution. It will, for instance, be able to emulate any other known operating system of any other computer, including Soviet ones, read any disk, tape, or cartridge drive from any other computer, and give us new communication facilities that were, until now, purely science fiction, taking us right into the next century. Senator, this update is an investment in the future of United States intelligence gathering and analysis . . ." Nixon marched on, listing the other, soundly based reasons gathered in the answer Rule had prepared for him.

Rule glanced at the assistant, Lee. He made as if to scratch an eyebrow and, in so doing, tossed her a tiny salute. She tried to look as smug as possible.

Later, as she made her way from the committee room, Lee fell in step with her. "Nicely anticipated, Mrs. Rule," he said.

She smiled sympathetically at him. "*Easily* anticipated, Mr. Lee."

He winced. "Ouch." He glanced about to be sure they were out of earshot of the others. "How about some dinner tonight?"

Rule stopped and turned toward him. "Mr. Lee, you

shock me. You know as well as I that there would be a clear conflict of interest in my seeing you socially—not that I would be interested, in any event."

"I've got some sweetbreads and some morels, and I've dug up two bottles of Krug sixty-six."

"Really, Mr. Lee, do you think you can tempt me into an illicit relationship with delicacies?"

"You betcha."

"What time?"

"Seven-thirty?"

"Make it eight; I've got some work to clear up."

It was nearly eight when Rule got home, and the phone was ringing. She raced down the hall to get it before the answering machine picked up. "Hello."

"Katharine?" Only one person could drawl her name in quite that way.

"Hello, Simon," she said impatiently, kicking off her shoes and starting to work on her buttons. "I'm just going out; is it important? Is Peter all right?"

"Oh, yes, he's just fine. He's out back; we're barbecu-ing." Simon took a deep breath. "Actually, it's Peter I'm calling about. Missy and I have been invited up to her folks' place, in Maine, for a couple of weeks, and I was wondering if . . ."

"Hold it right there, Simon," Rule said, in her lowest, hardest voice. "If you go, Peter goes; that's our deal."

"Well," Simon sputtered, "I didn't think you'd take that attitude; I even thought, however foolishly, that you might like to see your son for a couple of weeks in the summer, but I can see I've overestimated your motherly instincts."

"Don't try that hard-hearted-Hannah shit on me, Simon." She liked using bad language with him; it annoyed him so. "You're his father; try being fatherly for a change. I mean, Jesus, he's only been there for ten days, and already you're trying to unload him."

"I'm not trying to do any such thing, Katharine; it's just that Peter and Missy sometimes . . ."

"Don't try and lay it off on your wife, either. I know that Missy and Peter get along just great. It's *you* and Peter who have a hard time—or rather just you. That boy is the most eager-to-please child I've even seen; he'd walk over hot coals to get your approval, but you're so goddamned up-Eastern standoffish."

"Now, don't start that again, Katharine; I was just thinking of the boy."

"Sure you were, Simon; you wanted him stuck in the hell of Washington in the summertime, in some day camp, which is where you know I'd have to put him while I'm working . . ."

"So why don't you just stop working and live on the alimony and raise your son the way you should?"

"Because, as I've told you a hundred times, I don't *want* your fucking alimony; I've got the house and the child support, and that's all I need until you get him into Yale and start taking him to your tailor and buying him cars and all that. Until then, I can afford him. In the meantime, Simon, why don't you try to get to know your son? He really is a remarkably bright and charming boy, and if you'll just spend some time with him, you might even find you *like* him."

"I take it, then, you decline to take Peter for the two weeks."

"I decline to deprive his father of a much-needed experience in human relationships."

"Good-bye, Katharine."

"Tell Peter I love him," she replied, but he had already hung up. "SHIT!" she shouted as she padded up the stairs in her stocking feet, pulling at her clothes. She threw her suit at the closet, stripped off her underwear and tights, grabbed a plastic cap, and leapt into a shower. Ten minutes later, refreshed and clad in faded cotton slacks, kid loafers, and a tennis shirt, she let herself out of the house, then stopped. She ran back upstairs, took the Majorov photographs from her briefcase, and stuck them into her purse. It was worth a try.

She walked briskly down the leafy Georgetown street, swinging her bag and taking deep breaths, looking forward to her evening. The heat still rose from the pavement, but the worst was over, for the day, thank God; she hated heat. A man leaning against a tree on the other side of the street started to walk in the same direction, but more slowly, falling behind. She glanced at him: in his forties, short; chunky, blunt features; thick dark hair, black-rimmed glasses; tan poplin suit. It had been a long time, but once you'd had the Agency's surveillance-technique training, you were doomed to a lifetime of looking over your shoulder and remembering the details of people you'd never see again. She tried to think of it as practice, a game.

A block and a half down the street, she ran up the

steps of a Federal house much like her own, tapped the bell, and let herself in with her key. "Halloo!" she called, congratulating herself on not peeking from behind the curtains to see where the man had gone.

"Kitchen!" he yelled back, and she could hear the sounds of jazz mixing with that of a carbon-steel knife striking rock maple as she walked through the living and dining rooms to the kitchen, at the back of the house.

"Mmmm, onions," she said, walking toward him. There was an old Miles Davis album on the stereo.

"Onions, my ass," he said, switching the knife to his left hand and snaking his right around her waist. "Shallots." He kissed her. "You get onions with hamburgers, not sweetbreads." He kissed her again, dropping the knife and putting both arms around her. "I like it when you don't wear a bra," he said.

"I know you do," she replied, "and I thought you deserved a treat after tossing old Nixon such an easy one today." She liked having him wrapped around her, but if she wasn't careful, things would get out of hand, and she knew there was a good dinner in store. "What does a girl have to do to get a drink around here?"

"Nothing," he said, going to the refrigerator. "You get the drink now; then you do it later." He pulled a bottle of Champagne from the refrigerator and began opening it. "How was your day?"

"Oh, it would have been all right, but Simon was on the phone the minute I got home. I think he saw me leaving the office and timed me."

"Hazards of marrying a guy at the office. Nothing serious, I hope. Peter all right?"

"Oh, sure. His dad was just trying to unload him so that he could go away for a nice, cool couple of weeks in Bar Harbor and try to impress his new in-laws. They're loaded, you know, and getting old. Simon was always one for looking to the future."

"I should have thought that Peter would charm the socks off the old folks."

"Oh, he would. Simon just isn't smart enough to figure that out."

"Listen, if Simon is that much of a jerk, why did you marry him?"

"Oh, I don't know. I was young and stupid, I guess. He was a lot older, very smooth." She shrugged. "He was station head in Rome, and it was my first assignment out of the country. All very romantic, you know, two American intelligence agents, holding hands and wading in the Trevi Fountain at two in the morning. *La Dolce Vita Espione*. It wasn't until I got pregnant that he wanted to get married. Then he came over all traditional; his Eastern establishment blue blood began to flow. He expected me to quit work, serve on the symphony board, and give a lot of dinner parties. You wouldn't believe the number of cookbooks I was given. For my first birthday after Peter was born, I got a course at Cordon Bleu in Paris. He actually thought I'd leave the job for that."

"*I'd* leave my job for that." Will laughed.

"You would, wouldn't you?" It occurred to her that if she'd been cooking dinner it would have been pork chops and hearty burgundy, not sweetbreads and Champagne.

Lee filled two Champagne flutes with the wine. "Cheers," he said, clinking her glass.

"Wow," she said, wrinkling her nose at the bubbles. "Where'd you get your hands on this?"

"The senator. I was afraid to ask where he got it; might've been from some defense contractor's lobbyist."

"It's wonderful. I love old Champagne." She raised her glass. "To national defense."

"Well, it employs both of us, I guess. You sure did your part today in soaking up a few bucks for the effort."

"Listen, we need that computer—say, that reminds me." She took the Majorov photographs from her purse. "You ever run across this face in your sailing circles? Cowes Week, and that sort of thing?"

Lee took the photographs and went carefully through them. "Who is he? One of your spooks?"

"One of *their* spooks, name of Firsov. He'd be older by twelve or fifteen years, now, maybe graying, heavier. Talks teddibly British; sometimes plays at being a Polish count."

"What's the sailing connection?"

"He sailed in Stars for the Soviets in the 'seventy-two Olympics. He was based in London for a while, and a report says he sailed at Cowes."

Lee shook his head. "I don't know him. I was only in Cowes once before 'seventy-two, then at Cowes Week in 'seventy-nine and 'eighty-one—Admirals Cup years. The Soviets don't do that sort of sailing; neither does any of the Eastern Bloc countries, so it's unlikely I'd run across him at any of the regattas I hit. Bad guy?"

"He's KGB; is there any other kind?"

"What's he up to?"

"That's what I'd like to know. One of the things my

people do is keep track of their people, update their biographies, and for somebody who's as important as he may be, he's been out of sight for too long. It's just a hunch, but I figure that whatever he's up to is something we'd give our gold fillings to know about."

"Interesting work," he said. "You love it, don't you?"

She nodded. "I was annoyed, at first, when I had to give up covert work and come back to Langley, but to tell you the truth, although I was one of the few women trained for field work, I discovered pretty quickly that they weren't going to let me do very much of it. I wasn't much more than a clerk on the Rome assignment, and then, when I married Simon and he got promoted, Langley was the only real option. It's worked out really well, too; I have a much better overview of operations than I would have in some embassy somewhere, and I don't have to look under my car before I start it. Besides, I like the variety—one day I'm besting you in hearings; the next I'm hunting down guys like Majorov."

"Who?"

"Oh . . . well, that's Firsov's real name. I really shouldn't have mentioned that; I'm talking too much."

"Sorry, I'm prying."

"No, you're not; I guess I just feel like talking about it, and I know I can trust you. It's a rather unusual feeling, in my job, to trust somebody. I've missed it."

"How'd you get into this business, anyway?"

"Well, I'd finished Barnard and Columbia Law, and I suddenly discovered I didn't want to practice law, and I didn't want to go into business, either. My roommate

at Barnard, Brooke Kirkland, was in the Russian Studies program at Columbia, and she got me interested.
Halfway through my last year, one of my professors—I
was never sure which one—put an Agency recruiter onto
me, and a month after graduation I found myself at the
Quantico Marine Base firing submachine guns and learning to kill with a single blow."

"I'd better watch my step."

"Damn right."

"Do you think there's somebody in Moscow keeping
tabs on you, the way you're keeping tabs on Majorov?"

She laughed. "There probably is, since I've worked
abroad. The two sides nearly always know who the play-
ers are in an embassy. They probably have an embarrassing photograph of me scratching myself in Rome."

"Or of you and Simon wading in the Trevi Fountain."

"That *would* be embarrassing. Boris is probably still
trying to figure that one out."

He laughed and turned back to his cooking. "Listen,
go sit out on the terrace and let me do this. Ready in half
an hour."

Rule refilled her glass and wandered through the
French doors to the deck overlooking the paved garden
below. She arranged herself on a chaise so that she could
watch him moving about the kitchen. She liked watching
him cook; it seemed such an unlikely thing for him to
be good at. He was good at his work, good in bed, and
good, in general, at making her happy. He was just what
she needed for this time in her life: he was bright and
funny, but he could be serious; he was genuinely fond of
her without being oppressive; he wasn't divorced, thank

God—she'd had enough of divorced men, whining about their property settlements and wanting, desperately, to get married again. Will had never been married, and, while he didn't seem terrified by the idea, neither was he looking for it. He got along with Peter if they were together, but he wasn't always scratching at her door with a football, trying to endear himself to her through the boy. He was a big, husky man. She was five feet, ten inches tall, and he was taller, even when she wore heels; she liked that. He was thirty-eight, four years older than she, and that was about right, she thought.

He was security-safe, too, and for her, that was no small thing. They had met a couple of months before in the local supermarket; she'd thought he was just another legislative assistant, and she'd told him what she usually told people, that she was a lawyer for the Department of Agriculture (that usually stopped any further conversation about work). Neither of them had known quite what the other did until they had both turned up in the same committee hearing. There was a potential conflict of interest, she knew, since part of her job was getting more government funds, and part of his was making sure she didn't get too much, but forbidden fruit was tastier. Since the divorce from Simon, she'd had a rule against going out with Agency men, and she was sick of lying to outsiders about her work. Will had been the perfect answer; he had a top security clearance, and she had taken the precaution of reading his FBI file, something she felt secretly guilty about. They had rarely talked much shop, but once in a while when she was excited about something, like Majorov, it was good to let off a little steam, knowing it would go no further.

They'd been sailing a couple of times on Chesapeake Bay, where he had a boat, but they didn't go out much—not that it mattered, since only a handful of people in Washington would be likely to know who both of them were. Will liked to cook, and she liked it here.

He had laid the table in the dining room and closed the shutters to make the most of the candlelight. It was a perfectly beautiful dinner: the sweetbreads were crunchy on the outside and creamy inside, the flavor of the wrinkled mushrooms blended perfectly with them, and the Champagne was big and yeasty.

"God, this is wonderful," she said. "Listen, do I know you well enough to ask how you live so well on a government salary? I mean, you do own this house, don't you?"

He smiled. "Yes, I own it, and yes, you know me well enough." He sipped his wine. "I've got some capital, from the family, and I'm still a law partner with my father. Lee and Lee, the firm is called."

"Back in Georgia—what was the town, Delano?"

"You've got a good memory."

"Your father was, what—lieutenant governor? Governor?"

"Both. He's been out of politics for a while, concentrating on the law practice and the family cattle farm. He's a good guy; he should have been president."

"Why wasn't he?"

"Didn't want it badly enough to do what he had to do, I think. He wants me to run for the Senate next year, against the Republican, Abney."

"Why don't you? You'd make a terrific senator."

"Oh, I'd like the work, I think; I'm not sure I'd like the campaigning. I don't know if I can eat that much barbecue and live. Also, Abney is such a weak senator that half the Democrats in the state want to run against him. There's going to be a ferocious Democratic primary."

"Wouldn't you have your father's political friends on your side?"

"Some of them, I guess. I'd have all of his enemies against me, that's for sure."

"What about Senator Carr? Would he back you?"

"He might. I haven't asked him, but he's brought up the subject a couple of times. I guess I'm thinking about it." He seemed to want to change the subject. "Uh, Kate, do you think we know each other well enough to travel together?"

She smiled. "Sure we do. What did you have in mind?"

"Well, a friend of mine in London has bought a new boat. He'd planned to pick it up next month at the factory, on the west coast of Finland, and sail it to England, but work has cut into his holiday. I've said I'd sail it as far as Copenhagen. I've never sailed in the Baltic, and it should be nice in June. It's a nice boat, called a Swan; forty-two feet long, well equipped, including an autopilot. The two of us could handle it, easily; take us about a week, say ten days outside. Would you like to come?"

Rule thought for a moment. She'd enjoyed the outings on Chesapeake Bay, but she wasn't as nuts about sailing as Will was, and she knew she'd end up as cook, which he could do better, too. It didn't seem the most promising sort of vacation. "Tell you what," she said.

"I'll pass on the sailing until I've had more experience; but I'll meet you in Copenhagen. How's that?"

He grinned. "Okay, great. I guess I can scare up a crew somewhere."

She felt a sudden, jealous pang. She hoped he didn't mean a female crew.

A little after two in the morning, she eased herself out of bed without waking him, and got dressed. She loved falling asleep with him but hated waking up at his house; she wasn't sure why. Probably some qualm from her puritanical upbringing coming back to haunt her. She closed the front door quietly and started toward her house. There was a distant noise of traffic, but in the elegant little street there was no one but her. Or was there? Rule thought she heard a shoe scuff against the pavement across the street. She stopped. Had it been only an echo of her own footsteps? She walked a bit more quickly, the leather heels of her loafers clicking against the cement, making their hollow sound in the deserted street. As she reached the corner and crossed into her own block, she heard the noise from the other side of the street again, and, simultaneously, a car started somewhere down the block behind her. She took one quick look over her shoulder; if there was someone on the other side of the street, he was behind a tree; the street seemed empty. Further back down the block, though, badly lit by the infrequent streetlamps, she caught a glimpse of a car moving slowly toward her. Its headlights were off.

She moved still faster and thought. God knew Washington wasn't short of muggers, but in Georgetown? At this hour of the morning? Pickings would be awfully lean for a mugger. She nearly sprinted the last fifty yards to her house. She ran up the steps and fumbled with the key. The car had stopped fifty yards away; the driver was only a shape. She heard another sound from the other side of the street.

The door finally came open, and she slipped quickly inside. She went immediately to a small desk in the hall-way, opened a bottom drawer and took out a 9mm automatic pistol. She worked the action, flipped off the safety, and stepped to the front window. As she eased back a corner of the curtain, the headlights of the car came on, illuminating the figure of a man, crossing in front of it. Just a tiny second, but enough to know that it was the same man she had seen earlier.

The car drove away, unhurriedly; she heard it stop, then turn left at the corner. She leaned against the wall and let her pulse return to normal. Not muggers. For just a moment, she entertained the wholly irrational thought that Majorov knew she was after him, and now he was after her.

It was a stupid thought, but when she finally fell asleep, the pistol was still in her hand.

5

Helder hooked his toes more firmly under the hiking strap and sat even further out until he was using all the tiller extension and the Finn dinghy was screaming along on a plane, doing better than ten knots and casting spray everywhere. It was a new boat, and he knew he could get it to do even better if he had the time to tune it properly. Still, it had been four years since he had taken the helm of a Finn, and what he felt now was pure joy. He tried to remember the last time he had felt this way. He couldn't.

He couldn't remember the last time he had felt so relaxed, either; probably never. He had spent the last week running, reading, watching the amazing American television, eating wonderful Scandinavian and French dishes and screwing Trina Ragulin, all with an enthusiasm and sense of wonder that still filled him. There was but one cloud on an otherwise uncluttered horizon; he was soon going to have to do something to pay for this glorious existence, and, with the sense of pessimism instilled by a lifetime of dealing with the Soviet system, he could not but believe that the price demanded of him would be high. As if in reply to this thought, there entered his field of vision a gleaming white electric cart, driven by Colonel Majorov. The cart wound down the hillside toward the marina, and Helder somehow knew the man was coming for him. He'd give his new commanding officer a little display, he thought.

He turned the dinghy downwind and sailed toward the beach where the smaller boats were launched and recovered. Then he stood up in the notoriously unstable Finn and gybed, ducking easily under the low boom. A moment later he repeated the maneuver. He noted with some satisfaction that a group of his fellow officers ashore had stopped whatever they had been doing and were watching, transfixed. He continued to gybe and duck, tacking the dinghy downwind, still standing; then, when it seemed he would drive the boat right up onto the beach, he rounded up into the wind, let the boat stop, and stepped lightly into the knee-deep water. The group of officers stared silently at him for a moment, then turned back to their own boats.

As he pulled the dinghy ashore on its trolley, Majorov glided up in his electric cart. "Good morning, Helder," the colonel said. "That was quite a demonstration."

Helder feigned ignorance. "Good morning, sir. Oh, you mean the gybing? Well, the wind was in the right place."

Majorov laughed and waved him into the cart. The little machine began whining its way back up the hill. "It was just such balance and precision that brought you to my attention in the first place," the colonel said. "It may interest you to know, Helder, that in your entrance examinations for the naval college some years ago, you achieved the highest scores ever recorded on the spatial orientation tests, higher even than those of Yuri Gagarin, who had held the record up until that time."

Helder had not, of course, known his examination scores, but he remembered that his examiners had seemed impressed. No matter what machines they put him on or how they had spun or turned him, he still had known which way was up.

Majorov continued. "There was, in fact, a little battle between the submarine fleet and the space arm about your future. At the time there was something of a glut of cosmonaut candidates, so the fleet won. I am very glad they did, or you might be orbiting the earth today instead of being here with us."

"Thank you, Colonel," Helder replied, warming to the praise. There had been precious little of it the last few years, no matter how brilliantly he had performed. Majorov slowed the cart to allow a troop of men in sweat clothes, all jogging precisely in time, to cross the gravel path. "Have you been getting your land legs back? Getting some exercise?" he asked. "I want you fit."

"Yes, Colonel. I have been running every day. I'd like to get in some squash, but I haven't had a partner."

Majorov nodded. "I know you must have been feeling a bit isolated. The others are training in classes, and you will be joining some of them, beginning tomorrow. But I am afraid that much of your training will be rather solitary. Today, I want you to meet Mr. Jones." He swung the cart onto a new path and aimed it toward a low-lying building. "Mr. Jones is our name for your teller of tales, your legend-maker. Do you know what a legend is, Helder?"

"A historical myth, do you mean?"

"Exactly that, but in your case the meaning becomes more personal." Majorov stopped the cart in front of the building but did not get out. "It is just possible that your assignment may take you abroad for a time. Should this occur you must be able to give a plausible account of yourself. With that in mind, Mr. Jones has created a legend, or new identity for you. You must learn all that he tells you quickly and well, then you must begin to live it. We cannot have you fall unprepared into the hands of a foreign police force, and this identity will keep you safe for a few days, which is the maximum time you might ever need it." Helder followed as the colonel got out of the car and walked into the building, walking directly into an office. A man in a blue suit rose from behind a desk. "This is Mr. Jones. Mr. Jones, this is . . . ?" Majorov indicated Helder.

"Carl Bengt Swenson," Jones replied. "Please sit down, Mr. Swenson," he said to Helder. "May I call you Carl?"

Helder sat down. "Of course," he said.

"I will leave you in Mr. Jones's capable hands, now," Majorov said. "Tomorrow, in addition to more sessions with him, you will begin other classes. I'll see you then." Majorov left the room and Helder turned to face Mr. Jones.

"Please come over here, Carl," Jones said, walking to

a corner of the room where a camera had been set up. "Put on these clothes," he said, handing Helder a shirt, tie and tweed jacket that he recognized from the closet of his own room. He did as he was told and stood against a screen to have his photograph taken. Jones pulled the Polaroid film from the camera, stripped off the covering paper, and waited for it to develop. "Very nice," he said, "if I do say so." He turned over the sheet of four pictures and stamped something on the back of each. "Sam's Fast Foto, Grand Central Station, New York City," the print read. Jones cut the pictures apart, clipped two of them to a blank form, and pushed it across the desk to Helder with a pen. "This is an application form for an American passport. It needs to be filled out in your own hand and signed." He pushed across a typed sheet of paper. "This contains the correct information."

Helder took the pen and quickly filled out the application, learning in the process that he had been born in Duluth, Minnesota, to the former Helga Erikson and Bengt Swenson, both Swedish immigrants. He lived at 73 West Tenth Street in New York City.

Jones took the completed form, left the room for a moment, then returned. "Good," he said. "The application will be made the day after tomorrow at the passport office on Fifth Avenue in New York. It will be issued the same day, and you will have it by the end of the week. The appropriate entry and exit stamps will be entered later." Jones took a wallet from his desk drawer and handed it to Helder. It was of black lizard and slightly worn, bent, as if it had been in someone's hip pocket for a time. "Open it and sign the enclosed credit cards on the back."

Helder opened the wallet and removed an American Express card, a Visa card, and charge cards for stores called Bloomingdale's, Saks Fifth Avenue, and Barneys. He also signed a New York State driver's license, which Jones said would be laminated and returned to him, and a battered Social Security card.

"Some other possessions you must keep with you at all times," Jones said, pushing various items across the desk. "This is a class ring from the University of Minnesota, suitably worn; see if it fits." It did. "Here is a key ring from Tiffany's which contains the keys to your apartment and mailbox." Helder pocketed the keys. "And here is an artist's pen called a Rapidograph. I believe you draw." Helder nodded. Jones pushed across a sketching pad with the name of a New York art supply store printed on it. "Just sitting and drawing is an excellent way to pass the time in a strange place without calling undue attention to yourself. You may find it useful."

Helder picked up the pen and examined it. "Is this a weapon of some sort, as well?"

Jones laughed. "No, nothing as exotic as that. People who work with such a pen daily often use it for everything else, too. You are a commercial artist, you see." Jones thumped a thick stack of paper onto the desk. "This is a very detailed biography. You must memorize it, of course, but more than that, you must live it. You must invent the detail between the lines. Your mother, you will see, was a country school teacher with a nose broken in a childhood accident. You might extend that fact, for instance, to say that, although the broken nose gave her a tough-looking appearance, she was, in fact, the softest and kindest of persons. You must constantly imagine this sort of detail to flesh out the biography. Your legend will be greatly more convincing if you do that."

"I understand."

"Good. Now, let me take you through the biography in broad strokes to give you the picture. Your name, as I have said, is Carl Bengt Swenson. Your parents emigrated to the United States from Sweden in 1948, vouched for by cousins who had been in Minnesota for a generation. You attended the University of Minnesota as an art student. In the spring of your senior year, both your parents were killed when a tornado struck the family farm. You sold the land and went to New York City to be an artist. There, you spent some years trying to paint successfully, but failed, and when your inheritance began to run out, you turned to commercial illustration. It was tough at first, but gradually, you established yourself, and now you do quite nicely. You earned eighty-four thousand dollars last year. You live in the basement and ground floor of a Greenwich Village townhouse and work in your home studio. You have a girlfriend, whose picture is in the wallet, suitably signed. It's a quiet life, though, and you don't have many acquaintances, working at home as you do. An agent solicits work for you and delivers it on completion. Most of your clients have never met you."

"Tell me," Helder said, "what will happen if someone tries to check on any of this?"

"It will hold up perfectly," Jones said, "for the simple reason that Carl Swenson is real. For a short time, during your mission, he will leave New York for a holiday, and for that time, you will be he. He will cooperate perfectly, because he is addicted to heroin and cocaine, and his supply of these drugs is controlled by people who are sympathetic to our efforts. Oh, before I forget . . ." Jones took a small tape recorder from a desk drawer and handed Helder a sheet of paper. "Speak those words into the tape recorder, please, in your best Midwestern accent."

Helder picked up the paper and read, "Hi, this is Carl Swenson. If you're a friend of mine, I'm on vacation for a couple of weeks; just leave your name and number at the tone, and I'll call you when I get back. Oh, if you're a burglar, I was just kidding about being away; I'm out feeding the Dobermans at the moment."

Jones pocketed the cassette. "This will be in Swenson's telephone answering machine at the right moment." Helder spent the rest of the afternoon with Jones and made an appointment for the following day. By dinnertime, he felt oddly like a dual personality.

"Good evening, Carl," Ragulin said, smiling crookedly at him as she slid onto the barstool. They were dining at Caprice, Malibu's rendering of a good French restaurant.

He was surprised. "You know?"

She ordered a Campari and soda. "Of course. I'm meant to help rehearse you. Tell me, what fraternity were you in at college?"

Helder shook his head and tried to look bitter. "I didn't join a fraternity; the idea seemed stupid to me."

"Oh, really? I seem to remember seeing you at a rush party our freshman year."

He felt a sharp prick of what would have been panic had the situation been real. So this is what it would be like. "Oh, were you at Minnesota?"

"How soon you forget, Carl. Don't you remember the little fling we had during our freshman year? I'm a bit hurt."

Helder smiled. "I certainly would have remembered, I think. My freshman year wasn't that exciting. And you're right. I was at some of the rush parties, but I didn't get a bid. They were looking for athletes, not art students."

"Well," she said, opening the menu, "you've obviously been romantically deprived. I can see I'm going to have to make it up to you."

They dined on *pâté maison, coq au vin,* and a bottle of the Beaune-Grèves, then walked, hand in hand, back to Helder's room. It amazed Helder that he hadn't tired of making love to her; even more that she didn't seem to have tired of making love to him. Still, they were through the first rush of passion; the relationship was changing, somehow. He took her face in his hands and kissed her lightly, then again, more firmly. She came back with tongue and teeth, but he held her away, looked at her for a moment, and kissed her softly again.

She stared back at him, her eyes wide, her lips trembling. "This isn't supposed to happen, you know. It isn't part of your training. When this is over, we won't see each other again."

"Yes, we will," he said firmly. "I promise you. Believe it."

"I don't know why," she said, "but I do believe you. Is this possible? Can you make it happen?"

"Majorov has promised me that when this assignment is over, anything will be possible. I believe him."

She turned her head and put it on his shoulder. "Majorov can make it happen—there's no doubt about that."

"I'm going to give Majorov what he wants," Helder said. "I'm going to make it my business to amaze him with what I can do. And when it's over, he'll give me what I want."

"Yes," she said dully. "We must both give Majorov what he wants."

They stood for a long time in the dark, holding each other.

6

Rule sat down and inserted her key in the computer terminal that rested on the typewriter shelf of her desk. When the monitor had warmed up, the date and time appeared in the upper right-hand corner of the screen, and a single sentence was centered.

TELL OLD COSMO WHO YOU ARE, PLEASE.

She tapped a ten-digit number into the keypad. There was a brief pause while the computer, which was called COSMO for no other reason than that the name had popped into the mind of whoever did the original programming, checked the number against its files, and started to record. Rule knew that, at any time, somebody in the computer center could check the record of her computer usage and learn immediately what programs she had run and when.

GOOD MORNING, MRS. RULE. YOU'RE UP EARLY. WHAT CAN I DO FOR YOU?

Rule had long stopped being irritated that the programmers had a sense of humor; anyway, she had begun to think of COSMO as practically a person. She typed in IDMUG.

FILE DESIGNATION?

REVIEW, she typed. She didn't have a file number, but no one would think it odd that she was reviewing photographs. She did it a couple of times a week.

NATIONALITY? COSMO asked.

SOVIET, she typed back.

LOCALE?

D.C.

SEX?

M.

DESCRIPTION?

N/A.

LEGAL?

YES.

INTERVAL?

She typed a one.

TYPE P FOR PAUSE, C FOR CONTINUE, ESC TO LEAVE PROGRAM.

Mug shots of all male Soviet Embassy personnel began to appear on the screen at one-second intervals. Rule was so accustomed to this drill that she didn't need a longer look. She watched the faces closely as they went by, pausing now and then for a closer examination when the subject was the right age and shape. Nothing. She ran methodically through the legals in every Eastern Bloc embassy in Washington. Still nothing.

ANYTHING ELSE, MRS. RULE?

NO, she typed.

LISTEN, WHY DON'T WE HAVE A DRINK AFTER WORK?

COSMO said this to all the girls. She wondered if the director of the computer center knew it. Probably, she decided.

GET LOST, she typed, and switched off the terminal.

One thing about COSMO: you couldn't hurt his feelings. Sometimes she wished you could. The newly approved computer expansion would bring in voice activation, and Rule wasn't sure she was looking forward to it.

As usual, even before she had come to a rational conclusion about her problem, she knew how she felt about it: she was depressed. When she thought about it rationally, it didn't help. Nothing added up. First of all, the face didn't register. The face should have been there in the computer. Every visa photograph of every opposition legal was in the computer; it was updated daily. Surveillance wasn't the sort of work illegals did, ever; they were too expensive and too valuable to risk, so the guys had to be legals. And yet, the one whose face she'd seen just wasn't there. It wasn't Will they were tailing, either; they had been with her coming and going. And there were only two of them—that was inexcusably substandard work. Still, maybe they had expected her to be at Will's all night; maybe the other two were cooping somewhere, waiting for daylight. Maybe.

She knew what she had to do: she had to go down to Alan Nixon's office and report it. That was procedure; you went to your immediate superior, and you reported it. She stood up. She could already see the look on Alan's face: imagining things; intuition again. She gritted her teeth. Still, he'd have to go through the motions. They'd put a home team on her, day and night, until they made the watchers and figured it out. She hesitated. She wouldn't be able go to Will's, couldn't even phone him. They'd sweep her phones, then put in a tap. She didn't want his name turning up in the reports. She sat back down. She didn't want to stop seeing him, not even for a couple of weeks. With Peter at his father's, Will was the only company she had. Well, not the only company, but the only company worth bothering with. The home team would make her go out all the time, too; they'd want her on the move, the better to watch the watchers. She'd stir up the whole social cauldron, and when the incident was wrapped, it would still be bubbling; she'd be left with a lot of telephone calls she wouldn't want to answer, invitations she wouldn't want to accept. Shit. She picked up a stack of cables and started to scan them. She'd think about it tomorrow—that was what she'd do. Scarlett O'Hara had been nobody's fool.

She speed-read the cables, the stuff that came in from every embassy, every station every day; fodder, mulch, the compost of intelligence, not very much of it very interesting. How many facts like these were somewhere in her brain, waiting? When she had finished the stack, most of it was consciously forgotten. Only a few random pieces of information hovered in the front of her brain, for no particular reason: two thousand American-made Ingram submachine guns intended for the British Special Air Service commandos had been stolen from a depot near Aldershot, in Surrey, IRA suspected; a woman member of the German Bundestag had a girlfriend stashed in a Bonn flat, as well as a husband at home in her constituency; the Soviets had markedly increased the teaching of the Swedish language in their universities and language training centers, apparently beginning two years before; the vestibule outside the chemistry lab at Moscow University had a strong odor of urine; the laundries at two Soviet Marine Infantry training camps had had a sudden drop in the number of shirts laundered weekly, sixteen percent in one case, twenty percent in the other. There had been a further rash of what the Stockholm station called "periscope fever"—purported sightings among Swedes of Soviet submarines, minisubs, and frogmen—since the front-page story of the Swedish fisherman whose nets had become caught on what was claimed was a Soviet sub. It all seemed routine, as did the rest of her day, but when at six o'clock she packed it in and went home, she had had a better day than she knew.

All the way home, she kept looking in the rearview mirror. Nothing. Maybe they had dropped her. Or maybe they were getting better at their work.

7

Oskarsson looked with silent horror at what used to be his left hand. It was the first time he had been able to bring himself to do so. There was only a thumb left. There had been infection in the stumps and two operations in the weeks since he had lost the boat; now there were not even any knuckles left. When he had recovered enough from the initial loss of blood and the surgery, he had refused further painkillers. The pain seemed all he had left, the pain and the rage.

The doctor gently wrapped the stump in cotton padding and tied a sling around Oskarsson's neck. "There's no more need for a dressing," he said. "This is just to protect it from being knocked about until the healing is complete and the inflammation gone. I'd keep it in the sling until the soreness is gone. When you're feeling better, we'll see about getting you a prosthesis."

"Huh?" Oskarsson blurted.

"An artificial hand, or partial hand, rather. It won't

give you much more than something to oppose the thumb, but it will improve the aesthetics."

Oskarsson stared blankly at the young man.

The doctor held up his own left hand and waggled the thumb. "With the prosthesis, you'll be able to make more use of the thumb, and the stump won't look so . . . uh, it'll look better."

Oskarsson stood up and hitched his trousers with his good hand. The clothes hung loosely on him; he had lost a lot of weight. "Thank you, doctor," he said. "You've been very good to me here. I am grateful."

Gunnar was waiting for him in the hallway. In the parking lot a man took his picture with a flash camera, and another man tried to ask him questions, but he pushed past them and got into Gunnar's Volvo. There had been a lot about the incident in the papers in the beginning, but he thought they might have forgotten by now. Submarines were news in Sweden these days, and Oskarsson was the only person who had been harmed by one, except for poor Ebbe. "I want to go to the grave," he said to Gunnar.

Gunnar sighed and nodded. He threaded through the streets to the east of Stockholm and stopped at a large, municipal cemetery. Oskarsson got out of the car and followed his son to a plot squeezed between two others. He stood and stared at the plain stone with its name and dates. "Is this the best you could do?" he asked.

Gunnar bit his lip and looked away. "Papa, we don't belong to a church in Stockholm. This is the way everyone is buried; please don't make it sound as if we've neglected him in some way."

"I'm sorry, boy," Oskarsson said.

"Just remember that we miss him, too," Gunnar said. "Please keep that in mind with Ilsa. She's taken it well, but I'll need your help with her."

"I'll be out of her way," Oskarsson said. "I want to get home soon, anyway." He got back into the car.

"Listen, Papa . . . we want you to come and live with us. While you were in the hospital we sold the flat and bought a place out in the archipelago. You'll like it."

Oskarsson shook his head. "No, I know you'll want to be alone; I don't want to be a burden."

"Papa, I've brought your things up here and given up your room. There's nothing for you down there anymore."

Oskarsson felt suddenly uprooted and desolate. He had sold the house when his wife had died and moved into lodgings in the village. It had been strange at first, but he had had no one to keep house for him, and he had gotten used to it. Now, apparently, he was homeless.

"Come for a while, Papa. You'll love it out in the archipelago; we're right on the water, and it's beautiful. You'll have your own room. Try it just for a while; then, if you want to get a place of your own, well, there's the insurance money from the boat. I've opened an account for you at my bank."

Oskarsson said nothing. He leaned his head against the headrest and closed his eyes. Something had happened to him these last weeks. He had no will to resist Gunnar. He let himself be swept along, and gave himself to whatever was coming.

The house was out past Gustavsberg, and Gunnar

had been right; it was right on the water, and the place was beautiful. There were painters working in the living room, and Ilsa was supervising a man fitting cupboards in the kitchen. She looked nervous when she saw him. Ilsa had been a model in her youth, and even now, pushing forty, she held on to her fragile good looks. There were wrinkles here and there, Oskarsson could see, and she wore too much makeup, and her jeans were too tight, but she was still pretty. He allowed himself to be pecked on the cheek.

"Hello, Papa," she said.

He didn't like that, much, being called Papa by this woman he hardly knew. They had seen little of each other over the years.

"Your room's ready; come, I'll show you." She led the way upstairs and along a corridor, into a large corner room. It was comfortably furnished, more so than the rest of the house, he noticed. The furniture from their flat didn't fill the place. His clothes were hung in the closet and folded neatly into a chest of drawers. On a dressing table, there was a small, gold cup.

Ilsa picked it up and handed it to him. "Ebbe won it rowing last year. It was his favorite thing."

Oskarsson felt the smooth metal and read the inscription.

"We'll leave you to let you get settled for a bit, Papa," Gunnar said. "Maybe you'd like a nap."

"We'll have some tea as soon as they're done in the kitchen," Ilsa said. "Come down whenever you like."

Oskarsson nodded. There was a rocking chair facing the window. He walked over to it and sat down facing the water, still holding Ebbe's little cup. He might have arrived on a different planet. He had spent his life on a stretch of the south coast of Sweden among familiar people, places, and boats. Here, in this strange house, in this place, he was an alien. Even his son and daughter-in-law were strangers to him. He gazed out the window over the water, past the rocky islands, out to the Baltic. Here, only the water was familiar. The water and the rage. He held the little gold cup and rocked gently. The rage would never leave him, until he found some way to purge it. Tears spilled from his eyes and ran down his weathered face, now pale. It was the first time he had wept. He would never do it again.

8

Rule sat in her office and gazed disconsolately at the withering plants on the windowsill. Outside, in the Virginia countryside, a profusion of greenery mocked her efforts. She couldn't remember the names of these plants, but she had been assured by Molly, a department secretary whose cubicle resembled the National Botanical Gardens, that, "Even you couldn't kill these."

Wrong. She was convinced that her very pores exuded some invisible, toxic mist that choked any green thing unfortunate enough to fall within range. The original Black Thumb, she was. This ability to wither, it seemed to her, had begun to extend itself into her work, for the Majorov research had come to what, seemingly, was a dead end. She had raped the Agency's computer banks, running tapes extending back to the formation of the CIA in the early fifties. Before that, there were only the OSS files from World War II. In the thirties, when Stalin was decimating the ranks of the Red Army and the

Communist Party, only the State Department and the army had conducted anything like intelligence analysis; each had limited its efforts to its immediate concerns, and God knew where the records were.

She had been unable to locate a single fact about Majorov other than what she had presented to EXCOM TWO, and if she had meant that as an appetizer, nobody was hungry. She had sent memos to her counterparts at the National Security Agency and the Defense Intelligence Agency asking for any data, and there had been only silence.

She shuffled listlessly through the cables and reports on her desk. She had already handed out the morning's assignments to her researchers, and now she was faced with reading her own stack of material, sifting through it for a relevant fact on any one of hundreds of subjects, files, and cases. This, if the thriller writers only knew, was ninety percent of what intelligence was all about: reading, remembering, associating, analyzing, and occasionally, discovering. It was mornings like this that made her sometimes yearn for foreign duty, where there was, at least, the stimulus of outside contact. There was a rap on her open door.

She looked up to see a man she barely knew; Martin, his name was, one of those people in the bowels of the Agency who did God-knew-what.

"Morning, Mrs. Rule," the man said. "I've got something you asked for here." He held up a large brown envelope.

"Come in and have a seat," Rule said, grateful for any interruption. "What have you got?"

Martin slid a photographic print from the envelope. "Satellite shot, three days ago, the Latvian coast."

What had she asked for in Latvia, for God's sake? "Let's have a look," she said, gathering up her cables and reports and shoving them into a drawer, leaving her desk clear.

Martin laid the photograph before her. "This is the south side of the city of Liepaja."

"Mmmm," Rule said.

Martin pointed. "This is sort of a tidal lake, except there's not much tide in the Baltic. There's an entrance to the sea just here."

Rule pointed to a widespread group of buildings at the lake's edge. "This looks something like a college campus," she said, running her eyes over the photograph. "Is that a dock with some small boats?" She indicated the water's edge.

"Right, it's a little marina, sort of. Nothing but pleasure boats. Best guess on the adjoining area is it's some sort of all-service sports complex." Martin indicated various spots on the photograph. "Tennis courts, track, soccer field, pretty extensive. You've got a couple of dozen runners scattered around, too, and the nonathletic pedestrians are wearing both army and navy uniforms. We can actually read rank on some of them."

"Looks like a unit drilling," Rule said, pointing to a group of men formed in ranks.

"Nope, running," Martin replied. "They're all wearing sweat clothes."

Rule nodded. "What's here that I asked for?"

Martin pointed to a car park next to one of the buildings. "Exotic car. A Mercedes, either a 380 or 500 SE sedan, silver metallic paint. The Soviets don't use metallic paint on any of their cars, and apart from the German Embassy in Moscow and their various consulates, I'll bet there aren't three of the big Mercedes in the USSR. Whoever's driving it is important enough to turn down a Chaika or a Zil limo in favor of a foreign wagon. Never mind who has the juice to get one, who'd have the chutzpah to drive it around?"

Rule stared at the car. "Pity you can't see the license plates from overhead; that would tell us something. Listen, let's ask NSA for some more angle on this place. I'd like to see some building entrances—we might even pick up a face—and I'd sure like to see the designation on this car's plates. The Soviets tag everything with some sort of code—foreign diplomat, trade official, journalist, Central Committee—and the city of registration is on every plate, too."

Martin shrugged. "I've no idea when the next satellite pass will be over the area, and I don't have the authority to ask for the shots. The DDI, Nixon, will have to do that."

"Right. I'll handle the request, then. Thanks a lot, Martin, this is the first break I've had on this one. It may not go anywhere, but who knows? Can you leave this with me?"

"Sure, but I'll need a tight receipt to replace it in the file."

Rule wrote out a receipt, mentioning the file number and date of the photograph, and Martin went on his way. She dictated a memo to NSA for Alan Nixon's signature

and made a routine request to operations for any HU-
MINT, human intelligence, on the Liepaja site, and gave
the tape to her secretary. "Do this now, will you, Jeff?"
Some joker in personnel had given her a male secretary.
He liked it even less than she did.

"Don't you want the weekly summaries first?" he
whined, waving at what was already in his typewriter.

"Now, Jeff, please, and if you screw around, I might
miss a satellite pass, so move it, will you?"

He sighed and whipped the paper from the machine.

Rule went back to her desk and pored over the photograph. She couldn't shake the feeling that it was a campus, and she had learned to listen to her hunches. There
were too many buildings to just house athletes, given the
extent of the visible training facilities. They were teaching something here. She stared hard at the group of running men. Athletes didn't train in ranks, not even in the
Soviet Union; training was too individually planned for
that. This was a military unit of some sort; these men
were training together for something, and it wasn't the
next Olympics. She found a loupe in her desk, laid it
flat on the photograph, and worked her way around it.
There was not a sign of anything military; not a firing
range, even. That was interesting; an athletics training
camp would certainly have a firing range; shooting was
an Olympic event.

She ran the loupe around the perimeter of the facility. There was a double fence, and she'd bet the area in
between was mined. Who needed a double fence around
a sports center? She looked at the boats and wished Will
were here to tell her about them. They looked entirely

pleasure-oriented to her. There were some dinghies drawn up on a beach, and from a scale imprinted on the photograph, she reckoned the largest boat in the marina to be about thirty-five feet long. She was puzzled that a long stretch of the water's edge above the marina was edged with a what looked like a concrete curb. It reminded her of a lake's edge in a park, but there was no grass, just more of the same shale that made up the beach. She tried and failed to think of any good reason why anyone would want the water's edge curbed.

Jeff came in with the memo. "You want me to take this to Mr. Nixon?"

"No, I'll do it," she said, taking the paper from him. "You get back to the summaries." She hoofed down the hallway to Nixon's bigger, plusher office. The door was closed, and his secretary was filing her nails. "Anybody in there with him?" Rule asked.

"No, but he said he didn't want to be disturbed," the young woman said. She leaned forward conspiratorially. "Just between me and you, I think he's reading the new Len Deighton. Tell you what, I'll go to the john, and you just barge in."

Rule laughed, waited for the girl to disappear, rapped once on the door and opened it before Nixon could reply. His feet were on the desk, and he nearly spilled himself from the chair, taking care to drop the book in the process.

"Jesus, Kate, you scared me half to death."

"Sorry, Alan, I did knock."

He shuffled some papers on his desk. "What is it?" he asked testily.

"Just need your signature on a memo to NSA for some satellite shots."

"Shots of what?"

"I asked everybody for a sweep on exotic cars in the Soviet Union; one turned up in a satshot of the Latvian coast. Interesting place. Seems to be some sort of sports training facility, but it smells funny to me. There's a big Mercedes in the parking lot, too, and it's not the sort of place the German ambassador would be visiting. I'd like some angle to see if we can read the plate." She put the memo in front of him.

Nixon regarded it with distaste. "Kate, do you know what a satellite run costs?"

She did, and she knew he didn't. "Well, they're not going to bill us for it, Alan—it'll come out of their budget. Come on," she cajoled, "it'll give the layabouts over there something to do."

"This is that—what's his name? Finsov?"

"Firsov, aka Majorov. I sent you the sheet on him. I've also made a request to ops for HUMINT, but I'm not optimistic. The last couple of years, I seem to have had more and more trouble getting information collected at ground level. Sometimes I think Senator Carr and his committee are right—the Agency's putting too many bucks into hardware and not enough into training your good, old-fashioned spies."

"This Majorov is one of your intuition numbers, isn't it, Kate? Every now and then you get a wild hair up . . . ah, in your ear, and you go shooting off on a tangent."

"This is no tangent, Alan." She felt herself blushing. "Well, not exactly. This guy was deputy director in charge of the First Chief Directorate. He's within my province."

"'Was' is the operative word, Kate. He's not there anymore. Probably out in the Gulag somewhere, paying for his sins."

Rule shrugged. "Maybe. Then again, maybe not. Anyway, it can't hurt to know where he is. From the little I know about him, I'd prefer it if he were in the Gulag. He's a little too swift for my taste. I like plodders, and he sure ain't one of those. I can promise you, wherever he is, he's up to no good."

"Oh, all right," Nixon sighed, reaching for a pen, "but I'm probably just going to get a snotty memo back about allocation of resources. You know how those guys are." He signed the paper.

Rule snatched it up and started for the door. "Thanks, Alan, I'll get this right off."

"Kate!" He stopped her in her tracks.

"Don't come back to me for any more high-tech requests on this thing unless you can come up with something of substance, you hear? Sniff around, if it doesn't interfere with your other work, but I'm not going to start pissing away resources with nothing but your . . . intuition to back me up. Last time I went with that I got strung up by my . . . thumbs, you'll remember."

"Sure, Alan, I promise," she said, then fled the office with her cheeks burning. She had spent six weeks a year earlier chasing down a Soviet GRU man who, it turned out, had died of a coronary at his desk two years before. Nixon trotted that out whenever he wanted her leash kept short. This one wasn't like that, though, she thought. This was a live one; she knew it. Nixon had stopped himself short of saying 'woman's' intuition, but that was what he had been thinking. It was one of the things she had to put up with.

9

Helder filed into a small theater with some fifty other men and took a seat in the front row. In the two weeks since his arrival, it was the first time he had attended any training with others. He looked about him at the others, and there was a sameness he had not encountered before. In any Soviet military unit one could expect to see evidence of the multiethnic makeup of the Union of Soviet Republics, with its fifteen states and dozens of ethnic types and languages. He knew that the majority of many army units, in particular, did not even speak Russian and had to be commanded through a limited number of basic commands. But here everyone spoke not just Russian, but English and/or Swedish, and in appearance, the group looked quite uniformly Scandinavian or, at least, North European.

At the front of the theater, before a blank wall, was a table on which lay a number of small weapons, some of which he had never seen before. Hanging on the arm of each seat was a pair of industrial earmuffs, the sort worn by both civilian and military ground personnel around jet airplanes. As soon as they were settled, Majorov strode into the room, dressed in military-style coveralls and followed by a man carrying two metal ammunition boxes. Majorov walked to the center of the theater and stood in front of the table holding the weapons.

"Good morning, gentlemen," he said, smiling slightly. "We have now completed the acquisition of your small arms, and I would like to introduce you to them. In general, our operation will be conducted in three waves: the infiltrators, the shock troops, and the conventional troops." Majorov picked up two small automatic pistols and held them up to be seen. "Those of you who will lead infiltrator teams will be given sidearms only, for obvious reasons. Just as obvious, these arms must not excite undue interest should you or any of your team fall into opposition hands; therefore, you will be armed with either the well-known Walther PPK, which is, of course, very similar to our standard-issue Makarov—or should I say, vice versa?" There was a low chuckle from the group, who knew that the Soviet Makarov was a direct copy of the Walther PP. Majorov continued, ". . . or the Beretta Model 84 double-action pistol, both firing the 9mm short cartridge. All the weapons issue will appear used, but I assure you that each pistol has been dismantled and inspected and, when necessary, renovated. Most of you will have already fired these weapons at one time or another, so I will not waste your time with gratuitous information about them."

Majorov replaced the pistols on the table and picked

up another pistol, unfamiliar to Helder. "Now we come to the weapons to be carried by the shock teams, where we are unconcerned with weapons being identified. This, gentlemen, is the SIG-Sauer model P226 self-loading pistol, manufactured by the Swiss arms company Schweizerische Industrie-Gesellschaft, jointly with the West German firm of J.P. Sauer & Sohn. This pistol was developed by SIG for the competition for a new sidearm for the US armed forces and Coast Guard. The Americans were too stupid to adopt it. It is, in my very well-informed opinion, the finest automatic pistol available. The P226 fires the nine millimeter parabellum cartridge, loaded from a magazine containing fifteen rounds." There was a murmur of approval from the audience.

Majorov returned the pistol to the table and picked up a short, boxy weapon in one hand and a thick black cylinder in the other. "And now for the more interesting of your new weapons, gentlemen." He began screwing the cylinder onto the short muzzle of the weapon. "This is the Ingram Model 10 submachine gun, also known as the Mac 10, of which I am sure you have heard. We have procured some two thousand of these superb weapons by especially devious means. This weapon has a number of advantages. Although amazingly compact, like, say, the Israeli Uzi, it fires a forty-five-caliber cartridge, with all the resultant improvement in impact, from a thirty-round magazine at a rate of eleven hundred and forty-five rounds per minute. The cylinder, here, is not a conventional silencer, but a suppressor, which is designed to let the bullet reach its full velocity, thereby eliminating the usual thump from a silencer. All the opposition hears is the crack of the bullet becoming supersonic as it passes, which makes it impossible to tell from what position you are firing. I think you will agree that this is a distinct advantage in the sort of operation for which we are training. This weapon is to be carried by teams operating in open countryside, where noise and muzzle flash would give away our positions, and Sergeant Petrov here"—he nodded toward the man who had followed him into the room—"will be demonstrating it later and instructing you in its use. I think you will like it."

Majorov replaced the submachine gun and picked up another weapon, like nothing Helder had ever seen. There was a buzz of comment among the audience; apparently, no one else had seen one, either. It seemed to be a flat metal box, about three feet long, two inches wide at one end and six at the other. It would not have resembled a weapon at all had it not been for a trigger guard and pistol grip in the middle and a combination sight/carrying handle on top. Majorov cradled the thing in his arms and began to speak. "Now for the new weapon to be carried by teams operating in urban areas. In 1982, the American armed forces initiated something called the Close Assault Weapons System program, aimed at developing a new kind of combat shotgun. A number of weapons manufacturers expressed an interest in the project, and the West German firm of Heckler & Koch, whose work you all know well, developed a prototype, one of which, along with a complete set of drawings, ah, happened to come our way. For two years, now, a special team at Soviet State Ordnance has been developing and improving the idea, until we now have in limited production nothing less than a highly refined, highly reliable *submachine shotgun*." There was something like a gasp from the audience as Majorov held up the weapon.

Majorov continued. "We have also developed a range of highly effective ammunition, including a special antipersonnel buckshot, a CS gas cartridge, and a solid projectile that will defeat thirty millimeters (one and a quarter inches) of armor at a hundred and fifty meters." Another gasp from the audience. Majorov picked up a thick clip and shoved it into the stock of the weapon, behind the pistol grip. "It will fire, from a twenty-four-round clip, either single shot or on full automatic at a rate of five hundred rounds per minute. At a range of forty meters, shot will spread to approximately nine hundred millimeters (three feet), so in one second the firer can place eighty pellets into an area no more than one meter square, and at that range, each pellet will have a residual energy approximately fifty percent greater than that of a 7.65 millimeter pistol round. We estimate further that, in a confined area, say a city street, six men with two clips each would decimate a company of conventional infantry in less than ten seconds."

There was a moment's silence; then the audience burst into applause, and the troops were on their feet.

While they were still applauding, Majorov nodded to the weapons sergeant, who went to a panel and flipped a switch. The blank wall behind Majorov slid upwards to reveal a well-lit, fifty-meter firing range. The applause abruptly stopped. Helder, who had been drawn to his feet by the spontaneous action of the others, sank back into his seat, his stomach twitching. The other men immediately followed suit. Forty meters down the range, a dozen human figures were slung from the ceiling by ropes under their arms. For a moment Helder had thought they were merely unconscious, but something about their attitudes of hanging told him they were dead, and he was immediately thankful for that.

"Please put on your earmuffs, gentlemen," Majorov said; then as they did so, he wheeled, tucked the stock of the submachine shotgun under his arm, cocked it and, moving from left to right, emptied a twenty-four-round clip into the corpses. The figures jerked violently, spraying blood and gore onto the floor, sides, and ceiling of the narrow range. When the clip was exhausted, Majorov ejected it from the weapon, replaced it, and repeated the firing, this time from right to left.

Helder tried to close his eyes, but couldn't. The noise was incredible, even through the earmuffs; the bodies danced wildly, as if trying to elude the dense rain of shot. When the second clip was exhausted, three of the corpses were without heads; others were missing limbs; two had been cut in half. For a very long moment nobody moved. Then, as Majorov turned to face them again, the group sluggishly removed their earmuffs.

"Gentlemen," Majorov said quietly, "once the opposition has seen these new weapons used, they will fear you as they have never feared anything else in their lives."

10

Helder was now working flat out at whatever he was being trained for. He was drilled daily in his legend by Mr. Jones, who was ingenious at tricking him into blowing cover; he trained with both the Ingram submachine gun and the submachine shotgun, as well as with the Walther PPK, which he now carried, unloaded, in a soft holster clipped inside his waistband in the small of his back, to get used to it; he spent two hours each day in the language lab, polishing his American Midwest accent; he jogged and ran wind sprints twice a day; and he endured a punishing two-hour session each day with a squat, muscular Ukrainian, who taught a brand of unarmed combat that kept him permanently bruised and sore. He spent the evenings with Trina; they dined in one of Malibu's half-dozen Western restaurants and watched the news and movies on the cable television. She was, for all intents, living with him, though she kept no personal belongings in his room.

He was at the point of believing that his operational

naval career was over and that he was being trained purely for spying missions when Majorov turned up one day at the language lab and took him away in the golf cart.

"How are things going?" Majorov asked, as they whirred along toward the waterfront.

"Very well indeed, sir," Helder replied. "They're keeping me busy."

"Good, good." Majorov pulled the bill of his American-style baseball cap down a bit to exclude the sunlight. "Actually, you've had about all the training you're going to have ashore. Mr. Jones tells me you've got the legend down pat, and your weapons and other training has gone very satisfactorily. Now you're going to sea again, in a manner of speaking."

They passed without slowing through a gate manned by two men in sweatsuits and armed with Ingram Mark 10s and headed for the area covered by the water-filled roof that Helder had noticed on his first day at Malibu. The area was around a point of land from the marina, and Helder had never been able to catch sight of it, even when sailing the Finn dinghy. They descended below the level of the roof, and Majorov brought the cart to a halt. Helder followed him through a door set well back under an overhang. As they passed through it, he caught his breath. Rolling out ahead of him were about two hundred meters of submarine pens and workshops. There were three submarines in their berths, a Whiskey and two of the Romeo class, but Helder could see, as they walked briskly through the facility, two berths that would accommodate the gigantic Typhoon class, the largest subs in the Soviet fleet. There were also a dozen or so mini-submarines, mostly of Type Two and Three, the mass-produced workhorses of the Soviet minisub fleet, which were used for everything from seabed research to the carrying of troops. There were two Type Fours, as well, which were equipped with tracks for bottom crawling, and something odd, that looked like a truncated Type Four.

Helder was stunned. Even having been at Malibu as long as he had been, he had not had the slightest notion that the place was, in addition to a SPETSNAZ training center, a submarine base. He looked out across the water to where the tidal lake met the Baltic Sea. It was obvious that whatever left or arrived here did so submerged.

"I expect you see a lot that looks familiar," Majorov said.

"Yes, sir," Helder replied. "I've trained aboard everything here except"—he pointed at the shorter, track-equipped minisub—"whatever that is."

"It's just what it looks like," Majorov said. "It's a chopped-off Type Four." They walked up to the vessel and stopped. "And," Majorov said, "it's yours."

Helder stood and looked at the minisub. It was, essentially, a cylinder about two meters in diameter and six meters long, with a shaped nose and two large ports, which gave it the appearance of a huge caterpillar. Steel bottles of various sizes were attached to it on both sides, and there were two remotely operated grapplers situated at the front end.

"We took a Type Four, shortened it, and stripped it of everything not essential for its particular mission. The diesel is gone; so is the snorkel and the standard CO_2

scrubber. You've got a smaller scrubber and one small oxygen bottle, enough to keep two crew alive for the maximum operating period at cruising speed. You're left with a hundred and ten nickel cadmium battery cells weighing twenty kilograms each, which will give you three knots for twenty-four hours or six knots for two hours. As you know, the drain on the batteries increases exponentially with speed. Use of the tracks uses as much juice as full speed, which means for every five minutes you use the tracks, you lose an hour's running time. You must always keep that fact in mind; it's going to be very important to you."

"Yes, sir," Helder replied. He liked the Type Four. One man operated it, like flying a plane underwater, instead of sitting there and giving orders to two other men on the rudder and hydroplanes. Still, there was a lot for a crew of four to do on a Type Four. "You say there'll be a crew of two?"

Majorov nodded. "That's one reason we've stripped it down so much, to make it as simple as possible."

"Who's my man?" Helder asked. He had a feeling he wasn't going to have any choice in the matter.

Majorov walked to the bows of the minisub and looked into one of the ports. "Here's your man, now." He grinned, slapping his palm on the hull of the vessel. The hatch on top of the minisub opened and a familiar face looked out.

At first, Helder couldn't place him, and then as he climbed out of the vessel and down the ladder, it came to him. A lithe figure, dressed only in gym shorts and a tee shirt, jumped lightly to the ground, and in doing so displayed the body and coordination of a world-class athlete.

"Captain Third Grade Helder, Captain Lieutenant Sokolov," Majorov said, smiling.

"Sokolov," Helder said, extending his hand.

"Helder," Sokolov replied, grasping it.

The hand was hard, horny, and very strong. Helder could not stop himself from staring at the familiar short, pale hair, square jaw, and widely placed eyes, at the fine mustache above the thin, hard mouth. Helder's man was Valerie Sokolov, who had won the women's decathlon at the 1980 Olympics in Moscow, after astonishing the world by passing a chromosome test.

"Sokolov will be your second-in-command, your engineering officer, your communications officer, and your political officer, all rolled into one." Majorov grinned. "You will find her as competent in each of those areas as on the track."

"I am sure I will," Helder said, trying to smile at the woman.

"I hope so," Sokolov said. She did not smile.

"Sokolov has been working on the modifications to the sub," Majorov said, patting the machine proprietarily. "Now, let me show you what its purpose is," he said, leading Helder and Sokolov around to its other side. "You know, of course, that grappling arms are not standard equipment on a Type Four, but they are very necessary for your mission." They approached a stainless steel cylinder about half a meter in diameter and something over a meter high, resting near the sub. "This will be your payload," Majorov said. "Or rather, something

very like it. This particular example is filled with concrete, to approximate the weight of the real equipment,
which is virtually complete, but undergoing final testing.
It is a newly developed radio transmitter which, when
placed on the seabed in the proper position and depth
of water, will, on receipt of a sonar signal from a nearby
submarine, allow its top twenty centimeters to disengage
from the cylinder, rise to the surface and broadcast a
navigational beacon to special equipment on submarines,
surface vessels, and aircraft approaching the area."

Helder furrowed his brow. "I was under the impression that the current technology in inertial guidance systems and radio navigation was sufficient to navigate to
any spot within a matter of a few meters," he said.

"That is true, of course"—Majorov smiled—"but this
particular buoy, the only one of its kind, incidentally, is
to be placed in an area of magnetic anomalies that play
tricks on more conventional systems. It has also been
developed specifically for use in a particular spot which
has more than its share of hazards to navigation by other
systems—water density and salinity, shallow depths, et
cetera. You'll have to trust me on that; I can tell you no
more at this time."

"Of course, Colonel," Helder replied. "In any case,
my job is, as I understand it, to deliver the system, not to
question its purpose."

"Precisely," Majorov said. "You will be dropped from
a mother sub within range of your objective; you will,
after confirming your position by three means of navigation, place the buoy within fifty meters of the speci-
fied coordinates, then return to your mother sub. I am

satisfied that you and Sokolov are the best possible team for the job, you with your superb spatial orientation and outstanding navigational skills; Sokolov with technical support."

"Thank you, Colonel."

"We are fortunate in having excellent conditions for training just outside our tidal lake, in the Baltic," Majorov said. "I cannot yet give you the date of your mission—indeed, you may only have a few hours', even a few minutes' notice—but I can tell you that you must be ready to perform this task, ready in every possible respect, three weeks from today."

Helder nodded. "I can see no problem with that sort of schedule," he said, glancing at Sokolov, "providing the equipment performs as intended."

Sokolov turned her narrow eyes on Helder. "There will be no problem with any technical matter," she said, in a cold, light baritone. "You may be certain of that."

"Good," Helder said. "In that case, Colonel, you may rely on us absolutely."

"That's what I wanted to hear from you." Majorov smiled, clapping Helder on the shoulder. "Now, I want you to get started today, familiarizing Sokolov with the sub," he said.

Helder looked at him in surprise. "Excuse me, Colonel, but I thought you said that Sokolov had helped develop the sub's modifications."

"Of course," Majorov replied, laughing. "And she will familiarize you with the modifications and new equipment. But you are the experienced submariner; Sokolov has never actually been down in one."

Helder was speechless. He was supposed to pilot this ship to within fifty meters of a spot on the seabed, deploy a never-before-used navigational buoy, and return to a mother sub with a crew who had never dived in a submarine, and with three weeks for training?

His surprise must have been evident, for Sokolov leapt into the breech. "I assure you, Helder, that I will perform to your expectations. In my career, I have trained for many difficult tasks, and I have not failed, yet."

Helder turned to her. "I have trained men—ah, submariners for many difficult tasks, and I have never accepted failure from any of them," he said. "You are quite right, Sokolov. You will not fail."

Majorov smiled at them both, but not with his eyes. "Good," he said. "I see we all understand each other."

11

Rule arrived at the Agency on the morning of her thirty-fifth birthday to see, preceding her into the headquarters lobby, a familiar, bearlike figure. "Ed Rawls!" she called out and laughed at his quizzical expression as he turned.

"Hello, hello, hello!" Rawls rumbled, giving her a big hug and kiss. "How are you, Kate?" He had been in the Rome station when she was a glorified clerk.

"Never better, would be my best guess. And you? And Bette?"

He grinned. "Never better would describe us, too. Especially together." He shot her a wink. "I have a lot to thank you for."

Rule laughed at the memory of it. Ed Rawls had been banging the ambassador's wife in Rome, not the sort of thing the Company smiled upon, and his biggest problem had been not his employer, but his wife, a formidable lady who knew her husband well. In a scene right out of a French farce, Kate had snatched Rawls out of a dark embassy corridor in the wee hours, hidden him in her closet, and poured a drink for the pursuing Bette, while Ed sweated out an hour among Kate's dresses. The experience had, apparently, put the fear of God into Ed, or at least, the fear of Bette, which was enough.

"You sure do, sport," she laughed. "You'd be sleeping with the fishes in the Tiber if Bette had got her hands on you that night." She did not mention that he would be out of a career, as well, and it was a career fast becoming a legend in the Company. Ed Rawls, in his quiet, rumpled way, had, in recent years, brought off as many successful operations against the Soviets as any covert operator since the founding of the CIA. There were many in the Company who felt that the job of Deputy Director for Operations, now held by Simon Rule, should have gone to Rawls. "What brings you to Langley?"

"Business," Rawls replied, and Rule knew enough not to inquire further. "Listen, I was really sorry to hear about you and Simon."

"Then you were the only one who was," she shot back, "including me and Simon. Just one of those monumentally stupid mistakes the flesh is heir to. I got a nice kid out of it, though. He makes up for the worst of it."

"Well, I must say, being single seems to agree with you. You look sensational."

"Thank you, kind sir, just what a girl needs to hear on her thirty-fifth birthday."

"No kidding? Congratulations on making it that far in this game. I have to admit, I was afraid Simon was going to make a housewife out of you. I heard about it when you got the Soviet Office, and I cheered."

"Thanks, Ed, I'm loving it. Most of the time, anyway. Sometimes I'd like to be out there with you guys *doing* something, instead of jockeying a desk."

They passed through the lobby, and Rule waited with him for the elevator before continuing on to her ground-floor office. "Your kids must be in college by now."

Rawls nodded. "Millie is. Eddie finished this year. He's getting married in September."

"Good God! You're too young to be a grandfather, Ed!"

"Don't you believe it, sweetie; I turned fifty in January. That's it, look shocked, makes me feel good."

"So how's middle age? A few more years and I'll be there."

The elevator doors opened, and Rawls got on and held the door for a moment. "Listen, kid, when I was thirty-five, I thought fifty was middle-aged. But now that I'm fifty"—he let go the door—"I know that thirty-five is really middle-aged." The door closed on his grinning face.

Rule stood and thought about that for a minute, then continued to her office, shaking her head. Martin, from Imagery Analysis, was waiting for her, dozing in her most comfortable chair. Rule got a cup of coffee for both of them from the office machine before waking him up.

"Sorry about that," he said, blinking. "I had an all-nighter going last night, and this came in about half an hour ago. I gave it a once-over and thought I'd show it to you before I go home and get some sleep." He held up a brown envelope.

Rule cleared her desk and brought out her loupe.

Martin laid out the satshot. "There's more angle," he said, pointing. "But the Mercedes is now in profile, so there's no look at the plate. Some nice other detail, though. Have a look at that."

Rule moved the loupe to where Martin indicated. She went over the area quietly for a moment. "A golf cart?"

"That's what I make it, but the nearest golf course is in Finland, and anyway, have you ever heard of a golf cart on Soviet territory?"

"Nope," Rule said thoughtfully. "I haven't."

"See anything else interesting there?" Martin teased.

Rule looked again. "Two men, one wearing what seems like a golf or baseball cap."

"Yeah, but that's not what I mean. Look at the guy standing by the gate."

Rule looked. The golf cart was headed for a small gate which seemed to segregate one area of the complex from the rest. There was a uniformed guard with a weapon slung over his shoulder. Beyond that was nothing but the water's edge. "Where is the cart going?" Rule asked. "It doesn't make any sense. A guarded gate with nothing but a shale beach on the other side."

"That's not what I mean," Martin said impatiently. "Look at the weapon the guard has slung. You make it?"

Rule moved the loupe to the guard, who was saluting whoever was in the golf cart. His weapon could be seen resting across his back. "It's a little fuzzy, but . . . Jesus, Martin, it looks like an Ingram submachine gun."

"Could be an Uzi," Martin said, "but I've never seen that sort of suppressor on an Uzi. Looks like a Mac 10

to me. One more thing, then I'm getting out of here."
He pointed to the water, a couple of hundred yards from
the gate, an inch or so from the edge of the photograph.
"Have a look at that."

Rule moved the loupe to the spot and stared hard,
trying to make some sense of what she saw. There was
something on the water, something very small. It seemed
to be skimming the surface, creating a wake. "My father
is a fisherman," Rule said. "That looks a little like one
of his whatchamacallits . . . a plug. He used to have one
that moved along the surface of the water. This looks like
that, only bigger. I remember he never caught anything
with it."

"Yeah, it is a little like that," Martin agreed, "but
it's bigger. It looks to me like the attack periscope of a
submarine."

Rule looked sharply up at him. "Are you sure?"

Martin laughed. "Not even a little bit, but look at
this." He spread some sort of map out on her desk.
"There's no American, British, Swedish, or Finnish nautical chart for this area, but I found an aeronautical chart.
See the square I've drawn here? That's the area covered
by the coordinates of the satshot. Our bird is passing
from northwest to southeast, so the rectangle of the area
is tilted a little. Out here, you've got the Baltic, then the
Latvian coast, then, just inside the coast, another body
of water called Liepaja Ezers, a sort of tidal lagoon, shel-
tered from the Baltic by this narrow strip of land. There's
a narrow entrance, here, probably natural, but also probably improved to allow shipping to pass through. Maybe
they're moving subs in and out of there."

Rule stared at the object on the photograph. "It looks too small to be a periscope," she said.

"An attack periscope," Martin said. "Submarines have a regular scope for general use, but when there's hostile shipping in the area, they use a much smaller one, one that is less noticeable, that makes less of a wake. I'd say that object is just about the right size for an attack periscope."

Rule looked around the perimeters of the satshot. "Have you seen anything on this or any other shot to indicate submarine pens?"

Martin shook his head. "Nope, and that makes my identification of that thing as a scope very suspect, unless they've just run a sub into the lagoon, submerged for some sort of training exercise. But hell, who knows what they're up to over there." He got up and struggled into his jacket. "Well, it's not my job to guess. I just gaze at images—you're the analyst; you do the analyzing. I'm going home and get some sleep."

"Thanks, Martin," Rule said. "I appreciate your showing this to me before leaving, and thanks, too, for taking the trouble to dig out that aero chart."

"All part of the service," Martin said, tossing a wave over his shoulder. "Just part of your friendly CIA curb service."

Rule sat, staring at the satshot, at the golf cart, at the Ingram, maybe, at the periscope, maybe, at the Mercedes. Perhaps it was because it was early in the morning and she was fresh; maybe it was a message from outer space; maybe it was that least favorite thing of her superiors, her woman's intuition; maybe she was crazy; but half a dozen, eight, maybe ten isolated fragments of seemingly useless information popped together in her head, and she had something. It was like having some of the pieces of a jigsaw puzzle spread out before her, and from their accidental juxtaposition, suddenly visualizing the whole scene—and without even looking at the picture on the box.

She got COSMO up and running, called up indices of station reports, started gleaning. She hoped to God the computer input people were caught up with their work, because she'd never find the pieces of paper again, once they'd crossed her desk. She was lucky. She selected incidents from reports as they ran, and dumped them to her printer. She tapped into NEXIS, a computer news service, and extracted a dozen news stories dating back to October 1981. Before lunch, she had them all, the whole skimpy, ridiculous bunch of reports, facts and guesses, and during the morning she never stopped thinking. It wouldn't go away; it wouldn't fragment; it stayed and grew in her mind. She had it; she was sure of it; she believed it.

She grabbed the extracts, the satshot, the air chart, and all the hope she could muster and headed for Alan Nixon's office.

12

Helder sat in the uncomfortable plastic seat and ran through his checklist just once more. He had been thoroughly over the minisub with Sokolov, and he had to admit she knew what she was doing when it came to the electronics and the other equipment aboard. It still bothered him that she had no experience of submarines, but, with the way the sub's controls were laid out, that shouldn't pose any problem; he could steer and navigate the vessel and deploy the buoy; she would monitor the mechanical, electric, and electronic systems and handle communications. He was thankful that the seating was fore and aft; at least he didn't have to look directly at the implacable face, the nearly dead eyes all the time. There was a mirror mounted overhead and to his left, but it was awkwardly enough placed not to invite much use. With another crew he might have ordered it relocated, but with Valerie Sokolov, he was thankful for its placement. She smelled, too. They had not been screwed down in the sub for five minutes before it smelled like a locker room.

He glanced toward the forward ports and took in a divided scene. The lower half of the glass disks was underwater, the top half, above. The faces of the maintenance crew gazed back at him. One gave him a thumbs-up sign. He replied in a like manner. "Ready to submerge," he said, as much to himself as to Sokolov.

"Ready," she said.

It bothered him that she did not refer to him as captain or skipper, but he would not let his annoyance show. She seemed never to speak an unnecessary syllable. "Diving," he said, and reached for the rocker switches at the panel to his right. Blow tanks, he said to himself, then threw the switches. There was a rumble and the sub sank quickly. Level off at two meters, he ordered himself, and his fingers and the sub obeyed him. He was accustomed to giving orders to a crew. He would have to get over that; it took too much time. In an emergency, he wouldn't want to waste the fraction of a second required to give an order; he wanted just to react. He reached for the throttle—an electrical slide switch, really, but he thought of it as a throttle—and asked it for two knots. Less than his cruising speed of three knots, but sufficient for good control of the vessel. There was a low whine, and immediately, the sub moved forward and out of the pen. As they cleared the roof of the pens pale sunlight came into the sub, and the red interior lighting seemed unnecessary. "Switch off inside lights," he said.

Nothing happened. He turned his head and looked up into the mirror at Sokolov. She seemed to be staring straight ahead. "Sokolov! Switch off inside lights!" She jerked, looked confused for a moment, then hit the switch. "Thank you," he said coldly, "and when I give you an order I want it carried out immediately, do you understand?" He could nearly feel her flush behind him.

"Yes, sir. I am very sorry."

He held his course for a couple of minutes, to clear the end of the marina; then, glancing at his chart for a last confirmation of his position, he turned the sub south down the lake and pushed the joystick lightly. Four meters, then six showed on the fathometer. The interior of the vessel grew darker, and the instruments glowed green in the dimness. With a foot he pressed the right rudder, and the sub responded at once. He tried left rudder; the sub turned, then straightened to his touch. The controls were even lighter than on the unmodified version of the sub. He liked that; it increased the sensation of flying underwater. He pushed down on the joystick again and sank another two meters. His instruments now showed eight meters of water above him, four below. On the chart the lake deepened as it ran south. He continued to move the sub downward, keeping four meters of water under his keel. The dim light in the cabin faded even more.

"I . . . I can't see my control panel," Sokolov said. She sounded nervous.

"Well, switch on your bloody panel lights; you should have done that before we sailed." Good. She needed bringing into line.

"I can't see the switch for the panel lights," she said rapidly.

"Haven't you got a torch back there?" he asked harshly.

There was a rattling noise, and a few seconds later,

a bright light reflected off the white inside of the sub's hull. "There, I've found the switch," she said, and the torch went off, leaving them in total blackness.

Helder cut the throttle and let the sub sink until it bumped bottom. "Perfect," he said. "Now you've blown my night vision. We'll just sit here until it returns."

"I'm sorry, Captain," she said softly. "I'm very sorry. I didn't think."

Good. Now she was calling him captain, at least, and he hadn't had to ask her. He yanked back on the stick and pushed the throttle to full ahead. He heard Sokolov gasp as the sub reared back and shot toward the surface. He leveled off at two meters, grinning. He had subdued her, he reckoned; now he had to figure out if she was going to be anything more than a passenger on this mission.

13

Rule's heart slammed systematically into her rib cage as she seated herself across the desk from Alan Nixon. Just as she intuitively knew that she had hold of something very important, she instinctively knew that this meeting might determine whether anything ever came of it. They were very different, she and Nixon. She was trained and experienced at her work, brilliant, even, impulsive, daring. But she had difficulty assessing the political consequences of her actions. Nixon was trained as an executive, not as an analyst; he was politically motivated, and if he did not have her grasp of intelligence analysis, he rarely put a foot wrong when making a request for resources or a recommendation for action. If she could win his interest, now, he would know from whom to get a further hearing and how best to do it. She took a deep breath and started.

"Alan, I need your help." An appeal, not an announcement, seemed the best approach.

"Of course, Kate. Anything I can do." Nixon put his

feet on the desk and folded his hands across his middle, the most receptive possible attitude, Rule knew from experience. Then, "Is this about your Majorov?" Trouble. He was already impatient with her about that.

"Partly," she said, "but much broader. Let me go into some background, here. I know you know all of this stuff"—like hell he did—"but I need to piece this together as much for my own benefit as for yours, so bear with me."

Nixon nodded sagely.

"In October 1981, a Soviet Whiskey class submarine ran aground on the Swedish coast, near a sensitive military installation. It made worldwide headlines, you'll remember, and after that, there was a rash of periscope sightings in various parts of Sweden. A Swedish naval officer having lunch in downtown Stockholm spotted a periscope smack in the middle of the city, at a time when three American warships were visiting there, that sort of thing."

Nixon's eyebrows went up.

"Now, this was not an entirely new occurrence; there had been reports of Soviet subs in Swedish waters for years. We assumed they were there to give their crews some hard experience in waters which, if not exactly friendly, were not exactly hostile. They were running at about twenty a year. But since the 'Whiskey on the rocks' incident, they've been running at two hundred a year, and some of them have been very peculiar."

"How so?" Nixon asked, forgetting that he was supposed to know about this.

"First of all, when challenged, the subs have not broken and run the way they used to. As often as not, they've pressed *further* into Swedish territory, even under pursuit. Second, there have been credible reports, not just of subs, but of frogmen being landed from them and heading away from the sea. Some militiamen have taken shots at them, but have never caught one. But the most peculiar thing about all this is that nobody, not the Swedish government, not their military nor their intelligence, not our military nor our intelligence, has been able to come up with a credible hypothesis of why the Soviets are doing this. Oh, there are lots of theories—everything from training exercises to just fun and games—but none of them really adds up; none of them makes for any reasonable balance between what the Soviets have to gain from all of this and what they have to lose. They have, for instance, already been publicly humiliated in the world's press when their sub got caught aground in Sweden, but that didn't stop their incursions. As I mentioned, they have increased tenfold since that incident."

"Well, you're right, Kate. The whole thing certainly is baffling. Do you have a new theory on why they're doing it?"

Rule held up a hand. "Not a new theory; maybe some support for an old one. But hang on, there are some other points to bring into this. They're pretty scattered, but there may be a broad pattern emerging, which brings me to Majorov, who just might be the key to the whole thing."

Nixon took his feet off the desk and sat up straight. His expression had gone blank.

Rule spread out her two satellite photographs on

his desk. "What we seem to have here is a very special sort of military training base. It's at Liepaja, on the Latvian coast, and it's special because they've gone to so much trouble to make it seem like something else." She pointed out the drilling joggers and the double fencing. "We know that Majorov loves expensive foreign cars and gadgets, and here we have, on the same base, mind you, a Mercedes 500 SE, which simply does not exist outside of Moscow, and, would you believe it, a golf cart?"

Nixon pulled a large magnifying glass from his desk drawer and examined the golf cart.

Rule tapped the photograph. "I'd bet a year's salary that one of those two men in the cart, the one with the baseball cap, is Majorov, and Majorov's presence here increases the importance of this base to the nth degree."

"What else have you got, Kate?" Nixon asked.

"Little stuff, crazy stuff, but stuff that fits. Item: the laundries at two marine infantry bases are suddenly doing markedly fewer shirts—that means significant numbers of men are being transferred elsewhere. Item: last month, two thousand Ingram Mac 10 submachine guns were stolen from a British arms depot—this guard"—she tapped the satshot—"has an Ingram Mac 10 slung over his shoulder. Item: there isn't a known Soviet submarine base between Leningrad and Kaliningrad, down near the Polish border, but one of our best imagery analysts says that little thing right there is a submarine periscope. Item: now get this, please—during the last two years the Soviets have suddenly, dramatically increased the teaching of the Swedish language in their universities and language centers. Let me tell you something, Alan. Swedish is the most useless language in the world, unless you're in Sweden."

Nixon looked up sharply at her. "What are you getting at, Kate?"

Rule pulled a news story from her file. "This is a direct quote from Vice Admiral Bengt Schuback, who was at the time chief of staff of the Royal Swedish Navy, and who now is their equivalent of our chairman of the Joint Chiefs of Staff: 'A foreign power is preparing for war with Sweden.'" Rule put down the paper and looked at Nixon. "That's just one of the many theories about what the Soviet subs are doing in Swedish waters, of course, but I think what is developing here suddenly lends a lot of weight to it, don't you think?"

Nixon stared at her dumbly for a moment, then managed to speak. "But why? Why would the Soviets suddenly abandon their policy of expansion without armed conflict to do something that might start World War III?"

"Start World War III? With whom? With us? Sweden is as determinedly neutral as Switzerland; she has no, repeat, *no* allies. Suppose, for a moment, that NATO decided to intervene; how would we do it? We have no land forces in place to stop a Soviet invasion of Sweden; we'd have to use nuclear weapons. Do you think for a moment that NATO would start a nuclear war, risking the destruction of Europe, possibly the world, to save eight million Swedes from Soviet domination?"

Nixon's eyes seemed to go out of focus. He sat, frozen, seemingly speechless. Then he seemed to come to himself. "Kate, I'm going to have to talk with some other people about this. Is this everything you have?"

"It's everything I can get without a lot more authority. If you can get me the clout, then I know I can come up with a lot more." She made a determined effort to sound cool and calm. "Look, Alan, I don't want to sound like a crank about this; I know as well as anybody you're going to talk to that all I've got here is, at best, informed supposition. But intelligence analysis is not quantum physics; it doesn't operate according to some immutable natural law. Sometimes it's just a step away from fortune-telling, you know that. But I have to tell you, that based on my experience, I really believe something is going on here. I can't prove it, though, and I'm not going to be able to unless you can persuade somebody to launch some sort of covert initiative to turn up more raw intelligence."

"Just what sort of initiative do you want?"

Rule knew better than that. Simon Rule was director of Operations, and he would not be thrilled to hear her advice on the subject. "There are people in the company better qualified than I to decide that," she said. "When they see this stuff, they'll know the sort of information they need; they can put it out to the appropriate networks. Do you want me to go with you to put my case?" She knew he could do it better than she, if only he believed her. She thought he did.

"No, I think it's better if I handle it myself, at least for the moment." He gathered the photographs and her file together and stood up. "I'm going to see somebody now, so stay in your office until you hear from me. Does anybody else know about this?"

"Only fragments. You're the only person I've given it all to."

"Good. For God's sake, don't say a word about this
to anybody else." Nixon walked out of his office with her
file and left her standing there.

Rule took half a dozen deep breaths. She had done
it; she had hooked Alan Nixon, and now he was carrying
the ball. She walked back to her office with a light step.
She wanted Alan Nixon's job when he retired, and this
was the sort of operation that would help her get it. This
was original, brilliant work, she knew it, the sort of opportunity that came along once in a career, if you were
lucky. She had gotten lucky.

14

Helder walked once more around the minisub, the clipboard in his hand. He looked up to see Majorov striding toward him across the giant sub shed. Majorov wasn't going to like this. He was a planner, and he wasn't going to like being told his plan was wrong.

"Good morning, Helder," Majorov said. "Sokolov."

"Good morning, sir," Helder and Sokolov said in unison.

"What is the problem?" the colonel asked.

"I hope there may not be one, sir," Helder replied. "I'm hoping the actual buoy will weigh less than the dummy."

"Actually, it will weigh fifty kilos or so more. I'm sorry. I should have told you. Does that pose a problem?"

"Not really, Colonel," Sokolov broke in.

Helder wheeled on the woman. "Sokolov, stand at attention!"

Valerie Sokolov assumed the stance as slowly as possible.

"I will ask for your views when I wish to have them," Helder said. He turned back to Majorov. "Sir, I apologize for my crew. Are you certain about the weight of the actual buoy? What could weigh more than solid concrete?"

"Uranium 235," Majorov replied.

"What?" Helder asked, unable to contain his surprise.

"Don't worry, Helder," Majorov said. "It will be spent uranium. It is heavier than lead, and the buoy's designers want a very heavy base for purposes of ballast. The buoy must remain in an upright position in order to be effective. How will the weight affect the sub?"

"Sir, with the present weight of the dummy, the sub's maneuverability is marginal. With another fifty kilos added, I believe we must increase the size of the diving planes and the rudder in order to have a proper degree of maneuverability. Sokolov disagrees with me," he added. "Sokolov, state your position."

"I do indeed disagree, Colonel," Sokolov said, still at attention. "I have witnessed three days of trials with the dummy aboard, and the sub seems to be responding adequately to its controls."

"Helder?" Majorov asked, turning toward him.

"Yes, sir, the sub responds adequately under conditions in the lagoon, but it is my understanding that I am to assume combat conditions for this mission."

"That is so," Majorov said.

"Then I must assume that I might have to place the buoy while being hunted, perhaps even while being depth charged. Maneuverability is inadequate for combat conditions at present, even using the dummy. With another fifty kilos added, the sub will be very sluggish indeed. Incidentally, I presume the operating range figures you gave me were calculated for the actual weight of the buoy?"

Majorov nodded. "They were calculated to allow for the weight of the buoy for sixty percent of the mission. You would, of course, be free of that weight on the return journey."

"Sir, I must still disagree," Sokolov said. "The sub is responding adequately now, and I don't see that another fifty kilos will matter much."

"The reason you do not see it," Helder cut in, "is that you are not at the controls, and you have no operational experience whatever to support your opinion."

"Helder," Majorov said, "give whatever instructions you feel are necessary for modifications to the sub, and let me know the shortest possible time they will take."

"Sir," Sokolov broke in again, "to increase the size of the diving planes and rudder will take three working days."

"Wrong, Sokolov," Helder said. "They will take a day and a half, because you will not sleep until they are completed. Begin work now."

"Yes, sir," Sokolov said through clenched teeth, then wheeled and strode away, summoning the maintenance crew as she went.

"Colonel Majorov," Helder said wearily, "I must ask you for a replacement for Sokolov. Not only is she inexperienced in subs, she is constantly insubordinate. I must tell you that if I had her in a fleet sub training crew I would have fired her out of a torpedo tube by now."

Majorov laughed and clapped Helder on the back. "I know, Helder, I had expected something like this, and I must tell you, you are handling her very well. However, there were other considerations in making this assignment. Valerie Sokolov is a national heroine, because of her performance at the Olympics. I think you are aware of the role sports heroes play in our national life, and when this operation is completed, it will be important for nationally recognizable figures to have been a part of it. I can promise you, though, that once the operation is successful, you will never again encounter her in any operational capacity. She will be quite busy visiting factories and schools, inspiring the workers and students. Believe me, even with her reputation, I would not have assigned her to you if she were not fully capable of the work. I know she is inexperienced in subs, but her role is a technical one, and I know very well that a commander of your experience with green sailors can handle a single woman, no matter how arrogant and difficult." He clapped Helder on the back again. "Press on with your modifications and your training. You are still on schedule; you will be ready when the moment comes." He walked quickly toward the door, as if to avoid further discussion.

Helder turned back toward the sub with a heavy feeling in his chest. He had not had time to express his most important reservation about Valerie Sokolov. In the sub, underwater, Sokolov was afraid, and she did not seem to be overcoming it as the training progressed. Helder was afraid of her fear.

15

Rule drummed her fingers on the windowsill and looked involuntarily at the phone. It had been more than an hour. Nixon was getting a hearing somewhere upstairs, she knew, because she had called his secretary twice, and he wasn't in his office. The time was encouraging, she thought. She had put her case to Nixon in a few minutes. The longer they talked, the more credence they put in her theory. The time was creeping up on two hours when she called Will Lee.

"Hello."

"Hello!"

There was never any need for names; they knew each other's voices well.

"Listen," she said, trying to contain herself, "I'll buy you dinner tonight—and wherever you like."

"You're on. Let's make it Restaurant Lasserre, in Paris, about eight-thirty?"

She laughed. "You get us there by eight-thirty, and I'll buy."

"Oh. In that case, let's make it Maison Blanche on F Street, and I'll pick you up at eight."

"I hope they take credit cards; payday isn't till the fifteenth."

"Would I take undue advantage of your kind offer at a place that wouldn't take your credit card? Anyway, if they won't, I'll make them hold your personal check till payday."

"You're a regular prince."

"You know it. What're we celebrating?"

"I'll tell you tonight. By the way, it's black-tie."

"You really know how to get even with a fellow, don't you?"

"Eight o'clock. You book the table." She hung up, glanced around and jumped. Alan Nixon was standing in her office door.

"Alan, you scared me half to death."

Nixon said nothing; he closed the door and sat down. He tossed her file folder onto her desk. He was expressionless, but there were little splotches of color dotted about his face.

When he didn't speak, Rule did. "You struck out," she said.

"I didn't strike out," Nixon replied, rubbing the bridge of his nose. "I was thrown out of the game. Kicked out of the ballpark. Banned from the sport. I'm lucky the spectators didn't beat me to death with the chairs."

Rule slumped. "Simon didn't buy it, huh?"

"Simon hardly said a word. The director did all the talking."

"The director! Jesus, Alan, you didn't go to the director at this stage."

"No, I went to Simon. Two minutes into my little presentation, the director walked in. Just a sociable visit. Simon suggested I start again from the top, for the director's benefit, just to give him an idea of the sort of analysis the Soviet Office does."

"The bastard," Rule said, burying her face in her hands. "The director's an amateur."

"Funny," Nixon said, "that's what the director called *me*." His voice rose a little, and Rule began to see how angry he was. "He tore a very wide strip off my hide while Simon Rule watched," Nixon said, "and I didn't like it."

"I'm sorry, Alan. I'm sorry you had to go through that for me."

"So am I," he said, standing up, "and believe me, I'm not going to go through that again." He tapped the file on her desk. "Lose this, Kate. Cease working on it, and go back to your regular work. If something else comes in on Majorov, add it to your bio on him, but I don't want to hear about it."

"Look, Alan," she said in desperation, "there's just one other thing. Majorov wasn't mentioned in any of the digests of the Malakhov interrogations. I don't think anybody asked about him; there was no reason to, at the time, I guess, and Malakhov obviously didn't volunteer anything. Can't we request that from the interrogation team leader? Can't we just do that?"

"Listen, Kate," Nixon fumed. "Ed Rawls is the best interrogator this service has, and if it isn't in his reports, then it isn't in Malakhov's head."

So Ed Rawls was leading the team, she thought. That's probably what he was doing here, making his final report.

Nixon walked to the door. "I know you're not going to stop this," he said angrily. "I know you're too much of a goddamned Bolshevik to take a direct order. Well, let me tell you this, Kate; if I hear that you've spent so much as a minute on this, before, during, or after Agency hours; if someone comes to me and says he heard somebody else heard that you made so much as a single request for resources in pursuit of this fantasy, then I'll not only take the Office away from you, I'll kick you right out of this directorate, do you hear me? I'll see you in personnel, doing on-campus recruiting! Do I make myself clear?"

Rule nodded dumbly.

Nixon opened the door and walked out, closing the door behind him.

Rule leaned forward and cradled her head in her arms. She had flashed on something, then rushed into it too fast; she had let her intuition get the better of her judgment; she had ruined a relationship with her immediate superior that had taken years to build; her name had been brought to the attention of the political hack who was the director and, therefore, God Almighty, and in the worst possible light. This would go into her personnel package; it would dog her for years. Worst of all, it would give Simon something substantive to use as a crowbar to get her out of the Agency, something he had never had until now. She was in a lot of trouble, and she knew it.

But Nixon had been right; she wouldn't stop. She thought it was too important. She would just have to be careful, but she wouldn't stop. She picked up the telephone.

"Smith."

"Martin? Kate Rule."

He waited a beat. "Yeah, Kate?"

"Listen, will you copy me on any further satshots of the Liepaja area?"

A longer beat. "Listen, Kate, I'm sorry, but I've just gotten an exclusion order on you."

"What?"

"Yeah, not thirty seconds ago."

She couldn't believe it. "To what extent?"

"Scandinavia and the Baltic Basin."

"At what level?"

"One."

Shit. The director himself, probably. "What quoted authority?"

"Snowflower."

"Snowflower?"

"That's what it says here."

"Who or what is Snowflower?"

A long silence. "I don't know, Kate."

Rule flinched. In the Agency, a long silence followed by "I don't know" meant "You know better than to ask me that."

"I'm sorry, Martin. Thanks."

"I hope you get it sorted out, Kate. I wish I could help."

"I know you do." They both hung up.

An exclusion order on a Head of Office? It was unheard of. This was real trouble. She hoped it had only gone to Imagery Analysis; if the director were mad enough to make it general, she'd be a pariah by noon the next day. She stuck the file in her briefcase. She wanted to get out of there.

She drove home slowly, numb with depression. Once inside the house, she struggled upstairs and threw herself on the bed. Some time later, she woke. There had been a noise. The doorbell? She stumbled down the stairs in the half-darkness, trying to clear her head. The bell rang again, just as she reached for the doorknob. She opened it. Will Lee stood there, wearing a tuxedo.

16

Helder watched the needle on the radio compass and kicked the rudder right to correct two degrees. The sub came quickly on course; the enlarged rudder was doing its job. He was less happy with the diving planes. Something would still have to be done about those.

It was the first night drill with the mother sub, under simulated combat conditions, using no lights. He had only the coordinates of the submarine, the radio pulse, beeping erratically, so as not to attract the attention of an alert opposition listener, and, during his final approach, a tiny red light inside the launching chamber of the mother sub. He watched the compass and listened. Another beep came, and he corrected minutely. Then, in the murky darkness, the little red strobe winked at him. It was situated at the back of the chamber and could only be seen through the open doors, from dead ahead. If he approached at night from as little as five degrees off center, he might strike the sub's hull, making a very loud noise, or miss the sub entirely.

He throttled back and let the minisub sink to the floor of the lagoon, then engaged the track drive and tractored up the ramp. He could hear its low whine as the ramp closed behind him and felt the sub lift and move away. Behind him he could hear Sokolov's breathing, too rapid for his liking. They sat for another four or five minutes in the darkness, still surrounded by water, waiting for the mother sub to move away from the pickup point; then there was a hiss of compressed air, and abruptly, the floodlights of the chamber came on. Helder glanced quickly in his rearview mirror at Sokolov, in time to see her face bathed with sweat. He wished, once again, that he could replace her, that politics didn't matter. But politics always mattered, no less in the military than in the Party.

As the water level went down in the chamber, Helder could see Majorov through the glass inspection hatch, giving him a thumbs-up sign. He reached up to pop the hatch above him.

"No!" Sokolov said, sharply. "The chamber is not evacuated entirely."

He turned and looked at her. "Don't quote regulations to me, Sokolov."

"It is a regulation within my province, Captain," she said.

"Don't quote regulations to me in any circumstances," he said firmly, and held her gaze until she nodded. He spun the pressure wheel, popped the hatch, and stood up. There were still three feet of water in the chamber, but he had been longing to stretch. Even with the new seat he had insisted upon, the Type Four was still cramped. He hoisted himself through the hatch and sat on top of the sub until the chamber was dry. He saw the pressure wheel spin on the chamber's hatch, and Majorov stepped in.

"First rate, Helder," he said, smiling his languid smile. "You and Sokolov come to the wardroom when you've got the kinks out. I've some things to tell you." He stepped back into the sub proper, leaving the hatch open.

Helder, followed by Sokolov, slid down the minisub's hull to the wet steel deck of the launching chamber, and stepped through the hatch. They were immediately replaced in the launching chamber by two maintenance men, who began recharging the minisub's batteries. The Juliet class sub's forward torpedo room had been replaced by the launching chamber, and as Helder walked through the vessel, he was struck, as always, by how empty it seemed without the forward berths and the torpedo crews. The sub carried only the crew necessary to deploy minisubs, and they lived in comparative spaciousness. The captain had an actual cabin, as opposed to the alcove Helder had occupied when commander of the Whiskey, and the wardroom was larger, too. Helder and the sub's skipper waited for them at the table, and there was a large-scale nautical chart spread out. When they had been given cups of broth by the cook, the little group was left alone.

"Up until this time," Majorov said, "you have been training blind. Now it is time for you to know the details of your mission. It is, I am glad to say, fairly straightforward." He laid a finger on the chart at the edge nearest Malibu and began moving it toward the coast on the chart.

Helder was not surprised to see that the chart was the coast of Sweden, the Stockholm Archipelago.

"You will enter the approaches to Stockholm, following close upon the Viking ferry from Helsinki, to mingle your sounds with theirs." Majorov's finger traced the course of the ferry through the archipelago for about two-thirds of the way to Stockholm, then stopped. "The mother sub will leave the ferry's course here, in the bay called Trälhavet." He pointed to an open body of water amid dozens of surrounding islands. "Your arrival should be about oh-three hundred hours, but the time of day does not make a great deal of difference, since at this time of year there is very little darkness, anyway. There in the bay, the mother sub will rest on the bottom and immediately deploy the Type Four."

In the instant before Majorov began his next sentence, it suddenly came to Helder that what he was doing was finally, positively real. After his years of training, of exercises and maneuvers, he was now going to perform. He hung on Majorov's every word.

"Now, Helder, you will proceed in a southwesterly direction, following the marked route through the islands of the archipelago, past the town of Vaxön, emerging to the south in this larger channel, in more open water. This should be fairly easy, since the channel is buoyed, and the buoys are lit. There should be little traffic at this hour, and you will be able to move close to the surface, using your periscope frequently to find the next channel marker. I stress, though, that you are not to use your

periscope constantly, for obvious reasons." He smiled.
"We have given the Swedes good cause the last couple of
years to be periscope-conscious."

Helder agreed that navigating the channel submerged
should pose little problem.

Majorov continued. "Emerging here, you will turn
in a southwesterly direction again, still following the
main channel, past the town of Brevik, on your starboard
hand, to a point here, in the body of water called the Lilla
Vartan. Here you will deploy your cargo."

Helder felt a little shiver. Majorov's finger rested on
a spot no more than five kilometers from the center of
Stockholm.

"Then," said Majorov, "you will return to the mother
sub by the same route. She is to wait for you exactly
twenty-four hours, since that is the outer limit of both
your batteries' running time and your oxygen supply.
If you have not returned by that time, you will be pre-
sumed to have abandoned or to be casualties. As you
can see, the total distance you must travel is only twelve
kilometers, and at your standard operational speed of
three knots, that distance would consume less than three
hours of running time, so you would seem to have a very
comfortable safety margin. However, that margin would
presume an entirely uneventful passage, and that is very
unlikely."

Majorov rose and began to pace as he talked. "Since
the Whiskey-on-the-rocks incident in 1981, the Swedes
have been rapidly improving their sub-hunting capabilities. In 'eighty-one, when they had four of our minisubs penned up in the archipelago, all four escaped, but

you must remember that they are better now than then. You must be prepared for the worst conditions, and you must—I repeat, you must—complete the deployment of the buoy, no matter what happens. This buoy is absolutely vital to the success of our mission, and it is one of a kind; there is no backup equipment, no chance of a second mission if you fail. Should this buoy not be correctly deployed, the lives of hundreds, perhaps thousands of the cream of the Soviet military will be placed in the greatest jeopardy."

He paused, turned and looked directly at Helder and Sokolov. "That said, you should know that there is one possibility even worse than not deploying the buoy; that is if either of you should fall into Swedish hands. If, for any reason, you should have to abandon the minisub, each of you has a carefully prepared legend, and you will have further instructions which will make it possible for you to make your way to Finland, whence you will be transported back to Malibu. Should you find yourselves on the beach, you are to separate at once. Your legends have been based on traveling alone. You have each already been issued a handgun, and before your departure you will be issued two clips of ammunition and other aids for survival. The supposition is that, should you find yourself in a situation where you might use up two clips of ammunition, you will be unlikely to need more. You will also be issued with—how shall I put it?—aids for nonsurvival." Majorov shook his head. "No, euphemisms will not suffice in this situation. Let me put it to you bluntly. Should you find yourself in Swedish hands, you must take your own lives. If either of you has any doubts of your ability to perform that task, I must know now." He raised his eyebrows.

"No doubts, Colonel," Sokolov said, immediately.

"None whatever," echoed Helder. But he was damned if he'd kill himself. He was going to survive this mission, one way or another.

"Good," said Majorov. "Now there is just one more thing. I am pleased to tell you that work on the buoy has been completed. It will arrive at Malibu tomorrow, and Sokolov, you will immediately be certain that there are no mating problems between the grapplers on the mini-sub and the receptacles on the buoy."

"Yes, Colonel," Sokolov replied.

Helder was about to ask whether there could be prac-tice with the actual buoy, when Majorov interrupted him.

"We have good weather for the next three days, the met office tells me," he said. "You have worked hard in the past days, and you have proved yourselves ready. You go tomorrow night."

Helder's heart stopped. They weren't ready. He hadn't even been able yet to bring up the matter of further en-larging the diving planes, and he was very uncertain of Sokolov, whether she was going to hold herself together underwater. But he stopped himself from protesting. He could see that, whether or not he and Sokolov and the minisub were ready, Majorov was ready. He glanced at Sokolov. She, for once, was speechless. Helder forced himself to speak up. "Good, sir. We are ready."

"Fine, fine," Majorov said, rubbing his hands. "You are dismissed, now. Get a good night's rest, and take the morning off. The buoy will be in the sub pens by fourteen hundred hours."

Helder and Sokolov got up and started for the submarine's main hatch.

"Oh, Helder," Majorov said, seemingly as an afterthought, "stay for a moment; there's a personal matter I'd like to discuss with you."

"Of course, sir," Helder said.

Majorov waited until Sokolov and the skipper had left the wardroom before speaking. "Helder, there is one further task which you may have to perform." His face was expressionless. "Sweden, unlike the United States, competed in the 1980 Moscow Olympics, and the games received full press and television coverage in that country. Therefore, Sokolov's face is too well known in Sweden for her to be allowed ashore there. If you should have to abandon the minisub, you are to see that she does not leave the submarine. Do you understand? In those circumstances you are to kill her."

There was only a moment's hesitation before Helder replied. He wondered if he could do it. There had been times on every training exercise when he would have liked to kill Sokolov. But could he do it if the moment came? Could he become a cold-blooded assassin? He would have to think about that. In the meantime, though, he could leave Majorov with no doubts about his resolve. "Yes, Colonel, I understand completely," he said.

17

Rule gaped at the handsome man in the dinner jacket, trying to get her groggy mind into gear.

"Hi, remember me?" Will Lee asked.

Oh, God, she had a dinner date, a celebration, no less. In the midst of her depression she had forgotten. She was about to speak when two things stopped her; the ring of the telephone and the sight of the man who had been following her, now sauntering past her house on the opposite side of the street. She grabbed Will by the wrist and dragged him into the house. The telephone rang again. "Just a minute, Will," she said, grabbing for the phone. "Hello."

"Can I interest you in an impromptu dinner with a beat-up old spy?" Ed Rawls drawled. "I tried to get you at the office, but you'd already left."

Rule hadn't been expecting this, but her mind was suddenly clear, and she didn't hesitate. "Oh, yes, Ed, I'd love to have dinner with you tonight." She caught a glimpse of Will's face, which had twisted into an astonished frown, and waved an impatient hand to keep him from speaking. "Just tell me when and where." Her mind was racing.

"Well, I've taken a little place in Georgetown. It's no palace, but there's a grill out back. Why don't I do you a steak?"

"Sounds great," she replied, scribbling down the address. "You're only a few blocks from me. What time?"

"Soon as you like. Dress sloppy."

"I'll be there in twenty minutes," she said. She hung up and turned to Will, throwing up her hands in a defensive gesture. "Now wait a minute; I know this seems crazy; I know we had a dinner date . . ."

"A celebration, as I recall," he said, dryly. "Tell me, what were we celebrating when we still had a date? And who the hell is Ed?"

She took his face in her hands. "Look, I know I've screwed up your evening and all, but my reason for celebrating turned out to be more of a reason for a wake, and the guy who just called is an old friend on the covert side who may be the only person in the world who can help me fix it. Please understand, please. My whole career is in the wringer right now, and I've got to get it out."

His face dissolved into a resigned smile. "Okay, sure. I'll take a rain check. Is this something to do with Majorov?"

"It's everything to do with Majorov, and I wish I could explain it all to you, but I can't right now. I've got to get over there and persuade this guy to help me, and I'm not at all sure he will when he finds out what I want from him."

"Is there anything I can do to help?"

She thought for a moment. "Yes. Spend the evening here, watch TV, or read, or something. I may be able to get back early, but don't count on it. If I'm not back by, say, eleven, then go home, and I'll call you tomorrow. Okay?"

He shrugged. "Sure, I've got nothing better to do. Is there anything to eat in the house?"

"A freezer full of stuff, and there's some fairly old chicken in the fridge. I'm not sure it's edible."

"I'll make do. You get going."

"Right." She freshened her makeup in the hall mirror, grabbed her purse, started for the door, then stopped. The goon, as she had come to think of him, was out there in the street, and she didn't want him following her to Ed's. She went out her back door, through the ill-tended garden, pulled a plank off the fence that separated her garden from her neighbor's, and squeezed through. She walked through a carefully groomed garden to some French doors at the back of the neighboring house and rapped on the glass. An elderly man watching TV inside started, then came and opened the door.

"I'm Katharine Rule," she said to the stranger. "I live just behind you, and I didn't want to leave my house by the front door. There's this man who's been bothering me lately, you see, and I'd like to avoid him. Would you mind very much if I got to the street through your house?"

"Why no," the man said, baffled but courtly. "Please come in." He led her through his house and let her out the front door.

"Thank you so much," she said, waving.

"Not at all," he replied. "Anytime. It's been quite a while since a pretty girl tapped at my window," he called after her.

It took less than ten minutes to make her way to Ed Rawls's place, a basement apartment on P Street. She rang the bell, and Rawls answered the door in old khakis and a golf shirt. He kissed her on the cheek. "Come on in. It's not much; I just got it this week." He showed her quickly around the three-room flat, furnished in what looked like hand-me-downs from the owner upstairs. "It's a short let, until Betty can get down here and do some house hunting. I'll bet you want a drink."

"I'd kill for a bourbon on the rocks. You coming back to Langley, Ed?"

He nodded. "That's not for publication, though, not yet. I'm not due to start for a few days. Come on out back." He led her to a small terrace behind the house and installed her in a deck chair with her drink.

It was pleasant outside; there was still a lot of evening light at this time of year, but the heat of the day had waned. Bees buzzed about a garden as unkempt as her own. "I shouldn't ask, Ed, but what's the job?"

"Oh, it's okay; it's above the line. Assistant Deputy Director for Operations."

"That's terrific, Ed! Hell, you ought to be DDO, and everybody knows it."

Rawls laughed. "Now, now, pull your claws back in. I won't mind working for Simon. He and I have always understood each other. I've known him even longer than you have, you know, though maybe not as well."

"I'm sorry, Ed, I didn't mean to make a compliment an attack on Simon. I know you wouldn't be getting this job if he didn't want you, and you owe him your loyalty."

Rawls shrugged. "Anyway, I'll be off the street, now. I'm getting too old for that stuff, anyway, and Betty is sure as hell glad to come back to DC and unpack. We reckon to ride it out here until retirement."

"I guess she's tired of following you all over the world by now; I'd be glad to get back to the States if I were in her shoes."

"Oh, we've been back for a couple of years. I've had an assignment that's kept me in the East for a while. We've been in New York, took a place in the Village, and I got home on weekends. It was like being young again; we lived in the Village for a few months right after we were married."

"Malakhov must have been an interesting assignment," Rule said, and watched the surprise register on his face. Georgi Malakhov was the highest-ranking KGB officer ever to defect to the United States, a major general who had run their New York/UN station for four years, with a cover as a Deputy Director General of the United Nations. His defection had caused a major rift in US–Soviet relations and had been one of the biggest intelligence coups for the CIA since its founding.

Rawls shrugged. "It was absorbing work," he said, "and it kept me in the States. It was a nice assignment to go out of fieldwork on."

"I've been reading the digests. Fascinating. We're up-dating files every day with that material. You ought to be very proud. It's that sort of work that really gives an analyst something to get his teeth into."

"It fell into my lap, really. Malakhov asked for me."

"No kidding, why?"

"We knew each other slightly when I was in the Stockholm station. He was station head in the Soviet Embassy there, and we never made him. Thought he was first secretary, like his billing said. Betty and I once shared a table with him and his wife at a dinner at the royal palace. We both liked both of them, but, apart from bumping into him at a couple of diplomatic cocktail parties, we never really saw anything of them. Soviet diplomats don't mix much, as you know."

"What happened after that?"

"Nothing. Nothing for what, eight years? Then I'm station head in Belgrade, and I get this priority cable to get my ass to New York, pronto. Hell, I thought I'd screwed up and they were looking for my head. They met me at Kennedy, took me to a safe house in Manhattan, and told me Malakhov had approached our UN Ambassador at a cocktail party and said he wanted to defect. Langley and the president said, sure, great; then they told him he was going to have to work both sides of the street for a while, first. They had him, of course; he had no choice. He said he'd do it, but he wanted me to run him and nobody else. Stood his ground, too; wouldn't make a move until I was there in the flesh. I could've kissed him. I ran him for nearly a year, until Moscow Central started to get suspicious and he had to bail out. It was natural for me to debrief him."

"Christ, what a career break."

"You know it, babe. I reckoned I'd gone about as far as I was going to go in this man's service, you should excuse the expression, then, wham! Lightning strikes old Rawls, and here he is about to traipse into the executive suite at Langley." He chuckled loudly. "Tell you what; it's sure going to make one hell of a difference in my retirement pay. Bette's already talking houses in the Bahamas."

"That's terrific, Ed," Rule laughed. "And it couldn't happen to a nicer guy."

"Thank you, sweetheart." Rawls turned the steaks. "I was proud of you when I heard you'd got the Soviet Office."

"I got your note, Ed; thanks."

"There's hope for all of us when they start giving the younger officers some real responsibility. You like the job?"

Rule smiled. "There are moments when I'd like a bit more action, when I wish I'd never left the covert side, but I love it, really."

Rawls studied the steaks carefully. "You going to be able to hang onto it?"

Rule sat up straight. "You heard about this afternoon?"

"Heard about it?" he snorted. "I was there!"

"In the meeting with Nixon, Simon, and the director?"

He nodded. "I walked in at the height of the whole thing. I tried to back out, but they waved me on in. I didn't hear what your report said, but I heard the director's reaction. He was pretty hot." He forked the steaks onto plates, dished up a salad, and put the food on the table. "Come and get it."

Rule dragged up a chair as he poured the wine. "Alan didn't give me a blow by blow, but I got the gist of it, I think. They've slapped an exclusion order on me for satshots of Scandinavia—at least I hope that's the extent of it."

Rawls nodded. "I was there when the director did that. Scandinavia is as far as it goes. He wouldn't hang a general exclusion order on an office head; he'd just dump you someplace cold."

Rule sipped the wine Rawls poured. "Yeah, Nixon drew that particular picture for me. He mentioned on-campus recruiting."

Rawls leaned back and laughed heartily. "Yeah, that'd be just the sort of thing, wouldn't it?"

"Ed, is the director as big a jerk as he seems to be?"

"Probably. But directors come and go, and when the president goes, he does, too. He won't stand a change of administrations, let alone parties. I reckon he'll be a cross I'll have to bear for a while, but Simon will do most of the bearing." Rawls took a deep draft of the wine. "I think Simon would like that job," he said, "and if the president's successor opts for a professional instead of a crony like the present director, I reckon he'd have a shot at it."

"Oh, yes," Rule said, "Simon would love that." She had never really thought that he might get it, until now, and the idea rattled her. "And you'd get ops, wouldn't you?"

"Who can say? If Simon likes me as his deputy, then maybe." Rawls washed down some steak with more wine. "Question is, what's going to happen to you, Kate?

Are you going to prosper in the Agency with your ex-husband as Director of Central Intelligence?"

Rule shrugged. "To tell you the truth, Ed, I'm a lot more worried about the next few weeks than the next few years. Something's going on in Scandinavia, and—"

Rawls stopped her with an upraised hand. "Hold it right there, Kate. I don't want to hear a rump view of world events right at the moment. I drew you a picture of where things are going and who's going to be there. If I hear about this, I want to hear about it through channels."

Rule blushed. "You're right; I didn't mean to try to make an end run. It's just that I'm in a lot of trouble right now, and in the dark, and I've been denied work time and access to information on something that I've got a very strong gut feeling about."

Rawls nodded. "I've had a few of those in my time."

"What did you do?"

He laughed. "I kept at it. Made something of it, sometimes, too. Other times, got my ass in a wringer."

"That's about where I am, but I can't let go of this one. I think this is very, very important, Ed."

"I believe you," he said. "I know how bright you are, and although I haven't seen much of you lately, I've heard good things. If I were in the director's shoes, I'd listen, at the very least."

"Thanks." Rule waited until he had poured coffee, then leaned forward. "Listen, Ed, I understand why you can't listen to my theory right now, but I could use some advice, and some help, if you'll give it to me." She knew he was in her debt, but she didn't want to be too blatant in reminding him.

"Advice? Sure. Help? That depends on what kind."

Rule took a deep breath. "First of all, I need a computer security code for entry to COSMO. As things stand now, if I use my own code and they audit my online time, they'll know I'm still working on this, and I'll get shipped. I need somebody's unlock from another department entirely, preferably one they won't audit in the course of things."

Rawls grinned a small grin. "Okay, don't write this down, memorize it." He recited a ten-digit code. "Got it?"

Rule repeated it to herself. "Got it. It's not yours? I don't want to hang this on you."

He shook his head. "It's Simon's. Don't ask me how I got it."

She laughed. "You're pretty sneaky."

"They trained me to be sneaky. I'm too old to stop now. What else do you need?"

Rule thought about the goon hanging around outside her house. "I need a good mechanic, somebody versatile."

Rawls frowned. "You're not going to crank up something on the domestic side, are you?" The CIA was authorized to conduct operations only abroad. The FBI handled domestic operations, and although the Agency had run illegal projects at home, they had often got their fingers burned.

She shook her head. "It's only for defensive purposes, I promise."

Rawls thought for a moment. "There's a guy named Danny Burgis—he was Company a while back. Runs a security service in DC—alarms, guard dogs, whatever any-body needs. We used to fly light planes together. He's in the book; use a clean phone. Tell him Biggles sent you. That's what he used to call me."

"One more thing," she said, and this was the big one. "There was no mention of Majorov in the Malakhov in-terrogation digests. Surely the name came up. God, the man was the First Chief Directorate!"

Rawls shook his head. "If it isn't in the digests, we didn't talk about it."

Rule knew that was not so. It was Ed's way of saying he couldn't discuss it, that it was too hot. Ed was going by the book, but she had a feeling he might interpret the rules in her favor, if she could figure out what to ask for. "Malakhov is wrung dry, is he?" she asked.

"Bled white, believe me."

"Have you cut him loose yet?" If they had given him a new identity and planted him somewhere, she didn't have a chance.

"Soon," Rawls replied.

She knew that Malakhov must have been interrogated somewhere within a reasonable distance of New York, or Rawls wouldn't have installed his wife there and com-muted weekends. If they were about to move him there might be just a chance. She made a stab. "Ed, I want to talk with Malakhov. Give me an hour with him." To her surprise, Rawls didn't bat an eyelash.

"A mile outside Stowe, Vermont, going south on the main highway, there's a Texaco station. Be there at three o'clock Sunday afternoon, and be sure you haven't picked up a tail. Pull into the self-service bay and fill your tank. Pick up on a yellow Jeep driver only; follow him away from the station, and not too closely. He'll take you to a house. You'll be back at the Texaco station by four. That'll give you about forty minutes with him."

"Thanks, Ed."

"You'll be wanting to get home," he said, rising.

At the front door she stopped. "Ed," she said, "what's Snowflower?"

Rawls paused before he replied. "I don't know, Kate."

Rule hugged him and slipped out the door. She walked quickly back to her neighbor's house. He looked surprised to see her but let her into his garden. As she let herself in through her back door, she could hear Mozart coming from the living room. Will was dozing with a book in his lap. She woke him gently.

"So how was dinner?" he asked.

"A very decent steak, and a lot of help, thanks," she replied, kissing him lightly. "Did you eat anything?"

"A frozen diet pizza. You have about two dozen of them in there."

"That's what I eat when I'm not at your house; it's how I keep my figure. Listen, I'd ask you to stay, but my mind is humming; I'd be very bad company. Do you mind?"

"You're lucky I'm such an understanding guy," he said, standing up and stretching. "Most fellows would take exception to being invited out to dinner at an expensive restaurant, getting into a dinner jacket, and then end up dining alone on diet pizza while you eat steak with somebody else, not to mention being sent home in a sexually unfulfilled condition."

"I know how lucky I am," she said, slipping her arms around his waist, "and I can't even tell you about any of this, at least, not yet. It's extremely important to me, though, and maybe to a lot of other people, too." They strolled toward the front door. She stopped. "Listen, the rest of this week is going to be bad for me, and I've got to go out of town on Sunday. Can I call you the first of the week?"

"You're forgetting, I'm off to Finland on Sunday, by way of Stockholm."

"Oh, God, of course, and I'm meeting you in Copenhagen."

"By the way," he said, reaching into an inside coat pocket and retrieving an airline folder, "here's your ticket to Copenhagen and a hotel voucher, in case we don't arrive there absolutely simultaneously." He frowned. "You are still planning to come, aren't you?"

"Of course I am, Will. In fact, it might be the best thing for me to get out of the office for a while. You have to understand, though, that with this Majorov thing the way it is, I might have to cancel at the last minute."

"Well, okay," he sighed. "I know you'll do the best you can."

"Did you walk here?" she asked.

"Yes."

"I know this seems weird, but I'm going to leave the house first. You wait two minutes, then go, all right?"

"Whatever you say." He shrugged. "I'm too sleepy to even wonder about it." He kissed her.

She switched on the stoop light, let herself out of the house, and walked quickly away, in the opposite direction from Will's. A couple of minutes later, she found a newsstand, bought a paper, and walked home. She didn't bother looking for the goon; she knew he'd be there somewhere. At least he wouldn't follow Will home; if he didn't already know who Will was, he wouldn't find out tonight.

She didn't get much sleep that night. Her mind was still racing.

18

Helder lay on his bed, swathed in a thick terry cloth robe from Bloomingdale's, still wet from his shower, and tried to examine his feelings. What he felt was a mixture of pride, apprehension, excitement, curiosity, and the terrible tingle, from far away, of raw fear. It was oddly familiar.

He tried to match this sensation with earlier times: his first ascent in the escape tank at sub school; his first patrol; his first patrol as captain. It was not quite like any of them. This was not training, not maneuvers; this was military action. Even if no shot were fired, this was combat, Helder's first.

Now he knew the feeling, from a long way back: his first girl. He had visited an uncle and aunt on their farm south of Tallinn; he had been sixteen, and the girl was his cousin, their daughter, a year older. He had known from the moment they met that she would be his first girl, and for days he anticipated her as she teased and rubbed against him. They had finally had each other in the back of a wagon, on a tarpaulin, and the smell of canvas aroused him to this day. He was aroused, now, by that same odd mixture of feelings, and the memory.

There was the rattle of fingernails on the door; Trina let herself in and closed the door behind her. Then she laughed. "What are you thinking of?" She laughed, nodding at the bulge under the robe.

"Of you." He grinned. "Come here to me."

She came across the room, shedding clothes along the way, and tugged at the thick robe. "Off," she said. "I want this off." She threw a leg over him and took him immediately inside her. "You're going," she said. "You're going tomorrow." She moved slowly, rhythmically. "You want to go, don't you?"

"Yes," he said, moving with her, occasionally breaking their rhythm with a jab. "I want it very much. But I don't want to leave you."

"You'll be back," she said, and her voice rose to a little cry.

"Yes, yes, I'll be back. I'll be back for you."

"Promise me."

"I'll be back."

They came together. Later, instead of dinner, they made love again, then again.

When Helder woke the next morning, Trina was gone. Almost immediately, there was a firm knock on his door, and he scrambled for a robe. Mr. Jones came swiftly into the room.

"Ah, good morning, Mr. Swenson," he said, cheerfully. "I've come to help you pack." He held up a large, clear plastic envelope. "Everything goes into this. You are to take two complete changes of clothing, one pair of shoes, and the personal effects and weapon issued you." He held up two ammunition clips, then dropped them into the bag. "You are now armed. See that you don't get into any difficulty which requires more than thirty rounds of ammunition." He grinned. He held up a small plastic envelope. "Here we have what you are to use should you get into such a situation. You tear open the envelope and find inside a short length of pliable, pink material. You put it into your mouth, pressing between your upper gum and cheek; it will stick there indefinitely, without deteriorating. In extreme conditions, you pluck it loose, bite firmly into it, and swallow. You will lose consciousness almost immediately, and you will be dead shortly afterwards. Absolutely painless; in fact, quite pleasant, I'm told. Never tried it myself." He chuckled. "Now strip off. I have to oversee your packing and dressing."

Helder stripped and got into a light running suit and shoes. He packed a tweed jacket, a blazer, two pairs of trousers, underwear, and socks. Jones watched closely as he chose his toilet items and packed everything into a parachute nylon duffel. Jones went to the desk, retrieved a drawing pad, the Rapidograph drawing pen, and Helder's wallet. He checked the driver's license and credit cards carefully, then held up a slip of paper. "Here's a receipt from a Chinese laundry on Seventh Avenue in Greenwich Village." From an inside pocket he took an American passport and opened it. "Nice photo, eh? Sign the passport."

Helder signed the passport, then flipped through

its pages, glancing at the stamps. "I arrived in Sweden today?"

"Correct; first trip abroad," Jones said.

Helder packed the passport, wallet, and drawing materials into his duffel; then Jones dropped the bag into the large plastic envelope and closed it with a zipper. "There you are, Carl Swenson," he said. "Shall we go?"

Helder left with Jones in Majorov's golf cart; they drove down the hillside to the camouflaged submarine pens. The guards waved them through the gates, and Jones maneuvered the cart into the cavernous shed and stopped. Majorov came to greet them.

"Good morning, Swenson," he said, smiling broadly. "I see Jones has prepared you."

"Indeed he has, sir," Helder replied. "I feel like a new man."

"Good, good, now come and see your cargo." Majorov led the way across the shed and down a flight of concrete steps to the Juliet class sub. The forward doors were open, the Type Four minisub had been backed into the hold, and before it sat the squat, cylindrical navigation buoy, somewhat larger in diameter than the dummy Helder had been training with. Instead of steel, like the dummy, its surface was of a dull, plastic-looking material, one he had not seen before. There were brackets on either side to accept the grapplers from the minisub.

Helder was worried by the difference in size from the dummy. "How much does it weigh?" he asked.

Majorov looked momentarily irritated. "About sixty kilos more than the dummy. I trust you can handle it."

Helder wasn't at all certain that he could. He felt that

the Type Four had been working at the outer limits of its control functions on the last exercise. He couldn't be certain, of course, until he actually worked with the real buoy, and Majorov seemed in no mood for delays. He was about to reply when Valerie Sokolov's voice came from behind him.

"There will be no difficulties, Colonel," she said, firmly.

Helder turned and glared but did not speak to her. "I think I can handle it, sir," he said.

"Fine," Majorov replied. "Now, let's get on with it. Sokolov, do the brackets and grapplers mate properly?"

"Yes, Colonel. All is well."

"Get the buoy loaded, then."

Sokolov waved to three men in coveralls standing near, and they came and began manhandling the heavy object toward the grapplers of the minisub. Helder noticed, for the first time, that they were wearing yellow radiation badges, the type that turned blue if it received a significant dosage. He thought that spent uranium 235, with which Majorov had said the buoy was ballasted, would not require such care, but, he supposed, he could not quarrel with caution. Sokolov entered the Type Four and manipulated the grapplers until they mated with the buoy's brackets. Then, using the sub's power, plus the muscles of the three men, they lifted the buoy into its position, just under the ports through which Helder would see out of the sub. Underwater, the extra buoyancy would enable the grapplers alone to maneuver the buoy. Helder hoped so, anyway.

Sokolov came out of the sub, and the doors of the

Juliet whined shut. The sub's skipper came up to Majorov and saluted. "We are ready to proceed, Colonel," he said.

"Excellent, Captain." Majorov smiled. He turned to Helder and took his hand. "Well, Helder," he said warmly, "now you are ready to do what you have been trained for. I know you will do it well." Majorov glanced at Sokolov and squeezed Helder's hand slightly. "Remember all of your instructions."

"I remember, Colonel," Helder replied. "Thank you for this opportunity."

"Good luck, Sokolov," Majorov said, shaking her hand.

Helder and Sokolov followed the sub's skipper onto its decks, and two men removed the narrow gangplank. They climbed to the conning tower and stood as the sub backed out of its berth. As she backed around and turned her bows toward the lake and the Baltic beyond, Helder caught sight of an oddly familiar figure standing on the concrete jetty, wearing the uniform of a captain, first grade, chatting with Majorov. Helder was jolted by the sight and at first thought he must be mistaken. Then, as the man turned in profile to say something to Majorov, Helder knew he was right. They had been in sub school together and occasionally had bumped into each other at Murmansk and other sub ports over the years. His name was Gushin, and he was now one of the most famous—or rather, infamous—officers in the Soviet navy. In October of 1981, he had run a Whiskey class submarine aground near a secret Swedish naval base. For a week the sub had remained, caught there, while diplomatic negotiations went on between the Swedes and the Soviets over the fate of the sub and its crew. Finally, the Soviets had permitted a limited inspection of the sub by the Swedes, and it had been towed off the ground and had made its way home, escorted by Soviet ships.

Every Soviet naval officer knew the story, knew more than just the terse stories in *Izvestia* and the military newspapers. Gushin had been stripped of his rank, discharged dishonorably from the Soviet Navy, and given a long prison term at hard labor in the Gulag. His name was a synonym for what could happen to an incompetent naval officer. Yet, here he was, in the uniform of a full captain, chatting amiably with the commander in charge of Soviet submarine operations in Swedish waters. Helder climbed down the conning tower ladder of the Juliet and stood, baffled, as the sub's skipper ordered her crew to dive.

Just what the hell was going on here?

19

Rule left her house Sunday morning, drove to National Airport, and took the Eastern shuttle to New York. She was excited about her meeting with Malakhov and unconcerned with her rearview mirror. Shortly before the plane landed in New York, she got up to go to the john, and, halfway down the aisle, stopped in her tracks. Sleeping in a window seat, snoring lightly, was the man who had been following her. The goon. She stood for a few seconds and got a good look at him, grinding the features into her memory. Five-nine or ten, she estimated, heavyset—maybe one ninety—pale complexion with some old pockmarks, poor haircut, nearly bald on top, wearing a wash-and-wear summer suit, forty-fivish, typical of the sort of drone that did the dirty work in Washington's East European embassies. He probably had poor teeth and bad dental work. She briefly entertained the idea of taking the empty seat next to him and scaring the hell out of him when he woke up, but she continued to the washroom.

At LaGuardia, she hit the terminal moving fast. She had a little more than an hour to lose the tail and connect with a New England Air flight to Burlington, and she wanted to get into the taxi queue as far ahead of him as possible. It didn't work. As her cab drove away, she saw him handing the cab starter money, and the next man in line miming rage at the queue-jumper. She considered giving her driver a thrill by telling him to lose the cab behind, but she didn't want to let her tail know she knew he was there. "Metropolitan Museum," she said.

Traffic was light, and they were there in under half an hour. She trotted up the broad steps to the museum and inside, not bothering to look behind her. She knew he would be there. She flashed her membership card at the members' desk and got an entry badge. He, she felt fairly certain, would not be a member and would be forced into the public ticket line. She walked quickly past the guard into the central hallway, then turned quickly to her right, into the museum shop, and waited. The public line must have been long, she thought; nearly five minutes passed before she saw his reflection in a showcase, bolting down the hallway into the Sunday throngs. She gave him fifteen seconds to become hopelessly confused, then walked through the shop and out of the museum. It had been stupid of him to follow her into the place. He should have waited at the front door; there was only one entrance. She caught a cab discharging a woman and three small children and was back at LaGuardia in another half-hour, making sure the goon didn't have a partner tailing her. On the plane, she took deep breaths and tried to cool off. Had she not been able to shake the tail, she'd have missed her flight to Burlington and her appointment with Malakhov.

At Burlington, she rented a car and headed for Stowe, timing the drive nicely. She passed the scarred mountainsides that were ski runs in winter, passed pseudo-alpine motels that looked closed for the summer. She found the road south; when the Texaco station came into view, she pulled over and waited until a minute to three, then drove the last few hundred yards to the station and pulled in. Hers was the only car in the place. She got out of the car and filled the tank, which didn't take long, considering it was three-quarters full, looking up and down the highway for her contact. The road was strangely empty. She walked into the station and paid for the gasoline; when she got back to the car, there was a yellow Jeep wagon idling at the roadside. Ed Rawls was at the wheel. With no sign of recognition, he pulled away and drove south. She scrambled into her car and pulled away after him, keeping as far back as she could and still keep him in sight. Three or four miles further south, he turned left onto a graveled road, and she followed, marveling that, in the five or six minutes of their drive, she saw no other vehicle. Midsummer Sundays in skiing country were quiet, she thought.

Rawls turned left again, then right, and shortly pulled off the road into the paved forecourt of a schoolhouse, an archetypal New England little red schoolhouse, with a weather-vaned belfry and white trim. From a quarter mile down the road Rule saw him get out of the wagon and go into the school. She drove into the forecourt, parked next to the Jeepster, and got out of the car. It was hot, sunny, and still. The weathervane atop the building pointed east, unmoving. The front door was ajar, and Rule stepped inside. A short hallway led her past a closed door and into the single schoolroom. It became obvious that the building was no longer a school. There was a raised stage to her right, which, instead of a teacher's desk, now held a modern kitchen. The open floor of the schoolroom now held a dozen pieces of comfortable-looking, if dowdy, upholstered furniture. The blackboards around the room were still in place, and there was a pot-bellied woodstove in one corner. Her eyes were drawn back to the kitchen/stage by the sound of a refrigerator door opening. Ed Rawls bent over and peered at the lower shelves. "Want a beer?" he called.

"Got anything diet?"

He walked across the stage toward her, carrying a green beer bottle and a can of Diet Coke. "You wired?" he asked, coming down the steps to the main floor and handing her the soft drink.

"Nope."

"Good. You can't take any notes, either. Leave your bag here, and listen, Kate, this is deep background; you can't use anything you get here in any report or conversation at the Agency—you understand that."

Rule nodded. She wished that weren't a condition of the meeting, but she understood Rawls's need to protect himself. She put her bag on the edge of the stage and followed him back toward the front door. He stopped at the door she had passed earlier. "He doesn't know who you are or what you want, but he has an idea that where he goes from here might depend on the kind of answers he gives you."

"Thanks for that, Ed," she said.

"His appearance has changed, and I thought of hooding him, but he wouldn't have thought you were important if I'd done that. I thought of blindfolding him to enhance your status, but, in some of his early interrogation, that didn't work very well. He's more comfortable, more talkative, less mechanical, when he can see who he's talking to. That's natural, I guess. He's been accustomed to rank for a long time, and he responds to respect. Since the very beginning, I've been treating him as a senior colleague instead of a defector, and it's gotten results. He's had chats with half a dozen others, mostly technical people looking for stuff on communications and hardware, but he's done ninety percent of his talking to me and a tape recorder. You're the first woman he's seen, except the lady who's been doing the cooking and the housekeeping around here. He's pretty horny; that might be of some use to you, if you don't find it too chauvinist an idea."

Rule ignored that. "Does he have a pattern when he's lying?"

Rawls shook his head. "He's never once lied to me— or at least, I've never caught him at it. If he's lying, he's too good at it to have a pattern. Anything else?"

"Nope."

"Okay." Rawls looked at his watch. "You'll have to leave here in forty minutes to make the last plane to New York."

"I take it he's leaving soon, too." She didn't think Ed

Rawls would have let her come here unless Malakhov was about to depart.

Rawls grinned. "He'll be out of the state before you get to the airport." He opened the door and stood back. "Good luck."

Rule stepped inside and heard the door close behind her.

20

Helder opened his eyes and listened. The quiet whine of the submarine's engines was blotted out by the rumble of the Helsinki–Stockholm ferry, only a few meters above and ahead of the sub, as the two, like a whale and her calf, picked their way in tandem through the Stockholm Archipelago.

Helder thought he had heard the squeak of deck shoes in the corridor, but no one came for him. He looked at his watch. Soon, now. He had not slept deeply the whole night, but he had kept his eyes closed and made an effort to think about something other than his mission. Except for the intervals when Trina Ragulin had popped into his consciousness, he had failed. He had rehearsed every maneuver he might be required to make during the next eight hours; he felt he could reach his destination point without a chart by now. The chart was engraved on the frontal lobe of his brain, every characteristic of every buoy, every promontory, every shallow. No Soviet officer had ever been better prepared for a mission; he was sure of it. Still, the prickle of fear stayed with him, constantly stabbing, like the fibers of rough, Soviet service underwear. He thought every soldier who had ever raised his head from a foxhole to see an advancing enemy must feel as he felt now. The only way he could deal with the feeling, keep it at bay, was to resolve to do what he had been ordered to do, and the hell with safety; surely, that was how men had brought themselves to combat for centuries.

But each time he gathered that resolve, the thought of Trina broke it, and he had to start all over again. He had too much to live for, now, to put his safety aside. She was at Malibu, waiting for him, and he struggled to keep that from being more important than his mission.

The squeak of shoes again, and this time it was real. Helder swung his legs over the side of the pipe cot and put his feet on the deck as the rating brushed the curtain aside and spoke.

"It's time, sir. We've just disengaged the ferry and are going to the bottom, now."

"Tell the captain I'll be with him directly." Helder got into his tracksuit and running shoes, tied a rough pullover around his shoulders, should he need a bit of extra warmth, tucked the heavy, plastic envelope containing his emergency clothing under one arm and his chart case under the other, and stepped into the corridor. Valerie Sokolov, similarly equipped, stepped into the corridor from the adjoining cabin a moment later. He motioned her to follow him, and he was not happy with his glimpse of her face, which was drawn, haggard. He hoped she could get through this assignment without caving in on him. He wondered if he was capable of Majorov's orders to kill her, if circumstances warranted. No matter, he wasn't going to execute anybody in cold blood.

He led the way forward to the wardroom, where breakfast waited for them. There was hot porridge, smoked herring, black bread, and tea. He ate heartily, to his surprise; Sokolov did not. There was little conversation. Helder ate quickly, then stood. "If you're going to move your bowels today, you'd best do it now," he said to Sokolov, then went for the head. Ten minutes later, he was back, and so was Sokolov. The captain came into the wardroom.

"We're ready when you are," Helder said.

The captain nodded. "By the time you're buckled in, we'll have completed our sonar sweep. If there's nothing about, you're off."

Helder led the way forward again, through the sub to the specially constructed launch and recovery room where the Type Four minisub waited. He motioned Sokolov to board first; then he followed her up the ladder to the top-mounted hatch. He dropped his bag and chart case onto the seat below him, and swung his legs into the sub. Just as he was about to drop below, something caught his eye, something that was, somehow, the wrong color. It was lying on the floor of the chamber, and it was one of the yellow radiation badges he had seen the loaders wearing; only it was no longer yellow—it was blue.

"Sir," a crew member shouted through the open pressure hatch, "Skipper says you're all clear. Flooding chamber as soon as you're battened down. Good luck."

Helder jumped, not expecting the nervous boy's

shout. He gave him a thumbs-up, dropped into the mini-sub, and closed the hatch behind him, cranking the pressure wheel tight. He stowed his bag under his seat and opened the little chart case. As he clipped a strip chart to the little table at his elbow, he heard a valve crank open and water begin to rush into the chamber. He ran through a final checklist with Sokolov, as much to calm her with routine as to ensure that everything was ship-shape. He could hear the clicks of switches as she closed circuits, and the glow of red lights changed to green as they were completed.

"I've got a red light persisting on the main board," Sokolov said, suddenly. "That means malfunction of the grapplers."

Helder swore under his breath; the mission was off if the grappler wouldn't work. "Check the box," he said evenly. "Maybe it's just the switch and not the hydraulics."

Sokolov's hand came into view at his right, as she reached for a screwdriver from a set in a wall bracket. "Just a minute." He heard the switchbox open and waited impatiently for her answer. "Yes! Yes!" she said. "It's the switch; a wire has come adrift from the crimping."

"Fix it, then," Helder said, impatiently. Water had covered the forward ports, now, and Helder could see the red chamber lights casting wavering shadows over the dull, black skin of the buoy, which rested on its shelf, just under the ports.

"Got it," Sokolov said, a little triumph in her voice. "All lights green for go." Her hand came forward again and replaced the screwdriver.

A low whine rose from behind them somewhere, the forward doors of the launch and recovery chamber swung slowly open, and the steel-plate ramp unfolded and settled to the bottom. Helder switched on the mini-sub's forward lamps and cut in the track mechanism. He pushed the control lever forward, and the sub tractored out of the chamber, down the ramp, and onto the floor of the bay called Trälhavet. As soon as they had cleared the mother sub, he stopped the minisub and switched off the tracks, which used three times as much power as the props. He switched off the forward lamps, too. "Ten percent buoyancy," he said to Sokolov.

"Ten percent buoyancy," she repeated, and he heard her work the controls. The sub did not move.

Damn, he thought, it was the extra fifty kilos of the buoy. "Twenty percent buoyancy," he said, and she followed his order. The sub began to rise from the seabed, and Helder kicked in the twin propellers. The sub moved sluggishly forward; he pulled back on the joystick and got almost no response. Damned extra weight. He increased engine revs, and the sub slowly came up to a climbing altitude. On the way to the surface he checked responses to the controls. Everything was satisfactory except the upward response to the diving planes; the buoy's unplanned-for extra weight inhibited that. He could live with the situation, but it was going to cost him battery power; still, he had a lot in hand. He did some quick calculations; his six-hour mission would be increased to eight hours, and he had, he reckoned, nineteen hours of running power, even with the extra weight and the running speed required for good maneuverability on the outward leg.

The mother sub was lying in thirty-five meters of water, and watching his depth gauge, he allowed the minisub to rise thirty meters. Then, he operated the periscope and let the machine rise slowly until the scope broke water. He did a quick, 360-degree sweep with the periscope, its mirror mechanism allowing him to remain facing forward while it turned. There was no other craft visible in the half-light of the subarctic night. He brought the scope dead ahead, then swept the horizon in a 30-degree arc. There, there was his first light, kindly placed there by the Royal Navy of Sweden. Satisfied that his ship was alone and on course, he allowed himself his first look at Sweden. He saw nothing but distant, low-lying lumps of land. He would have another look in more confined waters. He lowered the periscope.

"We're on course, Sokolov," he said, half turning his head. "Report."

"Everything is in perfect order, Captain," she said.

He was surprised at her respectful tone, and she sounded calmer than she had looked before they launched. He relaxed a little.

Three hours passed uneventfully. Helder followed his course with ease, popping up the periscope for a few seconds at a time. He saw comfortable-looking houses ashore, some of them quite grand, and an occasional streetlight winked in the dim light, but no one stirred. The houses slept behind the thick blackout curtains that separate every Swede from the midnight sun. By full dawn, they were through the first narrow channel and into more open water. Moments after they left the channel, Helder saw the first patrol boat. He immediately cut his engines and let the sub sink a few meters before establishing neutral buoyancy.

"Two hundred meters' distance," said Helder, the sonar's phones pressed to his ears. "Two-fifty; three hundred; five hundred."

Helder restarted the engines and came to periscope depth again. A few minutes later, he encountered another patrol boat, and an hour later, another. After leaving the open water and entering his next channel, he saw no others. Leaving the island of Saint Hoggarn astern, he continued in a southwesterly direction, and, almost exactly eight hours after launching, he drove the minisub into the open water of Lilla Värtan, due east of Stockholm. He made one last periscope sweep. There were three merchant vessels ahead in the distance, and one mere dot behind him. The spires of Stockholm rose before him. He felt the thrill of trespass.

Reluctantly, he lowered the periscope and slowed the minisub, gaining depth rapidly. Then Sokolov spoke.

"Craft dead astern, seven hundred meters, closing rapidly."

Why the hell hadn't she heard it before he saw it? He didn't much care, now; he was at his destination. All that remained was to find a suitable site for the buoy and deploy it. He switched on the sub's forward lamps and waited. At thirty-one meters of depth, the bottom swam toward him. He slowed the sub's descent and let her take the bottom gently. He was on a nearly level, rocky seabed, ideal for his purposes. He switched in the tractor mechanism, moved it into forward, and stopped after no more than ten meters. Jesus, he was here! The bottom was perfect! What could be easier? "I'm deploying the buoy," Helder said.

"Craft at four hundred meters and closing more slowly," Sokolov said, a note of tension creeping into her voice. "Estimated speed fifteen knots and decreasing."

Fifteen knots? Patrol boat. What else would be moving that fast? He switched off everything and sat back. "Silence," he said, "except for reports."

"Craft at one hundred meters, speed steady at ten knots," Sokolov said.

Helder didn't need the sonar, now; the drum of the boat's engines was clearly audible. It passed straight over them.

"Craft departing at ten knots," Sokolov said, her voice relaxing a bit. "Three hundred meters and increasing."

Helder sat up. "Prepare to deploy the buoy," he said. "Switch to hydraulic power."

"Switching to hydraulic power," Sokolov replied, throwing switches. "Ready."

Helder grasped the control levers for the grapplers and lifted the buoy. With its additional buoyancy in the water, it came up easily enough. He pushed forward, and the buoy moved away from the minisub, off its storage shelf. He moved the grapplers downward, and the buoy settled onto the bottom, creating a small cloud of silt. He brought the grapplers back into their stowed position. "Switch off hydraulic power," he said.

"Hydraulic power off, full battery power available for propulsion," Sokolov said.

Helder checked the display on the inertial naviga-tion system. "Fifty-eight degrees, twenty-one minutes,

ten seconds north; eighteen degrees, twelve minutes,
two seconds east," Helder said aloud, simultaneously
writing the coordinates in his logbook and memorizing
them. The numbers burned into his brain; he thought he
would never remember anything so well ever again. God,
he had done it! He had piloted this ridiculous machine
into Swedish waters and dropped the bloody buoy on
the nose!

"Craft approaching from dead ahead," Sokolov said,
suddenly. "Speed approximately ten knots." Her voice
wavered. "My God, I think they've turned!"

Helder's first thought was to move away from the
buoy. He grabbed the controls, asked for buoyancy, and
when the sub had lifted three or four meters, pushed
the controls ahead. Freed of its burden, the Type Four
moved quickly forward, over the buoy, and into the open
waters of Lilla Värtan.

"What are you doing?" Sokolov nearly shouted.
"You're headed toward Stockholm!"

"I know that, Sokolov," Helder replied through
clenched teeth. "I'm not going back into that channel
until we're clear. We can't afford to be caught in confined waters. Now shut up and relax. Your job is over; it's
up to me to get us back in one piece."

"You're crazy!" she said, louder this time. "We've deployed the buoy—now let's get out of here and back to
the mother sub!"

Helder tried to concentrate on driving the sub as quietly as possible. "Godammit, Sokolov, shut up! That's
an order! Get back on the sonar and give me some
reports!"

There was a moment's silence; then Sokolov spoke again. "Now they're coming from behind! They must have gone over us and are coming back!"

Oh, Jesus, Helder thought, they've bracketed us.

"We've got to turn back toward the mother sub!" Sokolov shouted.

We've got to get as far away from that buoy as possible and into open water, Helder thought. "Silence except for reports," he said, and made a hard turn to starboard.

"What are you—"

Sokolov's cry was cut by an incredibly loud roar and the sudden, sideways thrust of the minisub. "That was a depth charge," Helder said. "Strap in and hold on!"

"You fool!" Sokolov screamed, clearly out of control, now. "You'll get us killed!"

"Shut up!" Helder screamed, and started to say it again, when an arm came from behind his seat and came tight against his throat. Sokolov's cries were unintelligible, now, and Helder, choking, could say nothing. He let go of the controls and grabbed the arm with both hands; the sub dived and struck the bottom at a shallow angle. He let go the arm with one hand and tried to manage the controls, while keeping Sokolov from choking him with the other hand. Sokolov was making infuriated little shrieks, but Helder could still hear the patrol boat's engines above them. He was having trouble breathing and turned his head to one side. That gave him some breathing space, but now the arm was pressing on the artery in his neck. Christ, the woman was stronger than most men!

He let go the controls again to devote both hands to

Sokolov, but the sub dived and bounced another time, and he had to grab at the joystick. Suddenly, Helder felt weaker, and he knew he was going to pass out unless he did something quickly. He freed his right hand and groped along the sub's side to where the tools rested in brackets, ready to hand. He got hold of something, he wasn't sure what, and jabbed backwards, toward where he thought her face must be.

Everything seemed to happen at once, then. In his last moment of consciousness, he struck something behind him and the arm's grip relaxed; then the loudest noise he had ever heard burst upon him, and the sub seemed to go berserk. His last sensation was of something cutting painfully into both shoulders. Then he passed out.

21

Rule found herself on a small landing, four or five steps above a long, narrow room, perhaps twenty-five feet by half that width. Light came from a row of highly placed windows that would be just above ground level on the outside. To her right there was a bin containing a dozen pairs of skis and poles. The place had probably been a storeroom in the past, when the schoolhouse was still a school. It was now, apparently, a ski lodge. There was a row of half a dozen steel army cots along each side of the room, and on one of them a man sat quietly.

She walked slowly toward him and took in his appearance. He was greatly changed. She remembered photographs of a tallish, slender man of about sixty with dark hair coming to a widow's peak, bushy eyebrows, and an aquiline nose that gave him a hawkish appearance. He looked ten years older. He had gained at least thirty pounds, the hair was now completely gray and had thinned enough to obliterate the widow's peak, and the eyebrows had been artfully plucked. The nose had been broken, not painfully, she hoped, and had not been cosmetically repaired. It was now flat, broad, and crooked. The mother of Major General Georgi Abramovich Malakhov would pass him on the street and not recognize him.

She sat down on the bunk opposite him. "Good afternoon, General Malakhov," she said.

"Please do not call me that," he said. "I am now . . . someone else, and I am certainly no longer a general." There was no regret in his voice.

"Of course," she said. "My name is Kirkland; I have come to ask you some questions about a man you knew in the Soviet Union."

"Have you a Christian name, Miss Kirkland?" he asked smoothly. "And might I call you by it?"

It was the sort of thing that a man might say to a woman at a cocktail party, and it disconcerted her in the circumstances until she remembered that he had not been around women for some time. She crossed her legs, leaned forward on her hands and smiled. "I would be pleased if you would call me Brooke," she said, feeling sure that her old college roommate would not mind the appropriation of her name, in the circumstances.

"Good. A good name. Brooke. It has a cool, clear ring to it, like its owner."

She laughed. "I must try and live up to it." She was surprised at the accuracy of his American accent. He pronounced his Rs very hard, as many Russians did in English, and the effect was Midwestern, Illinois or Ohio, perhaps. Still, his phrasing was not completely American. It seemed more European.

"So, Brooke. About whom have you come to ask me questions?"

"Viktor Majorov."

The eyebrows went up. "Aha! Viktor Sergeivich interests you, does he?"

She shrugged. "In passing. Can you remember the first time you met Majorov?"

Malakhov smiled. "Of course. Like yesterday. It was in 1959, in the office of Yuri Andropov. He was, at that time, secretary to the Central Committee. Andropov, not Majorov. Viktor Sergeivich was . . ." He paused and looked thoughtful. "I knew his parents. Would you like me to tell you of his background? It is quite interesting."

Would she? Oh, Christ, yes. "Please do," she said.

"Well, we must go back to the Revolution. Sergei Ivanovich Majorov was from a prominent, if not aristocratic, family of Leningrad merchants. At the time of the storming of the Winter Palace, he was a captain in the household cavalry, and he delivered his unit to the Revolution, gaining the personal attention of Lenin. A short time later, he became a bodyguard to Lenin. He was an attractive and charming man with a good education, and Lenin seemed to enjoy the contrast between him and some of the peasants surrounding him at the time. Lenin called him his favorite czarist."

Malakhov found a pack of small cigars in his shirt pocket and lit one while Rule tried to be patient. This was great stuff; she loved hearing it.

"He remained with Lenin until the great man had his first stroke, in the spring of 1922. After that, Lenin had less need of him, and he was approached by Dzerzhinsky, who was head of the Cheka, our first security police, but then you would know all about that, wouldn't you, being a Kremlinologist?"

"Please go on," she said, ignoring his curiosity.

"Sergei Ivanovich thrived under Dzerzhinsky, and later, under Beria. In about 1930, he met a young woman, a girl, really, named Natalia Firsova, who had been born in England to expatriate Russian parents, Bolsheviks who were fugitives from the czar. Stalin had invited Russians with technical skills to repatriate to help build the new motherland, and her father was an engineer. The girl had been trained as a dancer in London, and she very quickly auditioned for and was asked to join the Bolshoi Ballet. Majorov was in his early forties by this time, and she was eighteen or nineteen, I suppose, but it was a good match. They married, and she continued her career, becoming a principal dancer with the Bolshoi, until nineteen thirty-six or 'thirty-seven, when she became pregnant. Then things turned bad for Sergei Ivanovich."

"Stalin's purges?"

Malakhov nodded. "I forget what his offense was, but it hardly matters. Men were being executed daily on almost any pretext. There was an interesting rumor, though, that Stalin himself shot Sergei. I've often wondered if it were true."

"So what happened to Natalia and the baby?"

"There was no baby, yet," Malakhov said. "Sergei Ivanovich had many friends of long standing, and some of them were apparently brave enough to help her. I don't know quite how it was done, but she managed to get to Leningrad, and someone got her a job teaching the young dancers with the Kirov Ballet there. When the child was born, she gave him her name, Firsov, and called him Roy, after her father. Since it was important that nobody know who he was, he had to contend with being known as a bastard, a difficult thing for a boy in a puritanical, Communist society, I suppose. Still, I think he always knew who his father was."

"Did that inhibit his progress in the system?" she asked.

"It seems not," Malakhov replied. "I think his father's old friends looked after him. He got into Moscow University, where he excelled in languages and in Party activities. He was, in fact, chairman of Komsomol, the Young Communist League, at the university, and that is how he met Andropov. Yuri went to the university to address the Komsomol, and Viktor Sergeivich introduced him. Andropov was impressed with the young man and made some inquiries—Yuri always researched everything and everybody extremely well. While young Majorov was still at the university, Andropov offered him part-time employment."

"Doing what?"

"Teaching Andropov English," Malakhov replied. "Yuri Andropov had the widest-ranging mind of any man I ever knew. He was not well educated like many of his contemporaries, and I think he suffered from something of an inferiority complex in that regard. He wanted to read everything, know about everything, and much of what he wanted to know was written in English and not translated. Majorov, of course, having been brought up speaking English by his mother, spoke the language perfectly and was an ideal tutor for Yuri. When I knew Andropov during this period, he would clear his desk and his calendar three mornings a week for English lessons, and although his accent was never very good, he read the language fluently, without abridgments or translation help. It was one of his great personal strengths, I think, and he was always grateful to Majorov."

"And it was 1959 when you met Majorov in Andropov's office."

Malakhov nodded. "At Central Committee headquarters. I believe Viktor Sergeivich was about to graduate from the university, and he had expressed an interest in the KGB. Andropov asked me to come for lunch and meet the young man, and I was very impressed indeed. His skill with languages would have been reason enough to recruit him—apart from English, he spoke French, German, and Swedish fluently, and he got along in other Scandinavian languages, as well—but he clearly had an acute mind, and he seemed much older than his years, a serious young man. I marked him immediately for the First Chief Directorate, my own assignment. He was perfect for foreign espionage, absolutely perfect."

"So you recruited him that day?"

Malakhov smiled. "I think he recruited me, he and Yuri. He graduated near the top of his class, and within a week, we had him at the KGB foreign service school."

"Did you keep track of him during his training?"

"No, I was sent abroad soon after that, but on leave at home, I would always hear rumors around Moscow Central about his progress. He was dazzling, from all I heard. His skill with languages shortened his training time greatly, since much time is usually spent perfecting a candidate's language skills, and he was posted to Stockholm after only two years. I had no further direct contact with him until 1978, when he was made head of First Chief Directorate. I had a number of long meetings with him, sometimes alone, and he chose me for the UN assignment."

"Andropov made him head of First, then?"

"Of course. During the time when Yuri was studying English with Viktor Sergeivich, they developed almost a father-son relationship, although Andropov was only fortyish at the time. He was always Majorov's chief patron after that time, although Viktor Sergeivich took pains to ingratiate himself with others he thought to be on their way up."

"Who in particular?"

"Gorbachev, principally, who was a few years older than Majorov, but also a protégé of Andropov, and during his time at the UN I heard that he got along particularly well with Gromyko, not an easy thing to do."

"He did well with both generations, then?"

"Yes, indeed. He had the ambition of the younger generation to change things, but the cold hardness of the older. He could identify with both."

"It would sound as though, under the present leadership, he would have been in line to head the KGB."

Malakhov gave a massive shrug. "Who knows? I thought he was in line to succeed Andropov as head of the KGB when he moved up to the chairmanship; he certainly had Yuri's favor, but it didn't happen. It would have been the most natural thing in the world, given their relationship, but it didn't happen."

"Why not, do you think?"

"I have a theory, but I could be wrong."

Rule was anxious to hear this. "What is your theory?"

"I think he got something better."

Now her own theory was getting support. Her next question might advance it another stage. "What could be better than head of the KGB?"

"I think Majorov invented something for himself; nothing else could be better for him. He always liked freedom of movement."

"What could he invent for himself that would be better than head of the KGB?"

"I don't know, but it would have to be big; grandiose, even. Yes, grandiose, that would suit Viktor Sergeivich. It would have to be something big enough that, if it were successful, it would catapult him into the Politburo, perhaps even into the leader's chair."

"He thinks as big as that, does he? Pretty risky thinking."

"Majorov revels in risk, my dear Brooke. He is the sort of man who will either achieve everything, or destroy himself trying. He is not without his faults, if the rumors mean anything."

Rule tensed a little. "Tell me about the rumors."

"Well, on trips back to Moscow, I heard more than once that Viktor Sergeivich had . . . certain proclivities, sexual proclivities."

"You mean he's homosexual?"

"Indeed not. To the contrary, he was a consumer of women, often in twos and threes, that was common knowledge."

"What proclivities, then?"

Malakhov squirmed a bit. "I am an old puritan, I suppose, and these things make me uncomfortable, even to talk about them."

Rule leaned forward. "Please," she said.

"Well, the rumor was that things sometimes went too far, that he sometimes killed."

"Killed his sexual partners?"

Malakhov nodded. "That was the rumor, that it happened . . . more than once. And I must tell you, that when I heard this rumor, I did not have difficulty believing it."

"Why not? What in your experience with Majorov made you think he might be capable of sexual murder?"

"Murder is not hard," Malakhov said, somewhat sadly. "I have murdered. If you are in the KGB for very long, you will soon murder, one way or another. But not every murderer is capable of wielding the knife himself. But some men enjoy that. I saw Majorov enjoy it, once."

"Tell me about the occasion."

Malakhov looked at the floor. "Do you know how a military execution is carried out in the Soviet Union?"

"Firing squad, I suppose."

Malakhov shook his head. "No, for crimes that incur the death penalty, a firing squad is too good, too dignified for this sort of criminal. He is led to believe this is what will happen, though. A firing squad is selected, and the victim is marched out to meet them. Then, while the firing squad appears to be readying itself, a single officer with a pistol quietly approaches the victim from behind and shoots him in the head."

Rule said nothing.

"I saw Majorov perform such an execution, once," Malakhov said, still looking at the floor. "The victim was a KGB officer who had been found guilty of attempting to defect to the West. A firing squad was assembled, and as the officer chosen to perform the execution was about to approach the victim from behind, Majorov suddenly appeared and took the pistol from him. He walked slowly, crablike toward the victim, and the expression on his face. . . . He was very excited. He waited for a moment, then another, until the victim began to wonder what was happening, why the firing squad was not proceeding. Majorov held the pistol close to his head and waited . . . waited until the man thought he sensed something and began to turn toward him. Majorov waited until the instant the man caught sight of him, out of the corner of his eye, and then he fired, catching the man in the temple. Then he walked away and left him lying there, not dead. It remained for another officer to administer the coup de grâce. It was a terrible thing to see . . . a terrible thing to see a man *enjoy* the killing of another."

Rule still said nothing.

"I will tell you this, Brooke Kirkland." Malakhov leaned forward and spat the words. "In the more than thirty years I spent in the KGB, Viktor Sergeivich Majorov was the crudest, most ruthless man I ever encountered. It frightened me to be around him."

The door behind Rule opened, and she turned to see Ed Rawls standing in the doorway. "You've got to get going," he said.

Rule tried desperately to think of what she should ask. She had sat there, entranced, and let this old general control the conversation, spin his tales, and use up her time. Some interrogator she was! She stood up. "Coming, Ed." She turned to Malakhov. "Is Viktor Majorov capable of committing Soviet forces to a land war in Europe, if he could get the support of the Politburo?"

Malakhov stood, too. "You have not been listening to me, Brooke Kirkland," he said, shaking his head. "Viktor Sergeivich Majorov is capable of *anything—any* act that will further his personal ends. No man, no group, no *nation* is safe that stands between him and what he wants, and I do not exclude the Soviet Union herself from that assessment."

"Thank you," she said, and turned to leave.

"Brooke Kirkland," Malakhov called out as she reached the top of the steps.

Rule turned and looked back.

Malakhov grinned. "Whatever Viktor Sergeivich is up to, I can promise you, you will not like it!"

She could hear him laughing through the closed door as she walked from the schoolhouse with Ed Rawls. "Jesus," she said, "that was an education." She stopped at her car and turned to Rawls. "Ed, did you ever have some wild idea, and when you started to chase it down, everything you learned supported it?"

"Yeah," Rawls replied. "Once or twice." He grinned at her. "Pretty scary, isn't it?"

"It sure as hell is." She threw an arm around his shoulders and kissed him on the cheek. "Thanks, I appreciate this more than I can tell you."

"Remember," he said, "you cannot put today's stuff in any file—you cannot cite it to support any theory."

"I remember," she said, getting into her car and starting it. "See you around Langley, Ed."

"I hope so, Kate," he replied, not smiling. "I really hope so."

She drove to Stowe and turned toward Burlington and her plane. She had come up here for background, for confirmation, and she had gotten it, she thought. She wondered why, instead of feeling elated, she felt depressed.

22

Helder was wakened by a cold and wet sensation on the top of his head, followed instantly by the pain in his shoulders. He felt as if his face were about to explode, and it took several seconds for him to regain enough consciousness to understand his condition. He was hanging upside down from his airplane-style shoulder harness, and the straps were cutting badly. From a distance, there was the sound of water rushing under pressure, and he realized that the minisub was being flooded, and that the water had reached the top of his upside-down head.

He clawed at the emergency harness release in panic, thinking he would drown soon if it would not release. It released all too well, dumping him into a foot of water. He scrambled upright, spitting and choking and trying to orient himself to the sub's capsized condition. The instrument lights were still burning, and so was the overhead dome light, except that it was now underwater, and it cast distorted rays about the chaotic interior of the Type Four.

Helder looked about him. Valerie Sokolov was floating facedown a couple of feet from him. He grabbed at her and heaved her upright—she might still be alive—then he cried out and shrank from her. A screwdriver handle protruded from her right eye; the blade had been driven in to the hilt, directly into her brain. Her other eye stared blankly, and her jaw hung slack. Helder remembered grabbing something and jabbing at her to make her let go of him. He had succeeded.

It took a moment for him to recover from this sight and to begin to realize his situation. The minisub rested upside down on the bottom, at an angle of about ten degrees off the perpendicular, and water was coming in fast from the area of the hatch, which now rested on the bottom, making escape from the sub impossible. In the original Type Four, another hatch existed; in this truncated version, that had been eliminated. The main hatch was the only way out.

Helder tried to be calm and consider his position. The lights were still burning in the sub; that meant he still had battery power. He groped for the switch for the outside lamps, found it, and switched it on. The seabed outside the sub sloped gently downward in the direction of the sub's angle from the perpendicular, encouraging him to think he might be able to roll the machine at least partly over. He flipped off the switch, chose a part of the sub's hull on the downhill side and threw his weight at it. The sub rocked slightly, then settled back into its original upside-down position. He flung himself repeatedly at the hull, but the sub's attitude would not change.

Helder closed his eyes and tried to think what resources were available to him. Power, he had power. He thought for a moment, then reached up for the propeller controls. He took hold of the control handles and shoved the starboard throttle to full ahead and the port throttle to full back. The engines rose to a high whine, and the sub began to shudder. Then, slowly, the after end of the minisub skidded a few inches sideways, and the sub began to roll over. Helder had not been ready for this change of attitude, and he found himself clinging desperately to whatever handhold he could get as the sub rolled over to rest on its port side.

That cleared the hatch, he thought, if the sub's resting on it had not jammed it. Water sprayed violently from the breached hatch, sending out a painful, needle-like spray. Helder stood and started tearing at a locker door on the starboard side of the sub, now above his head. It came open, and two escape lungs fell on top of him. He grabbed one and inspected it quickly; it seemed to be all right. The lung consisted of a pressure regulator, a mouthpiece, a nose clamp, and a small bottle of compressed air, said in training to contain a ten-minute supply. Helder had used one once, in an escape tower at sub school. He snapped the strap around his neck and looked about him again. His emergency gear, still sealed in its heavy plastic envelope, floated at his feet. He picked it up, broke the seal, and squeezed as much air from the envelope as he could before rezipping it shut. He had to ascend to the surface as slowly as possible, and he didn't want the air in the envelope to pop him up too quickly. He looked around again; he seemed to have what he needed.

The spray from the hatch was driving him crazy. He waded aft past it, shielding himself from the needles, and opened the sub's seacocks. Water now streamed into the minisub in two columns that equaled the size of his wrist. The sub would fill quickly, now; when it was full of water and the pressure was equalized, he would be able to open the main hatch and escape, if the main hatch would open. He walked back to his emergency pack, picked it up, and leaned against the sub's hull. He slipped the regulator mouthpiece into his mouth and opened the valve. Air under pressure rushed into his lungs; the escape lung was working. He turned it off and waited, hoping against hope that when the sub was full of water, the hatch would open. If it would not, then he had hastened his own death by opening the seacocks.

The water was up to his chest, now, and he reckoned he had little more than a minute left. Trina Ragulin popped into his mind. He pushed away the thought. He needed to concentrate on his ascent, now. Suddenly remembering, he unzipped the pocket of his running suit and fished for the packet of cyanide. He threw it into the rising water. Not that way. He was going to be captured if he reached the surface; the area must be crawling with patrol boats by now. The water rushing into the sub drowned out any engines he might have heard. If he was captured, he would deal with that, but he would not kill himself, no matter what.

With the water at his chin, he bit at the regulator mouthpiece again, opened the valve and adjusted the nose clamp. He began to breathe forcibly out, ejecting the air pushed into his lungs by the pressure. He tried

to breath evenly and deeply, as the last air inside the
sub was denied him. He groped his way along the hull
until he came to the main hatch, then spun the pressure
wheel. It moved freely; thank God for that. He pushed
at the hatch and it opened about halfway, before stopping against an obstruction. It would move no further.
He grabbed his emergency pack, shoved it through the
opening, and squeezed in behind it. For a moment, he
thought he would not be able to get through, and panic
began to rise in him; then, suddenly, he was free and
floating.

He had been in something like thirty meters of water,
as well as he could remember. He let himself rise slowly,
breathing deeply, trying to count off the meters. The
water was shockingly cold, and he tried not to think
about it as he counted. When he reached thirty, it seemed
warmer, but he was still not at the surface. There was
light all about him, though, and he knew he would be
there soon.

Suddenly, the air from the bottle stopped, with no
warning, at a moment when his lungs were only half
full. That couldn't have been ten minutes, he thought,
no more than four or five. He held desperately onto the
breath, then, finally, began to release it. Where was the
surface? At the moment when he thought he would have
to inhale water, he broke into air, spitting out the mouthpiece and gulping. He looked around, treading water.
There was fog, thick fog, and it was raining lightly. Perhaps he would not be captured.

He could hear engines on two sides of him, one near,
one far away. Helder unzipped a corner of the plastic en-

velope containing his gear, blew air into it, and resealed it. Now he had something to support his weight in the water. He unsnapped the escape lung and let it sink away from him. He kicked off the running shoes and struggled out of the tracksuit. Naked but for a jockstrap, he could swim better. But which way to swim?

He waited until the engine noise of the boat nearest him receded; then he put two fingers into his mouth and whistled as loudly as he could. The noise died immediately, seemingly absorbed by the fog. He turned ninety degrees and whistled again. The noise died. He turned another ninety degrees and tried once more. This time, a hint of an echo. He threw his arms over the plastic pouch and started to swim, using the pouch the way he had used a kickboard when he had practiced for the school swimming team as a boy. He concentrated on kicking equally with both feet; he had no wish to swim in circles. He continued for half an hour by his watch, whistling occasionally. The echo grew more distinct and returned more quickly. He rested for five minutes, then continued. The next time he stopped, his feet touched a rocky bottom. He waded for a moment, lost the bottom, then found it again. A moment later, a patch of green appeared before him, a manicured bit of lawn. He crawled out onto the grass and peered into the fog. Up a slight incline, he could see the outlines of a small, white house. Afraid to stop and rest, he rose and staggered wearily along the water, looking for some sort of shelter. Shortly, a tiny boathouse swam toward him through the thick fog.

The door was not locked. He went inside and found a sports motorboat of about five meters moored along a catwalk. He stepped onto the boat and collapsed onto an upholstered seat. There were two damp beach towels in a locker under the dashboard, and he used them to dry himself as best he could, then gathered them about him. He was alive and, for the moment, safe. Nobody would be using the boat in this fog. Warmth washed over him, and sleep was not far behind. His cheek touched the upholstery, and he was gone.

23

Rule went to a pay phone as soon as she got into National Airport, thumbed through the yellow pages, and dialed a number. It was after nine on Sunday evening, but she reckoned there'd be a twenty-four-hour operator, and she was right. The woman asked her to hold while she switched the call.

"This is Danny," a man's voice said.

"Danny Burgis?"

"The very same. Who's this?"

"Remember Biggles?"

"Sure I do."

"He suggested I look you up for some work."

"What sort of work?"

"I want a house swept. Two houses."

"One of 'em yours?"

"Yes."

"You calling from there?"

"No. Biggles said to use a clean phone."

"Right. What's your address?"

DEEP LIE / 193

She gave it to him.

"How soon will you be there?"

"About half an hour."

"Thirty-five minutes okay?"

"You mean you want to do the sweep tonight?"

"If that's not inconvenient. I do some of my best work at night. I'm speaking from my car, now, and I've got everything I need with me."

"Okay. Thirty-five minutes, then."

"Right. What's your name?"

"Katharine Rule."

"Okay, Katie, when I get there, I won't ring the bell. I'll knock with my fist. When you let me in, don't say anything. I'm six-one, one-seventy, baseball cap, windbreaker, gorgeous. That's a town house, right? What's the layout?"

"Entrance, living room, and dining room on the main floor, kitchen and study one floor down, two bedrooms on the top floor."

"I'll start at the top of the house and work down; when you're clean, we'll talk. How many phone lines?"

"One."

"Extensions?"

"Uh, five—no, six."

"How many TV sets?"

"Two—bedroom and living room."

"Turn 'em both on before I get there. If there are any radios in other rooms, turn those on, too."

"One in the kitchen."

"Right. Thirty-five minutes."

Rule retrieved her car from the parking lot and drove

home. She went around the house, turning on TV sets and radios, then waited in the entrance hall. On the dot, there was a tap at the door. She opened it, and a man came in. He shook her hand and mouthed, "Hi." He was as described, and in addition, had short gray hair and about two weeks of gray beard. The letters BS stood out on his baseball cap. He started up the stairs, and she went into the living room and watched an old movie on TV. Forty minutes later, he came into the living room with a finger at his lips. He picked up the telephone, passed a meter over it, unscrewed both the mouthpiece and earpiece, then replaced them.

He walked over to where she sat, bent over, and whispered, "Where's the main phone box?"

Rule gave an elaborate shrug and shook her head. He nodded and left the room. Ten minutes later, he came back into the living room and switched off the TV.

"You're clean," he said, digging into a pocket and dumping two small electrical devices and a slightly larger black box with a short aerial onto the coffee table. "You had two bugs, on the master bedroom and entrance hall phones. Both of them could receive when the phone was hung up. Nothing else in the walls or electrical outlets or lamps."

Rule picked up the two devices and turned them over in her hand. "You're sure there's nothing else?"

"That's what you're paying me for, Miz Rule."

"Sorry."

"Not much of a bugging job, just the two. Either he was sloppy as hell or he got interrupted before he could finish."

"What sort of equipment is it?"

"It's adapted from some common Japanese components, the sort of thing you'd find at any RadioShack.
Nothing to indicate it's of any other foreign origin. It's
pretty good, but nothing special. The two little pickups
heard you on the phone or within a twelve- or fifteen-
foot radius in the same room, transmitted the sounds
over your telephone wires to your main box downstairs,
then to the black box, which transmitted a one-watt
VHF signal into the air, the sort of thing that could be
picked up, practically speaking, no more than a quarter
of a mile away. It's a pretty chintzy installation; your
man would sit in his car or in an apartment across the
street and listen or record. Only I doubt if he went to
the trouble to rent an apartment; that would be too big
an investment to support what he had in your house.
He's probably been tailing you. Your movements pretty
routine? Office, grocery store, night out, that sort of
thing?"

"That sort of thing."

"No point in a big stakeout, then. Better to tail you
home and listen in. Where's your car?"

"Out front a couple of doors down. BMW 320i." She
gave him the keys, and he left. He came back five minutes
later.

"Clean," he said. "This is minimum stuff. His assump-
tions are, you don't know he's tailing you, you think you
don't have anything to hide. You work with Biggles?"

"Sort of."

"You talk about your work on the phone, or around
the house?"

"Never."

"How about at the other house?"

Her ears burned as she remembered her conversations with Will about Majorov. "Never," she lied.

"You want me to check the other house?"

She gave him the address and dug Will's key from her purse.

"A friend?"

"Yes."

"Where is he now?"

"In Stockholm. He left this morning."

"Good. I'll do it now, if that's okay."

"Sure, go ahead."

"Be back in less than an hour," he said.

Rule got undressed and into a hot tub. She got the polish off her nails, shaved her legs, washed her hair, wondered what she'd been recorded saying. She was in a robe with her hair in a towel when Burgis returned.

"You forgot to tell me about the alarm system," Danny Burgis said.

"Oh, my God, I did! Did the cops come?"

Burgis shook his head and grinned. "Luckily, it was one of mine; I have a master code. My outfit has installed a couple of dozen systems in Georgetown. You could use one here, you know. This is a bad town for burglary."

"You're right. We'll have to talk about that. What did you find over there?"

"Exactly the same setup, bedroom and living room. That means two each was all he meant to install; he didn't get interrupted twice. You were lucky this time, though; his system was down. One of the two batteries in the black box was half out of its bracket. It didn't fall out; the guy was just sloppy. My guess is it hasn't been in long, and it's never worked. Your man hasn't had a chance to get back in and correct it."

"Danny, have you got some fix on who this is? I mean, the sort of people?"

"Well, it ain't one of yours and Biggles's colleagues; They like state-of-the-art stuff, the sexier the better. This is too simple for them. You in the middle of a divorce?"

"No, I was divorced two years ago. Why?"

"Well, I would have made this maybe a domestic matter, a private investigator, but if you've been divorced that long, that doesn't fit. You're not in a fight over custody or money?"

"No, that was all settled amicably at the time. He didn't want my kid, and I didn't want his money."

"Well, that leaves the opposition, doesn't it?"

"Does it? Anything to indicate he's foreign?"

"Nothing special. I've seen some of their work. Even a Russian might make his own stuff from locally available components, especially if he was worried about it being found. If it's the opposition, you're not very important to them; the effort isn't big enough. They're maybe trying to catch you in your friend's bed for some blackmail. That would add up. Maybe they hoped to squeeze you for some paperwork from your office. Anybody tried to lean on you?"

"No."

"Well, I reckon it's like this: if he's been in your bed, they might have some heavy breathing and some conversation. If you've been in his bed, you're okay, because their bug wasn't working. You know the people directly across the street from your house?"

"Yes. Elderly couple, been there for twenty, thirty years."

"Well, there's a shot from their top-floor window with an infrared camera and a long lens, but only if you didn't pull the shade. Impossible at your friend's house; the angles are wrong."

She felt vastly relieved. Will had never been in her bed, and what she had said at his house hadn't been overheard. "Well, thanks, Danny; what do I owe you?"

"Oh, a couple hundred, I guess. Tell you what: you let me put you in a good alarm system here for, say, eighteen hundred—and believe me, that's cheap—and I'll thrown in the sweeps. That'll make it tougher for them to bug you again, too."

"Oh, yeah? How'd they bug the other house, then?"

"One of two ways," Burgis replied with confidence. "Either they had the code, which is unlikely, or your friend didn't bother to arm the system one day, and they got lucky."

"The second one, I think. He's like that. Sure, Danny, do me a system." She went to a desk drawer in the entrance hall and gave him a key. "At your convenience," she said. "I'm at the office all day, every day."

"Right you are, Katie," he said, pocketing the key. "I'll try to get to it this week sometime. Do the work myself. Uh, listen, there's one other thing you can do about all this."

"What's that?"

"Let me tail you for a few days. I'll pick up whoever's on you and have a little talk with him."

She thought about that for a moment. "No, not yet, anyway. I don't want the kettle to boil any faster. I'll let you know if I change my mind, though."

"You do that. I'd sorta like to chat with him."

"Thanks, Danny." She let him out of the house, and leaned on the door. She felt better with him around. But who the hell was following her and bugging her house? She trudged up the stairs, drying her hair with the towel, wondering.

24

Helder awoke instantly, afraid to move. A noise had done it, a boat's engines. His cheek was sweaty against the plastic seat cover; he kept his head down as his bed rocked and bumped against its moorings, then settled as the engines faded into the distance. He sat up. The interior of the little boathouse was dimly lit from the outside. He checked his wristwatch; just past six o'clock, local time. But six in the morning or in the evening? Evening, he decided, of the same day he had begun his mission.

He felt a need to get somewhere else, quickly; he shouldn't be in this boathouse. He unzipped the plastic pouch and got at his nylon duffel. Since it was evening, he chose the darker outfit—navy blue jacket with brass buttons, gray worsted slacks, black loafers, white button-down shirt, striped necktie. He felt clean enough from his swim, but he needed a shave. Not here, though. He cracked the door of the boathouse and looked carefully about. There were lights on in the nearby house, but nobody around outside. He walked quickly away from the boathouse along the shore, through an opening in a high hedge. Another house greeted him, perhaps twenty meters away. There must be a road, he thought, and it must be at the back of the houses. He walked along the hedge, keeping an eye open for company. He heard the sounds of a tennis ball striking rackets and laughter; then he saw the court emerge from behind the house and a young couple at play. If they saw him, they took no notice.

He came to a tarmac road and looked in both directions. Did it matter? He checked the position of the sun and walked toward it. Stockholm would be west, and he wanted Stockholm, where he could blend in among thousands. He walked quickly, but not hurriedly, a man who knew where he was going but was not in a panic. Perhaps a kilometer along, he came to a crossroads and a bus stop with a little shelter alongside. He checked the framed schedule: a bus for Stockholm in twenty minutes' time. Good. He looked up and down the road. Two cars passed in rapid succession but no pedestrians were in sight. He sat down in the shelter, opened his bag, and began sorting through it, marshaling his assets.

He had eighteen hundred Swedish kroner, a hundred and seventy dollars, and a thousand dollars in traveler's checks, which he had already signed in the name of Carl Swenson. He had a wallet, a Visa card, and an American Express card, all suitably worn, but current; he had an American passport stamped for entry into Sweden that day and an unused return ticket from Stockholm to New York on Scandinavian Air Systems. He had another change of clothes, a toilet kit, and his sketch pad; he had a map of the city of Stockholm and a guidebook to Sweden; he had a 9mm automatic pistol and two clips of ammunition. He put all these things into his pockets except the pistol and ammunition. He didn't want them; they seemed foreign to his other possessions. He had no intention of shooting his way out of Sweden, anyway. He put them back into the bag; he would get rid of them at the first opportunity. He took a small, battery-operated electric shaver from his kit and ran it quickly over his face, then combed his hair carefully. His reflection in the mirror in the shaver's cap showed a surprisingly normal person looking back at him.

The bus came, and he climbed aboard. "Stockholm?" he asked the driver.

The man nodded. "Sixteen kroner," he said in English.

Helder gave him a fifty-kroner note and took the change, pleased that the driver would automatically speak English to him. He took a seat near the back of the bus. There were only half a dozen people on board. He was ravenously hungry, but he tried to put it out of his mind. He unfolded his map of Stockholm and went over it carefully, then turned to the guidebook. His concerns were food, shelter, and the docks. Satisfied that he had his bearings in the city, he gave in to fatigue and napped, surprisingly at peace with his circumstances.

He woke in the outskirts of Stockholm and watched, fascinated, as the buildings went past. Everything was so different from Soviet cities. The buildings were neat, clean, and in good repair, whereas in Moscow or Leningrad, only the public buildings were well kept, and not all of them. There were many more trees than he had expected. In Russia, city trees had been cut for firewood during the Great Patriotic War, and they had been only sparsely replanted. The great number of shops impressed him, too, and even though the streets were filled with people, there were no queues outside the shops. Traffic was heavy with private cars, and there were no military vehicles to be seen.

At the central bus station he found a taxi and asked to be taken to the old city. He got out near the royal palace and walked into the narrow streets of the old town, which dated, he knew, to the fourteenth century. Almost immediately, he came to a small hotel called the Lord Nelson. There was no room available, but the young woman in reception offered·to telephone to an associated hotel around the corner. "You are lucky," she said. "They have had a cancellation of a single room. Normally, we are very full this time of the year." She gave him a card with the hotel's name, the Lady Hamilton, and directions. In a few minutes he was housed in a tiny, but very handsome room, hardly bigger than a ship's cabin. He hung up his clothes and wondered what to do with the gun. In opening cupboards and drawers, he found a tiny refrigerator stocked with beer and spirits. He removed them and repacked the icebox, with the pistol and ammunition at the rear. He couldn't imagine that the Swedes routinely searched the hotel rooms of American tourists. At the desk, they hadn't even asked for his passport.

He left the hotel and found a restaurant, where he

wolfed down four courses and a bottle of wine. Then, sated and exhausted, he dragged himself back to his room and into bed, too tired to think of anything but rest. Helder's first night in the free world passed dreamlessly.

25

Rule overslept and had to hurry to reach the Agency in time for an EXCOM TWO meeting. The conference room was already in darkness as she tiptoed in and took her seat. Pegram from Imagery Analysis had a satshot on the screen and was droning on about it.

"You see here the Lenin Aircraft Fabrication plant at Pskov, in western Russia, near the Estonian and Latvian borders. Construction began on the plant four years ago, and it has been in use for more than two years, though greatly underutilized, by our best estimates. The building is nearly a mile in length and a quarter mile wide, making it big enough for the manufacture of the largest troop transports. The plant was to have been used for just that purpose, but due to a cutback in the building of such large aircraft, it has been used only for developmental work, which brings us to this." Pegram changed slides from an overall view to a closer view of one end of the building. The nose and a portion of the port wing of a large aircraft protruded from the building.

"Anybody care to guess what this might be?" he asked, laconically.

"Looks like a big, fat troop transport or cargo plane," a voice said from the dark.

"Anybody do better than that? Notice anything unusual about it?"

Rule spoke up. "Well, from what we see of it here, the wings look too short to give it enough lift to fly." She was getting an uncomfortable feeling.

"Pretty good, Rule. Now take a look at this." Pegram changed slides again. This time, the whole aircraft could be seen flying at a low altitude over what looked like water.

"Jesus, Pegram," Rule said. "It's not a WIG, is it?"

"A WIG it is, Rule. Tell us what you know about WIGs."

"Well, they said it couldn't be done, or rather, *we* said it couldn't be done, we and the British. The Soviets have been working on the idea since the fifties—we get a rumor now and then—but I sure didn't know they had one up and running."

"Come on, guys," another voice from the dark complained. "What's a WIG?"

"WIG is short for wing-in-ground effect," Pegram replied.

"Oh," the voice said. "Oh, that. Sure."

Pegram continued. "It works on the principle that an aircraft of a certain size flying at a low level, say under a hundred feet, builds up a cushion of air that might allow it to carry a payload of up to five hundred times greater than normal. Nobody on our side believed it would ever work; that's why we have no WIG program—not even on the drawing board."

"So what do we know about this one on the screen?" Rule asked. "What will it do?"

"Well," said Pegram, "the people at the Office of Scientific and Weapons Research have just pronounced on that, and here's what they say." He read from a sheet of paper on the lighted lectern. "The wing-in-ground effect aircraft pictured here is approximately two hundred feet in length, with a wingspan of only one hundred feet. It seems to be powered by two gas turbine engines, whose exhaust can be directed under the wings to provide additional lift, combined with a contrarotating airscrew mounted on the forward edge of the tail assembly. The nose of the aircraft seems to be hinged about fifteen feet behind the cockpit, leading us to believe that the entire forward section of the plane can be lifted for rapid loading and unloading. We estimated that the aircraft could ferry up to four hundred troops or several armored vehicles over a range of one thousand miles at speeds in excess of three hundred knots at altitudes of under one hundred feet over water and low-lying landmasses. It could take off and land at airstrips of under moderate length and could be adapted to do so on water, as well. The aircraft in the photograph appears to be carrying two SS N 22 missiles, similar to the French Exocet, one under each wing."

The room had become perfectly silent.

"Gentlemen," Pegram intoned, "what you are looking at is, if it works—and it appears that it does—nothing less than a quantum leap forward in amphibious warfare. The Soviets have two up and running—we've got satshots of them both. They've been testing them on a huge lake northwest of Pskov. What's more, they appear to have been up and running for at least two years. And we ain't got one."

There was a long silence in the room. Finally, a voice spoke. "I was just trying to think where they might use it against us."

The room broke up into half a dozen conversations on this subject. Finally, Rule spoke into the hubbub. "Pegram, how do we know there are two of these things flying?"

"Like I said, Rule, we've got satshots of them both. They have different numbers."

"Yeah, you said that, but what you've shown us is a mile-long aircraft factory built in a hurry, and you're saying that they're only using a couple of hundred yards of it to build two WIGs? Has any analysis of the materials being hauled into Pskov been done?"

"What're you getting at, Rule?"

"What I'm getting at is, what if they're using the whole mile to build WIGs, but they're only using two different numbers on the fuselages when they test them?"

It had become very quiet again in the room. Pegram could be seen, even by the lectern light, to redden. He shuffled the papers before him. "Don't you think we'd back this up with HUMINT?" he asked, rhetorically.

Jesus, I hope so, Rule thought. A little human intelligence on the ground would be very comforting in the circumstances.

The meeting broke up, and as Rule left the conference

room, a voice close behind her said, "Kate, you believe he's got HUMINT to back up that assessment?"

Rule turned, surprised to find Ed Rawls back at the Agency so soon. He must have handed Malakhov off to a settlement team, she thought. "No," she said.

"Neither do I," Rawls replied.

"Ed, from what he said about the capabilities of that thing, wouldn't the Baltic be a good theater of operations for it?"

"Ideal, I'd say. See you around, Kate." He turned and walked away down the hall.

Rule was deep in thought and almost to her office when she absentmindedly ran head-on into a man coming around a corner.

"Kate, how are you?"

Rule tried to reorganize her thoughts. "Jim Gill! I thought you were still in Rome. What are you doing here?"

Gill, a tall, stringy fellow with a pronounced Southern accent, looked questioningly back at her. "Sure I'm still in Rome; I'm just back for a couple of days for a meeting. Listen, I was just looking for you in your office. I didn't get an answer to my cable last week. Have you lost interest in Appicella?"

It took Rule a moment to register the name. "Appicella? Of course I'm still interested. I didn't get any cable from you; I haven't heard anything about Appicella since your original report." Emilio Appicella was the Italian computer pirate who, with his bragging about his visits with Majorov, had set this whole thing in motion.

Gill shrugged. "Well, shoot, I guess communications screwed up. I wondered why I hadn't heard from you."

Rule resisted taking him by the lapels. "What's happening with Appicella?"

"Well, ol' Emilio has got himself another invitation to go east."

"Invitation? From Majorov, you mean?"

"That's what he says. I sent you all this stuff, you know; cabled it last week. Maybe they just haven't gotten around to it in crypto or something."

The hell they hadn't decoded it, Rule thought. Somebody was screening her traffic. Somebody had stopped that cable. "Tell me, now, Jim."

"Emilio's flying to Vienna on—Jesus, what day is this, Monday?—Wednesday; he's connecting in Vienna with a Leningrad flight. I asked for instructions, Kate. Didn't hear from you; didn't hear from ops. The station's been a madhouse the last couple of weeks, and when I didn't hear, I just thought I'd take it up when I got back here."

"Has anybody in the Rome station dealt with Appicella besides you?"

"Nope, he's mine, all mine."

"When are you going back to Rome?"

"A week or so."

"Come on back to my office for a minute, will you, Jim?" She led him back down the corridor and closed the door behind them.

"Listen, Jim, have you talked with anybody in ops about this, yet?"

"Nope, I just got in this morning. Haven't even been up there, yet."

"Jim, I've got to talk with Appicella before he leaves for Vienna. Can you get in touch with him directly, without going through the Rome station?"

Gill produced a notebook. "Got his phone number right here. He works at home."

"It's extremely important that I talk to him, and I'm going to have to short-circuit the system just a little to do it. Will you wait until you're back at your hotel, then call him and ask him to see me?"

Gill looked thoughtful. "I guess you wouldn't want me to mention this to ops, huh?"

"I'd rather not. They'd only screw it up. You know how they are."

"You just want to talk with him, then?"

"That's it. Just call him for me, and give me his number."

"Well, hell, all right. If I wait until tonight to call, I'll wake him up. You don't want me to call from here, huh?" He grinned.

"I'd rather you didn't. Just tell him to expect a call from me, and tell him it's important."

"Okay, Kate, I'll hand him off to you. I'll tell him what a great-looking broad you are, and he'll be dying to meet you. He's a real ladies' man."

"Tell him anything—well, almost anything. Just get him to agree to talk to me."

"Okay, I'll call him."

"I owe you one, Jim."

"And one of these days I'll collect, you count on it." He wrote down the phone number and opened the door. "I'm due in ops. See you."

Rule grabbed her bag and walked out to where her secretary sat. "Jeff, I'm feeling like death. I'm going home and to bed. The way I feel, I don't think I'll be in tomorrow, either. Anybody calls, tell them I'm not answering the phone. If they want me badly enough, they'll send a courier."

"Okay," Jeff said, and went back to his magazine.

Rule left the building, got into her car, and stopped at the first gas station. She dialed Pan American. "You have a night flight to Rome, don't you? Good. I want one seat; I'll give you a credit card number."

26

Helder, exhausted and a little drunk, had slept sound-lessly until midmorning. He woke, sweating, his dreams back in the minisub, Sokolov with the screwdriver pro-truding from her eye, the hatch jammed. The sun on his face seemed like the light of heaven. He stood and looked out the little window at the spires of Stockholm. He was alive and safe.

He took a cool shower, washing away the sweat and the last vestiges of the dream, or rather, the memory. He dressed in his other clothes, a light tweed jacket, and linen trousers, packed his bag, retrieved the pistol from the fridge, and went down to breakfast. He ate greed-ily from the array of eggs, sausages, and herring, a good Swedish breakfast; then he paid his bill in kroner.

"Where would I go to book passage on the ferry to Helsinki?" he asked the girl at the desk.

"I can book it for you by phone," she said, and dialed a number. Soon she had booked him a single cabin on the evening sailing. "The ferry leaves at six and arrives in

Helsinki tomorrow morning at nine," she said. "Just pick up your ticket at the terminal an hour before sailing."

He thanked her and left. As he walked through the narrow streets of Stockholm's Old Town, looking at the fair Swedes and their city, something came to him that he had not had the time to consider. He was alone in a Western city with an American passport, credit cards, and a lot of money. It would be perfectly possible for him to take a taxi to Stockholm Airport and buy a ticket to any place in the world. Majorov would never find him. Or would he? Could the credit card charges be traced? Would the passport hold up under scrutiny? And how would he earn a living when the money ran out? He had been trained to survive in a foreign city for a few days, but did he know enough of Western life to survive on a long-term basis without tripping up? With luck, maybe, but probably not.

There was another alternative, though; he could take a taxi to the American Embassy and present himself to the authorities there. Better yet, he could board a plane for New York or Washington. With what he knew or suspected about Malibu and Majorov's plans, he would surely get a warm welcome. Still, he knew something about how the KGB worked, and the CIA would certainly not be much different. Would they believe him? Would they think he was a plant? Would they torture him for information he did not have? He suddenly felt very much alone and lost.

Then he thought of Trina Ragulin, and he didn't feel lost anymore. She was at Malibu, waiting for him, and where she was was where he wanted to be. If he went back, they had a future together. Majorov had promised him promotion and command if he performed well, and he had done that. The buoy was precisely where Majorov wanted it, and if Sokolov was dead, that would be all right with the colonel, too. His instructions had been to kill her if they had to abandon, and Helder had done just that, however inadvertently. By all rights, he should return as a hero, having earned Majorov's gratitude, and he had seen what patronage could do for an officer's career in the Soviet Navy. He could go back, marry Ragulin, rise in rank, and send their children to the best schools, ascend to that level of living which so few Soviets achieved. Could anyone in the West offer him more than that?

He emerged from the narrow streets into an open area and heard martial music. His map told him he was at the royal palace. He walked into a cobblestone courtyard and joined a crowd of tourists watching the changing of the guard. He followed the young men in their neatly pressed uniforms with their weapons held rigidly before them as they performed their routine. He wondered what they would do if they knew that he was a Soviet spy with an automatic pistol tucked into his belt. Probably drop to one knee and fire on him. He chuckled at the thought of the tourists scattering, the bullets ricocheting about the square.

When the performance ended he walked down a long flight of stairs to the water and looked about him. Stockholm reminded him a bit of Leningrad, with its expanses of water in the center of the city. He leaned against a stone railing and took his sketch pad from his bag. He sketched the palace, the water before it, the palace guards in their comic-opera uniforms, an old man on the street, whatever caught his eye. He felt a hunger pang and was surprised to look at his watch and see that more than two hours had passed.

He walked back up the steps and into the Old Town again. He had passed a restaurant in a little square earlier and thought he would go back. A girl seated him at an empty table for four on a glass-enclosed terrace which looked out over the square to the Swedish Academy across the way. The place was obviously popular, for it was filling fast. Helder ordered a beer and looked over the menu.

"Excuse me," a voice said.

Helder looked up to find the hostess who had seated him standing with a man at her side.

"Would you mind sharing your table with this gentleman? I'm afraid we are quite full."

Helder looked quickly at the man. He was tall, dark hair, late thirties; casually, but elegantly dressed; English, Helder guessed. He didn't look like a Swedish policeman.

"If it's inconvenient, I don't mind waiting," the man said, misreading Helder's hesitation.

"No, please sit down. I'm afraid I was daydreaming, and it took a moment for the penny to drop."

"Thank you," the man said, and sat down. He ordered a drink and picked up the menu. "Do you know this place? Can you recommend something?"

American, not English. Some sort of regional accent, Helder thought. Southern, maybe. "No, I'm a tourist; my first time here."

"British?" the man asked.

"No, American."

"Really? So am I. Where are you from?"

"Minnesota, originally. I live in New York, now."

"There's something about your accent I can't place. That business about the penny dropping is an English expression, so I thought you might be British."

"You're right. I picked that up from an English girl I know. As for my accent, my parents were Swedish; maybe that's colored it a bit."

"You speak Swedish?"

"Not really. The folks, once they were in America, wanted to be Americans. They insisted on speaking English when I was growing up. As for something to eat, you might try the gravlax; that's marinated salmon with a sauce of mustard and dill. My mother used to make it."

"Sounds good to me."

The waitress came back and they ordered.

"You're a New Yorker, then," the man said. "I love that city, especially the restaurants. Do you know Café des Artistes, on the Upper West Side?"

"No, I live in Greenwich Village, and I spend most of my time there, I guess."

"Good eating in the Village, too. Know La Tulipe, on West Thirteenth Street?"

"I'm afraid not. My girlfriend's quite a cook. We eat at home more often than not. I work at home, too, so I guess I don't get around as much as some people." The man was beginning to sound like one of Mr. Jones's legend drills.

"Can't blame you," the man laughed. "Me, I do most of the cooking for my girlfriend. What do you do?"

"Commercial artist. Illustrator."

The man craned to see Helder's sketch pad. "And a good one, too, I expect. That's very nice. May I see what you've been doing?"

Helder handed him the pad.

"Very good, indeed. Do you ever have a show?"

"Oh, no. By the time I finish doing advertising work and book jackets, I don't have much energy left for my own work. Vacations are the only time I have to draw for myself."

"Pity. Have you been in Stockholm long?"

"Arrived yesterday, and I'm off to Helsinki tonight. I have an aunt there I haven't seen since I was a child."

"Nice to have someone show you around in a strange city," the man said.

"What part of the country are you from?" Helder asked, anxious to turn the questioning from himself.

"Georgia; small town called Delano. I've got a law practice there with my father."

"You on vacation, too?"

"Yes, in fact, I'll be in Helsinki in a couple of days, but only to change planes."

"Where are you headed?"

"Place on the west coast called Pietarsaari, or by its Swedish name, Jakobstad. I'm picking up a new boat from a yard there for a friend; sailing it to Copenhagen."

Helder's interest was piqued. "What sort of a boat?"

"Sloop, forty-two feet, a Swan. You sail?"

"Oh, I did some dinghy sailing on the lakes in Minnesota. Finns, mostly."

"Single-handed, huh? I've done some of that myself, but in larger boats."

"I don't think I know the Swan," Helder said.

The man looked surprised. "No? They have the reputation of being the best production yachts in the world."

"Well, I guess there weren't many Swans on the Minnesota lakes," Helder laughed.

Their food arrived, and they chatted easily through lunch. Helder rather liked the man, and he enjoyed the mental exercise of holding up his end of the conversation, relying on the training Jones had given him and his own ability to improvise. They finished their coffee and divided up the check, then rose to go.

"Well, have a good stay, both in Stockholm and Helsinki," the man said. "And keep drawing. You're good."

Helder was grateful for someone to talk with and was sorry the lunch was over. "Would you like one?" he asked, holding up his sketch pad.

"Oh, thanks, but I'm sure you'll want them for the memories."

"I'd be very pleased to know one of my things was hanging in a lawyer's office in Georgia," Helder said. He really would, too. It amused him to think the man would never know who had done the drawing, and there would be a little of himself in America, even if the CIA didn't get him.

"Well, thank you very much. I'm partial to the one of the palace guards, I think. May I have that one?"

"Of course," Helder said, tearing the drawing from the pad. He signed it quickly and handed it over.

"We never introduced ourselves properly," the man said, "and I'd like to know whose work will be hanging in my office." He stuck out his hand.

"I'm Carl Swenson," Helder said, returning the handshake.

"It's good to meet you, Carl. If you ever find yourself in Delano, Georgia, look me up. My name is Will Lee."

They parted the best of friends.

27

Rule blinked in the dazzling Roman sunlight, shading her eyes with her hand, and searched the crowd in vain for Emilio Appicella. She was seated in an outdoor cafe in the Piazza Navona, feeling like death, and suffering a major continental disorientation. She had taken a night flight from Washington and arrived at the crack of dawn, gone straight to a room at the Hassler-Villa Medici, where they remembered Simon, if not her, and slept restlessly for two hours. The walk from the Hassler to the restaurant had passed like a stroll on another, but oddly familiar planet, waves of heat from the paving stones riffling through the throbs of her jet lag.

She had made a luncheon appointment with Appicella before leaving DC; he had agreed to see her with alacrity, even eagerness. What had Jim Gill told the man about her, anyway? Appicella had suggested lunch, suggested the restaurant, an old favorite of hers from her Rome station days, but he was twenty minutes late, and the ice in her San Pellegrino had melted. She waved at a waiter for a refill and searched the crowd in the square again, wondering what he looked like. ("I will find you," he had said when she asked.) She had a feeling he would be an Italian version of that well-known American breed, the computer nerd.

She watched a man walking slowly through the restaurant and smiled to herself. He was not her lunch date. He might have stepped out of a Mastroianni film. He was outrageously handsome, dressed in a white suit, the jacket draped over his shoulders, and a Panama hat. A pale yellow silk shirt was open at the throat, and the only spot of color was a wildly patterned silk handkerchief in the jacket pocket. He moved easily through the crowd, shaking a hand here, kissing another there, tossing a wave to somebody across the terrace. He had a habit of running a finger along his thick, dark mustache, which gave him a rakish air, and the waiters lined up to speak to him. He was a caricature of everything Hollywood believed about Italian men, and she wished forlornly that she was having lunch with him, instead of some half-baked computer pirate, who, she knew, would turn up in a wrinkled polyester suit with a lot of pens stuck in the jacket pocket. It was no way to spend her one day in Rome.

The man eyed her as he stopped a couple of tables away, and she returned his gaze frankly. If her man didn't show, what the hell? He exchanged a few words with the couple at the table, then moved toward her and stopped, removing his straw hat to reveal a dark headful of gorgeously barbered hair. She looked up into the dark eyes and tried not to giggle.

"Signorina Rule, I believe," he said smoothly, in comically accented English.

She was speechless.

"I am Emilio Appicella," he said. "I believe we have an appointment. May I sit down?"

"Of course," she said, recovering slightly. He lifted an eyebrow, and a waiter instantly materialized at the table. Appicella spoke to him for half a minute in Italian too rapid for her to follow, and the waiter vanished.

"I have taken the liberty of ordering for you," he said. "I hope you do not mind."

"No," she said, putty in his hands already.

"Well," he breathed, leaning back in his chair and looking at her, "you are certainly the loveliest CIA agent I have ever seen."

"Jesus Christ!" she hissed at him, rattled. "Will you keep your voice down!"

He laughed loudly. "Ah, Signorina Rule, nobody here is listening to us. Not on a day like today." He waved a hand. "They are all too busy making plans to take each other to bed immediately after lunch."

The waiter materialized again, bearing a tray with a pitcher of orange juice and a bottle of cold Champagne.

"It is a wonderful drink I am ashamed to say I discovered in England," Appicella said, supervising the pouring of equal measures of the two drinks. "It is called a Buck's Fizz, and it is far too cheerful and sunny a concoction for such a dismal place. They do not deserve it." He placed a glass in front of her and raised his own. "To successful missions," he said, conspiratorially.

"Mr. Appicella," Rule said quickly, "I think you must have the wrong idea about who I am. I—"

He held up a hand. "Please. First we will have a good lunch; then we will talk of spying and such things."

Rule tried to relax and enjoy herself, though she had a late-afternoon plane to catch. A huge platter of antipasti arrived, followed by pasta with sour cream, cheese, and flakes of smoked salmon, followed by tiny lamb chops and a salad. They chatted like new friends, about the heat in Rome and Washington, the best restaurants on the Amalfi coast, the best hotels in Venice. Appicella was familiar with them all.

Finally, over coffee, Appicella leaned back, belched discreetly, and said, "Now, to business. I expect you wish me to spy on Firsov for you—is that correct?"

"Yes," Rule replied. She was too surprised to say anything else. She had been preparing for a long exercise in subtleties and, perhaps, some batting of the eyelashes.

"All right," he said. "I will do it."

"You will?" she asked, weakly.

"Of course. Did you think I was some Communist, or something?"

"Well, no . . ."

"Do you wish me to photograph documents?"

"Emilio, I haven't brought you a camera or any other paraphernalia. It would be extremely dangerous for an ama—a nonprofessional to try that sort of thing."

He shrugged. "As you wish. I will be happy to take photographs if you like. I have a Minox of my own."

She shook her head. "No, I couldn't ask you to do that. I simply want to know where Firsov is and what he might be up to. Look, I don't have authorization for a fee, but I might be able to—"

He stopped her with a glare. "Do you think I do this for money? Good God, woman, didn't Gill tell you about my grandmother?"

"He said she was Russian, and that was why you spoke the language."

"My grandmother was a countess," he said, "married at nineteen, twenty when the Revolution came. The Bolshevik bastards murdered her husband and stole everything she had. She arrived in Italy in a third-class railway car, penniless; then she had the good fortune to meet my grandfather. Soon, she was an Italian countess. My parents were killed during the war, and I lived with her from my early childhood. She spoke nothing but Russian to me, and she told me everything I ever needed to know about the Communists. I will be very pleased to do whatever I can to hurry their downfall. I take their money"—he smiled, stroking his mustache—"in order to impoverish them. I do for them only small things, not things for war."

"I understand," Rule said, "and I am grateful for your help."

"What, exactly, do you wish me to find out for you?"

"Firsov's exact location and as much as possible about his activities. I want to know in what sort of place he is working, and what, if any, military equipment is in evidence around him. I want lots and lots of detail, whatever you see and can remember. It could be very important to a great many people. Lives could be saved, you understand?"

"Of course. I will do as you ask. How will I be in touch with you?"

She wrote down her home telephone number. "Please memorize this number; don't take it into the Soviet Union written down."

He gazed at the card for a moment. "Yes, yes, I have it."

"I will normally only be there during the evening hours, but there is a telephone answering machine, and you can leave a number or address for me to reach you. You can talk for as long as thirty minutes to the machine, and it is quite secure. Please don't try to call from the Soviet Union. Wait until you are back in Rome or in some other Western city. If it's possible, I'll come back to talk with you, but there may not be time for that."

"Do you know about computers, Kate?" he asked.

"I work with them a lot."

"Do you know what The Source is?"

"It's an information utility in Maryland. I've played with it."

"Good. I keep files in The Source at times. My account number is ZZP100, and my password is WHOP. Can you remember that?"

"Yes."

"If for some reason I cannot telephone, I will leave a message for you there in a file called KATE. Check it every day."

"All right."

"And now, my lovely spy," Appicella said, signing the bill, "will you come back to my villa and make love with me?"

Rule was not sure he was serious but thought he probably was. "It is not an unpleasant thought, Emilio, but I have a plane to catch."

"I am desolated," he said, and it made her feel good to believe him.

28

Helder stood on the deck of the Stockholm–Helsinki ferry as the ship was warped in to the docks. He was rested and well fed. The previous evening, he had enjoyed a sumptuous dinner, had danced with a couple of Swedish girls, and had slept well and alone by choice. He had risen early, had an excellent breakfast, and watched as the ship entered Helsinki harbor. It was a beautiful city, seen from the sea, but now his eyes were on the docks. He had made the required phone call from Stockholm but had been told nothing, and he hoped he would be met. Helder left the ship by an elevated gangplank that emptied into a terminal building. Inside, he walked slowly toward the street, wondering what to do next.

"Carl!" a voice somewhere behind him called. It took a moment for the name to register, and when he turned, Mr. Jones of Malibu was shaking his hand. "Carl, it's your uncle Jan! How are you?"

"Very well, Uncle Jan," Helder replied, astonished to see the legend-maker.

"Your aunt is dying to see you," Jones said. "Come, the car is outside."

Helder followed as Jones quickly led the way from the terminal to the car park. Jones motioned him into a blue Volvo station wagon, all the time smiling and keeping up a flow of banter about family and America and Helder's aunt. When they were under way, Jones said, "Helder, it really is good to see you. When you didn't return to the mother sub, we feared the worst. Where's Sokolov?"

"Still in the minisub," Helder replied. "She was unable to leave it."

"I see," Jones said, glancing into his rearview mirror. "Pardon me if we don't chat for a few minutes. I have some driving to do."

Jones drove quickly, then slowly, making turns in a seemingly random pattern. Once, he stopped for a red light, then drove straight through it, checking the mirror constantly. Finally, they pulled into a tree-lined street, and a man in civilian clothes opened a wrought-iron gate for them. Jones drove past a large, handsome house and parked in back. "Follow me," he said, jumping from the vehicle and racing up the back stairs.

Inside, there were marble floors and a lot of heavy furniture. They took a small elevator up two floors and emerged into a dingy and badly lit hallway. Jones stopped before a steel door and rang a bell. A small panel slid back, and a pair of eyes surveyed them both.

"What is this place?" Helder asked.

"It's the Soviet Embassy," Jones replied. "I thought you knew."

The door was open, and they were admitted by a man

in shirtsleeves to a large room filled with radio receivers and teletypes. It reeked of tobacco smoke.

"Show him how to work it," Jones said to the man.

"Over here," the man said, motioning them to a computer terminal. "You type?" he asked Helder.

"Yes," Helder replied.

The man picked up a telephone, punched out a number, listened for a moment, then placed the receiver in a cradle. A row of Xs appeared on the terminal's screen, then the words, "I am here."

"It's the colonel on the other end," Jones said.

The other man motioned Helder into a chair before the terminal. "All you do is type," he said.

"Come on," Jones said to the man, and they left Helder alone in the room with the glowing computer terminal.

Helder typed, "I am here, sir."

"Was your mission successful?" appeared on the screen.

"We successfully carried out our task, but we lost the sub to depth charges," Helder typed.

"Give me the numbers," the screen said.

Helder typed in the coordinates of the buoy's location. The screen spelled them out again.

"Are these correct?" it asked.

"Yes," Helder typed.

"Were you injured?" the screen asked.

"No, sir, I am quite fit," Helder replied.

"Did your companion survive?" the screen asked.

"No," Helder typed.

"Jones will drive you to an airport," the screen spelled

out, "where a plane awaits to bring you to Moscow. I will meet you there. There is aboard the plane a naval uniform for you bearing the insignia of Captain Second Grade. In addition to promotion, you will receive half your pay in a foreign currency of your choice. Congratulations and well done."

"Thank you, sir," Helder tapped back.

"Signing off. See you in Moscow."

Helder stared at the screen for a moment; then he got up and opened the door. Jones and the other man were standing in the hallway outside. "I'm finished," he said.

"Then we're off," Jones said.

At the airport, a small Soviet jet aircraft with no military markings waited. He shook hands with Jones.

"See you back at Malibu." The man smiled.

"Thanks for the lift . . . and for the legend," Helder replied. "I would never have made it without your training."

Jones shrugged. "It's my job. I like it."

Helder boarded the plane, and while it taxied to a runway, the copilot showed him a fridge with food and drink and gave him a small suitcase and a garment bag. When they were in the air, the man came back into the cabin. "You can move around, now, and get dressed if you wish, Captain. Do you need anything?"

Helder shook his head, and the man went back into the cockpit and closed the door behind him. Helder opened the garment bag and looked at the new insignia on his uniform. The case held shoes, shirt, and underwear, and a toilet kit. He changed into the uniform and repacked his traveling clothes. He felt a rustle in the tunic pocket and found a folded sheet of paper. "I have heard that you are safe, and I am glad. I sewed on your new insignia. Hope to see you soonest. T."

He sat back in his comfortable seat and heaved a great sigh. He was alive, safe, promoted, and loved. He could not think of any way to improve the situation.

On arrival in Moscow, however, the situation improved. When the aircraft taxied to a halt there was a Zil limousine waiting. A Zil! Helder stood at the bottom of the boarding steps and stared at it. It was said that there were fewer than one hundred of the handsome, hand-built cars in the whole of the Soviet Union. Only the very highest officials were entitled to them. As he stared, the driver got out and opened the door for him. Majorov was waiting for him in the backseat. The colonel shook his hand warmly.

"I am so very pleased to see you back, Helder," he beamed. I had begun to fear for you and your mission, but now you have returned to us to see it completed, and your timing is excellent." The car moved quickly away from the plane, through gates and onto a highway. "You have arrived just in time for me to be able to present you at a meeting of my superiors. I would also like you to assist me in a presentation—there are some charts and boxes of slides in the boot of the car."

"I am glad to be back, sir, and I would be very pleased to assist you," Helder replied. The car was moving rapidly through the suburbs of Moscow toward the center of the city. As they crossed the Moskva River, the spires of St. Basil's Basilica in Red Square loomed beside the Kremlin wall.

"There is the matter of Sokolov," Majorov said.

"Yes, sir."

"Do I want to know the details?"

"Lieutenant Sokolov went berserk when the depth charging started, sir. She was trying . . . I don't really know what she was trying to do; she was strangling me from behind. I . . . she was killed in the struggle. I was unconscious for a few moments; when I came to, she was dead. I left her body in the flooded minisub when I made my escape."

Majorov nodded. "I suppose I should have expected something like that. I was under considerable pressure to give her a key assignment."

"I understand, sir."

"I think it is best that she be declared killed by the depth charges. We'll say she struck her head. The sub will never be recovered."

"Yes, sir."

The car made a right turn into Manezhnaya Street, and a short distance later, turned right again, and drove up a ramp. Helder suddenly realized that they were entering the Kremlin. The hairs on the back of his neck began to move around. He had been inside the walls before, but only to the area open to tourists. Now they were through the gates and driving past the hall of the Supreme Soviet. Tourists, both Soviet and foreign, swarmed the sidewalks. Then the car drove, unimpeded, through another set of wrought-iron gates. The street was suddenly empty of anyone but a few uniformed soldiers standing guard. The Zil drove nearly to the Kremlin wall bordering Red Square and stopped. Majorov got out and Helder followed him. The driver went to the boot and removed two large cases and some boxes.

"Do you mind giving him a hand?" Majorov said, nodding toward the luggage.

The driver already had the two cases, so Helder picked up the stack of boxes and followed Majorov through an impressive entrance. Inside, they were met by a man in the uniform of a full general of the Red Army, who indicated that they should follow him. Majorov and Helder entered a small elevator with the general, while the driver with his cases took the stairs. They rose to the third floor and emerged into a broad hallway, lit by sunlight from a window at the end of the passage. They followed the general into a waiting room, then through double doors into a large, sunlit room furnished with a desk and a long conference table.

Helder thought that, the Winter Palace in Leningrad apart, it was the most elegant room he had ever been in. The walls were covered in pale yellow silk; there were four tall windows, with white silk curtains, looking over a handsomely gardened enclosed courtyard. There was only one picture on the walls, of Lenin. There were places set at the long table, with a crystal pencil holder and a writing pad at each place.

Majorov directed the huffing driver, who had now joined them, to place his cases at one end of the conference table. They turned out to be slide projectors, and Majorov's large briefcase was filled with stacks of apparently identical documents. The boxes Helder carried were trays of slides. When everything was set up Majo-

rov dismissed the driver, and Helder was left alone in the
room with him and the general.

"Well, Viktor Sergeivich," the general said, lighting a
cigarette, "this is your big day, eh?"

Majorov gave a modest shrug. "That remains to be
seen, General. Are you with me?"

The general's smile disappeared. "That remains to be
seen."

A door opened at the far end of the room; the general
hurriedly stubbed out his cigarette and came to attention, as did Majorov. Helder followed their example. A
dozen or fifteen men filed into the room, most of them
in civilian clothes, the rest in high uniform, and took
their places at the conference table, leaving only the head
chair vacant. Helder recognized the faces of a number
of the men from their photographs in *Pravda* and *Izvestia*, especially that of Admiral Gorshkov, for more than
twenty years the head of the Soviet Navy. A moment
later, a solidly built man, much younger than most at the
table, came into the room and took his seat at the head
of the table.

It suddenly came to Helder that he was in the presence of the General Secretary and the Politburo of the
Communist Party.

29

Rule was awakened by the persistent ringing of the phone. She had trouble seeing her watch in the darkened room, but it seemed to be eleven o'clock. The sun was trying to fight its way past the curtains into her room. Probably the office calling. They hadn't called while she'd been in Rome, thank God. She grabbed the phone.

"Hello."

The voice was clear, but the connection crackly. "Hello, sport. What are you doing home this time of day?"

"Will? Where are you?"

"I'm in Jakobstad, also known as Pietarsaari, on the west coast of Finland, where I'm supposed to be. That's more than I can say for you."

"Oh, I've had some kind of bug. It's had me in bed for a couple of days. You're the first phone call I've answered."

"Hope you're feeling better. I'm looking forward to Copenhagen."

"Me too, but I'm still not absolutely sure I can make it."

"Your problem continues?"

"Yes, but I've had a couple of breaks. I just don't know where they'll lead yet." He was being circumspect—that was good. She knew all too well how phone conversations abroad got plucked out of the air by the listeners. "How's it going with the boat?"

"The boat's great. She's in the water and fitted out. I did the provisioning today, and I'm sailing in the morning."

"Your crew work out okay?"

"Didn't work out at all. His wife decided to deliver prematurely, and he couldn't let me know until the last minute."

"What will you do?"

"It's going to work out okay. One of the young guys from the boatyard is coming with me for a couple of hundred miles south. I can sail night and day with him, and he'll help me get through an island group called Aland that's sort of in my way. I'll drop him on Kokar, and he'll get a ferry back to the mainland. After that, I'll be single-handed, but it's open-water sailing. I'll stop to reprovision in Bunge, on the big Swedish island of Gotland, then go on."

"Is this going to be safe?"

"Probably. I've done it before, you know. I'm looking forward to being single-handed again. The company's so good."

She laughed. "When will you make Copenhagen?"

"I'm figuring on a week from Sunday, with no problems. I'll call you from Gotland to report progress."

"You do that. I'll worry about you if you don't."

"I'm the one who's worried. Your problems are bigger than mine. Listen, if things get really tough, if you get boxed in, call my boss. Get a pencil and write down his private numbers."

She wrote down Senator Carr's private office number and home number.

"He's a good guy to have on your side in a pinch, and he's an admirer of yours from the hearings."

"Well, I hope it won't come to going outside, but it's nice to know there's someplace to turn."

"Listen, I've got to get going. I've got to stow all the food tonight and do some passage planning. I'll sleep aboard tonight, and we'll sail at the crack of dawn."

"Okay, you be careful, and be sure to call me from Gotland."

They hung up, and for a moment, she missed him terribly. She hoped to hell she could make Copenhagen. But how could she get to Copenhagen, when she couldn't even get out of bed? She had told Will that she had had a couple of breaks, and that was so; but she had not told him how little she had gotten from either one.

She was no interrogator; that much she had learned. Malakhov had fascinated her with his ramblings, and she had gotten just what he had wanted to give her, and no more. She was no field operative, either, in spite of her basic training and her brief service abroad. She didn't know how to run an agent. Appicella had ended up practically running her. She didn't know what to do next. What she needed was fresh information, and unless she heard from Emilio Appicella, she was only going to get that at the Agency. It both amused and annoyed her that she was, in a way, running her own agent. That was what ops was supposed to be doing, but the current Director of Central Intelligence loved the high-tech stuff, and good old Simon, the toady, was egging him on.

She struggled out of bed, determined to get back to the office and start looking again.

30

Helder sat, entranced, and watched Majorov's presentation to the Politburo unfold. Each man at the conference table had been given a summary of his plan, and they followed carefully through the manuscript as Majorov gave them a dazzling graphic representation of his document from the two slide projectors on two large screens. Helder replaced the slide feeders as they were used up and tried to absorb as much as possible of what Majorov was saying. They were already an hour into the presentation.

"Comrades, on the left-hand screen, you see a display of our primary targets for the first six hours of the operation. They are, not necessarily in order of importance, key military installations, the principal military and civilian airfields, and those gun emplacements in the Stockholm Archipelago which lie in our planned corridors of movement. There are, as I speak, some fourteen hundred handpicked SPETSNAZ operatives already in place on Swedish soil. They are now carrying out the final survey and planning for assaults on these objectives. Within seven days, with your approval, there will be eighty-two hundred SPETSNAZ troops in Sweden, enough to take twenty-seven percent of our initial objectives without further assistance.

"These would include such targets as the Stockholm Military District Headquarters at Strangnas, to the west of the city, and Stockholm Airport. Special squads of these troops will also see to the sequestering of the prime minister and his cabinet, plus some two hundred other key members of the government and civil service. Still other special squads will, upon landing, commandeer the state radio and television services, including several dozen low-power emergency radio stations scattered about the country for use in the event of mobilizations, and the national newspapers."

The Politburo members were as rapt as Helder, turning the pages of their summaries as the slides changed.

"Comrades, you will recall that Sweden claims a trained reserve force of eight hundred thousand, which can be mobilized in thirty-six hours. Their standing forces number less than ten percent of that number, and among our first objectives will be those associated with first, preventing a call-up of these forces, and second, depriving any who are called up of organization, arms and ammunition. There are hundreds of weapons caches located about the country, the locations of which are displayed on the right-hand screen. Eighty-one percent of these will be secured either before or within the first twelve hours of our operation, and the remainder shortly afterwards."

A voice rose from the darkness. "How have you obtained such detailed plans of the Swedish defenses?"

"Comrade," Majorov responded, "I can now reveal what has, up to this moment, been known only on a strict, need-to-know basis, that we have had, for some time, an operative high in the Swedish government. His code name is Seal, and he has been able to supply us with virtually the entire defense plans of the country. Those plans are what you see on the screens before you, the location of every coastal gun emplacement, every reserve weapons cache, every emergency radio station, every aircraft, tank, and missile installation, and every fuel reserve depot in the country. No invader in the history of modern military operations has ever been so well informed."

There was total silence in the room.

"As I said earlier," Majorov said, "at zero hour, we will already have in Sweden some eighty-two hundred crack SPETSNAZ troops, who will have infiltrated in night amphibious landings, and by such conventional means as commercial airline flights and the Helsinki–Stockholm ferries. By zero plus twenty-four hours, we expect to have one hundred eighteen thousand troops in the country. Our principal means of conveyance will be our new fleet of WIGs, our wing-in-ground-effect aircraft. I am pleased to tell you that we now have twenty-two of these superb troop carriers available, each capable of ferrying five hundred troops from our eastern Baltic bases at wave-top altitudes, in less than half an hour's flying time along corridors scrubbed clean of air cover, surface-to-air missiles, and coastal antiaircraft emplacements. They will land at airfields and on stretches of roadway previously secured by our advance parties, supported by amphibious forces landed from troop-carrying submarines."

"What provisions are you making for the effects of casualties?" someone asked.

"Since we intend operating only in conditions of complete surprise, we anticipate a very low casualty rate. However, even allowing for a worst-case casualty rate of twenty percent in every unit, we would expect to have secured eighty-four percent of our primary objectives before zero plus twenty-four hours. Well before that time, we will be landing troops in conventional air transports at secured airfields in Sweden."

For another hour, Majorov ran through summaries of troop movements, supplies, communications, and other logistics. Then, at a signal from him, the curtains were opened, and sunlight once again flooded the room.

"Comrades," Majorov said, "you have been very patient, and I have only one other brief aspect of our planning on which to make a final report. Our accelerated Swedish studies program in our universities and KGB training establishments have produced a hard core of some twelve hundred men and women who are fluent in the Swedish language, and who have been intensively trained in the administration of the Swedish civil services, both at the national and municipal levels. Within twenty-four hours of the consolidation of our military position, there will be Soviet administrators overseeing the operation of every essential government service and state-owned industry. There will be Soviet editors supervising the content of the radio and television services and the national and local newspapers and magazines. The plan is to be very light-handed in this supervision, since the Swedes are such good administrators, anyway. The editorial content of the news services will be allowed to remain as much as possible as before; we will interest ourselves only in news of the Soviet participation in Swedish society.

"We expect to resume international flights to and from Sweden within seven days of taking control, and many Swedes, especially those connected with export sales, will be allowed to travel much as before. We believe that reasonably free travel by a large number of Swedish citizens will help to assuage fears of domination, and we want to encourage whatever flow of foreign currency into the country that we can. But I don't want to go into detail, now. Tomorrow, we will have a full-scale presentation by the KGB of our plans for Swedish life in a postinvasion society. I think you will find it fascinating. If there are no questions . . . ?"

"Viktor Sergeivich," a voice said, and from the movement of every head and body, Helder knew it was that of the Chairman. "We have heard you mention worst-case casualty estimates; we do not wish to hear of worst-case estimates. We have made our position very clear on this operation from the very beginning of its planning, during the tenureship of our beloved Yuri Andropov: unless this invasion can be conducted with total surprise and without any general mobilization order from the Swedish government, it will not be conducted at all. We have carefully calculated the political liabilities of this affair, and they are monumental, even in the best of circumstances. But if the Swedes are alerted even minutes before the operation begins, if they are able to broadcast a mobilization order, then we are immediately faced with the prospect of hot and bloody resistance, and a holocaust of world opinion. I will not preside over the humiliation of the Soviet State in such circumstances, and I tell you once again, in the presence of these comrades, that the final order to invade will come only from me, when I am satisfied that we can move with total confidence of absolute surprise. Is that clearly understood?"

"It is most clearly understood, Comrade Chairman," Majorov said, with considerable humility. "And now, before adjournment, I would like to introduce to you a Soviet naval officer who has just returned from a most important minisubmarine mission in Swedish waters, which you have no doubt been reading about in your intelligence summaries today. Comrades, may I introduce Captain Second Grade Jan Helder."

Helder stood stiffly to attention. To his astonishment, the entire group then stood and roundly applauded him. When they had finished, they remained standing, and the Chairman spoke.

"Captain," he said gravely, "on behalf of my colleagues in the Party, I wish to express the deep gratitude of the Soviet nation for your heroic efforts. I know that you, as we, were saddened by the loss of your fellow officer, Captain Lieutenant Sokolov, and I assure you that, at an appropriate time, she will receive the public gratitude of the people."

"Thank you, Comrade Chairman," Helder managed to say.

The men began to file out of the room behind the

Chairman, and Majorov motioned Helder into the waiting room. "Now, Helder, you will proceed back to Malibu by the car and aircraft, which brought you here. Rest yourself. I will be back in a couple of days, and we will discuss your further part in this enterprise. You have only begun to win glory, I can promise you. I need hardly tell you that you are to discuss your Swedish mission or today's meeting with no one." He shook Helder's hand, then returned to the conference room.

In the car on the ride to the airport, Helder examined the leather upholstery and fine appointments of the Zil in minute detail. He was a lover of cars, though he had never owned one. On the plane ride to Liepaja, he slept soundly.

He arrived at Malibu after midnight, and went straight to his quarters, hoping Trina would be there. He let himself into the room, and groped for the bedside lamp. There was a rustle of sheets.

"No," she said. "No lights."

He sank to the bed and reached for her. As his arms went around her and brought her close, she gave an involuntary gasp of pain.

"What is it?" he asked. "What's wrong?"

"Oh, Jan," she whimpered. "I didn't think you would be back so soon. I didn't expect you for at least a couple of days. I just wanted to sleep in your bed."

He touched her face and she recoiled with a little cry. "What on earth is the matter?" he asked. "I'm back, Trina." He found the lamp and switched it on, then stared. One side of her face was badly bruised, and she turned it from him.

"I didn't want you to see me this way," she said. There was another bruise on her bare shoulder.

He grasped the bedsheet and pulled it away. "My God!" He gasped. "What has happened to you?" There were more bruises, and she tried to cover herself with her hands.

"I'm so sorry," she said. "I can't make love to you. I want to so, but I can't. I hurt too much."

"What happened?" he demanded. "I want to know right now."

"It was Majorov," she said, "and the others."

"What?"

"There was a party two nights ago, and he insisted I come. He said it would cheer me up. There was a general and some of the other girls. I didn't want to make love to them. They beat me. Then Majorov forced me . . . from behind . . . then the others. . . . Oh, Jan, it was horrible." She sobbed, clinging to him. "I thought it would never end."

"Oh, Trina," he said, holding her gently.

"I used to like the parties," she said, trying to stem the sobs. "Then you came here, and they weren't the same, anymore. Majorov stopped making me come after a while, after he gave me to you, but I think he thought you weren't coming back from your mission, that it didn't matter anymore." She began crying again. "I was so frightened. He killed a girl, once. I heard about it."

Helder stroked her hair and tried not to think of what had happened to her, tried to contain the anger growing inside him. He forced it away from him and tried to give all his thoughts to her, but he could not. The mission, the promotion, the Kremlin meeting bled away. All he could think of was her pain and his own betrayal by his benefactor, this monster.

He held her until she was asleep, but he, himself, did not sleep for hours.

31

Appicella felt a tingle of excitement the moment he first laid eyes on Malibu. It had been an extremely boring flight on Aeroflot from Vienna to Leningrad, and an even more boring flight to wherever he was, since the second plane had had its windows blacked out. He did not know where he was, but the sea glinted in the distance as the car descended the hill toward what seemed like a town nestled against a lagoon separated from the sea by a narrow strip of land.

After passing through a heavily guarded main gate, Appicella was surprised by the appearance of the place—it seemed so Western—and he was further surprised and intrigued by three large satellite dish antennas situated on the roof of the low building into which he was being escorted by an extremely comely young woman. He passed through an open work area where other, equally comely young women were working on the terminals he had installed for Firsov in Moscow, then through a reception area and into a handsome office. Firsov came from around a desk with his hand extended.

"Emilio! How are you? So very good to see you."

"Roy!" Appicella returned the greeting with equal enthusiasm.

"Come and sit down. I have a lot to tell you," Firsov said. He mixed them both a drink, then joined Appicella on the sofa. "First of all, I am known here not as Roy, but Viktor, Viktor Majorov. I won't bore you with the reasons, but I would be grateful if you could make the adjustment."

"Of course, Viktor," Appicella replied. "After all, if Lenin and Stalin could change their names, why not you?"

Majorov laughed heartily. "Well, now, let me tell you why I needed you so badly at this time."

"Please do. My fees being what they are, I certainly don't want to delay getting down to business."

"Look over there," Majorov said, pointing across the room to a conference table.

Appicella looked. The Russian had not been kidding when he had called. He had got hold of an IBM PC AT computer. "Well, good for you, Viktor," he said. "Those things are in short supply; there probably aren't more than half a dozen of them in Europe, outside the IBM organization."

"You said on the phone you had worked with one before," Majorov said, a little worriedly, Appicella thought.

"Of course." He smiled. "I have one of the half dozen

in Europe; I've been doing some development work on it."

"What do you think of it?" Majorov asked.

"It's quite a nice machine—512k of memory in the basic machine, expandable up to two megabytes; a 1.2-megabyte floppy disc drive, and a twenty-megabyte hard disc. I've put together a board that will make it support twelve terminals, instead of the standard three."

"That is exactly what I want," Majorov said, excitedly. "I want to switch from the CPM-based equipment you put together for us last year to this system, and I want to transfer all the files we have accumulated. Can you do that?"

"Well, I can get the equipment up and running and expanded with what I have brought with me. Are all the files you want to transfer written with the WordStar word processing program?"

"Yes."

"Good, then using them after they are transferred should not be a problem."

"How long will it take?"

"A few days, if I don't run into hardware problems. I've brought the board with me, but there is still work to be done on it. I assume you have a copy of the operating system and the manuals."

"Yes. Can we use our existing terminals with the AT?"

"Yes, no problem. Where will I work?"

Majorov led him through a door to an adjoining conference room. "How's this?"

"It will be fine. I will need a drawing board and a lighted magnifying glass, in addition to my own toolbox. Please have the AT moved in here, and you will either have to have the terminals moved in here, or, if you want your girls to go on using them as long as possible, I'll have to run some cabling to the existing central processing unit."

"We'll run the cabling then," Majorov said. "The girls are quite busy at the moment. Speaking of girls, I assumed you'd like some company this evening."

"Indeed, yes." Appicella smiled. "Tell me, is that little blonde still with you—what was her name? Trina?"

Majorov frowned. "Yes, but I'm afraid she's not very well at the moment. What about the girl who brought you in, the tall redhead?"

"She's lovely. She'll do very nicely."

"Let's get you quartered then, and I'll give you a little tour on the way."

Appicella followed Majorov from the building, and they got into an electric golf cart.

"This place is a sports center, a training facility for various athletes," Majorov said, steering the cart down the hill. "There are whatever athletic facilities you might like to use, but as I remember, you prefer indoor sports."

"You are right, my friend," Appicella replied.

"Down there is a small beach, next to the marina, if you'd like a swim. The Baltic is quite pleasant this time of year." Majorov pointed to a gate across the way, where a guard stood watch. "I'm afraid I must ask you not to wander in that direction. That's off-limits, and the guards are nervous."

"Whatever you say. The beach does sound appealing, though."

Majorov steered the cart up a paved path, and they came to a small, detached house set in some trees. "This is one of our guest cottages; I think you will find it comfortable." He produced a piece of paper. "There are restaurants on the grounds," he said. "This is a little map and a list of the facilities. We're quite isolated here, so there's no point in looking for entertainment outside the main gates. Anyway, the guards have instructions to allow no one to leave without a pass. It would be simpler if you stayed on the grounds." He led the way into a comfortably furnished sitting room, then showed Appicella a small kitchen and bar and a bedroom with a large bed.

Appicella could hear some sort of motor running. "What's that noise?" he asked.

"Ah"—Majorov smiled—"that's coming from the bathroom. Your bags are already here. I'll have your equipment cases put in your workroom. I'm afraid I can't dine with you tonight, but you'll be in good company. In fact, we may see very little of each other while you're here. I'm very busy at the moment."

"That is all right, Viktor. I understand."

"Tell Olga if you need anything. She'll let me know."

"Olga?"

"She's the noise in the bathroom," Majorov laughed. "Have a pleasant evening. Perhaps I'll see you tomorrow." He let himself out of the cottage.

Appicella walked into the bedroom and toward the bathroom door, and the noise grew louder. He opened the door and peeked inside. The redhead was sitting in a large Jacuzzi bath, smiling at him.

"Hello, Olga," Appicella said, working on his buttons.

32

Rule arrived at her desk just before two, to find a memo waiting, asking her to be in the director's conference room at two o'clock for a meeting of office heads. She arrived breathlessly on the executive floor just in time to turn everyone's head and interrupt the director as he was about to begin. They were all gathered around the long table, the director standing at the end. At his right hand sat Simon Rule; at his left, Alan Nixon.

The director had been a big-time tax lawyer in Washington before his former client, the President, had appointed him Director of Central Intelligence. His previous experience in intelligence work had been when he had parachuted into occupied France on a mission for Wild Bill Donovan's Office of Strategic Services, the World War II predecessor to the CIA, and he had never let anybody forget it.

"Now that we're all here," he said pointedly, looking at Rule, "I want to have a little chat with you all. As you know, I'm testifying before the Senate Intelligence

Committee tomorrow on the subject of our request for funds to expand our technology. As you also know, Senator Carr, the chairman of the committee, has something of a little crusade on these days about our use of technology, as opposed to HUMINT. The senator is a bit of a romantic, I believe, and he thinks we should be devoting more of our resources to cranking out James Bonds and less to the high-tech stuff and disinformation operations that have proved so productive since I became Director of Central Intelligence. He claims that you people, the best intelligence analysts in the world, can't analyze unless you hear from some supersleuth out there on his belly in the grass. Well, I think that's a lot of horseshit, and I intend to tell him so tomorrow.

"Now, I also intend to tell him that my analysts are behind me on this, and that's why I've called you here today. I do not want to pick up the *Washington Post* the day after tomorrow and read that so-called informed sources are saying that there's dissent on this in the Directorate of Intelligence. In short, I don't want any leaks to the press on this. I . . ."

The director paused. Harmon Pool, the head of the Central American Office, was on his feet. Rule knew him well enough to know he was angry. "Mr. Director," Pool said, in a low, even voice, "forgive me for interrupting, but can you cite a single instance of a leak from the Directorate of Intelligence, ever?" He remained standing. Harmon Pool was retiring soon, and he apparently was in no mood to take any crap from a political appointee.

The director looked flustered. "Now, uh . . ." He leaned toward Alan Nixon, who said something without moving his lips. "Pool, yes. I know how loyal you people are, and I certainly didn't mean to imply that security was lax in the DI."

"Thank you, sir," Pool said, and sat down.

"What I mean is, I want unanimity on this issue, and I just want to say to you people that if there are any complaints about my position on this, I want to hear them now." He looked defiantly around the table. "Anybody?"

The group exchanged glances or looked away from him, but nobody said anything. Rule knew of at least two other office heads who had been complaining about a shortage of HUMINT coming in, but nobody had been prepared for this sort of bullying from the director.

"Come on, let's hear it," the director said, sensing victory in their silence. "Can anybody cite so much as a single instance of a critical absence of HUMINT on a tech-based report?" He looked slowly around the table, his jaw set. "Good," he said. "I expect that . . ." He stopped, his eyes narrowing. "Ms. Rule?"

Rule was surprised to find herself on her feet, but now that she was, she had no intention of stopping. "Yes, sir, I think I can do that; in fact I can cite two instances in less than thirty days. In the first, a satshot came through showing what I think might be a new Soviet SPETSNAZ training base on the coast of Latvia, disguised as a sports facility. There are indications that it might also be a submarine base, and although I have requested HUMINT from ops, we apparently have no one on the ground, not a cleaning lady, not a garbage collector, who can confirm or dispute it." The director was glaring at her, his eyes slits, his nostrils flared. "In the second instance," she went on, being careful to keep her tone informative and civil, "satshots have confirmed the existence of at least two wing-in-ground-effect aircraft which are operational, although we didn't believe such a plane was feasible. That work must have been going on for years, and our technical facilities didn't detect it until the aircraft were flying, and we don't really know whether the Soviets have two or two hundred of them." She sat down.

The director continued to stare at her. Simon was staring at her, too. Alan Nixon had taken off his glasses and was rubbing the bridge of his nose, his eyes tightly shut.

"That's all," the director said, suddenly; then he turned on his heel and left the room.

A moment passed before anyone realized they had been dismissed. Finally, people began silently filing out. Rule got out of her chair and started for the door.

"Katharine," Simon's voice said from behind her.

She turned.

"Stay a moment, please."

She sat down again. Simon and Alan Nixon remained seated at the opposite end of the table. Simon turned to Nixon.

"Alan, I don't want to trespass on your directorate, but I wonder if I might have a moment alone with Katharine."

"Of course, Simon," Nixon said. He left the room.

Simon stared silently at her for a moment. He was aging well, she thought. The yellow hair was streaked with gray, now, and his neck bulged around his button-down collar a bit, but he remained a handsome, even distinguished-looking man.

"How's Peter?" she asked into the silence.

"He's very well, thank you. He and Missy have become quite good friends." He was silent for another moment. "Katharine, I think you should resign from the Agency." His voice was flat and without expression, which made it seem menacing.

She was shocked. "You have no right to say that to me," she was finally able to say.

"I'm speaking professionally, not personally," he said. "I don't believe you are suited for this work."

"What?"

"You are beginning to show signs of instability, and you know as well as I that the Agency cannot tolerate instability in its people."

"Oh? And just how is this instability manifesting itself?"

He placed his hands on the table, palms down, as if to steady himself, but his tone did not change. "You are publishing wild, unfounded theories. You are becoming insubordinate."

"I believe I can support my theories, given time and resources, neither of which I'm getting," she said, hotly. "And you think I was insubordinate just now? He asked a question, and I answered him, as respectfully as I know how. Did he really expect to be able to drag us all in here and browbeat us into accepting a position that, I know for a fact, half a dozen of the office heads in that meeting have the gravest reservations about? Do you think that was a reasonable thing for him to do?"

"The director's ability to reason is not in question," Simon replied, his tone still unchanged, that of a psychiatrist speaking to an unruly patient. "Yours is. Your conduct calls it into question."

"My conduct? What conduct?"

"The day before yesterday, you left the country without authorization. That, as you well know, is a serious breach of Agency rules."

It was, and she knew it. She wanted out of this room. "Simon, you are way out of line. I don't work for you, and you have no right to question my conduct, let alone my stability. I am a loyal, hardworking member of this establishment with an outstanding record of accomplishment." She stood up. "If you have any accusations to make against me, make them before a review board. I may not be a politician, but I'm a lawyer, and I know how to defend myself." She walked to the door and turned back. "Tell me something, Simon," she said. "What is Snowflower?"

He seemed to redden slightly. "You know better than to ask a question like that."

"I have the highest security clearance the Agency can award," she said. "What is Snowflower?"

Two small wrinkles appeared between Simon's eyebrows. "You don't have a need to know," he said.

"Well, I'm going to find out," she said, and started out the door.

"Katharine!" he called after her.

She stopped.

"You are digging your own grave here. Get out while you can still do it with some remaining shred of an honorable career. You owe your son that much."

She left the room, slamming the door behind her. She walked back to her office in a haze of rage, breathing hard, closed the door, sat down at her desk and switched on her computer terminal. When COSMO came to life, she tapped in a ten-digit code, not her own, Simon's, the one Ed Rawls had given her.

GOOD MORNING, MR. RULE. WHAT CAN I DO FOR YOU? SNOWFLOWER, Rule typed.

SEARCHING . . .

She stared at the screen, waiting impatiently.

TYPE (S) FOR SUMMARY, (F) FOR ENTIRE FILE, (X) TO RETURN TO SYSTEM.

She typed S.

TYPE (P) FOR PRINTER, (S) FOR SCREEN.

She typed S.

SNOWFLOWER IS A DISINFORMATION OPERATION DESIGNED TO CAUSE THE SOVIET UNION TO COMMIT A DISPROPORTIONATE NUMBER OF TROOPS AND MATERIEL TO THE EASTERN BALTIC, WHERE NO REAL THREAT TO THEM EXISTS. IF THIS CAN BE EFFECTED, IT IS ANTICIPATED THAT THE BULK OF THE FORCES DEPLOYED THERE WOULD BE DRAINED FROM EASTERN EUROPE, PARTICULARLY THE EAST GERMAN BORDER REGION, THEREBY REDUCING THEIR ABILITY TO LAUNCH A WESTWARD THRUST IN THAT REGION, IN THE EVENT OF HOSTILITIES. THE THRUST OF THE DISINFORMATION IS TO BE THAT SWEDEN,

HERETOFORE DETERMINEDLY NEUTRAL, IS
SECRETLY PREPARING TO JOIN THE NORTH
ATLANTIC TREATY ORGANIZATION (NATO).
DO YOU WISH TO SEE THE ENTIRE FILE?
Y/N

Rule gaped at the screen, reading the summary again.
"Jesus Christ," she said aloud. Everything was clicking
noisily into place in her mind. She typed Y.

TYPE (P) FOR PRINTER, (S) FOR SCREEN.

She switched on her printer and typed P. She sat and
read from the screen, appalled, as the printer whirred
back and forth. The fools, she thought, as the amber
lines moved up the screen. The goddamned fools.

33

Appicella gazed intently through the lighted magnifier and carefully soldered a microchip onto the computer circuit board. He had been at Malibu, as they called it, for three days, and he had been astonished and intrigued at what he had seen here. He had made more than sixty trips to the Soviet Union over the past fifteen years, mostly dealing with the foreign trade people; he had visited factories, laboratories, homes, and the dachas of very highly placed Soviets, including Majorov's, and he had never seen such an allocation of resources as had been invested at Malibu.

Quite apart from its restaurants and shops filled with Western goods, the place had every technological innovation available to the Soviets, and some he had thought were not available. It did not surprise him very much when Firsov, or rather Majorov, as he now called himself, telephoned him to say he had one of the newest American computers, one that was in short supply even in America. He knew from past experience that Majorov was resourceful and determined when it came to getting what he wanted, especially with regard to the technological. What did astound him was that Malibu was equipped with the latest digital telephone exchange, made by Western Electric in the United States, one that allowed Majorov, via his own satellite station, to place and receive calls nearly everywhere in the world. The Soviets had, years before, after a brief experiment, ended personally placed telephone calls outside the country, and the equipment installed in this relatively small place would normally have been used to serve a large city. The satellite television reception surprised him, too, not so much because of the technology involved, but because of what the system received—uncensored American television newscasts and films. Only a person in a very particular position of power in the Soviet Union could possibly have access to that sort of privilege.

What he had seen at Malibu made Appicella absolutely certain that Majorov was KGB, and that frightened him. It also made him extremely curious. Even if he had not promised the beautiful American woman information about his visit, he would have been curious enough to explore for himself. Appicella had no intention of climbing over fences or peeping through keyholes for this information, though. He reserved his bravado for his relations with women. But he knew that whatever this Majorov and his incredible "sports center" were about would be recorded in the storage devices of his computers, which Appicella knew well, having stolen or designed their workings himself.

He finished the last of his soldering and fitted the

circuit board into its intended slot in the computer. He booted the system and typed the word INSTALL into the keyboard, then watched with satisfaction as the installation program he had written checked each of the computer's components and reported it working satisfactorily. That done, he installed his specially modified, multiuser software, then moved back and forth between two terminals, checking their access to the central computer. All was perfection, but then, this miracle had been performed by Emilio Appicella, had it not?

Now came the part he had been itching for. He plugged the waiting cables, which led from the old computer system, into the serial port of the IBM, put a floppy diskette containing his communications software into the IBM's floppy drive, and tapped in a few instructions. Having satisfactorily got a systems prompt from the old computer, he typed in the word TREE. Immediately, there began to scroll up on his monitor a list of all the directories and subdirectories on the old computer's ten-megabyte hard disk. He was now operating Majorov's system remotely, from two rooms away. Abruptly, he stopped the scrolling. There was a subdirectory called WAR. War? It must be an abbreviation or an acronym, surely. Still, he looked at the sub-subdirectories branching off it. AMPHB, AIRBRN, LOGIS, SUB, ARMR, AIRCRFT, SUM. Amphibious, airborne, logistics, submarine, armor, aircraft? SUM must be summary. He typed in instruction to open the file. Then, on the screen before him, he read, in English, SUMMARY OF PLANS FOR AN INVASION OF SWEDEN

Appicella quickly scrolled through a few pages of the file. He was stunned. Could this possibly be real? He quickly removed the communications diskette from the floppy drive and inserted a blank diskette, then instructed the computer to copy the file SUM. In seconds, the file had been copied onto his floppy diskette.

"How is it going?" Majorov's voice suddenly asked from immediately behind him.

Appicella jumped. Majorov had entered the room from his adjoining office and was now looking over his shoulder. "I've just this moment got the whole thing together," he said, quickly typing in other instructions. "I'm ready to copy from your old ten-megabyte hard disk to your new twenty-megabyte one. Watch." He hit the return key and the message, DISK COPY IN OP-ERATION. STAND BY, came onto the screen. "There," Appicella said, "it's copying now."

"How long will it take?" Majorov asked.

"Well, I don't know how much is on your old disk. If there's a lot, it could take several hours. It's transfer-ring information at 9600 baud, though, and that's fast." Appicella pushed back his chair. "Well, there's nothing to do but leave the equipment to do its work. I think I'll call it a day."

"Come on into my office," Majorov said. "I'll buy you a drink."

"I could use one," Appicella replied, following him. In the next room, he sank into a sofa, while Majorov got together an iced bottle of Stolichnaya and opened a tin of caviar.

"I think this calls for a celebration," Majorov said, "completing your work so quickly."

Appicella shrugged. "It was all pretty straightforward," he said, "given the development work I had already done. You certainly came to the right man."

Majorov smiled and lifted a glass. "I'll drink to that," he said. "You've done your usual fine job."

"Thank you, Viktor. I've also installed a new internal modem, for transmitting data over telephone lines. Your old one only worked at 300 baud. The new one works at 300, 1200, or 2400 baud, and you can install your own password to prevent any tampering with your data."

"That sounds great, Emilio. Will it be very secure?"

"Of course. You can change the password as often as you like with a few keystrokes. Not even I could crack it from outside. I'll show your secretary how it works. Then I'll have a couple of hours' instruction for your girls tomorrow morning, and that'll be it. Since they'll still be using the WordStar software, there will be very little new for them to learn, just how to gain access and so forth. I'll like to be on my way by lunchtime, if you can arrange some transportation for me."

Majorov said nothing for a moment, merely gazed at the Italian. Then he said, softly, "Emilio, I'd like you to stay on for a few days more, just in case there are any bugs in the equipment."

"There will be no bugs," Appicella protested. "Everything has been thoroughly tested, hardware and software. It was perfectly straightforward, I told you. In any case, I've a great deal of work waiting for me in Rome, and

I must get back." He smiled. "You can't expect to monopolize all the time of the fantastic Emilio Appicella."

Majorov smiled, and his voice remained very soft. "I'm afraid it won't be possible for you to leave tomorrow," he said. "We're in rather a remote location here, and there is no scheduled air service. Because of other events, there is a great demand for aircraft, and the plane that brought you here from Leningrad is not available."

Appicella began to feel a distinct chill. "I see," he said.

"Don't worry—we'll keep you occupied and entertained, and, of course, we'll pay you your usual daily fee, since your continued presence here is our fault. It's the least we can do."

"Thank you. This is going to cause me some problems, though. Can I telephone my office from here? They'll need to know that I'm going to be late returning."

"Of course. Simply ask the operator for an international line, then dial 0101, the country code, the code for Rome, and your number."

"Good." He tossed off the vodka and stood up. "Well, I must clean up some odds and ends, and I don't want keep the lovely Olga waiting any longer. You will let me know as soon as there's transportation, won't you?"

Majorov stood with him. "I will, indeed. Don't worry—it will only be a matter of a few days."

Appicella excused himself and left Majorov's office. He went back into his workroom, closing the door behind him, and pretended to tidy up. He removed the floppy diskette containing the summary file, and with a craft knife, opened the paper envelope meant to permanently contain the diskette. He removed the five-inch disc of thin mylar plastic, and looked around for a place to conceal it. His eyes fell upon a penlight which he used for seeing into tight places in computers. He unscrewed its cap and shook out the batteries. Then he wrapped the plastic disc tightly around the batteries and reinserted them into the penlight. It was a close fit, but when he replaced the cap and switched on the light, it worked. He clipped the penlight into his inside jacket pocket and congratulated himself on his ingenuity.

He left the building and strolled down the hillside toward the sea and his cottage. It seemed to him that in the past couple of days, there were a lot more people about. A troop of young men in sweat clothes jogged in step past him toward the gymnasium. Appicella was afraid. He didn't believe for a moment that a man who could put together this place would have the slightest difficulty in summoning an aircraft whenever he pleased. When he reached the cottage, he picked up the telephone and asked for an outside line. On hearing the dial tone, he punched in the numbers for his Rome workshop. His secretary answered.

"Hello, Angelica? This is Appicella." He enunciated very carefully. "I'm afraid I'm going to be stuck with Mr. Firsov for a few days. Apparently there is a lack of transportation at the moment. Do you understand?"

"Yes, Mr. Appicella. I'll cancel your hairdresser's appointment for the day after tomorrow, then, and your luncheon engagement with the young lady."

"Yes, yes. Oh, do you remember the young lady I lunched with last week?"

"The Amer—"

"Yes, that's the one. Please call her and tell her I am having difficulty keeping our appointment, that I am stuck here. I will call her when I can, though. Tell her, if she doesn't hear from me by the end of the week, she should forget about our appointment, but please, not to forget about me. Tell her that, exactly, all right?"

"Yes, Mr. Appicella. Is there anything else I can do for you?"

He thought desperately for some other message he could leave that would alert someone to what was happening, but he could not. "No, that is all, but please call the young lady right away. She will be so disappointed, I know."

He hung up and took a deep breath. He had not the slightest doubt that he was a prisoner, now, and he could not imagine what, if anything, Katharine Rule could do when she received his message. He felt very alone and frightened.

34

Will Lee lay back in the cockpit, a cushion under his head, and sipped a cold beer. The sun warmed his face as the breeze cooled it. He thought he had never felt so perfectly content. He and the boy from the boatyard, Lars, had cruised in a leisurely fashion down the Finnish coast, then among the islands of the Aland group, stopping where they liked, and using the local cruising club's saunas ashore. The boy had been good company, although his English was scanty. They had tuned the boat together, getting the best performance out of her, and made the small adjustments and repairs that any new craft demands. At that moment, Lee thought, he should have been lubricating a sticky bottom swivel on the headsail reefing gear, but the sun was so pleasant that he could not bring himself to budge.

He had left Lars to catch a ferry on the island of Kokar, past the main island group, and now he was sailing south in open water, single-handed, and not running into as much shipping as he had imagined he would. With a reaching wind, he had come a hundred miles in fifteen hours, about as fast a time as he could have wished for in a boat of this size, some forty-two feet, considering he was not pushing himself. Sweden was off to starboard somewhere, and Soviet Estonia was off to port, no more than about seventy miles, he mused. He had never been to the Soviet Union; he wondered if this was as close as he would ever get. He and the boat would be in the port of Bunge on the Swedish island of Gotland by midnight, he reckoned, and there he would reprovision before setting off on the last leg to Copenhagen. Kate would be in Copenhagen, and he looked forward to her. He fell asleep with that thought, and with conditions so perfect and the beer lulling him, he slept longer than he should have.

He woke only when he felt cold, and the sun had disappeared behind scudding clouds. There was little enough blue sky left as he sat up and scratched his head. The boat was going like a train, and the horizon to starboard looked ominously dark. The wind was up, too, and he would have to shorten sail if it continued to rise. He looked at his watch. Christ, he had been asleep for nearly three hours! Two beers in the afternoon had not been a good idea. He was lucky he had not been run down by shipping. He scanned the horizon quickly for a sign of anything on a collision course. Nothing, thank God, and he relaxed a bit. Then he tensed up again. He was twenty degrees off course to port. The wind had backed to the southwest, and, since the autopilot was being operated by a wind vane, the boat had simply changed course. He had an off-course alarm aboard, but he had not set it. How long had the yacht been off course?

He went below and checked the Decca navigator, an instrument that, from a network of special radio transmitters, plotted the boat's position and gave a constant readout of longitude and latitude. He wrote down the numbers, then plotted them on his chart. Lee stared at the X his pencil had made. It couldn't be, he thought—it simply couldn't be. Then he thought about it, and realized it very well could be. He was more than twenty miles off his proper course, twenty miles closer to the international boundary than he should be. He was using a fairly small-scale chart for the open-water sailing, and there was no boundary marked on it. Still, he felt he must be in Swedish waters, even with the three-hour run in the wrong direction. The yacht lurched as it took a wave, a bigger one than he had seen all day. He'd better shorten sail and get back on course in a hurry.

Fortunately, that would be relatively easy, with the headsail reefing system. All he had to do was ease the sheet and winch in on the reefing line; the sail would roll up around the forestay like a window blind. He did that, then took a reef in the mainsail, as well. All this took another twenty minutes before he could point up toward Gotland. But when he had sheeted everything in tight, he still wasn't pointing high enough. Screw Gotland; he'd go there another year.

He continued to sail south with a little west in it, safe on the Swedish side of the international boundary, he reckoned. The boat was flying along, and he found himself enjoying the brisker weather. He'd been too lazy these past days. He went below to make himself a cup of coffee and had a glance at the barometer. It was falling like a stone. He looked at the chart. He had sea room, in the usual sense, but the boundary was out there some-where, and that might be more dangerous than a rocky lee shore. He might end up getting his friend's yacht confiscated, if he wasn't careful. The boat took a larger wave, lurching enough to spill his coffee. He put it down in the galley sink and climbed into the cockpit.

The wind was still rising, and the boat was overpressed again. He'd have to reef further. First, the headsail, then the main. He loosened the sheet and started to winch in the reefing line. The line came taut, and the rotating headstay refused to budge. Damn, these things always went wrong at the worst possible time. He went below and slipped into a safety harness, then came back on deck. He hooked onto a wire jackstay and walked along the windward deck, staying crouched to keep his bal-ance on the bucking foredeck. At the bow, he knelt and grasped the forestay, which was wrapped in several turns of sail. He took a grip on it and tried to turn it. Noth-ing. It wouldn't budge. If he couldn't get the forestay to rotate, he wouldn't be able to use the headsail at all; it would just flog in the wind until it destroyed itself. He took a deep breath, summoned all his strength, and put his weight into turning the forestay.

It moved a fraction, then a bit more. Then there was a crack like a rifle shot, and Lee found himself flat on his back on the deck. What the hell had happened? He looked up into the sky and saw a giant flag waving from the top of the mast. It was the headsail, still attached to the forestay, which had pulled right out of the deck, even while he was trying to turn it. He was on his feet like a cat and running toward the cockpit. The mast was now entirely unsupported from forward, and he had to let go the mainsheet to get the pressure off, otherwise the mast might go. Even as that thought passed through his mind, even as he was throwing himself into the cockpit, reaching for the mainsheet, he heard another, much louder crack; then, suddenly, everything seemed to go quiet.

The wind had dropped, and the seas seemed not nearly so bad. No wonder, he thought. They were no longer sailing, pounding into the seas. They had been dismasted. The spar had broken cleanly perhaps four feet from the deck and was lying in the water to leeward, still attached to the boat by the steel wire rigging. The yacht was now drifting rapidly to leeward, in exactly the direction he did not want to go.

The next hour and a half was a time of hard work and bitter self-recrimination. This was his own fault. It had been his job to grease the swivel at the bottom of the forestay, and he had not done it. He could not imagine that the swivel could have corroded in such a short time; it must have been loose to begin with, and had he taken the trouble to get off his ass and lubricate it, he would have seen the problem and tightened it before it became critical. Thank God he had a good engine; now he would have to use it to get the yacht to the nearest port. But first, he had to cut loose the mast. There was no way he could get it and the boom back aboard, alone as he was; the sails would just have to go with it, and Lloyd's of London could pay for new ones. He dug a pair of bolt cutters from a locker and went to work on the rigging. Ninety minutes later, his hands and forearms aching, he watched the mass of spars, sails, and rigging sink out of sight, freed from the boat.

Exhausted, he went below and rested, sucking a sugar cube for quick energy. Things could be worse, he thought. At least he had a brand-new Volvo diesel engine at his disposal. He did some quick calculations and reckoned he could make four or five knots, going straight into the seas. It wouldn't be very comfortable, but he could make Gotland by morning, maybe. He climbed wearily back into the cockpit, switched on the ignition, made sure the engine was out of gear, pushed the throttle forward, and hit the starter. The engine turned over for ten seconds or so, but didn't catch. He stopped to let the batteries recover. Come on, dammit, start! He hit the starter again. Immediately, this time, the engine caught and raced. Lee throttled back and let it idle for a minute or so, then pushed it into gear.

He came onto a course for Bunge, then set the autopilot. It was heavy going, dead into the seas, but the boat was making five and a half knots through the water, and that wasn't bad at all. He suddenly felt very hungry. He looked carefully around the horizon for signs of shipping and saw none. That was a relief; he would be hard to spot without sails up. He started below for a snack. As he put his foot onto the companionway ladder, the engine noise suddenly shot up into a shriek, then stopped completely. What the hell? The silence was pierced by the buzz of the oil pressure warning. He reached to switch off the ignition; then he saw it. Running from the starboard winch over the side, bar taut, was the windward sheet, the rope that had once controlled the headsail. Lee knew without a doubt that it was wrapped around the propeller.

He started the engine again; he had to know for sure. It ran perfectly well in neutral, but when he shifted into forward, it immediately began to labor. There was one hope; he tried reverse. Maybe it would unwind. In reverse, the engine ran smoothly for a few seconds, then began to strain again. Lee shifted back to neutral. The yacht came off the wind and lay beam on to the seas, rolling with them.

There was a word that described his circumstances, Lee thought, a short but expressive word that said it all. Fucked. He was fucked, and completely. He couldn't sail; he couldn't motor. He lay, drifting downwind at perhaps three knots, toward the waters of a country hostile to uninvited visitors, toward God-knew-what sort of shore, for which he had no large-scale chart. Fucked.

Wearily, he switched off the engine and went below. The locker under the navigator's seat yielded a packet of three parachute flares. It had been all the little chandlery in Jakobstad had had. They were expecting a shipment, they said. Three had seemed enough; now he wished for twenty. He climbed back into the cockpit and looked around him. Nothing. Not a ship, not a fishing boat, not a yacht. He opened the packet of flares, removed one, stripped off the top and fired it. It arched high into the sky, then exploded into a red light, which wafted slowly downward, supported by a tiny parachute. If there was a ship just over the horizon, perhaps the flare would be seen. On the other hand, it didn't get very dark at night at this latitude at this time of year. It wouldn't be easily seen with this much ambient light. He looked at the two remaining flares; they would have to be saved until he could actually see another vessel.

He went below to the chart table. The VHF radio was useless; its antenna had gone with the mast, and he had no emergency antenna. The Decca navigator still worked, though. Its antenna was fixed to the stern pulpit, not the mast. He read off the latitude and longitude, then plotted the position on the chart. He was about forty miles west and slightly north of a town on the Latvian coast. He had never heard of the town. Its name was Liepaja.

35

Rule shuffled listlessly through the morning's bag of cables and raw intelligence. She had not slept well the night before, and she had a headache. Simon wanted her out of the Agency; he had bluntly told her so. He had complained about her working when they had been married, and after the divorce, his complaints had never stopped. Simon had long ago conceived an idea of what a mother should be, and she knew she had never filled the bill. Even divorced, he wanted her at home, carpooling with the other mothers, ready with milk and cookies when Peter came home from school. What had kept her awake was wondering how much Simon wanted that, how far he would go to make it happen.

She opened an internal mail envelope and shook out some sort of publication in Russian. It was the journal of the Soviet Navy, and it had been folded back to show a marked item. It was nothing more than a list of promotions and assignments, but the item leapt out at her. An appointment had been made to the chairmanship of the Third Department of the Intelligence Directorate of Soviet Naval Headquarters. The name was that of Viktor Sergeivich Majorov, Captain, First Grade. She looked at the date on the newspaper: August 18, 1983.

Rule was flabbergasted. Majorov had been the darling of Andropov, had had the plum job of head of the First Chief Directorate of the KGB. Then, more than six months before the death of Andropov, he suddenly became a commodore in the navy and was transferred to a job three or four ranks lower than his previous one. While it was certainly not uncommon for a highly placed Soviet to fall from grace and land in an ignominious place (she remembered that Malenkov, once coleader of the party, had ended up running a pencil factory) she could not remember any occasion when a civilian had been moved to a military job. Nothing she had so far learned about Majorov had indicated any sort of naval background. It was baffling.

She went to a filing cabinet, found a Pentagon phone book, looked rapidly through it, then dialed a number. The phone was answered on the first ring.

"Naval Intelligence, Captain Stone's office."

"May I speak with Captain Stone, please? This is Katharine Rule, Soviet Office, CIA."

"Just a moment, ma'am." She was put on hold.

"Kate? How are you? It's been a long time."

"Hello, Doug. Yes, it has. I heard about your promotion. Congratulations."

"Thanks. This business or social?"

"Business. Just a quick question. I'm a little rusty on

the Intelligence Directorate of the Soviet Navy. What does the Third Department cover?"

"That's an easy one. The Third Department is SPETSNAZ."

Rule's heart lurched. "Who's in charge there?"

"That's easy, too, if a little mysterious. Name's Majorov. It's mysterious, because nobody here ever heard a thing about him until he got the job. I did a computer search of the service journals, and he'd never had a promotion or a reassignment announced. It was like he'd just joined the navy and then got put in charge of SPETSNAZ."

"Thanks, Doug . . . oh, is anything brewing with SPETSNAZ these days? Anything unusual, I mean?"

"Nope. Well, they're bunched up in Poland and the Baltic Republics at the moment, but that's to be expected."

"Why?"

"Operation Hammer. At least, that's our name for it. The Soviets run major, interservice maneuvers every four years in a different region, and it's the Baltic's turn. I'm glad, too; it makes me nervous when they do it in East Germany, like last time."

"Thanks, Doug, that answers my question. Take care." She hung up. Military intelligence was not in her bailiwick, but she knew about the Soviets' quadrennial maneuvers; she just didn't know that this year it was the Baltic. Maneuvers in East Germany made Doug Stone nervous; maneuvers in the Baltic at this moment made her very nearly crazy. She got up and walked to Alan Nixon's office. He received her icily.

"Yes, Katharine?"

"Alan, I realize that you're probably not in a mood to hear about this, but it just came across my desk in a routine way this morning."

Nixon sighed. "Is this about Finsov again?"

"Firsov. I'll tell you what I've learned, and you can draw your own conclusions. In August of 1983, Majorov—which, as I've mentioned, is Firsov's real name—was moved out of his job as head of foreign operations of the KGB, was apparently inducted into the Soviet Navy as a commodore, and was put in charge of the special marine infantry, SPETSNAZ. The assignment was published. At the moment, the Soviets are preparing to hold interservice maneuvers in the Baltic Republics, and SPETSNAZ forces have been grouped there, ostensibly for the maneuvers. So, I expect, has a rather large chunk of the Red Army, and one hell of a lot of materiel, if their war games are anything like ours." She started out of the room. "I just thought I'd lay that on you, see if there was any interest."

Nixon said nothing. She stopped at the door. "By the way, Alan, when was it exactly that the Snowflower operation ran? I forget."

"May or June of 'eighty-three, I think."

She nodded. "Right. I couldn't remember the dates." She left before it might occur to him that she wasn't supposed to know about Snowflower.

Back in her office, she switched on the computer and went to the word processing mode. She typed a memo to Alan Nixon, Deputy Director for Intelligence, outlining what she had just told him, referring to their earlier conversations on the subject, and recommending further investigation by operations. She gave the memo a file number, then printed out a hard copy and saved the file for central records. She dropped the hard copy into an interoffice envelope, wrote Nixon's name on it, and put it in her out-box.

Now she was on the record. This thing was going to blow, she knew it, and it was time to start covering her ass.

36

Will Lee looked around him and saw nothing. The short Baltic night had long ago given way to morning, but with it had come fog. The wind had dropped to a light breeze, but there was still a leftover sea running, making life aboard the yacht uncomfortable, with relentless and unpredictable rolling. He had fired another flare at midnight, in the hope of being seen by some Western craft before drifting into Soviet waters, but no one had come to his aid. He was saving the last flare in case everything got even worse. The Decca navigator was still working, placing him close to the Latvian shore, and his depth sounder readings had steadily decreased to what was now only twenty meters. He had an anchor and warp on deck, but there was no point in using it, yet. It would keep him off a rocky lee shore, though, if that was what the yacht drifted onto.

A noise came to him across the water from the east, a low rumble, like the engine of a fishing boat. Maybe, he thought, just maybe, they'll be Swedish fishermen, who might tow him back to their own waters. The noise grew louder, and Lee looked out to see an odd white line on the water a few hundred yards away. Fishermen's nets? A detergent streak? He glanced at the depth sounder: eight meters, suddenly. He looked back at the white streak. It was surf. It was time for the last flare.

He fired it and watched it arc into the sky, not high enough to disappear into the fog. He had had more visibility than he realized. He was drifting inexorably closer to the line of surf, and now he could see the land behind it, low, gray, and rocky. He watched it come closer for a few minutes, glancing every few moments at the depth sounder. It was down to six meters, now, about twenty feet, and the yacht drew seven. He stepped out of the cockpit, walked forward on the deck, and started to unlash the anchor. He wasn't sure what sort of bottom was under him, but he guessed rock, and he hoped the anchor would hold. He had chosen the old-fashioned fisherman's anchor, which was better in rock than either of his other two, even if there were no guarantees. He stood next to the anchor, sorting out the nylon warp attached to it and watching the line of surf. Now was as good a time as any, he thought. He picked up the anchor.

Then, to his surprise, a bright yellow runabout with a big outboard motor suddenly appeared between the yacht and the surf. There were four young men dressed in foul-weather gear aboard, and they turned as they spotted the yacht, two of them pointing and shouting to the driver. The motorboat raced toward the yacht, leaping across the still considerable waves. He hoped the driver knew what he was doing. It slowed as it approached, and swung around in his lee about ten yards off. One of the men shouted something in what, to his surprise, sounded like Swedish. Lee shook his head.

"I don't understand!" he shouted back. "Do you speak English? French?"

"Yes, I speak English," the young man called out. "I see you are in difficulties. We will tow you to the dockside. Do you have a line?"

"Yes," Lee called back. "One moment." He went forward, unshackled the anchor, and tossed the warp to one of the men, who cleated it at the motorboat's stern and gave him a thumbs-up sign. The line came taut, and Lee returned to the cockpit to steer the yacht in the runabout's wake. He was fortunate to have run upon someone who spoke English and, apparently, not military or police. He doubted the authorities hereabouts ran around in yellow pleasure boats. Maybe he could talk his way out of this, yet. If he could get the line untangled from the prop, he could motor back into Swedish waters, maybe to Gotland, before his fuel ran out.

The boat towed the yacht south, parallel to the shore for half an hour or so, then began a turn into what looked like the narrow entrance to a large bay. Once inside, they turned north and kept to the middle of the bay. The fog was lifting, now, and Lee could see that the body of water was much narrower than it was long. A couple of miles up the bay, a small forest of masts appeared, and he could see that they were headed for what appeared to be a marina. He dug mooring warps and fenders out of his stern lockers and made them up at the stern and bow. As they approached the nearest pontoon, he saw a couple of dozen small yachts moored, and two other young men stood, waiting to take his lines. The motorboat slowed, and Lee steered the boat alongside and tossed his lines to the waiting men.

The man who had called to him from the motorboat jumped onto the pontoon and ran over. "Please stay aboard your boat. I must speak to my . . . boss to receive his instructions."

"Right," Lee called back. "I'll just make myself some coffee."

He looked at the two men who had taken his lines. "Would you like some coffee?" he asked. They looked interested in him and his boat, but they said nothing. Probably didn't speak English, he thought.

Lee went below and put the kettle on. While he waited for it to boil, he looked out the galley port, which was of a blue-tinted Plexiglas. He could see out, but the men couldn't see in. What he could see didn't seem to be much. There was a small beach to the right of the marina, and there were a number of people there launching dinghies. The land rose behind the docks, and he could see a cluster of modern-looking buildings around a large, sloping, grassy area. It looked like the campus of a small college. The young men had looked a bit too old for students, but who knew? He hoped they weren't calling the cops, or worse, the KGB. He knew that the KGB was responsible for internal security in the Soviet Union, guarding the borders. Suddenly, it occurred to him that he knew a great deal more than that about the KGB, and about the Central Intelligence Agency, as well. He had better start thinking about what he was going to tell the "boss" when he showed up.

The truth, he decided immediately. Well, most of it, anyway. If he were going to talk his way out of here, there had better be no mention of Washington or his work for Senator Carr on the Senate Intelligence Committee. That could only lead to a call to some higher authority, and he had no wish to talk with any higher authority, especially not the KGB. Those people would be all too interested in what he knew. He knew, for instance, a great deal about the budget and operations of the Central Intelligence Agency; he knew the names and titles of a number of its key personnel; he knew the head of the Soviet Office of the Directorate for Intelligence very well indeed; he had an appointment with her in Copenhagen in three days' time. The kettle began to whistle.

He made himself some instant coffee, but suddenly it seemed too hot to drink. He was already sweating. He shucked off his foul-weather jacket and mopped his brow, taking deep breaths to calm himself. He thought about dosing the coffee with brandy, but decided against it. He might be too talkative with a drink inside him. He had to keep his head and just be who he was, with only a few omissions—the innocent yachtsman, not well enough prepared to keep from losing his mast, too stupid to check for lines overboard before starting his engine. He chuckled ruefully to himself. Playing that role should be easy enough.

He glanced back at the campus beyond the marina and saw a white golf cart carrying two men making its way down the hill toward the docks. It stopped at the marina entrance, and the two men came walking toward the yacht, followed by the young man in foul-weather gear who had gone to fetch his boss. Lee took his coffee cup and climbed into the cockpit. The two men stopped on the dock and looked carefully over the boat. One was slender, in his fifties, glasses, sandy hair going gray; the other was in his late forties, taller, with thick, dark hair now half gray, and rather handsome. Lee thought he looked oddly familiar but dismissed the thought. Whom would he know in Latvia?

The taller man finished his look at the boat, then turned and spoke to Lee in what sounded like Russian. Lee looked blankly back at him. The man tried again, this time in Swedish, Lee thought.

Lee spread his hands. "I'm sorry," he said. "My only languages are English and French."

"Which is your native language?" the man asked.

"English. I'm American."

"Very well, we'll speak English," the man said. "May we come aboard?"

"Yes, please do. May I offer you a cup of coffee below?"

"Thank you, yes," the man said.

Lee followed them below.

"My name is Will Lee," he said. They were standing in the space between the galley and the chart table, looking carefully around the yacht.

"My name is Kramer," the tall man said. "This is Mr. Mintz."

"The kettle is already hot; this will just take a moment. Please sit down."

The two men made themselves comfortable at the saloon table, still thoroughly examining the interior of the boat. "This is a very handsome yacht, Mr. Lee," Kramer said.

Lee thought Kramer sounded very British. "Thank you. I wish it were mine."

"You are not the owner then?" asked Mintz, speaking for the first time.

"No, I'm delivering it for the owner, a friend of mine from London, from where it was built in Finland to Copenhagen. My friend will pick it up there and sail it to England."

"I see," Kramer said. "And how did you come to be our guest?"

Lee gave them their coffee, got the chart and showed them how he had first gone off course, and then been dismasted, drifting down onto their coast. "I'm very grateful for the assistance of your people this morning. I might have ended up on the beach."

"Yes, I can see that," Kramer said, looking intently at the chart, making some measurements with his fingers and comparing them to the distance scale on the margin.

"Look, Mr. Kramer," Lee said, "I'm very much aware than I'm an uninvited visitor to your country, and I'm very sorry about that. It's my hope that I can be allowed to get my boat going and leave as soon as possible. If I can borrow a diver's mask, I can get the line freed from the propellor, and I have enough fuel to motor to Sweden. I hope it won't be necessary to involve a lot of officialdom in this. I'm aware that the boat could be confiscated, and I would have a very difficult time explaining that to the owner. I suspect that my insurance coverage lapsed as soon as I entered your waters, and it is a very expensive boat."

"Yes, I can see that," Kramer said. "Well, I will do what I can to help you, Mr. Lee, but you must understand, the question of your leaving may not be entirely up to me. I must ask you some questions, and it is most important that you give me entirely truthful answers."

"Of course," Will replied earnestly. "I'll be happy to tell you anything I can."

"First of all, may I see your passport and any other identification you may have, and your ship's papers?"

Lee got his passport and wallet from the chart table and handed them over. Mintz produced a notebook and began jotting down details.

"I see you are a Southerner," Kramer said, looking at the passport. "I am familiar with Georgia, from maps, but where is Delano?"

"About eighty miles south of Atlanta, in the west central part of the state, in Meriwether County."

"And how does a person from a small town in the American South come to have a friend in London?"

"My mother is Irish, and since I was a child I've traveled often to England. My friend is the son of a friend of my father."

"What are the names of both these people?" Mintz asked.

"My friend's name is Spencer Wilks; he is a barrister in London. His father's name is Sir Martin Wilks; he is a member of Parliament, the Labor Party. My father flew bombers out of Britain during World War II. Their friendship dates from that time." In answer to Mintz's request, Lee gave him the addresses of both men.

"What is your work, Mr. Lee?" Kramer asked.

"I'm a lawyer; I'm in partnership with my father in Delano. The firm is called Lee and Lee." He produced a business card from the wallet.

"What sort of law do you practice?" Kramer asked.

"A bit of everything. It's like that in small towns. Wills, divorces, business law, the odd criminal case." Lee could not shake the feeling that Kramer was familiar, and his English accent seemed to make him even more so.

Kramer continued to question him, and Mintz continued to make notes. In the hour that followed, Lee gave him what amounted to his life story. Then, as they talked, Lee suddenly thought he knew where he had seen the man, but he dismissed the idea as preposterous. But as the session wore on, he changed his mind. Kate had shown him a photograph of this man. This was Majorov. The man was KGB. Lee was grateful for the chance to recite facts; it kept him from being nervous.

"Well, Mr. Lee," Majorov said, standing. "I think that is all we need to know for the moment. I will take your passport and other identification with me and make a couple of phone calls to my superiors. In the meantime, I will have a diver clear your propeller. If you have told me the truth, I think we may be able to help you further. Is there anything you would like to add to what you have said?"

"No," Lee said, "but I will be happy to answer any

other questions you may think of. I can only assure you that I am who I say I am, and not some sort of spy. I know there is a lot of distrust between our countries, but I have told you the truth. I only want to be on my way."

"We'll see," Majorov said, climbing into the cockpit and stepping back onto the dock. "I must ask you to remain aboard your boat. Will you be comfortable here? Do you need anything?"

"I will be perfectly comfortable, thank you. I've been up for a long time, and I could use some sleep."

Majorov nodded, then walked away down the dock. It was then that Lee saw two things that made him uneasy. At the head of the dock stood a soldier armed with some sort of machine gun. This was no college campus. The other sight that caught his eye was of a man on the beach beside the marina stepping out of a dinghy. Lee went below, got his binoculars, and trained them through the galley port onto the figure of the man. He was all too familiar.

Lee put the binoculars back into their box and sat down heavily at the chart table. It had been worrying when he had recognized Majorov from the photograph Kate had shown him. But he was absolutely baffled to see the American he had met in Stockholm, Carl Swenson of New York, sailing a dinghy in this place. If Majorov was KGB, Swenson had to be a spy. Just what sort of place had he fetched up in? He glanced at the drawing of the Royal Palace in Stockholm, which he had tacked up over the chart table. Now, though he had seen it constantly, he noticed something new about it. He took it down and stuck it among the charts in the chart table. Then he stretched out on the saloon settee and tucked a pillow under his head. In the short time he had been in this place he had seen far too much. He didn't want to see any more.

37

Appicella had seen from his window Majorov driving toward the marina in his golf cart. This might be his moment, he thought. He left the guest cottage and walked quickly up the hill toward headquarters. He was a familiar sight around Malibu by now, and no one questioned his movements as long as he stayed away from prohibited areas. In the headquarters building, he walked past the switchboard operator who sat in the reception room onto which opened both Majorov's office and the conference room Appicella had been using.

"Good morning, my dear." He smiled at the switchboard operator. "Is Majorov in?"

"Not at the moment, Mr. Appicella," the girl said, returning his smile. "He's down at the marina."

"Yes? He's going for a sail on a day like today? Not very inviting, is it?"

"No, apparently a foreign yacht has turned up here, and he's gone to speak with the captain. I'm not sure when he'll be back."

"No matter," Appicella replied. "I have some testing to do on modem operation. Will you please connect the conference room extension to an outside line?"

"I'm sorry Mr. Appicella," the girl said, "but I must have express instructions from Majorov before connecting any outside calls."

"Of course," he said, his pulse hammering. "I don't want to make any calls; I just want to test modem transmission. You can listen in on the line, if you like." He gave her his most dazzling smile. "Not a word will be spoken, I promise."

"Oh, all right," she replied, "if I can listen in."

Appicella went into the conference room, leaving the door open, so as not to look suspicious. From his briefcase, he took the diskette containing his file transmission program and loaded it into the computer. He picked up the desk-type telephone next to him, disconnected the instrument, and with a coupling device, connected it directly to the computer. Then he brought up a menu for the file transmission program and typed in 0101, for overseas dialing to America, 212 for New York, and the local number for the New York area access line to The Source, a computer time-sharing information utility, located in Silver Spring, Maryland.

He left the file transmission program and opened a new file on the same diskette. When he had a prompt, he typed,

MY DEAR,
I AM HERE ON THE SHORES OF THE BAL-
TIC, IN A MOST LUXURIOUS FACILITY, SUR-

ROUNDED BY A GREAT MANY HANDSOME,
ATHLETIC, YOUNG MEN AND WOMEN.
I KEEP SAYING I HAVE TO GET BACK TO
ROME, BUT MY HOST KEEPS INSISTING I
STAY, AND I AM UNABLE TO RESIST HIS
INVITATION. THERE IS SAILING HERE, AND
SWIMMING, AND GOOD SUNSHINE, AND
MY HOST IS HIS USUAL, HOSPITABLE SELF,
THOUGH HE IS VERY BUSY INDEED THESE
DAYS. I DO SO WISH YOU COULD MEET HIM
AND SEE THIS WONDERFUL PLACE! THERE
IS SO MUCH MORE I WOULD LIKE TO TELL
YOU, BUT THAT WILL HAVE TO WAIT UNTIL
WE CAN SEE EACH OTHER AGAIN. I WISH I
KNEW WHEN THAT WILL BE. FORGIVE THE
BREVITY OF THIS NOTE, BUT IT IS THE BEST
I CAN DO AT THE MOMENT.
EMILIO

Appicella closed the file, and invoked the transmission
program again. "Okay," he called out to the girl through
the open door, "give me the line."

"You've got it," she called back, then left her switchboard to come and stand in the doorway. "What is it you
are testing?"

"Just the modem transmission capabilities of the new
computer." He typed, RUN SOURCE. "Listen," he said
to the girl. "You can hear it testing itself." From a speaker
inside the computer, there was, first, a dial tone, then the
sound of a number being dialed, then a tone, then silence.

This meant the computer had reached The Source and was now giving the host computer an account number and password. On the screen before him appeared the words: WELCOME TO THE SOURCE.

Appicella quickly held down his control key and typed P. A system prompt appeared. He typed:

NEW FILE
NAME OF NEW FILE? the computer asked.
KATE

The screen went blank. He hit the escape key on the computer, then typed:

SEND KATE

There was a brief clicking noise from the disk drive as the file was transmitted, via an American communications satellite, from the computer at Malibu to the computer in Maryland; then Appicella typed control P again, and was returned to the system prompt. He typed:

OFF

SIGNING OFF, the host computer sent back, TIME CONNECTED :25 SECONDS; then the screen went blank again.

Into his own computer, Appicella typed:

ERASE KATE

1 FILE ERASED, the computer replied.

It was done, and there was no trace of it. He would have liked to transmit the summary of the invasion plan in the files, but he had no way of knowing what sorts of electronic intercepts the Soviets had. If they were any good at all, they already knew that an overseas phone call had been placed from Malibu, but that probably happened all the time. If they were really good, they would be able to decipher the message. He hoped it would seem innocuous enough not to excite interest.

"That's it," he said to the girl. "Everything is in perfect order."

"Good," the girl replied. "Oh, and Mr. Appicella, if you should tire of Olga's company, please let me know, will you?" ,

"My dear, what a pleasant thought," he said. "You may count on it." He got up from his chair and tidied up the work area. The sun was now streaming through the windows. "Well, it looks as though the weather is improving. I think I will go for a swim. Join me?"

"How I wish I could," the girl replied, pouting.

"Another day, then." He started from the room, then stopped. "Tell me, lovely, what is the number of the incoming computer line here, including the country code? Majorov asked me to test the modem transmission from the other end, as well."

She looked up the number, wrote it on a pad, and gave it to him.

He kissed her hand, exciting the appropriate response, then left the building. The sun was out at odd moments, now, and the sky was rapidly clearing. He could see Majorov's golf cart still at the marina entrance. He went back to the cottage, changed into a swimsuit, grabbed a towel, and walked down to the beach. There were half a dozen of Malibu's young men there, lying in the sun or launching dinghies. He spread his towel a few yards away from the group and sat down.

"What's going on out there?" he called to one of them, pointing to the strange yacht.

"Some yacht got dismasted and blew in here. One of the fellows who towed him in says he's an Englishman or an American."

"Imagine that!" Appicella laughed. "How many aboard?"

"He's single-handed, I think. He must be crazy."

Appicella leaned back on his elbows and gazed out to sea, occasionally glancing at the yacht. An armed soldier appeared and stood guard at the marina entrance. Eventually, Majorov and the man called Jones left the boat and drove back up the hill in the golf cart. Appicella got up and walked back to the cottage. He could still see the marina from there. He settled down on the terrace with a cup of coffee.

38

Helder arrived at Majorov's office in response to a summons. He didn't know what the meeting was to be about, but he was not anxious to see Majorov. It would be the first time they had met since they had both returned from Moscow, and Helder was still filled with what was now a cold anger over what the man had inflicted upon Trina Ragulin. As Helder presented himself outside Majorov's office, Majorov and Jones also arrived.

"Ah, Helder," Majorov said, "come in, come in." He seemed preoccupied. He led the way into his office. "Sit down, and excuse me for a moment; we have a little situation to resolve." He turned to Jones. "Now, Mr. Mintz, what do you think?"

"I think we should send him to Moscow immediately for a thorough interrogation at Central. It is surely too great a coincidence for an American to turn up at our gates at this particular moment, is it not?"

Majorov picked up a small card from some papers he

had thrown on his desk. "Perhaps you are right. Still . . ." He glanced at his wristwatch, seemed to do some mental calculation, then picked up the telephone. "Give me an outside line." Glancing at the card, he dialed a series of digits, then switched on a speakerphone.

Helder could hear some static, then a number ringing; then a woman's voice answered.

"Good morning, Lee and Lee."

"Good morning," Majorov said, and his accent became even more British. "May I speak with Mr. Lee?"

"Which Mr. Lee would you like? Billy or Will?"

Majorov shot a glance at Jones. "Mr. Will Lee, please."

"I'm sorry, but Will is out of the country. His father is in; could he help you?"

"No, it's a personal call. I'm an old friend, calling from London. Can you tell me where I might reach Will abroad?"

"Oh, just a minute, let me get his itinerary." There was a pause and a shuffling of papers. "Here it is. Well, if he's on schedule, he should be sailing a boat right now, but he's due in Copenhagen in three days. I have the number of the hotel there."

Majorov took down the number. "Thanks, I'll try him there. Good-bye." He broke the connection and stared at the card, looking thoughtful.

Helder was stunned at the name of Will Lee, too stunned to speak.

"That's no confirmation," Jones said. "It's the simplest sort of cover, if he's an agent. No doubt, the hotel in Copenhagen will have a prepaid reservation in his name."

"No doubt," said Majorov, "but there's something else. When I was in First Directorate, we routinely kept files on American politicians, especially those who might be presidential material. There was a governor of Georgia in the sixties who was frequently mentioned as a replacement for Vice President Lyndon Johnson on the 1964 Democratic ticket with John Kennedy. His name was William Henry Lee, known as Billy. This man in the yacht appears to be his son."

"It's all cover, I tell you," Jones said, vehemently. "They've covered him with a real person, that's all. It's exactly like our cover for Helder, here, on his mission."

"Excuse me, sir," Helder said, "but I think I know this man, Will Lee."

"What?" asked Majorov, nonplussed.

"It was when I was in Stockholm. Quite by accident, we shared a table in a restaurant."

Majorov demanded a full account of the meeting, and he and Jones listened raptly. When Helder had finished, Jones spoke first.

"This is too great a coincidence to be real," he said. "We cannot possibly allow this man to leave Malibu, except to go to Moscow."

"No," Majorov said. "This is too great a coincidence *not* to be real, don't you see? In order for this meeting to have been staged, someone would have had to know in advance of Helder's presence in Stockholm. Not even *we* knew Helder would be in Stockholm. Not even *he* knew he would be there. It was unpredictable. And even if it had been predictable, even if the meeting were not a coincidence, they would never have al-

304 / Stuart Woods

lowed him to leave. He would have been arrested on the spot."

Jones seemed to have no answer to that. "Perhaps you are right. But we still cannot allow him to leave. We are too close to moving."

"Perhaps we are too close to moving not to let him leave," Majorov said. "He has seen nothing here; he has not left his yacht. The submarine pens are invisible from the entrance to the lagoon and from the marina. He may have seen one or two people in uniform, but that's all. And the very fact that we are willing to allow him to leave makes us seem all the more innocent. It would be a needless complication to hold prisoner the son of an American politician." Majorov slapped his palm onto his desk. "No, we'll get him out of here today. I'll take care of it myself, but first, I have to speak to Helder. Please excuse us, Jones."

Jones got up and left, shaking his head.

Majorov turned to Helder. "Jan, we go tomorrow."

Helder blinked. "Tomorrow? On such short notice?"

Majorov smiled. "No, the notice is not short at all. For weeks, we have been moving troops and supplies into the Baltic region, on the pretext of regularly scheduled maneuvers. Our intelligence tells us that the Western services are not alarmed at these movements, that no unusual precautions have been taken in Sweden or anywhere else. Conditions are ideal for our operation, and you, my boy, are to have the single most important assignment in the whole plan."

"Sir?" Helder had forgotten about Trina Ragulin. He was too caught up in the drama of this moment.

Majorov walked to the maps behind his desk and flipped a switch that illuminated them. He pointed to the map at the approaches to Stockholm. "Here. You will follow the identical route that you took on your earlier mission, on the heels of the Helsinki–Stockholm ferry. Except this time, you will command a Whiskey class sub, and you will follow the ferry for a few kilometers further, to a point, here." He paused for effect. "And here you will run the sub aground."

The effect was fully received. "Aground, sir? Deliberately?" There was no faster way for a submarine commander to end up in a penalty battalion, Helder thought. Then he remembered his classmate, Gushin, who had done just that, and whom he had seen in the submarine pens at Malibu, fat and happy.

"And then," said Majorov, "this is what you will do."

Lee was awakened by a sharp rap on the yacht's deck. He jumped up from the settee and climbed into the cockpit. The KGB man, Majorov, was standing on the dock.

"Come with me," Majorov said.

Lee followed him down the dock, worried, and then he noticed that the soldier with the machine gun was gone. He followed Majorov off the dock and into a long shed adjacent. A yacht of some size was chocked up in the shed, having her bottom painted with antifouling by four men. Next to the yacht lay a mast.

"I reckon this to be a couple of feet shorter than your mast," Majorov said, "but I see no reason why, with new rigging, it couldn't be made to fit your boat, do you?"

"No, Mr. Kramer, I don't," Lee replied. "Of course, I've lost my boom and sails, as well."

"We will lend you this yacht's boom and sails, which are cut to this rig, anyway," Majorov replied. He began barking orders in Russian, and the men painting the yacht's bottom dropped their tools and began scurrying about. "This fellow here understands a little English," Majorov said, pointing to one of the men. "We'll get your boat brought alongside the shed and use our crane to step the mast. They can cut the rigging to the required length, and with a few adjustments to your deck layout, you'll be in business."

"You are very kind to be so helpful, Mr. Kramer," Lee said earnestly. "I cannot tell you how grateful I am for your assistance in getting me out of here. I would like to reimburse you for the equipment."

Majorov smiled. "Just put it down to East-West détente," he said. "But you must go as quickly as possible." He looked at his watch. "I think we can have you on your way by midnight."

"That's fine with me. I'll get right to work."

Majorov shook Lee's hand. "Good-bye, Mr. Lee. We will not be seeing each other again."

That was fine with Lee, too.

39

Rule waited until just before leaving for work before trying The Source again. She had had the telephone call from Appicella's secretary, which puzzled her. The woman had said he couldn't keep their date, that he had been delayed. She took that as a hint that he wasn't doing well or needed more time. Perhaps, she thought, he had had second thoughts about his "mission," once he was on the scene and in what must be the pretty daunting presence of Majorov. Still, she had checked Appicella's files in The Source twice a day. Nothing.

Now, she sat down in her study at her little Apple computer and got connected with The Source, using Appicella's account number and password.

WELCOME TO THE SOURCE, it said.

She got to a systems prompt and typed FILES.

The list scrolled up the screen, the same list she had seen for days; then it stopped. At the bottom of the list was KATE. He'd done it! Quickly, she read the file. Clearly, he was afraid of its being intercepted; it read like a postcard. Still, it was obvious he was with Majorov, and something was up in the Baltic. It was also obvious that he wasn't being allowed to leave. She printed a hard copy of the message and signed off The Source.

All the way to Langley, she watched the rearview mirror, but she saw nothing of her tail. She had spotted him once or twice the past few days, but at odd hours. She was sure she was being only sporadically followed. It was raining, so she parked in the underground parking lot at the Agency; she switched off the engine, but before she could leave the car, the passenger door opened and Ed Rawls got in.

"Hi, kid," he said. "I was on my way in and saw you. How's it going?"

"It's frustrating, Ed. Pieces keep falling into place, but I still don't have enough to force anybody to make a move." She told him about Majorov's appointment to commander of SPETSNAZ forces and about the concentration of troops gathering in the Baltic.

"You're right," he said. "That's not enough to move anybody. Tell me, just what sort of action do you want?"

"Well, before, I wanted ops to get its people on the ground to look for corroborating evidence. I thought maybe some light shined on what the Soviets seem to be doing might put a stop to it. Now, I think it's too late for that. I think they're going to make a move soon. I think the best thing now would be to take it to the president and ask him to direct the State Department to warn the Swedes. Either that, or get him to call the Swedish prime minister personally and let him know what we think's going on."

"What *you* think's going on, you mean."

"Well thanks, Ed. A cold shower was just what I needed."

"Why do you think the Soviets are about to make a move? You got something new?"

She nodded. "I've got a man in Majorov's camp."

Rawls's eyebrows went up all the way. "You've *what?*"

She dug Appicella's message from her briefcase, told him about the Italian's visit to Majorov, and explained how the message had come.

Rawls laughed. "Boy, would Simon be pissed off to know that you've put an agent into the USSR!" He read the message. "Pretty swift, this guy. He's got balls, I'll give him that. Still, this reads like a letter home from camp, and you've got no way of proving how it came to you. Anybody with the right password could have stuck this message into the computer, and for all you know, he could have sent it from the beach at Portofino."

She nodded. "I know. I believe it, though. I don't think the man is jerking me around. Listen, Ed, I've been thinking about going to the *Post* or the *Times*, or maybe both with this." She waited for him to yell at her, but he didn't.

"Listen, Katie," he said. "Maybe that's the right thing to do, I don't know, but you've got to think ahead a bit, you know. If you're thinking about becoming the Deep Throat of the eighties, you should realize that you'd have to live with it for the rest of your life. It will be impossible to stay anonymous, because the Agency will know immediately who you are, and it'll leak. If you're right about what's going on, then you'll

310 / Stuart Woods

be the heroine for a while, but what kind of a life would it be? You'd be right, but nobody you know would ever speak to you again. They'll maintain that you should have been able to do it through channels. You'll spend the rest of your life turning down invitations to speak to left-wing student groups on abuses in the CIA." He took a deep breath.

"On the other hand, if you're wrong—and you have to face the fact that no matter how good this looks, you may be wrong—then the sky is going to fall. The Agency and the administration will crucify you, you'll look like a fool to the world, and you might very well end up in Leavenworth. You've already left the country without prior authorization, and that's a very big no-no. If you had to, could you prove that you weren't sending information to Majorov using the Italian as a conduit? If you go public, you'll have to, believe me. The Agency is going to set you up as a Soviet mole, and it won't be all that tough to make plausible. Even if they couldn't get a conviction, you'll spend the rest of your life trying to prove you aren't a Communist spy."

There was a big knot in Rule's stomach. "I can't argue with any of that, Ed."

"But either way, right or wrong, your whole life is going to change forever. Nothing is ever going to be the same again. You might give some thought, also, to what it's going to do to your friend over at the Senate Intelligence Committee."

"He doesn't know about this . . . well, not much, anyway." She shook her head. "Jesus, I'm supposed to meet him in Copenhagen the day after tomorrow. I did get authorization for that trip."

"Can I make a suggestion?"

"I need a suggestion, Ed."

"Meet the guy. Have a fine old time in Copenhagen. Come back refreshed. In spite of what you may think you've deduced, I doubt if anything is about to blow. Even if the Soviets are cooking up what you think they are, there'll be time to anticipate it." He put a hand on her shoulder. "Look, I've started the new job. I'm in a position to keep an ear to the ground for you. I'll have access to stuff that you won't. I'm also in a position to do something if anything breaks. Leave it with me and go off to Copenhagen with a happy heart. Give me your itinerary, and I'll call you if anything startling happens. We'll set up a scrambled line to the embassy there, if necessary."

She thought about that for a moment, then shrugged. "Maybe you're right, Ed. God knows I could use a few days off, and the way Nixon and Simon have got me boxed, I'm probably not going to get anything new, anyway." She scribbled on a pad. "Here's the name of our hotel. I'll leave word there if we move."

"Great. I'm glad you're doing this."

She smiled. "I feel better already, knowing you're backing me up on this." She wasn't sure why he was; a week ago, he'd been keeping her at arm's length. Still, she was grateful for the only help that had been offered her.

"Now listen," he said, holding up a finger, "I'm not convinced myself, and I'm sure as hell not about to urge the director to go to the president. But if something else comes in that supports your theory, you have my promise that I'll pursue it to the hilt. That's all the backing up I can give you."

"That's all I need, Ed." They got out of the car, hugged briefly, then made separate entrances into the building. She spent the rest of the day trying to concentrate on routine work.

40

Oskar Oskarsson squinted into the late-afternoon sunlight and spoke to his dead grandson.

"There, Ebbe!" he said, pointing, then shook his head. "No, no, it is only a stick, not a periscope." The big twin outboards on his son's modern, eight-meter motor cruiser thrummed along at half-throttle, easily propelling the boat at twenty-five knots. Oskarsson knew the boat would do forty at full throttle; he had tried it.

"Everyone looks, Ebbe," the old man said. "But we will find it. It is there, and you and I will find it."

The waters near his son's home in the Stockholm Archipelago had been busy these last couple of weeks, first with the Royal Navy's patrol boats, searching for the minisub, then, after they had given up, with pleasure boats. A rash of periscope spotting broke out after every sighting of a sub, and especially after this most recent sighting, when the navy had been so sure they had the sub bottled up. But as before, nothing had come of it. Somehow, the Russians had managed to elude them again. Since the "Whiskey-on-the-rocks" incident of 1981, none of the submarines had been captured, killed, or even photographed, but everyone knew they were Russian.

There was no keener periscope-spotter among the pleasure boats—nor even in the Royal Navy—than Oskarsson. No man was better motivated. The Russians had taken everything he loved, and he meant to have his revenge. It was good, being out on a boat with Ebbe again. His son didn't mind the fuel bills he was running up; he even encouraged the old man's sub hunting. Oskarsson had heard them talking in the kitchen one night, when they thought he was asleep.

"I don't care how much it costs," his son had said to his wife. "It's the only thing that's got him out of that chair in his room since Ebbe's death, it's the only thing he cares about, and if I can give it to him, I will."

Oskarsson had smiled to himself and slept better that night. Then, the next time he had taken the boat out—and he was taking it out every day the weather was decent—Ebbe had been with him, and he had been happy. Or, at least, he would be happy when they finally found a sub, as he knew they would.

Oskarsson spun the wheel without throttling back and reveled in the boat's performance as it tracked through the turn. He had never owned a boat like this, a boat this fast. He liked it. He would find a sub in this boat, he and Ebbe, and when he did . . . well, he was not quite sure, but his son's double-barreled shotgun rested on the seat beside him. In the end, he would *do* something.

He pointed the boat back up the channel. He would be home, soon. He thought of his son's house that way, now. There would be hot chocolate and brandy, and tomorrow—tomorrow he and Ebbe would hunt subs again.

41

Will Lee watched from the yacht's deck as the replacement mast was swung toward his boat by the crane. He and Yuri, who was the English speaker among the crew of workers, caught the end and guided it into the opening in the yacht's deck; then Lee went below and guided it into the mast step over the keel. Everything was a reasonable fit, although the slightly smaller replacement mast left a gap around it at deck level, which would have to be chocked there and at the mast step, then sealed to keep water out.

The new wire rope, which had been attached at the top of the mast, now had to be cut to the proper length and swaged to the deck fittings of the yacht, then tightened. When it was all done, it was nearly midnight, and Yuri helped Lee bend on the sails. There were only two, a mainsail and a working jib, but with some adjustments to the sheet leads, they were a good enough fit. The boat was sailable again. The propeller had been freed by a diver, too, and the boat was ready. They moved her back to her original berth at the end of the pier, and Yuri and his crew topped up the fuel and water tanks.

"How far to Copenhagen?" Yuri asked. He looked as if he wished he could come along.

"If I don't stop, I guess about two and a half days' sail, with a decent wind."

Yuri looked carefully about him. "Uh, Will . . . you have magazines?"

"Sure, Yuri. Let's see what we've got here." A brief search produced a *New Yorker* and a *Time*.

Yuri looked disappointed. "Ah, Will . . . you have maybe *Playboy?*"

Will thought maybe he had. A search of the berth of his former crew, the Finn, Lars, produced a worn *Playboy*, an even more worn Swedish girlie magazine, and, what caused even more excitement, a British car magazine.

"Thank you very much, Will, is good," Yuri said, stuffing the magazines into his coveralls.

Will searched the boat for anything else he might give the crew and found some chewing gum, some ballpoint pens, and a bottle of Jack Daniel's whiskey. All were received with gratitude. "Would you and the fellows like some coffee, Yuri?" Lee asked.

"No, please. You must go. I have orders you must go on the time the boat ready. But first, you must write for mast."

"Write?"

Yuri made a scribbling motion. He wanted Lee to sign for the equipment he was taking.

"Sure, Yuri, where do I write?"

"At bureau."

Lee and the four men left the boat and walked back to the boat shed, to a small office at one end. There, Yuri made a neat list, in Russian, of all the gear he was taking. Lee signed the document, then gave Yuri his business card. "Tell your boss, send me a bill here, okay?"

Yuri smiled broadly, revealing a row of gold teeth. "Okay," he said. "Now, I take little boat—you follow me." He strode off down the dock. Lee walked back to the boat, started the engine, and the others cast off his lines. As Lee left the dock, he saw Majorov drive up in his golf cart and stop, watching him. He waved and shouted his thanks; Majorov waved back. Lee felt lucky to be leaving at all. With Yuri leading the way, the yacht made its way to the entrance of the bay; then, with a wave, Yuri turned back.

Will set a course of due west, so as to cross the boundary into Swedish waters as soon as possible. From there, he would set a new course, southwest toward Denmark. He steered the boat until he was well clear of the land. When the lights of Liepaja had faded behind him in the half-light of the northern night, he set the autopilot and went below to make coffee. He had had little sleep during the past twenty-four hours, and he was going to need coffee. The wave of relief he felt at being out of Latvia was soporific, and he struggled to stay awake while the kettle came to a boil. When it had, he stepped into the hatch for a quick look around the horizon, then made a cup of coffee and sat down at the chart table.

He finished the coffee, then, in spite of himself, dozed for a while, sitting up at the chart table. There was a small, unaccustomed noise from forward which caused him to open his eyes for a moment. He closed them again, thought, then looked across the cabin, wide-eyed. A man he had never seen before stood at the other end of the saloon.

Neither man spoke for a moment, one shocked, the other uncertain. "Good evening," the strange man said, in accented English. "I am Emilio Appicella."

Lee was still too stunned to speak.

"You are English?" the man asked.

"American," Lee was finally able to say.

"Good, very good," the man replied. "I am Italian. I am a spy of your country."

"You are *what?*"

"I am a spy of the American Central Intelligence Agency," the man said, as if he had been asked about his work at a dinner party. "I must go to an American embassy, the closest one, please."

"Hang on a minute," Lee said, recovering. "How did you get on this boat?"

"I have been waiting all day for an opportunity," Appicella said. "I thought perhaps the Russians would not leave it unguarded, but finally, when you went to the boat building together, I managed to get aboard." He motioned toward the forepeak. "I hid under the sailbags, there."

"Well, look, I can't take you out of this country. I . . . What was that you said about the CIA?"

"I have been spying for some days here at this place for your CIA. Now, you must help me go to an American embassy. You are an American."

"Now, hold on a minute, do you have any idea what those people would do to me if they found you aboard this boat?"

"Yes, I think so," Appicella replied. "I know a great deal of what this man, Majorov, who runs that place, would not like me to know. I think it is better if I don't tell you these things, but if they caught up with us, they would never believe I had not told you. You and I would listen to each other's screams down the halls of Lubyanka prison, I think."

Lee stared at the Italian, dumbfounded. "Swell," he finally managed to say. "What do we do now?"

"We go to the American embassy, as I said before," Appicella said, as if talking to a child. "I am afraid I don't know exactly where we are. Do you?"

Lee waved him toward the chart table. "There," he said. "We've just left Liepaja, and we've been sailing due west for about an hour."

"Mmmm," Appicella mused. "I think we must go to Stockholm. It looks closer than Copenhagen. Where were you bound?"

"To Copenhagen, and I still am, but I'd like to get rid of you as soon as possible, I think. Stockholm, is that where you'd like to go?"

"If you please," said Appicella. "I wonder if I might go on deck for a moment," he said, looking queasy. "It was very close under the sailbags."

"By all means," Lee said, earnestly, "and if you have to toss your cookies, for God's sake, do it over the leeward rail, will you?"

Appicella hurried past him, climbed into the cockpit, and did as he had been told. "I feel much better, now," he said, taking deep breaths.

Lee looked quickly about them. "Well, you can't stay

up here for long," he said, worriedly. "If we're spotted by another boat, it's going to have to look as though I'm alone."

Appicella nodded. "Yes, I think I will be comfortable below now. Might I have a glass of milk, please?" He climbed back down the companionway ladder.

Lee followed him. "I haven't got any milk left; how about orange juice?"

Appicella nodded. "If that is all you have."

"Listen, uh . . . what's your name again?"

"Appicella, Emilio Appicella," he replied, extending his hand. "Please call me Emilio."

"I'm Will Lee, Emilio," Lee said, feeling absurd. "Call me Will."

"Well, Will, I don't know quite how you fetched up in Malibu, but I am very glad you did."

"Yes, I suppose you must be. What did you call the place?"

"Malibu, as in California. It's what the Russians call it."

"Have a seat, Emilio." They both sat down at the saloon table. "How long had you been there?"

"Only a few days. I came to do a small job for this Majorov, one his people could not do themselves. When I finished, they would not allow me to leave."

"What is that place, a college or something?"

"Perhaps, I do not know everything they do there, and I think it is better that you do not know what I know of it, since I do not know if the CIA would find you trustworthy." Appicella spread his hands. "Forgive me. It is nothing personal, you understand."

Lee laughed loudly. "You're forgiven, Emilio, and

you're right. I shouldn't know about all this. Look, I would take you to Stockholm, but I've got a date in Copenhagen, and I'm already going to be a day late. You're just going to have to put up with my company for about two and a half days."

"No, no, that is not possible," Appicella said with finality. "Do you have a radio?"

"Yes, but the antenna was lost with the original mast. It's useless."

Appicella got up and went to the chart table. He pointed. "This island, Gotland, is it Swedish?"

"Yes."

"Then please take me there. I'm sure I can get from there to Stockholm. I must get to the American embassy there at once. In two days, it may be too late."

Lee looked at the chart. It was only about seventy-five miles to Ostergarn, on the east coast of Gotland. They might make that by lunchtime tomorrow. He ought to call Kate, too; she would be in Copenhagen first and might worry, and she should be told about his sighting of Majorov. "Oh, well, all right. I'll drop you in Ostergarn; that looks big enough for some sort of airport. Do you have a passport?"

"Oh, yes. It won't have an entry stamp for Sweden, though. Where have you come from?"

"Finland."

"Good, I'll just say the Finns didn't stamp it."

"Won't it have an entry stamp for Russia?"

"No, the Russians don't stamp your passport. They give you a little visa booklet, instead, and they take it back when you leave the country."

"Good, I don't want to have to explain where I found you." He thought for a minute. "Maybe Ostergarn isn't such a bad idea. I've got to order a new rig for this boat. They can ship it on to Copenhagen from the factory. You ever done any sailing, Emilio?"

"Alas, no. But I will do what I can to help."

"Well, what you can do right now is go sit in the cockpit and keep a lookout for any boats. We don't want to bump into anything."

Appicella went into the cockpit, and Lee plotted a course for Ostergarn, then went on deck, reset the autopilot, and adjusted the sails. They were moving along nicely in a fresh breeze.

"Okay, everything's shipshape. I'm going to get some badly needed sleep. You keep a sharp eye out and call me if you see another boat, okay?"

"Of course," Appicella replied. "I will do exactly as you say. And Will . . ."

Lee stopped on the companionway ladder. "Yes?"

"You have probably saved my life, and perhaps, a great many others, too. Thank you very much."

"Don't mention it," Lee replied. "I take stowaways out of the Soviet Union all the time. Anyway, we're not in Sweden, yet."

"I feel sure we will make it," Appicella said.

"I hope you're right," Lee said back, then headed for a bunk. He slept the sleep of the ignorant.

42

Rule woke up at four in the morning and couldn't go back to sleep. She had felt relieved when Ed Rawls had offered to back her up while she was in Copenhagen, but now she was worried again, and worse, guilty. Everything she knew, every instinct, said the Soviets were going to invade Sweden very soon. As cockeyed as that sounded, even in her own thoughts, it was more important than running off to Copenhagen. Come to that, she concluded at six in the morning, it was more important than her career or her privacy. She had a friend who knew Ben Bradlee, at the *Washington Post*. She picked up the phone and dialed her friend's number.

Then, before he could answer, she hung up. There might be a better way. She got out of bed and dug in her handbag for her notebook. She found the number scribbled on a page with a lot of trivia. She'd read that he was an early riser; she hoped so. She dialed the number.

"Hello." The voice didn't sound sleepy.

"Senator Carr?"

"Yes."

"My name is Katharine Rule; I'm the head of the Soviet Office in the Directorate of Intelligence of the Central Intelligence Agency."

"Yes, I believe you were at a hearing with Mr. Nixon recently."

"Yes, sir, I was. Senator, Will Lee gave me your private number and suggested I call you if it became necessary."

"You met Will at the hearing, too?"

"Uh, no, sir, Will and I . . . have a personal relationship not connected with our work."

"I see. How can I help you Miss Rule . . . Excuse me. I believe it's Mrs. Rule, isn't it?"

She could hear the wheels turning in his head. "Yes, sir, I'm divorced from Simon Rule, who is Deputy Director for Operations."

"Ah, yes, divorced. Well, what can I do for you, Mrs. Rule?"

"Senator, there is a matter of what I believe to be the utmost importance, that I would like to discuss with you at the earliest possible moment. May I see you this morning at your home before you leave for your office?"

"I have a nine o'clock appointment with the president, Mrs. Rule, but if you could be here by, say, seven o'clock, I will see you then."

"Thank you, sir. I can be there by that time." She wrote down the address. "And, Senator, I hope you will keep this in confidence, at least until you've heard what I have to say."

"Of course. I'll see you at seven."

Rule showered and dressed with a feeling of excitement mixed with unease. Before the day was over, she might well be unemployed, or worse, under arrest.

Before leaving the house, she went to her study, switched on the copying machine, and made two copies of everything she had collected in her files. She was pleased to see that the satshots copied very nicely. She drove quickly through the still-empty streets of Washington, conscious that she was about to take an irrevocable step. Carr's house was on Capitol Hill, one of a row of Victorian structures that had been gentrified during recent years. He had lived there long before it was fashionable.

He answered the door himself, already in a necktie, but wearing a silk dressing gown over his shirt. "Come into the study," he said, leading the way to a sunlit room at the back of the house. They sat next to each other on a leather Chesterfield sofa, while he poured her some coffee. Then he got right to the point. "Now," he said, "what's this about?"

Rule put down her coffee and tore her attention from the oak-paneled room, with its floor-to-ceiling bookcases and photographs of the senator with half a dozen presidents. She opened her briefcase. "It's hard to know exactly where to start, Senator, but I suppose this is as good a place as any." She handed him a sheaf of papers. "This is a copy of an Agency document describing a disinformation operation called Snowflower, which ran, or at least, began, in the early summer of 1983. As you can see in the summary paragraph, the idea was to convince the Soviets that Sweden was secretly considering joining NATO, in the hope of scaring them into moving forces into the Baltic, where there is actually no threat to them. The Agency hoped that some of these units would be moved from East Germany, where, as you know, there is a heavy concentration of Soviet ground forces."

The senator's eyebrows went up as he read. "As *you* know, the Agency is obliged to come to the committee for approval of covert operations, but they never came to us with this. I suppose they could argue that since this didn't involve troops, it didn't count, but I wouldn't buy that. This could have all sorts of ramifications."

"I believe it already has. I believe that this operation may have resulted in an entirely unanticipated course of events." She took him carefully through everything she had—the running aground of a Whiskey class Soviet submarine near a Swedish naval base in October of 1981, and the subsequent sharp increase in submarine sightings in the Stockholm Archipelago; the background and discovery of Firsov/Majorov and his odd removal from high position in the KGB to the command of SPETSNAZ forces; the indications that what appeared to be a sports complex might really be a submarine and SPETSNAZ base; the marked increase in Swedish studies programs in Soviet universities; the successfully secret Soviet development of a wing-in-ground-effect troop transport, previously thought unworkable; the massing of Soviet forces in Poland, Lithuania, Latvia, and Estonia, ostensibly for long-planned maneuvers; the recruiting of Emilio Appicella and his electronic message to her.

The senator listened intently to her presentation, occasionally asking a question. "I take it," he said when she paused to sip her coffee, "that you believe the Soviet

Union is considering some sort of military adventurism in Sweden, is that it?"

"Senator, I believe they have been considering it for a long time; I believe a full-scale invasion may now be imminent."

Senator Carr blinked. "That is a very startling statement, Mrs. Rule, coming from someone in your position."

"I know, sir, and I hope you will believe that I have not come to that belief rashly."

"You don't seem like a rash person to me, Mrs. Rule, although I expect there must be people in your Agency who would regard such an assessment as rash, coming, as it does, from a woman."

"I am afraid that is entirely true, Senator."

"It is my assumption that you have already brought these facts and suppositions to the attention of your superiors, and they have not reacted as you believe they should."

"That is correct."

"Have they taken any action at all?"

"Not so far as I can determine, and my sources are good."

"Why not? Well, never mind their reasons for not acting; why do you *believe* they have not acted?"

"First of all, because of Snowflower. This was a highly secret operation, one that I am not supposed to know about. To admit that the Soviets are about to act would be to admit that the Agency may have provoked their action."

The senator nodded. "Yes, I can see how that might prove just a bit embarrassing, if it came out."

"Beyond that, Senator, I don't really know why my superiors have reacted the way they have, except for the fact that my ex-husband seems to find my presence in the Agency an embarrassment and may have had a tendency to ridicule the theory, because it came from me. I do know that the Director of Central Intelligence, himself, has seen or heard most of the material in this file, and that he reacted very angrily to it. My immediate superior has indicated to me that if I continue to pursue the matter, even on my own time, that I might expect to be removed. My ex-husband has suggested that I resign and implied that if I don't, I might be dismissed."

"Mrs. Rule, forgive me if I ask this, but I must, and I must ask you to be perfectly truthful with me."

"Yes?"

"Mrs. Rule, might a thorough investigation of your employment at the Central Intelligence Agency reveal grounds, quite apart from this Swedish business, that might suggest that you are in trouble there, that you might be a candidate for dismissal in any case?"

Rule sat up and felt her face flush. "Senator, I am thirty-five years old, and I hold the Soviet Office of the Directorate of Intelligence. I am the youngest person ever to do so, and I am a woman. Does that answer your question?"

The senator burst out laughing. "Yes, I believe it does. I am very sorry, indeed, but you can see why I had to ask that."

"Yes, I suppose I can," Rule replied, somewhat mollified.

The senator looked at his watch. "There are a great

many other things I would like to ask you, Mrs. Rule, but I have an appointment with the president in less than half an hour. It does not take much thought to see that the Soviets might perceive many advantages in controlling Sweden, but let me ask you, why, with all they will have to endure from the rest of the world—military, economic, diplomatic sanctions—why, in the light of all that, do you think they would do it?"

"Let me ask you a question in reply, Senator; do you believe that the United States would use nuclear weapons to defend Sweden from a Soviet invasion?"

The senator looked at the carpet. "No," he said, finally. "I don't believe so."

"Well, sir, there is no other way to prevent them."

"What about the Swedes themselves? They have a much-praised system of defenses—a fine air force, a navy, hundreds of gun emplacements along their archipelago, a very large and well-trained reserve army—why would they not defend themselves?"

"Senator, the Swedes are very well set up to repel a D-day-type invasion from the East. They claim they can raise an army of eight hundred thousand—that's ten percent of their population—on thirty-six hours' notice. But it won't be a D-day-type invasion, and they won't have thirty-six hours. SPETSNAZ forces will knock out concentrations of their shore gun emplacements and missile stations early on, and the Soviets will enter quickly through relatively narrow gaps in the shore defenses. And from what we know about SPETSNAZ operating techniques, they'll already have a sizable force in place on Swedish soil, knocking out communications and destroying the Swedish air force on the ground. I'm no military expert, but I believe it could all be over very quickly, if the Soviets have surprise on their side."

"All right, you've told me how you think they'll do it; now tell me *why.*"

"Because they've always been paranoid, and they think they're threatened by NATO in the Baltic; because we won't go to war to stop them, and neither will anybody else; because they're in critically deep economic trouble, and they could harness the Swedish economy to their very substantial benefit; because the Soviets have never lost a man nor a square yard of soil to public opinion; because they have a great deal to gain and not much to lose; *because they can get away with it.*"

The senator stared at her for a moment, then got up and walked to his desk. "Mrs. Rule, what is it you would like me to do? I probably have a great deal less scope than you believe."

"Take a copy of this file to the president. Ask him to warn the Swedes, to telephone the prime minister personally, if possible. I don't think an invasion can work unless the Soviets have the advantage of absolute surprise. If the Swedes mobilize, the Soviets will have to back down. It would be too expensive and bloody a move if the Swedes are warned. Tell the Swedes. That's all I want."

"That's *all?* You want an entire country to go on a war footing because of what's in your file?"

"That's not my decision, Senator—that's not even the president's. All we can do is tell the Swedes, and then it's their decision. But can you imagine what will happen if we suppress this information and the Soviets do invade?

Never mind history. What would it do to this country right now, let alone to the balance of power in Western Europe? We'd have to pour troops into Norway and Denmark and Germany; we'd have to deploy a whole new series of Cruise missiles, with all the political consequences that entails; it would cost us tens of billions of dollars. Not only that, but our armed forces would be at full alert for months, and so would the Soviets. The chances of an accidental nuclear launch would increase exponentially. And need I mention world opinion? We're having a tough enough time as it is. *We've got to tell the Swedes, Senator.*"

"That's all you want, then? For somebody to tell the Swedes?"

"That's all."

"Well, I can't go to the president with only what you've got here. First of all, he would suspect it, coming from me, in the opposition party. Second, even if I convinced him it was worth looking into, he'd want the advice of everybody in sight—the Pentagon, in particular, and not least, your own Agency. That would take time, and if this is as imminent as you think it is, well . . ."

Rule stood up. "Thank you for your time, Senator. I won't trouble you again."

"No, wait, wait," he said, taking her arm and steering her to a chair. "I didn't say I wouldn't help. I just can't go to the president. Maybe there's a better way."

"What's that?"

"Maybe we can arrange for you to tell the Swedes yourself."

"How?"

"Are you the young lady Will is meeting in Copenhagen tomorrow?"

"Yes."

The senator walked around his desk and picked up the telephone. He looked up a number in his address book, glanced at his watch, and dialed a lot of digits. "Go to Stockholm instead," he said. "Hello? Hello? Is that Mr. Carlsson's office? This is United States Senator Benjamin Carr calling. May I speak to Mr. Carlsson, please?" He put his hand over the phone and turned to Rule. "This fellow is Head of Chancery at the Swedish Ministry of Defense . . . Hello, Sven? This is Ben Carr, in Washington. How are you? Good. Yes, I'm well. Listen, I'm calling you on a matter of some importance. A friend of mine is going to be in Stockholm"—he looked at Kate—"tomorrow?"

She nodded.

". . . tomorrow, and I would be very grateful if you would take the time to see her. Her name . . ."

Rule was waving frantically at him. "No, not my name over the phone!"

". . . just a minute." He put his hand over the phone. "What name should I give him?"

"Brooke Kirkland."

"Sven, her name is Brooke Kirkland—have you got that? Good. Now listen, Sven, I want you to understand that this lady is a serious person, and I hope you will listen to what she has to say. Please take my word that she is who she says she is, that's very important, and her information may be of great value to your people there. I think you might want her to meet your minister. I'm sorry I can't be more specific, but you understand. Yes, I hope we'll see you in Washington again, soon. Thank you, Sven, and good-bye."

He hung up and turned to Rule. "Sven Carlsson, as I said, is Head of Chancery, the top civil servant in the Swedish Ministry of Defense; his office is right across from the minister's. We've met a number of times; he's been a guest in my home. You heard what I said to him. When you see him, explain that this is being done unofficially, that it is not a message from our government. But when he's seen what you've shown me, perhaps he will be impressed enough to take you to his minister, and perhaps he, in turn, will go to the Prime Minister. I'm sorry I can't do more, but at least, this way, they'll have your information tomorrow and not next week."

Rule stood up and gathered her papers together. She handed the senator a large, brown envelope. "This is a copy of everything I showed you. Make whatever use of it you wish."

He took the envelope. "Thank you. If I have the right opportunity . . . and I'll try to keep your name out of it."

"I appreciate that, Senator, but I understand that it may not be possible. Do what you must. And thank you so much for listening to me, and for your help."

"Call me when you've talked to Carlsson. I'll let you know what's happening here."

She left Carr's house, drove to a pay phone, and booked herself on an SAS night flight to Stockholm, canceling her seat to Copenhagen. She called the Grand Hotel in Stockholm, the only hotel there she knew about, and booked a room. She called the hotel in Copenhagen and left the Stockholm number for Will.

She got back into her car and drove to Langley. Somehow, she had to get through an ordinary workday. Then she would be free, free to try and stop this thing.

43

Helder sat in the first row of the theater and watched Majorov take his audience through an abbreviated version of the slide show he had given the Politburo some days before. It was bold—he had to give the colonel that; in fact, it was brilliant. The country would fold before its people had known what had happened; the prime minister, or somebody who looked and sounded like him, would appear on television and radio, asking for calm and no resistance. There would be outbreaks of fighting, Majorov conceded, but they would be isolated pockets, militiamen with nothing more than small arms and soon-to-be-shattered hopes. The major population centers, though—Stockholm, Göteborg and some smaller cities—would be taken very quickly, indeed, as would major military centers, such as the Stockholm Military District Headquarters, at Strangnas. Command of Swedish forces would be lost during the first hours of invasion, taken by crack units already in place. All this would happen if the element of surprise could be kept intact.

Majorov did not mention his orders that, if surprise were lost, the invasion would be immediately canceled, and troop movements explained away as maneuvers.

"And now," Majorov was saying to his obviously excited audience, "you will report to your division and regimental commanders for your final instructions. Remember, if you and your troops perform as you have been trained, you will write a page of Soviet military history that will be read and reread for centuries to come. And the Soviet people will shower upon you such honor and privilege as you cannot now conceive."

The audience was on its feet, cheering, then singing the SPETSNAZ anthem in lusty voices. Majorov beamed at them, then, catching Helder's eye, motioned him to a side door. "Come," he said to the younger man. "I'll walk you to the sub pens."

The two men walked briskly down the hill together, toward the guarded gates. Helder felt light-headed and short of breath. He had said his good-byes to Trina Ragulin the night before; she had recovered enough from her bruising to make love to him repeatedly. He promised her that he would return, but he had no way of knowing that. He was going into battle, and he did not feel invulnerable. Death had come too close on the first mission. In spite of himself, his anger at Majorov had diminished somewhat, as he had been swept along in the excitement of this monumental military exercise. He knew, now, that if he could but survive, he would spend the remainder of his career in a position he had never dreamed of achieving.

"Helder," Majorov said, "this is to be your day, more

than any of the others. But for you to realize that, you must know a bit more than you have been told so far. This goes back to a blunder on the part of the American CIA, one so stupid that it was hard to credit, at the time. They made an effort to convince us that Sweden was about to become an enemy, a member of NATO, and by the time we discovered it was a lie—a discovery we made from inside their own ranks, I am glad to tell you—I had put a plan to the Politburo, then under Andropov, and had been given SPETSNAZ as the means of realizing the plan. Ever since the Great Patriotic War, we have been sending submarines into Swedish waters for reconnaissance, and after the development of the mini-subs, we began sending SPETSNAZ units in for training, as well."

Majorov scooped up a stone from the path and sent it skimming across the lawn. "Swedish sub-hunting technology was extremely poor, and we had little difficulty in penetrating their waters. Their capabilities in this regard were so small, in fact, that I believed we could endure even a major upgrading of their techniques, and I was right. My plan began and will end with provocation. In the autumn of 1981, I ordered a Whiskey boat to be put aground near the base at Karlskrona. The resulting uproar was all I could have wished for. Swedish public opinion turned against the Soviet Union, their parliament launched an investigation into the incident, and their prime minister, who had been most conciliatory towards us, was greatly embarrassed. It was wonderful."

"I don't understand, sir," Helder said.

"The provocation was necessary to create an antagonistic atmosphere between our two countries," Majorov replied. "I have continued to build on that antagonism in the meantime. It is that which will give us our rationale for defending ourselves against them." He chuckled to himself. "But I am getting ahead of myself. After the so-called Whiskey-on-the-rocks incident, we increased our penetrations of their waters; we sent groups of minisubs in; we put SPETSNAZ units ashore, to live in the country for weeks at a time, establishing safe houses and bases, and returning with better and better intelligence; armed with detailed plans of the Swedish defenses supplied by Seal, our man in their government, we mined shoreline gun emplacements and military harbors, and because our mines are made of new materials which are extremely difficult to detect, they have not been detected. Just as the buoy you placed near Stockholm has not been detected."

They reached the gates and passed through, then walked into the submarine pens. Majorov stopped at the mooring of a Whiskey class submarine, its crew and officers lined up on deck. "Since your mission, the attitude of the Swedes has bordered on hysteria, and now, in great part thanks to you and Sokolov, they are ripe for one final, unbearable provocation."

Helder's eyes widened.

"Exactly, Helder." Majorov smiled. "That is your mission. When you put this sub aground in the Stockholm Archipelago, you will create a frenzy of naval activity in the area; you will rivet the attention of all Sweden to one tiny island in the approaches to Stockholm." Majorov paused for effect. "And then," he said, "we will send a rescue party—a rescue party they will never forget."

Majorov boarded the submarine and, ignoring the crew, climbed the conning tower and dropped down the main hatch, closely followed by Helder. They went to the chart table at the navigator's station. "Here," said Majorov, pointing a finger to a tiny island, Höggarn, that Helder had passed on his previous mission. "Here is where you will put her aground, as I told you earlier. The southwestern shore of the island is sandy, and you will drive her well up. We don't want her to drift off later. You will be discovered in due course, although last time we had to wait for a local fisherman to ring the police, and you will quickly be surrounded by everything they can muster in the area."

Majorov turned to face him. "Now, listen to me carefully. You are not, under any circumstances, to allow any Swede to board this vessel, and when you begin to communicate with them, you will make that very clear. From the moment the first Swedish naval forces arrive, you are to keep the deck gun and the conning tower machine guns manned at all times. If any attempt is made to board the sub, you are to fire on the boarders. Is that clear?"

"Yes, sir, it is clear," Helder replied, "but you realize that I cannot defend a grounded submarine against attack indefinitely."

"I realize that, but I expect you to put up a fight, for a time, anyway, before you surrender."

"Surrender?" Helder was shocked.

"You have already said that you cannot defend the sub indefinitely, and I don't want you all to die trying. Don't worry. You will not be in Swedish custody for very long;

when we receive the signal that they have fired on your vessel, we will move very quickly, you may be certain."

"I understand, sir."

"Good." Majorov took an envelope from an inside pocket and opened it. "Here are three code words," he said, holding up the paper. "WHALE, you will send when you are successfully grounded; FOX, you will send when Swedish forces arrive on the scene; BEAR, you will send when you have been fired upon. It is all written in this order."

"I understand, sir."

"There are three other coded instructions, which you may or may not receive, but which you will not send." He produced a small card from his pocket on which there were three five-digit groups of numbers written. "Look here," Majorov said, moving to the communications room. "This special piece of equipment has been fitted to the sub. Its only purpose is to display five digits. If you receive this five-digit group"—he pointed to the card and the group, 10101—"you are then immediately to fire on the Swedes with the deck gun, at an important target of your choice. Do you understand?"

"Yes, sir."

"And if you receive this group"—he pointed to the card and the group, 10201—"you are to surrender your ship to the Swedes at once. If you receive this group, 10301, you are to order the sonar operator to transmit a continuous signal on this frequency." He produced another card. "Do you understand?"

"Not entirely, sir. Of what use would a sonar transmission be?"

Majorov led him back to the chart table and pointed. "This is the spot where you deployed the navigation buoy on your first mission."

"Yes, sir, that is the spot." Helder followed Majorov's finger in a straight line back to the island where he was to run the sub aground.

"As you can see, you will have a line-of-sight transmission of the active sonar signal to the buoy. In its present position, lying deep in the channel, it cannot be reached by radio transmission, but only by sonar, and only on this specific frequency. When it receives the sonar signal, it will release its top portion, which will rise to the surface, attached to the base by a cable. The floating top of the buoy serves as an antenna, which can receive satellite transmissions."

"*Receive* transmissions, sir?" Helder's understanding was that the buoy was to broadcast, not receive.

Majorov appeared momentarily flustered. "Forgive me. I meant to say send, not receive. It will send to our satellite, which will broadcast the relevant data to the incoming force. Come with me again, Helder."

Majorov climbed to the conning tower and levered open the catches of a waterproof case bolted to the steel bulkhead. Inside was an instrument identical to the one Helder had seen in the communications shack. "Here, as you can see, is another receiver of the five-digit groups, so that you will know, whether you are below or in the conning tower, the moment these signals are sent." He replaced the cover and latched it shut again. "Now, I want you to repeat all the instructions I have just given you."

Helder ran through the instructions. WHALE, aground; FOX, in contact with Swedish forces; BEAR, have been fired upon. A signal of 10101 on the special receiver, an instruction to fire on Swedish forces; a signal of 10201, an instruction to surrender the sub to the Swedes; a signal of 10301, an instruction to broadcast a sonar signal to activate the navigation buoy.

"Excellent," Majorov said, clapping him on the shoulder. "Now we will introduce you to your crew." Majorov started to climb down from the conning tower, only to be met by Jones, coming up.

"Colonel," the legend-maker said, out of breath, "I'm sorry to interrupt your briefing, but Appicella is gone."

Majorov's brow furrowed. "Gone? What do you mean?"

"I mean, sir, that he appears to be gone from the base."

"That is impossible," Majorov said, firmly. "No man could possibly get out of here."

"I hope that is true, Colonel, but nevertheless, he cannot be found. The girl, Olga, reported him missing this morning, and I ordered an immediate search of the base."

"He will turn up here, somewhere; wait and see," Majorov said.

Jones looked uncomfortable. "Colonel, the girl says he spent the afternoon yesterday sitting on the veranda of the guest cottage, watching the repair of the American's yacht. He even took his dinner there. She went to bed without him around eleven; when she woke up, he was no longer there."

Majorov appeared stunned. He looked at his watch. "The yacht has been gone since midnight. It is in Swedish waters by now, perhaps even in Sweden. They could make Gotland by this time."

"Yes, sir," Jones said. "But, in any case, Appicella knows nothing. How could he? He was kept out of sensitive areas."

Majorov winced. "He was not kept out of the most sensitive area of all," he said. "He had access to the computer." He thought for a moment. "If he has learned about our operation, they would not go to Denmark; it's too far. They'd go to Sweden, and then to Stockholm and contact either the Swedish government or the American Embassy."

"Shall I start a sea search for them?"

Majorov chewed on a knuckle for a moment. "No, we're too close to jump-off to send boats and helicopters into Swedish waters. Chances are they don't know anything, anyway. Appicella was probably nervous about being kept here and decided to run for it."

"There's something else," Jones said. "We've had a signal from Seal, in Stockholm. An American senator, Carr, is sending someone named Brooke Kirkland there. She has an appointment at the ministry tomorrow. Seal thought the name might be a cover, so I queried Ferret. He has confirmed that this Kirkland is the woman, Rule. He also confirms that Appicella is Rule's man."

"That would be very unfortunate, indeed," the colonel said. "Does Seal have any reason to believe that Rule might expect to meet Appicella in Stockholm?"

"No, and it doesn't seem likely. Appicella's escape was

a fluke, caused by the accidental presence of the American yacht. She can't possibly know if he's headed there. The impetus for Rule going to Stockholm is the senator. She obviously intends alerting the ministry."

"Appicella may or may not have information that would confirm Rule's guesses, but we can't take a chance. Even without confirmation, Rule might be able to impress someone at the ministry. We have a unit in central Stockholm, don't we?"

"Yes, sir, Group One; their mission is parliament and the royal palace. The other two Stockholm units, groups two and three, are responsible for Stockholm Military District Headquarters at Strangnas, to the west."

Majorov nodded. "Signal Group One to place one member each at Stockholm Airport, the American Embassy, and the Ministry of Defense. If there is a woman on any flight incoming from the United States named either Kirkland or Rule, kill her at the first opportunity. If anyone fitting Appicella's description shows up either at the airport or at the embassy or the ministry, he is to be killed immediately. The same for the American, Lee. We must assume that Appicella knows and has told Lee. Tell them to do it quietly, if possible, but it must be done, at whatever cost."

"Yes, sir."

Majorov turned to Helder. "I'm sorry, but I must go now. There is your crew," he said, gesturing toward the men formed on the deck. "They are handpicked, every one of them, and they are yours." He stuck out his hand. "Good luck, Helder. See you in Sweden."

"Thank you, sir," Helder said, taking the hand. Then

Majorov and Jones were gone. Helder looked down on the crew below. "Give me your attention," he said. They all turned to look at him. "My name is Helder. We have not sailed together before, but we have been well trained. I will run this cruise by the book. Take your stations and prepare to sail." They disappeared through the deck hatches, leaving only enough men on deck to cast off. Helder began barking orders, by the book. But as he did, he worried. This cruise would be anything but by the book. There was something he didn't understand, something that kept eating at him, but he had not had time to come to grips with it. He'd do that when they were safely under way. It was something to do with the last mission, something he couldn't remember. But there'd be time. He'd figure it out.

Then, something else occurred to Helder. He, himself, had been present when the First Secretary of the Communist Party had instructed Majorov to cancel the invasion if the element of surprise were in any way compromised. Yet, in all the instructions Majorov had just given Helder, there was no code for an order canceling the invasion.

44

Rule worked most of the day organizing the Soviet Office to function smoothly in her absence. At four, she held a meeting of her key subordinates to make specific assignments. Just after five, as the meeting broke up, Alan Nixon's secretary appeared in the doorway.

"Mrs. Rule, Mr. Nixon would like to see you in his office," she said.

Rule thought it odd that the woman would come for her, instead of telephoning. "I'll be there in two minutes," she said. "I've got some files to lock up first."

"Please don't be long," the secretary said, and left.

Rule refiled the folders on her desk in the combination-lock cabinet, then walked down to Nixon's office.

"Go right in," the secretary said.

Alan Nixon sat behind his desk. A man she didn't know had pulled a chair around to Nixon's side of the desk and sat next to him. "Come in, please, Katharine," Nixon said, "and close the door."

Rule closed the door and sat in the single chair facing the two men.

"This is Charles Mortimer of Internal Investigations," Nixon said. "He has some question to ask you. Are you willing to answer his questions?"

She regarded Charles Mortimer evenly for a moment. Internal Investigations served much the same function in the Central Intelligence Agency as did the internal affairs units in big-city police departments. Mortimer hadn't spoken yet, but Rule hated him already. Everybody hated Internal Investigations. "Are you reading me my rights, Alan?" she asked.

Nixon flushed. Mortimer spoke quickly. "Now, Mrs. Rule, I don't think that's necessary at this point in time. We can talk informally, here."

"Informally?" Rule asked. "Tell me, Mr. Mortimer, is this conversation being recorded?"

Nixon got even redder, but Mortimer did the talking. "Would it disturb you if we were being recorded, Mrs. Rule?"

Rule knew she was on shaky ground, here. Employees of the Agency had the same rights as other citizens, but to invoke them could be a very bad idea. She might end up suspended from her job for weeks or months, and the whole investigative weight of Internal Investigations might fall on her. She didn't need that, just at the moment. She smiled slightly. "If I were invited in for an informal chat by my immediate superior, and I learned later that the conversation had been recorded, that might disturb me," she said, taking care to keep her tone even. "Would you be disturbed, in the same circumstances, Mr. Mortimer?"

It was Mortimer's turn to flush. He said nothing for a moment; then he reached forward, opened a drawer in Nixon's desk, and pushed a button, making a soft click. "This conversation is not being recorded," he said. "Now, I would like to ask you some questions, informally of course."

"Of course," Rule replied. "What would you like to know?"

Mortimer leaned forward in his chair. "Mrs. Rule, since you have been an employee of the Central Intelligence Agency, have you ever done anything to violate the terms of your employment contract?"

Tricky, Rule thought. A yes answer could get her suspended immediately; a no could lay her open for what amounted to an internal charge of perjury, never mind that she hadn't been sworn. Who hadn't taken a file home to work on, or leaked some tidbit over dinner or in bed? Everybody did that stuff. "That's an awfully general question, Mr. Mortimer," she replied. "Why don't you be specific?"

Alan Nixon could contain himself no longer. "You're not making this easy, Katharine," he blurted.

"What am I supposed to make easy, Alan?" she asked.

Mortimer held up a hand. "All right, we'll be specific. Have you ever removed classified material from the Agency premises without authorization?"

Why were they picking at her like this when they knew she had left the country without authorization? At least Simon had told her they knew. Had he been bluffing? She couldn't allow them to nail her with anything now; she had to fly to Stockholm tonight. "Mr. Mortimer," she said, allowing herself to sound a little exasperated, "I am a loyal citizen of the United States and a loyal employee of this Agency. If you have any charges to make against me, make them, and I will respond appropriately." Put up or shut up. If he put up, she was suspended and grounded. She held her breath.

Mortimer sat back in his chair, and she hoped that was body language for backing down. "As I said, Mrs. Rule, this is just an informal chat among colleagues." Swell, now they were colleagues. "Let me put it this way: if I charged you with removing classified materials from Agency premises, would you deny it?"

"Hypothetically speaking?" she asked.

"Of course." He smiled.

"Hypothetically speaking," she said, "if you charged me with removing classified materials or, for that matter, with anything else, I would immediately request a formal hearing with counsel present."

His smile disappeared. "I see," he said.

Quickly, before Mortimer decided to charge her with something, she turned to Nixon. "Alan, I'm leaving on vacation tomorrow morning, a trip that you approved some time ago, and I've got a lot to do." She pointed at Mortimer. "If this jerk thinks I'm a Soviet mole, or something, tell him to arrest me now. Otherwise, I'm going home to pack." She stood up.

Mortimer leaned over and whispered something to Nixon. "That will be all, Katharine," Nixon said. "For the moment. Have a nice vacation. We'll see you when you get back."

She turned and walked toward the door, breathing

hard. "I'll look forward to it," she said, without turning her head. She opened the door and closed, almost slammed, it behind her. Her heart seemed to pound two or three times for each footstep as she strode quickly to her office, grabbed her briefcase and walked out of the building.

That had been a near thing, she thought, as she made her way home through the rush-hour traffic. They weren't sure of themselves, yet, but they were leaning hard. By the time she got back, they might have something on her. Her only defense, if any, was to be right. She laughed nervously to herself. The only thing that could save her career was if the Soviet Union invaded Sweden!

45

Helder took the Whiskey boat out of Liepaja submerged and set a course north to intercept the Helsinki–Stockholm ferry. Some of his crew were familiar from the Juliet mother sub on his previous mission; one officer was not.

"My name is Kolchak," the man said. He did not offer his hand. "I am assigned as political officer." He was taller than Helder and thin, with a bland, gray face, the sort of face that was difficult to read.

"Kolchak," Helder said, nodding. He was surprised to find the man aboard. One of Malibu's features had been the remarkable and complete lack of political officers. Every military unit in the Soviet armed forces had a political officer, who reported not to the unit's commander, but to his Party superiors. Political officers were a pain in the ass and were despised by every military commander, and Helder was no exception. Why, after all this time, had Majorov saddled him with a Party hack?

"My instructions are to remain with you at all times during this operation," Kolchak said.

"I see," Helder said. "Why are you armed aboard my ship?" he asked, nodding at the pistol in the shoulder holster visible under Kolchak's bridge jacket.

"I am instructed to be armed," Kolchak replied.

Majorov obviously intended to see that Helder carried out his mission. Helder had little doubt that, if he varied from Majorov's orders, Kolchak had been instructed to shoot him and complete the mission himself. Helder was in no mood for a political officer. If he completed his mission, he would be beyond the reach of such people; if he didn't complete it, he'd be dead. "Fine," said Helder. "Carry out your instructions, but stay out of my way. See that I don't bump into you as I move about my ship."

Kolchak blinked. He obviously was not accustomed to being addressed in this manner by military commanders. "What is your course?" he asked.

"You worry about Party doctrine," Helder snapped. "I'll worry about the course." He pushed past Kolchak and went to the communications shack. The radio operator, in his tiny alcove, didn't bother to rise, since he couldn't. "Sparks," Helder said, "in certain circumstances you may be required to transmit a sonar signal on this frequency." He handed the operator the card Majorov had given him.

"Yes, sir," the radio operator replied, glancing at the card. "I have been told of this and of the special receiver, but I have not been told the codes."

"I have the codes," Helder said. "You are to transmit

on my order alone, as long as I am alive. Do you understand this?"

The man glanced over his shoulder at Kolchak and smiled. "Yes, Captain, I understand. Only on your order."

Helder clapped him on the shoulder. "Good man." He walked aft to where two young men, the helmsman and the planesman, sat before two large wheels, watching dials before them. "Helmsman, have you been told that we will follow the Helsinki–Stockholm ferry into the archipelago?"

"Yes, sir. I was at the helm during your last mission, Captain. I know the drill. The planesman, too."

"Good." Helder motioned for the officers to gather round the chart table; then he explained the mission in detail to them. "Any questions?" he asked.

No one spoke. Kolchak started to say something but stopped himself.

"Good, let's get on with it, then."

The sub continued north through the afternoon, staying in Soviet waters until they were past the Estonian island of Hiiumaa, nearly into the Gulf of Finland. At their rendezvous point with the ferry, Helder slowed the sub and used the periscope frequently, until he had the large ship in his sights. Issuing commands in a calm, quiet voice, he brought the sub into the ferry's wake, then closed slowly on it until the noises of the submarine would be indistinguishable from those of the ferry.

"Number one," he said to the executive officer, "take the conn; I'm going to my cabin for a while. The ferry will slow to six knots when it enters the archipelago. See you don't stick this sub up her ass. Call me if anything even slightly unusual occurs."

"Aye, aye, sir," the man said.

Helder stopped for a moment and studied the chart again, memorizing its every feature. With his finger, he traced the straight line from where he would ground the sub to where the navigation buoy lay on the seabed. He looked at the area surrounding the buoy. Stockholm lay five kilometers to the west, and the low-lying islands of the archipelago surrounded the site. The buoy was landlocked, except for the relatively narrow channel through which he had taken the minisub. Helder went back to the captain's cabin, pulled the curtain shut and stretched out on the bunk.

Everything was in perfect order, he thought, except that some shadowy fear still gnawed at him, a fear not connected with the ordinary apprehension before a mission. He did not like the feeling, and he tried to trace its origins through the maze of his mind. It was the buoy that bothered him. He had placed it himself, at great risk, and normally, when he had completed a task, the thought of it gave him satisfaction. But now, instead of satisfaction, he felt apprehension. Why? What was his subconscious telling him?

He dozed off and on, playing with the thought, letting it find its own way through the maze; then his eyes came open, staring. Three questions about the buoy nagged at him; together, they triangulated on a single answer. He dismissed the idea as insane, but when he ran through the process again, he was led to the same place. He had watched and admired Majorov's determination through

356 / Stuart Woods

all of this, but now he believed he had underestimated that determination. Helder suddenly knew that Majorov had not the slightest intention of halting the invasion of Sweden, surprise or no surprise. If the Swedes caught on too soon, and the Kremlin tried to back out, Majorov had a means of committing them irrevocably to the invasion, and he, Helder, was Majorov's instrument.

He remembered the yellow radiation badges worn by the men who had loaded the buoy at Malibu, and now he remembered finding one of those badges in the launching compartment of the Juliet sub. The badge had turned blue. True, Majorov had told him that the buoy was ballasted with spent uranium 235, but that would have been insufficient to irradiate the badge. He had served aboard nuclear subs, and he knew what sort of radiation dose it took to change a badge from yellow to blue.

He remembered Majorov's mistake, when he had said the buoy's antenna was meant to receive satellite transmissions. He had then corrected himself, and said the buoy would send, but a navigational buoy wouldn't send to a satellite, but to ships in the area equipped to receive. Helder remembered the satellite dishes on the roof of the headquarters building at Malibu. *They* could transmit signals to a satellite, which could then be received by the buoy. But only after Helder had ordered the sonar transmission that would release the buoy's antenna and allow it to surface.

He remembered Majorov's unwavering determination; he remembered that none of the codes he issued to Helder was associated with aborting the mission. They were on radio shutdown, except for the burst transmission of the WHALE, FOX, and BEAR code words; the sub could receive nothing but the three five-digit number groups. *There was no way to recall the Whiskey boat.*

Helder's conclusion was finally inescapable. The "navigation buoy" was a *nuclear device*.

He got up and went back to the navigator's station again. Motioning the officer out of his seat, he sat down and looked again at the locale around the buoy. The device sat, more or less, in the center of a basin. On the east of the basin was an outlet, the channel through which Helder had piloted the minisub; on the north and south were islands; and to the west lay the city of Stockholm, crossed and recrossed by waterways.

The bomb wasn't big; it wouldn't need to be. Half a kiloton—a kiloton, at the most. When Majorov triggered it from Malibu, after Helder had signaled the release of the antenna, it would release an enormous force in all directions, but since the water surrounding it would yield more easily than the rocky seabed beneath it, most of the force would be transmitted outward and upward. The sea to the east of Stockholm would rise, and the outward force would propel a massive wall of water in every direction. To the north and south, the low-lying islands would take the brunt of the wave, though, no doubt, some of it would carry straight across the land to other islands beyond. To the west, Stockholm would be struck by a tidal wave that would rake people, vehicles, and buildings from its streets, then recede, leaving the waterlogged skeleton of a beautiful city. No, the bomb would not be very big. Majorov would have calculated the force so that the essential city would be left standing for occupation, even if few of its inhabitants would survive. He would have the place up and running again in no time.

Then, there was the area to the east of the bomb, the channel down which the sonar transmission would travel. A high bore of water would be shot down that channel like a shell from a cannon, sweeping all before it. Helder's submarine was before it, directly in its path. It would be picked up from the sandy ground where it rested and flung into hell.

Helder rested his forehead in his hand and tried to think. Maybe the invasion would go smoothly, as planned; maybe he would never receive the five-digit group 10301. Maybe. But what if it came? What then? If Helder didn't send the sonar signal, then Kolchak, the political officer, would shoot him and do it himself.

Helder kept trying to think, but he could not. He was numb with fear.

46

Rule threw her bag into the trunk of her car and darted back into the house. It was starting to rain, and she grabbed a folding umbrella from the stand in the entrance hall. God knew what the weather would be like in Stockholm.

She drove the two short blocks to Ed Rawls's little apartment, parked across the street, and grabbed the fat envelope lying on her briefcase. When Rawls answered the door, she thrust the envelope into his hands and said, "Here. This is a copy of everything I've got, if something comes up."

"You're off to Copenhagen, then? Good." He smiled.

"No, I'm off to Stockholm, Ed. I've found a private channel to a man named Carlsson, who's Head of Chancery at the Swedish Ministry of Defense. I'm seeing him tomorrow, and I hope I can accomplish what I want without raising a ruckus."

Rawls looked doubtful. "That's risky, Katie. You're contacting a foreign government directly, and short of defecting to the Reds, there's nothing you could do that would make the Agency madder."

"Yes there is; I could go to the *Washington Post*, which is the other alternative. I don't want to do that; that's why I'm taking this chance."

"Okay, kid, but you'll be out there on your own, you know. You'd better not go near the Stockholm station."

"Don't worry. I've no intention of involving them. I'm going to do this in Stockholm, then meet Will Lee in Copenhagen, and come back from my vacation the following week as if nothing had happened. I don't see what else I can do."

Rawls nodded. "Maybe you're right. In any case, I'll keep an ear to the ground here for you. Call me and let me know how you do in Stockholm. If you call me at the office, tell them you're my sister, Trudy."

"Okay. Listen, I've got a plane to catch. See you." She kissed him on the cheek and ran for the car. She pulled out of her parking place and started her drive to the airport. The rain came down harder, and it got darker. She switched on her headlights. She was stopped at a traffic light when she saw him, one car back, but not entirely hidden from view, craning his neck to be sure he hadn't lost her. Shit, what a time for her tail to show up again.

She glanced at her watch. She had less than an hour before her plane to New York, where she would connect with her SAS flight to Stockholm, not time enough to lose him without letting him know she knew she was being followed. She crossed the Potomac and headed toward National Airport, while he stayed a car or two back. Rule started to get mad.

At the airport, she whipped into the lower-level parking deck, waited a moment for him to pass her and park a few cars away, then got out of the car, taking her umbrella with her, and walked briskly away. She could hear him hurrying to keep up. The garage was deserted, and that suited her. She kept looking for the right spot; then there it was. She passed the restrooms, then ducked around a corner and waited. He was only seconds behind her. She hefted the umbrella in her hand. In its folded state, it packed its bulk into about a pound of tightly compressed fabric surrounding a steel shaft, soft on the outside, solid on the inside. He walked past where she waited and, bless him, stopped.

Rule stepped from around the corner, already starting her backswing, and hit him hard at the base of the skull, just the way they'd taught her at Quantico, when she was being trained for the covert service. He made a tiny sound; then his knees sagged and he collapsed in a heap at her feet. She looked quickly around, then grabbed him by his raincoat collar and started dragging him. The men's or the ladies'? The ladies', she decided, praying there was no one in there. She shouldered open the door and looked quickly around. Nobody. She dragged him across the restroom and into one of the booths. Mustering all her strength, she hoisted him onto one of the toilets and leaned him against the wall.

Quickly, she went through his pockets. The first thing she found was a gun, and not an ordinary one. It was a Heckler & Koch nonferrous 9mm automatic, made of stainless steel and alloys, designed to be walked through an airport security system without ringing all the bells.

She shoved it in the waistband of her skirt. She ran her hand around behind him, feeling for his wallet, and found a pair of handcuffs clipped to his belt. Jesus, she hadn't coshed a cop, had she? She popped the handcuffs, pulled his hands behind him and cuffed him to the plumbing. Then she found the wallet.

Gerald Marvin Bonner, the Virginia driver's license said. He lived in Alexandria. Then a business card. Federal Bureau of Investigation, it said, G. M. Bonner, Special Agent. Oh, shit, shit, shit! Then she found another business card: Gerald M. Bonner, private investigator, ex-FBI. She heaved a great sigh of relief. But why a PI? She shook him.

"Come on, Gerald, wake up. We have to talk," she said. Bonner drooled from a corner of his mouth. She pinched his cheeks. "Wakey—wakey, Gerry. Speak to me!" Bonner made a little mewing noise. Rule drew back and slapped him hard across the face. "Wake up, you prick!" she shouted at him. "You're in the ladies' room!"

"Which?" Bonner said, suddenly. He opened his eyes and tried to focus.

Rule slapped him again.

Now he could focus on her. "What the hell . . . ?" he managed to say.

"Look at me, Bonner," she said. "Know who I am?"

He tried to move and found himself handcuffed. "What is this, lady? What are you doing? I never saw you before in my life."

"I'm losing my patience, that's what I'm doing, and I want some answers."

"Go to hell. I've got nothing to say to you. I'll have the cops on you!"

Rule pulled his gun out of her waistband and worked the action. She stuck the barrel in one of his nostrils and pushed his head back hard against the tile wall. "You know who I am, and you know where I work, don't you? You know that I can shoot you right now and have an Agency team here in fifteen minutes to pick up the pieces. You'd vanish into thin air." That was a lie, but he probably didn't know it.

"All right, all right," he said, sounding odd, with his nose blocked that way. "What d'you want?"

"I want to know who hired you to follow me the last few weeks," she said, pushing a little harder on the gun.

"Ow!" he yelled. "Don't! It was Rule hired me. Your ex-husband."

"What?" she yelled. "You'd better do better than that, you little creep!" She shoved the gun a little farther up his nose.

He yelled again. "No, I swear, it was him—it was Rule. He wanted something on you. He wants your kid!"

She stopped pushing the gun. So it was Simon. He didn't want Peter, though, he just wanted some dirt. He wanted to force her out of the Agency. "What have you told him, so far?" she asked Bonner.

"Not much. Not much to tell. He knows about the boyfriend."

"Did you bug my phone?"

"Yeah. His, too. I didn't get anything, though. The bugs never worked right."

"Okay, so you know about the boyfriend. What else are you looking for? Why are you still following me?"

"He wants pictures, your ex-husband does."

"Pictures of what?"

"You know. Of you and the boyfriend. In bed."

"So you were going to kick the door down, huh? A real artist, you are. So why didn't you take the pictures?"

"I never had a chance. Then the guy left town. I didn't have much else in the way of business, so I kept following you, thought something might turn up."

"You're a real sweetheart, Bonner. I'll bet you got canned from the Bureau."

He looked away.

"Well, so long. I'm due at a dinner party on Capitol Hill."

He sat up. "Hey, wait a minute! I told you what you wanted to know, so unlock me. The keys are in my watch pocket."

"Don't worry," she said. "I'll send somebody to unlock you." She shut the booth door. "Now, if you're real quiet, maybe the next lady who comes in here won't know you're not a lady."

"Oh, Jesus Christ, please unlock me!" he yelled from behind the door.

"Have a nice rest," she called back. "Somebody will come for you soon." She left the restroom, tossed Bonner's wallet into a trash can, went back to the car for her bag, and walked to the main terminal, looking for the departures board. She found a San Francisco flight that was leaving in ten minutes, then went to a phone and dialed the Virginia Highway Patrol. "Hello," she said to the trooper who answered, "this is Detective Sergeant Brooke Kirkland of the San Francisco PD. I'm out at National Airport, and I just tried to use the ladies' room in the parking lot, and some guy jumped out of a booth and tried to rape me. I managed to overcome him, though, and I handcuffed him to a toilet. That's the ladies' room in A lot, lower level. Yeah, I've got to catch a plane home in ten minutes, so I can't hang around, but I'll telex you a statement as soon as I check in tomorrow, okay? You can mail me the cuffs." She hung up before the startled trooper could ask any further questions.

Then she remembered the gun. Looking carefully around her, she unbuttoned her jacket and slid it around to the small of her back. You never knew. She waltzed through security, ringing no bells, and ran for her flight.

Two hours later, she was taking off from Kennedy Airport on SAS. She had a drink to relax, then had two glasses of wine with dinner, and a brandy to follow. She fell asleep as soon as the movie started.

47

Helder called for the attack periscope and flipped down the handles as the column came up to meet him. A boiling sea met his eyes. "Reduce speed by one knot," he barked.

"Speed reduced one knot," the second officer called back.

Helder watched through the periscope as the ferry pulled ahead, and the water became smoother. He quickly swung the scope right and left; they were emerging from the narrow channel into open water. Slightly to the right of his course was an island; beyond that was another island, his destination. "Increase speed two knots," he ordered, and the command was answered. When they had caught up to the ferry again, he reduced speed to keep pace.

Twenty minutes later, Helder knew they were there without even using the periscope. They ran on for another ten minutes. Helder swept the horizon with the periscope. There was no vessel in sight in the near-daylight of the early-morning hours. It was one day after midsummer's night, the longest day of the year. There had been a lot of drinking done in Scandinavia the night before; this night, the drinkers would sleep gratefully and well. "Hard right rudder," Helder said, and the sub came around. "Hold that course," he said, when the island and its beach appeared, dead ahead. "Prepare to surface," he called out. "Surface."

Helder glanced at the depth sounder. The bottom was rising under them. He left the periscope and climbed a ladder to a point just under the main hatch. As the sub broke water, he cranked the pressure handle, then heaved open the hatch. Water spilled down on him and on Kolchak, who was on the ladder immediately under him. Helder climbed the remaining rungs and emerged into the conning tower, at the top of the sub's sail.

Quickly, he confirmed his position and his course. The island and its beach lay dead ahead, and close. He wrenched the cover off the conning tower squawk box. "Hold your course; full ahead!" he shouted. A tinny voice confirmed his order. Helder glanced at Kolchak; the political officer was staring straight ahead, wide-eyed. The island was rushing toward them, now, as the sub gained speed. She could do eighteen knots on the surface, but they hadn't the distance to gain that speed before grounding. Helder shouted into the squawk box. "All hands to collision stations!"

He grabbed the railing in front of him and braced his shoulder against the bulkhead. He couldn't help laughing; Kolchak had dropped to the conning tower sole and had his back braced against the bulkhead. Not a bad idea, Helder thought, but it was too late to change positions, and, anyway, he wanted to watch. He had spent his career avoiding putting subs aground, and now that he was about to do it, he wanted to see everything. There was brief thud and a buck as the sub touched a shallow place, then forged on, still picking up speed. Then the sub struck sand and lurched. Helder clenched his teeth and waited for a hard impact, but it never came. The sub continued forward, though in contact with the sandy bottom, then, with one long groan and shake, drove herself to a halt. There was one massive lurch; Helder was pressed forward into the bulkhead, then thrown backwards as the vessel came to a halt. He recovered, then grabbed the squawk box. "Stop engines!" he yelled.

Then everything went quiet. There was utter peace in the conning tower. Kolchak struggled to his feet and stood next to Helder. The second and third officers asked permission, then came up into the sail. Helder looked around him. There was a house down the beach about a quarter of a mile, but no sign of anybody. Then, as he watched, a yacht of about thirty feet came sailing from behind the point at the western end of the island, about a mile away. Helder picked up his binoculars. The helmsman was shouting something to whoever was below. A young man and woman spilled into the cockpit and, following the helmsman's pointing arm, gaped at the stranded sub. The young man dived back below.

Helder raised the binoculars slightly; at the top of the mast, he could see a VHF antenna. It wouldn't be long, now. Then Helder looked back toward the house. A man was walking down the beach from that direction, wearing pajamas and a dressing gown. He stopped at the water's edge, no more than fifty yards away, cupped his hands and shouted, in Swedish, "Good morning!"

Helder took a megaphone from the third officer. "Good morning," he called back. This was ridiculous.

"Do you need assistance?" the man shouted. "Should I call someone for you?"

"I don't think that will be necessary," Helder called back. "It might be best if you went back to your house; I think there will be a lot of boats here soon."

The man stood, looking, for a moment, then nodded, and started back toward the house.

Helder reached for the squawk box. "Sparks," he said.

"Yes, sir?" a voice came back.

"Send WHALE."

48

Rule got off the plane in Stockholm feeling worn and a bit hungover. She endured the line in immigration a couple of places behind a tall, slender American woman of about forty-five, with a loud laugh, who held up things for a moment by flirting with the immigration officer.

The luggage came quickly, and she headed through the nothing-to-declare exit at customs, still behind the American woman. Then, as she came through some swinging doors into the main terminal, she stopped, and she was suddenly afraid. A few yards in front of her, a man in a dark suit and a chauffeur's cap, one of a number of such men, was holding up a hand-lettered sign with two words written on it, KIRKLAND and RULE.

She would not have been terribly surprised if Carlsson had sent a car for her, since she had been introduced by a United States senator, but the only name Carlsson had for her was Kirkland. He could not, from what Senator Carr had said to him on the phone, have known her real name. No one in Sweden, in fact, not a soul, knew that anybody named Rule was arriving, and it was not a common name. Her passport and ticket were in the name of Callaway, her maiden name. She had never bothered to get a new passport after she was married.

To Rule's surprise, the tall American woman walked straight up to the chauffeur and said, in a loud voice, "Hi, my name's Eleanor Kirkland. You looking for me?" The man nodded and took her bags. Rule watched them disappear around a corner. Baffled, she went to the foreign currency window and exchanged some dollars for kroner, something she hadn't had time to do in New York. She had just finished the transaction when there was a piercing scream from across the terminal.

Rule looked up from her purse to see a chunky woman in a smock standing a few yards down the corridor, in the act of being hysterical. She was screaming something in Swedish and pointing around the corner. Rule, in company with a dozen other curious people, was drawn to where she was standing. Around the corner, the door to a maintenance closet was open. Inside, on the floor, amidst a great deal of blood, lay the American woman. Her throat had been opened with something sharp.

Rule backed away through the crowd, then turned and headed for the outside doors and a taxi stand, trying not to scream herself. She tried to stay calm through a two-minute wait for a taxi, then got into one and said, "Grand Hotel, please."

The cab pulled away. "You are English?" the driver asked, pleasantly. She jerked her head up and found his eyes in the rearview mirror. He was young, blond, bland-looking, everything an American expected from a Swede. He was watching her carefully in the mirror.

"Yes," she said. "English."

"You stay at the Grand?" he asked.

"No," she said. "No, I'm meeting friends there. I'm staying in the country with them."

"Where?" he asked. "I am from the country, too."

She searched her mind for the name of some Swedish town and came up dry. "I can't remember the name," she said, finally. "Your Swedish names are difficult for me. How long a drive is it to the hotel?"

"At this time of day, perhaps thirty-five, forty minutes."

She laid her head back on the seat and closed her eyes. He seemed to take the hint. She saw little of the city on the drive. She was confused and frightened and thought nothing of her surroundings until the taxi stopped. "What?" she said, sitting straight up.

"Grand Hotel," the driver said.

She jumped as the taxi door opened. A uniformed doorman stood, waiting for her to leave the cab. A man and a woman waited impatiently behind him. She paid the driver and got out. A porter took her bag and led her to the reception desk.

"My name is Katharine Rule," she said to the receptionist. "I have a room booked."

He consulted a card file. "Yes, Miss Rule, your room is ready. May I have your passport, please?"

She gave it to him, explaining about her name. "Have I had any telephone calls?" She had booked the room under Rule. She prayed nobody had called.

"Yes," said the receptionist, taking a slip of paper from a pigeonhole, along with a key. "A Mr. Lee called from Copenhagen. He will call again later."

"Thank you," she said, relieved. "I would be very grateful, in the event that anyone else should call, if you would list my name with the operator as Callaway. My friends here know me by my maiden name."

"Of course," the man said, scribbling a note.

"And if anyone should ask for Katharine Rule, please tell them there is no one registered here by that name."

The man stared at her for a moment, then scribbled again. "If you wish it, of course, that is what we will say." He handed her a key. "You are on the top floor, with a view of the water," he said. "I am sorry I don't have a clerk to take you up at the moment, but if you will kindly take the lift up, then turn right, the room will be a few doors down on your right. I will send a porter up with your luggage shortly."

"Thank you," she said. She walked to the elevators. The door opened and she got on. A man got on behind her, and the doors closed. He was taller than she, with a strong jaw and a muscular build. Blond again, and bland. He looked at her and said something in Swedish. She smiled tightly and ignored him.

"I am sorry," he said in English. "You are American?" He had hard, cold eyes.

"English," she said, and looked away toward where the floor indicator lights were slowly blinking.

"Welcome to Sweden," he said with a small smile.

Oh, God, please let this thing move faster, she prayed. She edged a hand behind her as if rubbing her back. The hand rested on the butt of the pistol. "Thank you," she said. The elevator stopped, and the doors opened.

"After you," the man said, making an ushering motion.

She walked quickly out of the elevator and turned right, shooting a glance over her shoulder. The man had turned to the left.

Her heart pounding, she walked down the corridor, looking for her room. The door opened into a vestibule; another door opened into what looked like the living room of a suite. She hadn't reserved a suite. Then she heard a man's voice, speaking softly, from the room. She couldn't make out the language. She checked the key number with the number on the door. This was her room, and a man was in it.

Rule got a firm grip on the pistol, flipped off the safety, took a deep breath, and stepped through the door, the gun held out in front of her with both hands, as she had been trained. Two men were sitting at a table, having breakfast.

"Kate?" one of them said. "Jesus Christ, Kate!"

"Will!" she cried. "Appicella!" She was shouting, now.

"Calm yourself," Appicella commanded. "And put down that pistol at once."

49

Helder looked at his watch, then at the waters about him. It had been three-quarters of an hour since he had grounded the sub, and still no vessel had hove into view since he had seen the yacht. He turned to the exec. "I'm going below for some coffee," he said. "Call me the moment the first naval vessel appears."

Kolchak, the political officer, gaped at him. "How can you go below at a time like this? It is desertion of post."

"Oh, shut up, Kolchak," Helder said, wearily. "See if you can't do your miserable job without opening your yap again."

Kolchak looked as if he might explode. Helder, for one, didn't give a damn if he did. Judging from the smirks of the other officers, neither did they. Helder climbed down the companionway ladder, motioned the navigation officer out of his seat, and sat down at the chart table. A cup of coffee materialized beside him.

Helder stared at the large-scale chart before him. Apart from navigating on his two trips into the archipelago, he had never paid much attention to the surrounding territory. Now, with his finger, he traced the towns and cities scattered among the islands. Stockholm was a very big city, at least a million people, he thought, but there were other places, as well, towns, villages, hamlets. The chart even showed individual houses in the area. Comfortable houses they were; he had seen them through the periscope, and one of them lay only a quarter of a mile from where the sub had grounded. He had talked briefly, comically, with the owner less than an hour before. These people had no idea what he had brought with him to this place. No one on the sub had any idea, either, not even the reptilian Kolchak. Kolchak understood only that an order would be received and another given. Helder understood all too much more.

He had avoided giving too much thought to the invasion, to what it would mean to the Swedish people. He had been swept along in the excitement of his own role, of the heights to which he had ascended, of the luxuries he had been shown, of his future rank and career. Soon the Swedes would be like the Czechs, the Poles, the Hungarians. He winced. Like his own people, the Estonians. His parents had been socialists; they had hated the Germans and welcomed the Russians—at least, at first. He wondered what they would think of his role in all this if they were alive today. No, he didn't have to wonder; he knew.

Now, at last, he was confronted with the consequences of his actions. The bomb, waiting out there on the seabed, forced him to face what was at hand. He was an accomplice in a plan to dominate a small nation; he had let his greed overwhelm his scruples when he saw what Majorov had dangled before him. He had acted willingly, enthusiastically, at every step of the way. But now, he had come as far as he could go. He could not even bring himself to doubt that a bomb lay out there; he could no longer rationalize. Now he was responsible.

"Captain!" the shout came over the squawk box. "Contact!"

Helder got to his feet, more slowly than he should have under the circumstances. He climbed the ladder and stepped into the conning tower. The exec handed him the binoculars. Up the channel, from the direction of Stockholm, a patrol boat raced. Helder could see the faces of the young men above the windscreen. To his right, coming up another channel, appeared another boat. The two converged and raced toward his position.

They slowed as they came closer, then stopped, perhaps a hundred yards off. A young officer aboard one of them picked up a loud-hailer. "Captain of the Soviet submarine, I am an officer of the Royal Swedish Navy. I require you to assemble your crew on deck and prepare to receive boarders for an inspection. Do you understand?"

Helder picked up the microphone of his own loud-hailer and said, in Russian, "I demand to see a representative of the Soviet Embassy at once. I will not acknowledge any other communication until I have spoken with this representative." He released the transmit button, then leaned close to the squawk box. "Gun crew, stand by to take your positions on deck."

The Swedish officer consulted a book which someone had handed him. Then, in execrable Russian, he read,

"Your ship has invaded Swedish territorial waters. You are under arrest. Prepare to receive boarders and surrender your weapons."

Helder spoke into the squawk box. "Gun crew on deck."

The forward hatch flew open and men spilled onto deck. They unlashed the gun, and shells were handed up. The crew chief came to attention, facing Helder.

Helder nodded. "Lock and load one round; sight on the vessel to your left." He watched with admiration as they swiftly carried out their orders. When they were loaded and ready, he spoke into the squawk box. "Sparks?"

"Yes, sir?" the voice came back.

"Send FOX."

50

Rule sat as quietly as she could and listened to Will and Appicella tell their story.

"Emilio and I were equally astonished to learn that we both knew you," Will said. "Then, when we got to Ostergarn and I called the hotel in Copenhagen to leave a message for you saying that I'd be late, I got your message. We caught a seaplane to Stockholm and checked in here. I got a suite and canceled your room. Emilio is sleeping next door. Would you like some breakfast?"

"Yes, I believe I would," Rule said. "In spite of everything."

Will ordered her breakfast. "Well, I'm glad we haven't put you off your food, at least. I thought you'd be glad to see us."

"Oh, I'm sorry, Will. I am most certainly very glad to see you both, but . . . well, I'd better bring you up-to-date."

"Please," Will said. "What are you doing in Stockholm?"

"Yesterday, I went to see your boss, told him everything, asked him to go to the president."

"And?"

"He was impressed, I think, but cautious. He wouldn't go to the president, but he put me in touch with a man named Sven Carlsson, who's high up at the Ministry of Defense here. I'm hoping I can convince him to go to his minister and maybe the prime minister. Emilio, where is this material you stole from Majorov's computer?"

"In my pocket," Appicella replied, "but we'll have to find an IBM computer in order to be able to read it. I know a fellow at a computer shop in Stockholm where we might be successful." He looked at his watch. "He will be open at ten. Have your breakfast; then we'll go to see him. I think what I have brought will help to convince this fellow at the ministry. I may be able to get you a great deal more. We'll see."

"Fine," she said.

"Listen, Kate," Will broke in. "You're reacting oddly to all this. I would have thought you'd be extremely happy to get what Emilio has brought you."

"Oh, Will, I am happy about that but I haven't told you everything." She told him what had happened at the airport earlier that morning.

"And you think he was waiting for you?" Will asked.

"I haven't the slightest doubt he was waiting for me. No one in Stockholm, except you, knew that anyone named Rule would be here. Don't you see what that means?"

"It means somebody found out, I guess."

"Exactly. And they found out from somebody in Washington."

"Who knew you were coming?"

"I'm not sure, anymore; I've no way of knowing who's talking to whom. The point is, somebody wanted very badly for me not to reach Carlsson."

"You got any idea who?"

Rule explained about Snowflower. "It was Simon's operation. He's terrified that it will come to light. He's trying to force me out of the Agency."

"But Jesus, Kate, he wouldn't resort to killing you to get you out of the Agency, would he?"

She shook her head. "No, at least not for any personal reason."

"What other reason could he have?"

"Well, there's Snowflower. He certainly doesn't want any light thrown on that. But Simon wouldn't kill me to save his career. Not his career with the Company, anyway."

Appicella spoke up. "I think maybe something is rotten in Denmark."

"I was just thinking back," Rule said. "When Simon was head of the Rome station—that's when we met, you'll recall—he was friendly with one of the Soviets in their embassy. They did quite a lot of drinking together. It isn't all that unusual in the field; if one of our people can cultivate one of their people, sometimes we can turn him."

"Or the other way around," Will said, slowly.

There was a knock at the door. A waiter wheeled in a tray and bustled about, setting it up. He switched on the television. "You have not seen the excitement?" he asked. "Look."

Rule, Lee, and Appicella stared at the television set. The shot was from a helicopter. In the upper right-hand corner, a Soviet Whiskey class submarine sat, immobile. The remainder of the screen was filled with a variety of Swedish naval vessels.

"None of us speaks Swedish," Rule said to the waiter. "Where is this happening?"

"It is a little island in the archipelago, called Hoggarn. Only about seven or eight kilometers from Stockholm." He went to the desk and got a tourist's map of Sweden. "It is just about here," he said, pointing. "The submarine has been there since early this morning." He left them staring at the map.

"Well," Rule said, finally, "it's starting."

51

Trina Ragulin reported to work for the first time in a week. The bruises on her face had faded to the point where a little makeup would cover them, and the bruises on other parts of her body were better, too. She could walk without pain.

She was sent to a building in the headquarters complex that she had never before visited. When she entered the building, she found it was one large room, a sort of theater, with wide tiers holding desks with telephones and computer terminals, and they all faced a wall filled with three large screens. The center screen contained a huge map of the entire Baltic area, and there were dozens of markings scattered over it, in Sweden and in Poland, Lithuania, Latvia, and Estonia, apparently designating different sorts of military units—air, armor, ships, submarines, and troops. She was surprised to see that one of the symbols for a Soviet submarine was placed in the Stockholm Archipelago, only a few kilometers from the city itself. In the center of the room, at a desk which was clean except for a black telephone console with many buttons and a single, white instrument, sat Majorov.

"We have the Swedish television transmission," someone called to Majorov.

"Put it on screen three," Majorov replied.

An image appeared on the right-hand screen, and to Ragulin's astonishment, it was of Jan Helder. He was being photographed from a distance, standing in the conning tower of a submarine. There were other men with him, but she did not recognize them. Then the screen changed, and she was watching an aerial view of a large area. The submarine was prominent, and it was surrounded by a number of other vessels.

"Trina!" Majorov's secretary called to her. "Man the galley, there, in the center. Keep coffee and food coming to whoever wants it."

She went to a freestanding galley area placed in the center of the theater, toward the rear, and made herself busy. She had known about plans for the invasion, since she had been working at headquarters for more than a year, and even though she had not worked for a week, she had known from Helder that it was about to go. Still, she was rattled by the idea that it was really happening, and stunned to find Helder at the center of it. She took a tray to Majorov's desk.

"Thank you, Ragulin," he said, smoothly, smiling at her. "Glad to see you back. I hope you had a nice rest."

"Yes, thank you," she managed to say through her anger. The bastard. He had nearly put her into the hospital.

Jones was at a desk next to Majorov's. "Colonel," he

called, "we have a report from Stockholm. The woman, Kirkland, was intercepted at the airport and liquidated."

"Excellent," Majorov said, smiling broadly. "My compliments to Ferret in the next transmission to him." He laughed. "Well, no, perhaps not. They were once rather close; we don't want to upset him, do we?" The white phone on his desk rang; its tone was distinctive, and instantly, the room became hushed. Majorov picked up the phone. "This is Majorov," he said.

There was a pause while he listened. "Yes, Comrade Chairman," he replied. "We are at FOX, now. Helder is refusing all cooperation; he is speaking to them only in Russian. We are holding at the moment, waiting for WIG units in Estonia and Poland to report back, and for confirmations from SPETSNAZ units in Sweden to signal that they are in position. I estimate conditions will be ideal to go very soon." He smiled. "Yes, indeed, Comrade, thank you." He hung up and said to the room at large, "The First Secretary of the Party sends his regards to you all."

There was an excited murmur in the theater. Ragulin continued on her rounds with food and coffee. Suddenly, there was a chorus of shouts. She looked up at the screen receiving Swedish television. A larger ship, a destroyer, was steaming into the fleet surrounding the submarine. There was scattered applause in the room.

"Well, well," Majorov called out. "They're getting serious. Let's see how long it will be, now, before somebody fires a round, eh?"

Ragulin stared at the colonel. So that was why Jan's submarine was where it was; Majorov was using him to provoke the Swedes. She stared at the image on the screen. What would become of her if Jan were killed? Without his protection, she would be back in Majorov's stable, an animal to be regularly used and abused. And sooner or later, she knew, Majorov would kill her. And he would enjoy doing it. She finished her rounds and stationed herself at the galley, from which she had an excellent view of everything and could easily overhear Majorov's conversation.

"Has there been any sighting of Appicella or Lee?" Majorov asked Jones.

"No, sir," Jones replied. "Perhaps they have not gone to Stockholm at all."

"Perhaps not," Majorov replied, "but we will take no chances. I want a watch kept on the American Embassy and the Ministry of Defense until we jump off."

"Group One still has watchers at both places, sir. I have not recalled them."

"I want them killed on sight," Majorov said. "We are at too late a stage to worry about manners on the streets of Stockholm."

52

Rule waited impatiently. She, Appicella, and Will were in the cramped service department of a computer shop near the center of Stockholm. Appicella and the shop owner, a man named Rolf, were lifting a new computer from a box and setting it on the workbench.

"I knew," Appicella was saying, "that if anyone in Scandinavia had an IBM PC AT, it would be you, Rolf." He turned to Rule. "Rolf has always run the hottest shop in Europe," he said.

"That is so much bullshit, if you will forgive me," Rolf said jovially to Rule. "Every time Emilio is in Stockholm, he wanders in here wanting to use my equipment to make money for himself. All I ever get for my trouble is flattery."

"And an occasional very clever modification," Appicella said. "I might even have something new for you, if this works the way I expect it to." He connected the monitor and keyboard to the computer, then connected it to a printer next to it on the workbench.

"This machine has never been turned on, let alone burned in," Rolf said, worriedly. "If you screw it up, I won't get hold of another for months. I'm counting on this as a demonstrator to pull in orders."

"Fear not," Appicella said. "By the time I have finished here, it will be not only burned in, but thoroughly checked out by an expert and, perhaps, even enhanced."

"Oh, my God," said Rolf, rolling his eyes.

Appicella took a blank diskette, pried open its paper flap with a small screwdriver, and removed the disc of mylar plastic from inside. Then he took a penlight from his pocket, unscrewed it, and shook the batteries out onto the bench. With them came another mylar disc. He inserted the mylar into the plastic envelope and taped the envelope shut. "There," he said. "Now we will see if this piece of plastic has weathered a bit of abuse, plus a seaborne crossing of the Baltic." He booted the computer, inserted the disc into its floppy drive, and typed something. A list of files came up on the screen. He typed something else, and the printer went into action.

Rule stood and watched, wide-eyed, as the document was printed. "Good God, Emilio," she said, "how did you do this?"

Appicella shrugged. "I simply robbed Majorov's computer," he said. "And when this is finished printing, I am going to rape it."

"Who is Majorov?" Rolf wanted to know. "I thought I knew everybody in the business here."

"He is in quite another business, my dear Rolf," Appicella said. "If you will forgive such a liberty in your own place of business, I think my friends would like a bit of privacy. Do you mind?"

Rolf threw up his hands. "Mind? Why should I mind? We won't get any repair work done this morning, and half a dozen customers will want my head, but what the hell? If I can make Emilio Appicella happy . . ." He walked out and closed the door.

"Emilio," Rule said, reading the document as it was printed, "you should be a full-time spy, you know." She looked up at him. "What were you talking about, raping his computer?"

"That will take a little longer, I am afraid," Appicella replied. "I'll explain when I've done it."

The printer stopped, and Rule began tearing the continuous pages of the document apart. "Look, I've got to get over to the ministry and see Carlsson. Emilio, you'll be working here for a while, right? I think it's important that you not leave here and go wandering around the city. Majorov has surely missed you by this time, and he can't be very happy with you."

"Don't worry," Appicella said. "I have plenty to keep me busy while you save Sweden from the Russians."

"Will," she said, "I don't like asking you to take risks, but will you come to the ministry with me? You work for Senator Carr, and you might enhance my credibility with Carlsson."

"Risk? What risk?"

"I think you ought to consider that there might be people looking for you around Stockholm, even as we speak. They took a swipe at me this morning and hit somebody else instead, so maybe they think I'm dead. On the other hand, if they've found out they hit the wrong person, they might still be looking for a woman alone. I think we might be less conspicuous together. They're probably not looking for a couple."

"Okay, I'm with you," he said.

Rule asked Rolf to look up the address of the ministry, and they got a cab in the street.

"Shouldn't we telephone ahead?" Lee asked.

Rule shook her head. "I don't trust the telephone right now," she said.

The cab drove them to what seemed a side street off a small square and stopped in front of an unprepossessing doorway. "This is the address," the driver said.

"Not very impressive, is it?" Lee said, as they got out of the cab. "I was expecting a sort of Scandinavian Pentagon, I guess."

Rule didn't respond. She was busy seeming not to notice a car parked down the street, with the silhouette of a man at the wheel. They went inside and found themselves in a small vestibule, faced with a set of double doors. To their right was a small window at which sat a man in uniform.

"Good morning," Rule said to the guard. "Would you please tell Mr. Sven Carlsson that Brooke Kirkland of Washington, DC is here to see him?"

"And the gentleman's name?"

"Mr. Lee. Would you say to Mr. Carlsson that he works for Senator Carr?"

"Is he expecting you?" the guard asked.

"Yes, but not necessarily at this hour, and he is not expecting Mr. Lee."

The man made a telephone call and spoke in rapid Swedish for a few moments, then waited for what seemed a long time. Finally, he hung up. "Someone will be down for you directly," he said, then went back to his work.

Perhaps three minutes passed; then a woman appeared on the other side of the double doors. There was a buzzing sound, and the doors opened. "Miss Kirkland? Mr. Lee? Would you come with me, please?"

They walked a few yards down a hallway, then took an elevator up a couple of floors. They emerged into a hallway that was a balcony supported by marble columns, overlooking a large work area filled with desks, on the ground floor.

"It looks more like a bank than a ministry," Lee said.

"It used to be a bank," the woman replied.

The sounds of the work going on below were a distant murmur, barely penetrating what seemed an unnatural quiet. The woman turned left into an oak-paneled reception room, onto which two sets of double doors opened. She knocked at the doors on her right, then opened them and ushered Rule and Lee into a comfortably furnished office overlooking the square through which they had passed. A man rose from a desk and came around to meet them.

"Miss Kirkland, I believe? I am Sven Carlsson. Senator Carr told me to expect you, but I did not know at what time." He had quite gray hair over an unlined face, and the combination made his age difficult to guess. Somewhere between thirty-five and fifty, Rule thought. He wore rimless glasses of a modern design.

"Mr. Carlsson, it is very kind of you to see us on such short notice."

"Please," he said, motioning them toward a leather sofa across the room.

"How can I be of service?" Carlsson asked, when they had arranged themselves.

"It is we who wish to be of service to you, Mr. Carlsson," Rule said. "First of all, I should tell you that my name is not Kirkland; the senator and I thought it would be better, in the circumstances, if I used that name." She produced her identification card. "My name is Katharine Rule, and I am an official of the Central Intelligence Agency of the American government. I am the head of what is known as the Soviet Office, the department charged with analyzing intelligence from the Soviet Union."

"I see," Carlsson said, examining the card carefully.

She gestured toward Lee. "This is Mr. Will Lee, who is Counsel to the Senate Intelligence Committee, and who is, as such, an assistant to Senator Carr."

Will handed Carlsson his own Senate identification.

"Mr. Lee," Carlsson said, "I believe I have heard Senator Carr speak of you when I was in Washington a short time ago."

"We are here," Rule said, "because we have important information concerning Swedish defense which has been developed by my department at the Central Intelligence Agency. Because of the shortness of time, and for other reasons too complicated to go into at the moment, I felt I should not wait until this information could be transmitted through normal governmental and diplomatic channels. I went to Senator Carr, and after hearing what I had to say and examining my evidence, he advised me to come directly to Stockholm and present myself to

DEEP LIE / 393

you, in the hope that you would bring this evidence to the immediate attention of the minister of defense and the prime minister."

"Well, Miss Rule," Carlsson said, "you have certainly gained my undivided attention. What is it you wish to tell us?"

Rule handed him the document Appicella had stolen from Majorov's computer. "If you will read the summary at the head of this document, that will explain the essence of what I have to tell you."

Carlsson quickly read the brief summary, then read it again without expression. He then quickly flipped through the other pages, glancing at the contents. Finally, he looked up at Rule. "I am flabbergasted," he said. "If you are who you say you are, and not a writer of spy fiction . . ." He seemed to grope for words. "May I ask the origin of this document?"

"It was taken from a computer at a secret Soviet military installation on the Latvian coast less than forty-eight hours ago," Rule replied. "I have every reason to believe that it is a serious statement of Soviet intentions, and not simply a training exercise or a war game. Let me show you other corroborating evidence which has come from divergent sources."

Rule quickly took him through the same presentation she had given Senator Carr the day before. Carlsson listened with apparent growing concern, occasionally interrupting with a question. When she had finished, Carlsson was quiet for a moment.

"Tell me," he said, finally, "do you have any indication of when this plan is to go into effect?"

"I believe it may already have begun," Rule replied. "I believe the Soviet submarine which your navy now has at bay in the archipelago may be a part of it, perhaps intended to provoke an incident. Mr. Carlsson, the first document I showed you states that the invasion would only be carried out under conditions of absolute surprise. If you can persuade your minister and your prime minister to issue an immediate mobilization order, you may very well force the Soviets to abort their operation. I hope it is not already too late."

"I see," Carlsson said, gazing toward the windows.

"Something else," she said. "This morning at Stockholm Airport, an American woman named Kirkland was murdered. I think I was the intended victim. Somebody knew I was coming to Stockholm. Did anyone else in Stockholm besides you know that I was coming?"

"No. No one," Carlsson replied.

"Have you spoken to Senator Carr again since his initial call yesterday?"

"No."

Rule slumped back into her seat. "I see," she said.

"Miss Rule," Carlsson said, "I must ask to borrow for a few minutes this material you have just shown me. Will you please wait here until I return?"

"Of course," Rule replied.

Carlsson gathered up the file and left the room.

"I think the minister's office must be just across the reception room," Rule said to Lee. "Senator Carr told me their offices are adjacent."

"I think you convinced him, Kate," Lee said. "He looked pretty shaken."

"I hope so," Rule replied. "I hope I shook him to his roots."

"You think Simon alerted the Soviets that you were coming to Stockholm?"

"I hate to say it of the father of my child, but it looks that way. If Senator Carr didn't tell Carlsson my real name, then that information had to come from Washington, and Simon is shaping up awfully well as the source. I haven't had a chance to tell you this, but he's had a private investigator following me for weeks. I had a little confrontation with the guy at the airport on my way here. I persuaded him to talk to me, and he says Simon wants his son, which I have every reason to disbelieve. He wanted information for entirely different reasons, I think."

"I'm sorry, Kate," Will said. "I know you don't like the guy, but still . . ."

"Right, it won't be very good for Peter when his father is exposed as a spy for the Soviets. There's never been a mole in the Agency, you know. All hell is going to break loose when I get back."

The two of them sat, then paced around the office for another twenty minutes before Carlsson returned.

"I've talked with the minister," he said. "He's on the phone to the prime minister now. He has already given the order to mobilize. By dinnertime tonight, every important military and civilian target will be secure. We cannot thank you enough, Miss Rule, Mr. Lee."

Rule was suddenly very tired. She had come all this way, and she had been too worried to hope that her story would be believed in time. "Mr. Carlsson, I am grateful for your trust. Is there anything else I can do to help you in this matter?"

"I don't believe so," Carlsson said. "But I would be grateful if you would hold yourself in readiness for another twenty-four hours, in case we need to talk with you again."

"May I ask you, please, to keep my name and that of Mr. Lee out of this? I am here entirely unofficially, and any sort of publicity would cause me very serious problems at home."

"Of course," Carlsson said, "I understand completely. You may be sure that we will not broadcast that we learned of this from the CIA. There are any number of people in our government who would be happy to take the credit, believe me." He handed her back the documents she had brought. "We have copied these, so you may have your originals back. May I suggest that you return to your hotel and wait for word from me there? My car is waiting for you downstairs."

"Thank you. Yes, we'll go back to the Grand," Rule said.

Carlsson walked them down the hall to the elevator.

"I can't believe it's over," Rule said as the elevator took them down. "I think I had begun to believe that it would never end, that I would go on and on, trying to convince somebody of what was happening."

"You've done a sensational job," Will said. "And there'll be more to do when you get home."

The elevator stopped and they got out. "I know, and I'm not looking forward to it."

They walked toward the front door. As they reached

it, Rule stopped and nodded toward the street. A car had pulled up to the door, and a chauffeur stood next to it, waiting.

"That'll be Carlsson's car," Will said. "He said it would be waiting for us."

"Yes, he did," she replied tonelessly. "And the driver is the man who was at the airport to meet me this morning."

53

Oskar Oskarsson had slept late, as had become his habit in recent weeks. This morning, when he came downstairs, his daughter-in-law was setting the table for lunch. The television set was on, which was not unusual, since the woman kept it on all the time, whether she was interested or not. Oskarsson thought she liked the noise. He rarely watched it himself.

But this morning, as he glanced at the set while he poured coffee, he was riveted. There was a Russian submarine on the screen. "What is it, Ilsa?" the old man asked his daughter-in-law. "What is happening?"

"Oh, God, I should have turned it off," she said, and went to do so.

"Stop!" he commanded. "I want to see this."

"Oh, Papa," Ilsa said, "it will only upset you. You shouldn't watch."

"I am watching," Oskarsson said. "Go about your business."

She stood and watched with him. "It can't be an accident," she said. "Not this time. I think I believed them when the one was stuck at Karlskrona that time, but not this time."

"Hush, woman!" Oskarsson ordered. "I must hear this."

Oskarsson listened, his eyes widening. He learned that the sub was aground on an island called Hoggarn. He knew this island; he had passed it many times on his patrols. It was less than three kilometers from his son's house.

Ilsa had turned away to get plates for lunch. When she turned back, her father-in-law was gone.

Oskarsson heard her call, briefly, over the rumble of the engines. Then her calls were behind him, fading, as he roared down the archipelago.

54

Rule leaned against the marble wall and tried to slow her breathing.

Will stood next to her. "Listen, are you sure it's the same guy, and not just another man in a chauffeur's uniform? Maybe he really is just Carlsson's driver."

"You're damned right, I'm sure," Rule said. "And another thing—I doubt very much if civil servants in this country are entitled to chauffeured cars. They take their socialism seriously here."

"We've got to find another way out of here," Will said, looking about him. They were standing in a hallway, which seemed to lead only further into the building.

"And then what?" Rule asked. "Where are we going to go? Carlsson is obviously working for the Soviets; he'll have the town scoured for us. We can't go back to the hotel. We can't even go out onto the street!"

There was a buzzing sound, and a large man in naval uniform came through the front door, accompanied by a civilian carrying a briefcase. Both men glanced at Rule and Lee as they brushed past. The navy man said something in Swedish. Rule smiled and nodded. The two men stopped, and the officer spoke again.

"I'm sorry," Lee said. "We don't speak Swedish."

"Good morning," the officer said in English. "May I ask what you are doing in this building?"

"Good morning, Captain," Lee said, guessing at the man's rank. "We had an appointment this morning . . . Excuse me. May we introduce ourselves? My name is Will Lee," he said, showing his Senate identification. "I am employed by the Intelligence Committee of the United States Senate. This is Katharine Rule, who is an official of the American Central Intelligence Agency." Rule showed her identification card.

"Do you know Senator Benjamin Carr?" the civilian asked.

"Yes, indeed," Will replied. "I work for Senator Carr; it was he who sent Miss Rule to Stockholm."

"On what business?" the captain asked, looking puzzled.

Rule started to speak, to blurt out her story, but Will interrupted. "We have some important information concerning the Soviet submarine which is now aground in the Stockholm Archipelago," he said. "We have just communicated this information to Mr. Sven Carlsson, Head of Chancery, but . . . tell me, Captain, do you know if Mr. Carlsson has at his disposal a car and driver?"

"He does not," the civilian said. "Carlsson rides a motorbike to work every morning."

"Have you ever seen the man in the chauffeur's uniform standing just outside the front door?" Will asked.

Both men walked a few steps back to the door, looked out, and came back. "No," the captain said. "He is not an employee of this ministry."

Rule spoke up. "Captain, we believe there may have been a very serious breach of security in the Ministry of Defense, which is connected with the Soviet submarine in the archipelago. I wonder if there is somewhere we could talk about this for a few minutes in private."

The captain again inspected their identification, then looked questioningly at the civilian, who nodded. "Will you follow us, please?" the officer said. He led the way to the elevator and up to the floor they had just left. To Rule's alarm, they were proceding in the direction of Carlsson's office. Then, to her horror, they turned into Carlsson's reception room. The secretary at her desk looked up, surprised to see them. "Good morning, sir," she said, standing.

"No calls for a while," the civilian said, turning to his left and into the office across from Carlsson's.

They emerged into a very large, paneled room, elegantly furnished. "Now, Mr. Lee, Miss Rule," the officer said. "I am Captain Holmquist of the Royal Swedish Navy." He indicated the civilian. "This is Mr. Bjorn Westberg, the minister of defense. What is it you wish to tell us?"

Rule was too overcome with relief to speak immediately, but Lee filled the gap. "I take it, you have not spoken to Mr. Carlsson this morning, Minister?"

"I have been at Stockholm Military District Headquarters at Strangnas all morning," the minister said.

"Minister," Rule said, recovering. "Please read the summary at the head of this document." She took it from her file and handed it to him.

Westberg read the page, then handed the document to the captain, while Rule began to spread her file on a small conference table. It was the third time in two days she had made this presentation, and she was becoming practiced. She went through it quickly, emphasizing the need for an immediate mobilization of Swedish forces. Jet lag and a lack of sleep were preying on her, now. "May I?" she asked, picking up a crystal water decanter and a glass.

"Of course," Westberg said. "Miss Rule, I would like to telephone Senator Carr before I proceed further."

Lee spoke up. "I'll give you his home number," he said, scribbling it on a page of his notebook and ripping it out. "It's early in Washington, but I don't believe he'll mind being waked."

"I don't believe we need disturb the senator." The voice came from behind them, and they all turned to face the door. Carlsson was standing there, holding a pistol. "I believe I can confirm the essence of what Miss Rule has been telling you. Its all quite true, and she is to be complimented on her work." He stepped further into the room.

"Thank you, Mr. Carlsson," Rule said, wearily, pouring herself a glass of water, "but you've been working on this for longer than I have, haven't you?"

"That's quite correct, Miss Rule," Carlsson replied. "For a very long time, indeed, and I will not allow my work to be ruined by an order to mobilize. Minister, I will shoot and kill all of you, if you make it necessary, but I would rather just have you all sit down quietly and wait with me. In an hour, maybe less, this ministry will be under Soviet control, as will Stockholm and most of Sweden, and I will be heading a provisional government. While we wait for that to happen, I will fill you in on the details." He stepped up to the conference table, picked up the telephone, and pushed a button, watching them all carefully. "Miss Holm," he said to the secretary in the adjoining room, "there is a chauffeur waiting at the front of the building. Would you please ask the security guard to send him to me here? Show him directly in, please. Thank you." He hung up the phone.

As Carlsson did so, Rule threw both the heavy crystal decanter and the glass at him, pushing them away from her like a basketball. Carlsson flinched, but the decanter struck him in the face, smashing his glasses. As he fell backwards, his gun fired, shattering the telephone on the desk. Rule had her pistol in both hands, ready to fire, but it was unnecessary.

Lee had reached Carlsson first, and Captain Holmquist was not far behind. Carlsson struggled wildly, yelling in Swedish, but in a moment the two large men had him facedown, with his arms pinned behind him. The captain cuffed him hard across the head. "Shut up, you bastard," he said in English.

"The man downstairs is probably a Soviet SPETSNAZ assassin," Rule said to the minister. "He killed a woman at Stockholm airport this morning, thinking she was I. Something had better be done about him at once."

The minister picked up the phone and began speaking in rapid Swedish. "The security guard had not yet admitted the man. I've told him to call the police and have them deal with him."

"Are you convinced, Minister?" Rule asked. "Or do you still want to call Senator Carr?"

"As Carlsson said," the minister replied, "it won't be necessary to disturb the senator." He turned to the naval captain. "Holmquist, transmit an order to military district headquarters that, under no circumstances, is the Soviet submarine to be fired upon, no matter what the provocation. Then get us a helicopter here at once. I'm going out to the archipelago and take personal charge of operations there. Then call the prime minister, tell him what is happening, and be sure that security is airtight around him. Also, call the counterintelligence department at the state police and get them over here to interrogate Carlsson. I want to know everything he knows." He picked up a phone again, dialed a number, and began barking orders in Swedish.

A pair of security guards, pistols drawn, appeared at the door, attracted by the gunshot. They quickly handcuffed Carlsson.

The minister hung up the phone. "Take Carlsson to his office," he said, "and keep him there for questioning." He turned to Rule. "Every military installation and critical civilian facility will be placed under heavy guard immediately, and a general mobilization will commence." Outside, a distant siren began to wail; then another and another. "There it goes." He smiled. "It's nice to get such quick attention to an order. I hope it's not too late.

Miss Rule, would you and Mr. Lee like to come with me?"

In the distance, and growing closer, the chop-chop of a helicopter could be heard.

"It might be safer than Stockholm," Rule said.

55

Trina Ragulin watched, fascinated, as, one by one, the symbols on the theater's central screen changed from red to green.

"WIG Group One is go," Jones called out, and Ragulin watched as the figure of an airplane in Estonia changed colors.

Majorov punched a button on his black phone. "Group Five in Göteborg is go!" he called. "Group Seven at the Norwegian border road is go!"

"We have enough to move, Colonel," Jones shouted. "We can go now."

"No," Majorov said. "We have five units to hear from, and I want them fully deployed and ready before I ask the chairman for a go order."

"Group Four at Karlskrona has reported, sir!" someone called out, and its symbol went green.

Majorov was standing, now, and he suddenly looked worried. "We don't have a go from Group One in Stockholm or Group Three in Strangnas. What reports do we have from them? We can't go without those two."

"I don't understand it," Jones said. "Group One has been in place longer than any other. What can be keeping them?"

"They are still looking for Appicella and Lee," Majorov said, sitting down again. "Signal them to forget the surveillance and regroup at once. I want them ready, now!"

Jones answered a ringing phone, said a few words, and turned toward Majorov. "We have a signal from Group Three in Strangnas. Stockholm Military Headquarters appears to be conducting a drill. Gates have been sealed and troops are being deployed at the perimeter in armored carriers."

"That's not possible!" Majorov cried. "There is no drill scheduled there for another week! Carlsson gave us the schedules!"

Jones punched another button and listened. "Colonel, Group One is reporting civil defense sirens in Stockholm! What the hell is going on?"

As he spoke, Ragulin watched the screen on the right-hand side of the theater change from the scene of the grounded submarine in the Stockholm Archipelago to a man behind a desk in a studio.

"Give me sound on screen three!" Majorov shouted.

". . . to our central studios in Stockholm," a voice said. The man behind the desk shuffled his papers and began. "The Ministry of Defense, a few moments ago, issued a call for a general mobilization of all Sweden. All military leave is canceled. All members of the armed forces are ordered to report to their units immediately. All members of the military reserve and civil defense units are ordered to their preassigned positions at once. All Swedish subjects who are not members of military reserve or civil defense units are asked to remain at their current locations until requested to move. Office and factory workers not called up are instructed to remain at their places of work. All private motor vehicles are to be immobilized in order to leave streets and roads clear for military and civil defense vehicle movements. All Swedish subjects are requested to limit their use of telephones to cases of serious emergency. The government and Members of Parliament have already begun to disperse to preassigned, secure locations. The minister of defense is flying to the island of Hoggarn, in the Stockholm Archipelago, in order to take personal charge of dealing with the Soviet submarine which ran aground there early this morning. For further mobilization instructions, tune in to your local radio stations." He began to repeat the bulletin.

Majorov was standing again. "I don't believe it. This can't be happening!" he shouted. The white telephone on his desk, with its distinctive ring, suddenly brought the room to a halt. There was an immediate hush. Majorov stared at the telephone as if it were a poisonous reptile, while it continued its loud ringing. Finally, he picked it up.

"This is Majorov. I know, Comrade Chairman. We have just seen the report on Swedish television. I have reason to believe it may be a defensive hoax. I request permission to hold my forces in readiness while I receive reports from my units in Sweden. Yes, Comrade Chairman, no more than thirty minutes." He put the phone down.

"Defensive hoax?" Jones was standing at his desk, calling to Majorov. "Group One has already reported a general alarm in Stockholm, and Group Three has reported the sealing of the Strangnas headquarters. There can be no hoax!"

"Shut up!" Majorov shouted at him. "I want reports from all units on Swedish soil at once! Broadcast in the clear, if necessary!"

Jones returned to his phones, punching buttons and issuing orders. Ragulin grabbed a bottle of vodka and a glass from the galley, strode the few steps to where Majorov sat, and set them on his desk. She poured a glass of the vodka. "Here, Colonel," she said, hardly disguising her glee. "I think you need this."

"Get away from me!" Majorov shouted, but he picked up the glass in a trembling hand and tossed down the vodka, then poured another. "Reports, Jones!"

"Colonel," Jones called back, "reports of other units confirm Group One. There is a genuine, nationwide, general alarm. Reserve troops have begun to take positions around key targets. I am afraid it is true, Colonel Majorov. Sweden is mobilizing."

Majorov sat stock-still, staring blankly toward the central screen. Red symbols for Swedish military movements were beginning to flash on the screen. The white telephone rang.

Silence quickly blanketed the room again. The piercing ring of the white telephone filled the silent theater. Every man's eyes were on Majorov.

Majorov ignored the ringing of the white telephone. "Jones," he said, quietly, "transmit to Helder's submarine the code 10301."

"Yes, Colonel," Jones replied. He picked up a telephone and spoke into it, then hung up. "Code 10301 has been transmitted, sir," he said.

The white telephone on Majorov's desk stopped ringing.

56

Helder stood in the conning tower of the Whiskey boat and looked about him. Something was wrong. It had gone very quiet.

Kolchak had noticed it, too. It was early afternoon, now, and the wind had dropped, leaving the surface of the sea as placid as a lake. It was very warm, too, and the crew on the deck gun looked drowsy. Then, from across the water, there came a noisy whine. Helder and Kolchak turned in unison to look at the Swedish destroyer steaming slowly along half a mile away. Her guns, previously lowered and trained at sea level toward the grounded submarine, were elevating. On two patrol boats a couple of hundred yards away, gunners stood back from their weapons and let them point at the sky.

"What is it?" Kolchak asked. "What is happening?"

It amused Helder that the man was whispering. "They are backing off," he answered. "They have been told not to fire on us."

"Then we must fire on them," Kolchak said, nervously. "Our orders are to provoke a battle, if necessary, before surrendering."

Helder had no intention of provoking a battle. He did not intend to lose a single man, Russian or Swedish, to Majorov's monumental ambition. "I'll wait for the coded order on that," he said. "That is my prerogative."

"I'm not at all sure that it is," huffed Kolchak. "Surely, we cannot allow this situation to fizzle out."

Helder cocked an ear. "What is that?"

"What is what?" Kolchak asked. "I don't . . . Yes, I do."

From somewhere in the distance, down the channel toward Stockholm, a siren wound up to a pitch.

"A fire in one of the hamlets in the archipelago," Kolchak said.

"A fire in two of them," Helder said, turning to look south. Another siren had started up. Then, as the two men stood listening, the sirens were joined by others, near and far.

"What is going on?" Kolchak demanded. "Is this some sort of trick to unnerve us?"

Helder smiled. "Unnerve you it may, Kolchak, but it is not a trick. The Swedes have tumbled."

"You mean the balloon is going up, as planned?"

"The balloon is not going up, Kolchak. Instead, the penny has dropped."

"Stop speaking in English riddles, Helder; what do you mean?"

From the east, Helder noticed a new sound. At first he thought it another siren, but then it changed, grew into something else. It was coming closer.

"I mean there will be no invasion," Helder said. "The Swedes have sounded the alarm; they are mobilizing. Surprise is lost. There will be no invasion."

Helder leaned over the rail and looked to the east. A boat was coming, and very fast. It looked like some sort of fancy pleasure boat. Probably some excited Swede was coming to have a look for himself. Another sound behind him caused him to turn. A helicopter was approaching, low, from the west, toward Stockholm.

"Of course there will be an invasion!" Kolchak insisted. "Majorov has told us so!"

"As it happens, Kolchak, I was present when the First Secretary of our beloved Party told Majorov that there would be no invasion if surprise was lost." Helder reached for the squawk box. "Number One."

"Yes, sir?" the exec's voice came back.

"Bring up a white flag, and prepare to hoist it."

"What are you talking about?" Kolchak nearly shouted. "Your orders were not to surrender the ship until there had been an exchange of fire!"

Helder turned to watch the fast-approaching powerboat again. "You haven't been listening, Kolchak. It's over. Now we are going to be eating Swedish meatballs for a while."

Another sound stopped Kolchak from replying. A loud, electronic beep ricocheted around the conning tower, followed by another, then another, five in all.

"We've got a code!" Kolchak said, crossing to where the radio receiver was mounted.

Helder followed him. The light-emitting diodes on the receiver spelled out a number: 10301.

"That's it!" Kolchak said. "The invasion is still on! Send the sonar signal!"

The exec came into the conning tower, carrying a white flag.

"Hoist it," Helder said to the man.

Kolchak stepped over to the squawk box. "Radio man!" he shouted into it. "Send your sonar signal!"

"Who is speaking, please?" the voice came back.

"This is Kolchak, dammit, your political officer! Send the sonar signal!"

"I am sorry, sir," the radioman replied, "but I can only send that signal on the captain's order."

Kolchak whipped out his pistol. "Helder!" he shouted. "Give that order at once, or I will shoot you where you stand."

The exec looked on, dumbfounded. Neither he nor the captain was wearing a sidearm.

Helder was looking again at the approaching power-boat, now much closer. He could see a single man, perhaps an old man, aboard. The thing must be doing between forty and fifty knots, he thought. He turned back to the political officer. "Kolchak, if I send that signal, shortly afterwards a nuclear mine will be detonated in the archipelago only a short distance from where we stand."

"What?"

"I know. I placed it there myself. If it goes off, not only will Stockholm be virtually wiped out, but so will you. It will send this submarine and all of us on it straight to hell, do you understand?"

"I understand my orders!" Kolchak yelled. "Give the

instruction to the radioman, or I will kill you and do it myself!"

Helder looked at the astonished executive officer, standing, holding the white flag. "Hoist it," he said.

Kolchak raised the pistol and fired at Helder's head.

RULE looked down from the helicopter and saw a speeding powerboat coming from the east toward where the submarine lay. "Minister, look at that," she said, pointing.

The minister, Lee, and the pilot all craned their necks. The powerboat, with a single man aboard, came flying across the water, parallel with the grounded submarine, then began to execute a ninety-degree right turn, directly toward the sub. A Swedish patrol boat, belatedly, began to give chase. Men aboard other boats pointed, and officers and crew aboard the destroyer rushed to the rail and leaned out to look.

"Jesus Christ," the minister said, "he's going to ram the sub."

Oskarsson came out of the turn at full throttle, both levers jammed all the way forward. The two giant outboards rose in pitch to a scream as they were pushed to maximum revs. Oskarsson chose his course, straight between the conning tower and the deck gun, then looped a length of shock cord over a spoke of the helm. He grabbed the loaded shotgun on the seat beside him, and stepped to the rail. The boat ran, straight and true, over the still water, gaining speed and holding rock steady. Oskarsson hooked a foot under a seat, rested the barrels of the gun on his maimed hand, reaching over with the thumb, and took careful aim. The boat was seventy yards out, then fifty, then thirty. Oskarsson followed the change of angle to a point where a tiny bell rang in his brain.

"Now, Ebbe, now!" he said to his grandson, then pulled both triggers.

Helder staggered, then turned away from Kolchak and looked at the powerboat, coming directly at the sub. The bullet had seared the back of his head as he had turned, and taken away his cap. Now even the enraged Kolchak turned to look at the approaching boat. He rushed to the rail beside Helder.

It was coming dead at them at what seemed an impossible speed. The crew of the deck gun, as a man, flung themselves forward or overboard to escape the onrushing white projectile.

Helder saw the shotgun microseconds before it went off. It seemed to fire at the same moment the hurtling boat struck the deck of the sub.

Rule, with the others, gaped as the uplifted prow of the powerboat struck the low-lying, sloping deck of the submarine. The boat reared at a steep angle and shot across the sub's decks like a water-skier over a jump. It struck the water, perhaps thirty yards the other side of the sub, its stern landing first, then the full length of its bottom slamming into the sea, throwing water to all sides. It barreled on toward the island, and, seconds later, drove straight up through shallow water onto the beach, skidding sideways and coming to rest on the sand. Rule thought she could see a man lying in the back of the boat.

"Pilot," the minister said, "set down on the beach."

Helder thought he must have been out for only a few seconds. He came to, lying on the sole of the conning tower, the exec bending over him.

"Captain! Captain, can you hear me?" the exec was saying.

Helder got up onto one elbow, and immediately was struck by pain from his jaw.

"You've taken a couple of pellets in the neck," the exec said, "and two or three more in the face. I don't think it's bad."

Helder thought it hurt like it was bad; his jaw seemed to be broken. Not as bad as Kolchak, though. He had taken the full force of the shotgun blast in the face, and there were brains and hair spattered over the red star and the numbers painted on the conning tower.

Helder, with the help of the executive officer, struggled to his feet and leaned on the rail of the conning tower. He looked toward the beach, where a helicopter was landing, and people were running toward the big powerboat, now high and dry. A light breeze had sprung up, and the wind ruffled his hair. "I don't know who that fool was," he said to the exec, "but I hope his are the only shots fired in this ridiculous war. Run up the fucking white flag, and be quick about it!"

57

Trina Ragulin watched, with the others, flabbergasted, as the big, white powerboat flew over the submarine. The Swedish television camera angle changed to a close-up of the sub's conning tower. She saw Helder, blood streaming down his face, struggle to his feet and bark an order to another officer. Moments later, a white flag appeared above the sub.

Majorov was on his feet again. "Dammit, Jones, I ordered you to send that signal!"

"It was sent, sir," Jones came back, "and confirmed electronically. But we've had no contact with the buoy via satellite."

"The sub has not sent the sonar signal!" Majorov said, banging a fist on his desk. "Contact them on the radio—do it in the open, if you have to!"

"But sir," Jones said, "they are under radio shutdown, and on your orders. They will not be listening. Their radio is switched off."

"Damn Helder!" Majorov shouted, hammering repeatedly on the desk. "Damn him! I want him shot! Contact Group One in Stockholm. I want him found and killed before he can talk! He has flagrantly disobeyed my most specific orders! He did not signal the mine!"

"Mine, sir?" Jones asked, looking bewildered.

"Contact Group One!" Majorov shouted.

"We can't, sir; they will have already followed their contingency plan in case of a Swedish alarm. They will already have disbursed."

"I want Helder back here! Contact the Stockholm Station, and have them put their men on it!"

"We have no way of directly contacting Stockholm Station, Colonel," Jones replied. "Any contact with the embassy will have to be through Moscow Central."

It was the first time Ragulin had ever seen Majorov other than perfectly composed. She looked back at the screen. Swedish sailors were swarming over the Soviet submarine, and she saw a stretcher being handed down from the conning tower. She could see Helder's face, still bloody, being dabbed at by the other Russian officer. He was in Swedish hands, now. They would never let him go, not after this incident.

The white telephone rang. Majorov stood, apparently trying to compose himself, while it rang again and again. The whole room had stopped, and all eyes were on the Colonel.

Finally, he sank back into his seat and picked up the telephone. "Majorov," he said. "No, Comrade Chairman, we have confirmed that the alarm was not a hoax.

I have given the order to stand down from the invasion plan. No, Comrade Chairman, not a single man has fallen into Swedish hands . . . yes, except for the submarine crew. They had no alternative, of course, but to surrender. I request that the Foreign Ministry begin negotiations at once to recover them, especially the captain. He is one of our best men. . . . You met him in Moscow. Yes, Comrade Chairman, tomorrow morning, I shall be there."

Majorov hung up the phone and slumped in his chair. "Give the order to stand down from the invasion plan," he said to Jones. "I have been called to Moscow for a meeting tomorrow. The plan is not dead, Jones, merely postponed. You will see."

"Yes, Colonel, of course," Jones replied quietly.

Ragulin stood and watched the big screen. The green symbols, one by one, changed to red, then went out. The atmosphere in the theater had changed from enthusiasm to depression. Quietly, people went about the work of clearing up. Soon, the main screen went dark, and only the television screen remained on. Ragulin watched as the stretcher was handed into a boat and driven toward the island in the background. Helder would not come back, she knew, even if the Soviet diplomats were able to negotiate his release. He had disobeyed some important order of Majorov's, and he could not now come back. She was alone again, and more so than ever before.

Lights began to go off in the theater. A soldier in uniform came up to the galley where Ragulin stood. "How about some coffee?" he asked, leaning his weapon against the counter. Ragulin poured the coffee and looked at the weapon. It was the submachine shotgun she had heard about from Helder. She looked at it closely, found the bolt, located the safety. There was a clip already in the weapon.

58

Rule and Lee were standing on the front porch of the beach house on Hoggarn when the submarine commander was brought in on a stretcher. The house had been turned into a command post by the Royal Navy and the press and was teeming with people. The bemused owners were trying to help by making coffee and sandwiches. The place was buzzing with the story of Oskar Oskarsson, the fisherman, who was now inside, holding court for the press.

Two sailors set the stretcher gently on the porch while waiting for instructions. Rule looked down at the bloody and swollen face, which had not yet been bandaged. The man was trying to speak. She bent down, but he seemed to be looking past her.

"Hello, Lee," he managed to say.

"Good God," Will said, bending down. "It's . . . Helder, isn't it?"

The submariner's eyebrows went up. "How did you know my name?"

Lee smiled. "The sketch you drew in Stockholm, the one you gave me; you signed it 'Helder.'"

The man managed a kind of laugh. "Oh, no! And I worked so hard on my cover!"

"Your cover was great," Will said. "I didn't notice the signature until yesterday."

Rule gaped at the two men. "What is going on here?"

"I'll explain later," Will said.

"Lee, I am not going back to the Soviet Union," Helder said. "I will ask to stay in the West."

Will fished his Senate business card from his wallet. "Here's where you can find me. Let me know if I can help."

Helder looked at the card. "A country lawyer, eh? Your cover was pretty good, too. You fooled Majorov."

"I didn't lie to him," Will said. "I just didn't tell him the whole truth."

"Just as he didn't tell me all the truth," Helder said. "He didn't tell me about the bomb."

"Bomb? What bomb?" Rule asked.

"There is a bomb, a nuclear mine, in the archipelago, not far from here."

"Minister!" she called through the front door. "You'd better come out here."

The minister joined them, and Rule listened while Helder explained and gave him the longitude and latitude of the bomb and the frequency of the sonar signal that would release its antenna. "Don't worry," Helder said to the man. "I think it cannot be detonated until the antenna is released."

The minister disappeared into the house.

A man wearing a press badge approached Rule and Lee. "Aren't you Will Lee?" he asked.

"That's right," Lee replied, surprised.

"I'm Fred Allen, Scandinavian correspondent for Cox Newspapers, which include the *Atlanta Constitution*. Don't you work for Senator Carr in Washington?"

"Uh, yes, but I'm just on vacation at the moment."

"Vacation?" the reporter snorted. "What kind of vacation would dump you in the middle of all this?"

The minister walked up. "Oh, this young man is the hero of the story," he said, "and . . ."

Rule caught his eye and shook her head.

"Well, look," the reporter said, "I want to hear all about this."

"Not now," Will said. "Why don't we talk about this later, okay?"

"Only if you promise me not to give it to somebody else first. I want the whole thing from the horse's mouth."

"I promise, nobody else first." He turned to the minister. "Mr. Westberg, I understand all the airports and ports have been sealed. Do you think you could assist us in getting on a plane to New York tonight? I think there's an SAS flight at seven o'clock."

"Of course, Mr. Lee," the minister replied. "I'll send someone with you to the airport to clear the way." He pulled Rule and Lee away from the reporter. "Miss Rule," he said quietly, "I've had a report that there is an Italian at the Grand Hotel in Stockholm holding some sort of auction of what he claims is the Soviet plan to invade Sweden. Do you know anything about this?"

59

Trina Ragulin looked around the theater. It was nearly deserted, now, and without the illumination of the center screen, the lights were low. A few more people shuffled out, and only Jones, Majorov, and the guard were left in the large room with her. The guard had turned to watch the television screen.

Helder was gone from the screen, taken away by the Swedes. He was gone from her, too, and she was left with Majorov.

Majorov spoke into the silence, seeming to think himself alone with Jones.

"By this time next week, I would have been elected to the Politburo," Majorov said. "It had been promised to me by the Chairman himself."

"I am sorry, sir."

"Oh, it will still happen," Majorov said. "But not next week. Tomorrow, I will go to Moscow and stand before the Politburo and put the best face possible on what has happened. I will launch an investigation of how the Swedes learned of our plans, and that will occupy me for some time."

"You don't fear—"

"Punishment for failure?" Majorov interrupted. "Certainly not. I will have the protection of the First Secretary, and of two other members, about whom I have, shall we say, interesting documentary information. Anyway, I have achieved an expansion and upgrading of SPETSNAZ forces that would not have been possible under any other Russian. That will not be forgotten, especially by Admiral Gorshkov, who is the immediate beneficiary of this achievement. No, Jones, I have a great deal in my favor. I still have Ferret, in Washington, and I have run him personally. Ferret alone, with his high position in the CIA, would be enough to guarantee any man's career. I will survive and prosper, Jones, and I will take you with me, fear not."

"You will not survive," Ragulin said, and she immediately had everyone's undivided attention. The soldier came at her, and she shot him once. It was quite enough. She stepped away from the galley, holding the submachine shotgun. Jones had frozen, and now Majorov had stood and was turning to face her.

"Ragulin," Majorov said, quietly, "put down that weapon now, and nothing will have changed. The soldier is of no consequence; I can fix that. You will still have your place here."

"Do you believe that I still want my place here?" Ragulin asked. She turned slightly and shot Jones. He tumbled over the railing behind him and landed on a desk on the next tier down. "Do you believe I would like to spend the rest of my youth as an animal in your stable, available to you or any visitor, beaten and whipped at your command?"

Majorov was edging around his desk, now, his eyes locked on hers. Ragulin could hear footsteps pounding down the stairs that led to the theater.

"They are coming, now, Trina," Majorov said. "Put down the weapon, and I will protect you from them."

"I have previously enjoyed your protection, Majorov," Ragulin said. "And I have no wish to repeat the experience." She flipped the weapon to automatic and squeezed the trigger.

By some weird combination of physical forces, the burst caused Majorov to dance backwards along the railing of the tier, even as he received the rain of antipersonnel buckshot. A second burst lifted him over the railing and bounced his body from tier to tier, down into the well of the theater, where it lay, pieces missing from it, pouring blood into the carpet.

The theater door opened, and two uniformed soldiers burst into the room. Trina Ragulin reversed the shotgun, took the hot barrel into her mouth and pulled the trigger. She never heard the shot.

60

Rule let herself into the suite at the Grand, with Lee close behind. The sitting room was empty, but it was littered with empty glasses and cigarette butts. The furniture was in disarray.

"Jesus," she said, "this place looks like San Juan during the hurricane season. Emilio!" she yelled.

"In here," came a muffled voice from the next room.

She pushed open the door to the adjoining bedroom and went in. Lee followed her. The bedroom was empty.

"In here! Please come in!"

"You'd better go first," she said to Lee, pointing to the bathroom door.

Lee stuck his head in and laughed. "I think it's all right," he said. "You're not all that shy, anyway."

They both walked into the bathroom. Emilio Appicella was up to his ears in a huge bubble bath, with a big cigar stuck in his face.

"Hello!" he said around the cigar. "I hear you have been successful in your mission!"

"Emilio," Rule said, "what's this I hear about your selling the Soviet invasion plans to the press?"

A hand snaked out from under the bubbles, wiped itself on a towel, and removed the cigar from Appicella's face. "Ah, yes," he said, revealing all of his beautiful teeth, "I rang up a few people and organized a little auction. Got thirty thousand dollars from an American wire service. Isn't capitalism wonderful?"

"Emilio, that document was the property of the Central Intelligence Agency," Rule said, sternly.

"Oh, yes?" Appicella hooted. "How much did they pay for it?"

"Well . . ." Rule was flustered. "I'm sure I could have gotten you a very nice gratuity from the Agency."

"Thank you very much," Appicella said, "but I don't accept tips. Anyway, there is no reason for you to be upset. I have a great deal more stuff for you."

She sat down on the toilet lid. "Yeah? What stuff?"

Appicella pointed the cigar. "There is a briefcase on the bed."

"I'll get it," Will said, and came back with a cheap, plastic case.

Rule opened the briefcase. Inside were two fat stacks of computer diskettes and a brown envelope. "What is it?" she asked.

Appicella took a long puff on the cigar before replying. "When I was working on Malibu's computers," he said, finally, "I installed a very special circuit board of my own design. I told Majorov it was a modem, which allowed telephone communications with the computer.

It was that, of course, but much more. With a matching board in Rolf's computer in Stockholm, I was able to telephone Malibu's computer at Malibu and operate it from the keyboard here. Further, I was able to instruct their computer to think of Rolf's computer as just another hard-disc drive." Appicella took another puff and blew a perfect smoke ring. "Then, I simply copied everything on his hard-disc drive to Rolf's hard-disc drive. *Capisci?*"

"Capisco," Rule said, her face lighting up.

"And those floppy diskettes in your very pretty lap contain the entire contents of Malibu's computer," Appicella said, pointing with the cigar. "There are two sets, of course; one should always have a backup copy of everything."

"Tell me," Rule said, narrowing her eyes, "does Majorov know that you have done this?"

"Absolutely not," Appicella said. "He now has a multi-user system. I am simply one of the users, and I can go on using as long as his computer works."

"Is this a gift, Emilio?" Rule asked suspiciously.

"From me to you." The Italian smiled. "Only, please, if the CIA should wish to continue to use Malibu's computer, I will require one hundred thousand dollars for my very special, one-of-a-kind circuit board."

"I will be happy to put that proposition to the Agency on your behalf, Emilio; I don't think there will be any problem."

"Good," he said. "I will ship the board to you on receipt of the money in my Zurich account—ah, the deposit number is written on the envelope, there." Then his face grew serious. "I am afraid I have another gift for you, my dear. In the envelope."

Rule removed a sheaf of papers from the envelope. "What is it?"

"In copying the files, I discovered that some of them were coded. It was quite easy to break into them, of course, since it was I who devised the coding system, on an earlier visit to Majorov. They turned out to be Majorov's personal files, and among them was information about two moles he was personally running, one in Sweden, and one, I am afraid, in the United States. Their names are not mentioned, but the Swedish one is referred to as Seal and the American as Ferret."

"Seal is undoubtedly Carlsson," Rule said, flipping through the pages.

"And Ferret?" Lee asked.

Rule stopped flipping and started reading. "There is an account of how he was recruited," she said, "that identifies him beyond any doubt." Reading the pages, she felt an overwhelming sadness.

"I'm sorry, Kate," Lee said. "I know this isn't very pleasant for you."

Rule stood up. "I need a few minutes to think, Will." She walked back into the sitting room and collapsed in a large chair. For half an hour, she thought the problem through and weighed her alternatives. Finally, she picked up the phone and asked the operator for the dialing code for the United States. She dialed the main switchboard of the Central Intelligence Agency and asked to be connected with the director's office.

"Office of the Director of Central Intelligence," a male voice said.

"This is Katharine Rule," she said, "of the Soviet Office. Let me speak with the director at once, please."

The voice became chilly. "The director is not available at the moment, Mrs. Rule. What is this about?"

"Kindly tell the director that I am telephoning from Stockholm," Rule said. "I believe he will want to speak with me."

"One moment, please," the man said.

There was a delay of a few seconds; then a husky male voice said, "Stockholm? What the hell are you doing in Stockholm, Mrs. Rule? Don't you watch television? Haven't you any idea what's going on there?"

"Is that the director speaking?" Rule asked, politely.

"You're goddamned right it is, and I want to know right now what you are doing in Stockholm. And is this a secure line?"

"It is not a secure line, but we are not going to speak of classified matters during this conversation. I will tell you what I am doing in Stockholm in New York tomorrow morning," Rule said.

"I have a meeting of the National Security Council tomorrow morning, and I have no intention of being in New York."

"Listen to me very carefully," Rule said. "This is very serious. I want you, Simon Rule, Alan Nixon, and Ed Rawls in the first-class lounge of Scandinavian Airways System at six o'clock tomorrow morning."

"What on earth are you talking about, woman?"

"Let me put it this way: there is going to be a very

large contingent of the free American press just outside the first-class lounge. If you are not there, I will talk to them, and believe me, you will not like reading about this in the newspapers."

There was a long moment of silence. "Do you know what you are doing, Mrs. Rule?" the director asked, finally. "Do you know what sort of shape your career is in at the moment? Do you have any idea what is going to happen to you when you return to Langley?"

"I will not be returning to Langley unless you and the group I have requested is in New York tomorrow morning at six. If you are not there, I will be spending a lot of time on television during the coming months. Do we understand each other?"

Another long silence. "All right, Mrs. Rule, we'll be there."

"Something else," Rule said. "None of the others is to know about the meeting until tomorrow morning. Call them at home only just in time to make the chopper."

"Anything else?"

"Yes. I want two FBI agents there. They shouldn't come on the chopper with you, and the others are not to know they'll be there. And you should know that if any attempt is made to arrest or detain me, I have made provisions for the press to be fully informed of all my news."

"All right, godammit!"

"Just one other thing," Rule said. "Tell Simon to bring my son to the meeting. Either Peter is there, or we don't talk. Understood?"

"Understood," the director said, sounding defeated.

"Good-bye," Rule said, and hung up.

She pressed her hands to the back of her neck and rubbed. If she didn't get a bath and some sleep, she wouldn't have the wit to bring this thing off in the morning. And she had to bring it off.

61

Rule felt oddly refreshed as they landed in New York. She had gotten her first real rest in two days in the huge first-class sleeper seats. She turned to Lee, beside her.

"Okay, now, we've got everything straight?"

"You bet."

She handed him a set of the computer diskettes, and a dozen copies of the Majorov files. "Just hang around outside the lounge until we leave. Those press people you called had better be there."

"They'll be there—all three New York dailies, the *Washington Post*, *Time*, and *Newsweek*, the wire services, and all three networks. Senator Carr said to use his name."

"Okay, if I'm taken, kicking and screaming, from this meeting, you talk to them and spread Majorov's files around. You know as much about this as I do now, so I'm depending on you to spread the word if I don't get out of that meeting with my head."

"I like your head where it is; hang on to it."

The pilot's voice came over the loudspeaker system. "Will Mrs. Katharine Rule please identify herself to a flight attendant?"

Rule waved at a stewardess, who came over.

"Mrs. Rule? We've had a message that you are being met at the gate. We'd like you to be first off the plane, please."

"Fine," Rule replied, rising from her seat. She winked at Will. "Better pretend you don't know me for a while," she said.

He pulled her down and kissed her. "Buy you dinner tonight?"

She squeezed back. "If I'm a free woman tonight, *I'm* buying. I owe you one, remember?"

He grinned. "I'll book at Maison Blanche. Black-tie?"

"You bet." She turned and followed the stewardess, steadying herself as the plane rolled to a stop at the gate. The door came open, and a man in a blue suit stepped aboard.

"Mrs. Rule?" he asked, showing her an ID card. "I'm Special Agent Madison, FBI. Will you come with me, please?"

The agent walked her through immigration and guided her to the SAS first-class lounge. As she came through the door, she was forcibly struck by the weight of a small boy.

"Mom, oh Mom!" Peter yelled, drawing chuckles from the other occupants of the lounge. "I'm so glad to see you! Where have you been?"

Rule hugged the boy for dear life, then held him back

to look at him. "I'll tell you all about that later," she said. "In the meantime, here's something for you." She pulled a wrapped package from her carryall.

The boy tore at the wrappings. "A camera!" he cried. "Oh, boy, how did you know I wanted one?"

"A lucky guess," she said. "Listen, Peter, I want you to have a seat over there for a little while. You read the instructions for the camera while I have a short meeting; then you and I will be leaving together, all right?"

"Listen," he said in a loud whisper. "Dad's pretty mad about something. I don't think he liked getting up so early, and he's pretty nervous, too. I never saw him so worried."

"Thanks for telling me, love. Now you go and have a seat, okay? I think I see some sweet rolls over there, too, and some orange juice."

The boy bounded off with his camera.

Agent Madison indicated a closed door. "Conference room, there," he said.

"Has it been swept?" she asked.

"We think of everything." The agent grinned.

"I'd like you and your partner inside, please. There'll be an arrest to be made. You'll hear the evidence."

Madison beckoned to another man sitting in the lounge. "This is Special Agent Ward. Ward, we're going to the meeting. There'll be an arrest."

"Are you armed?" Rule asked.

"Yes, ma'am," Madison replied.

"Good," Rule said, "let's go." She opened the door and walked into the room, followed by the two agents. The director sat at the opposite end of a small conference table, with Alan Nixon on his right and Ed Rawls on his left. Simon stood to one side behind the director, leaning against the wall. Rule sat down at the end of the table. The FBI men stood behind her.

"All right, Mrs. Rule, let's have it," the director said.

"Good morning, gentlemen," Rule said. "Thank you for getting up so early to meet me."

"It wasn't by choice, Katharine," Nixon blurted. "Now let's get on with it."

Rule unsnapped the plastic briefcase she had placed on the table. "Gentlemen, by now you are aware that the Soviet Union attempted to launch an invasion of Sweden yesterday."

Simon spoke up. "We're getting all sorts of reports. We haven't put it all together yet."

Rule ignored him. "The invasion was planned and was to have been directed from a Soviet base known as Malibu, on the Latvian coast, at Liepaja, by a man named Majorov, once head of foreign operations for the KGB."

"Yes, yes, Katharine, we know all about your theory," Nixon said.

"It's no longer a theory, Alan," Rule replied, taking the stack of computer diskettes from her briefcase. "These represent all of the data stored on Malibu's computer—including all of the plans for the invasion. I assure you that the closest inspection will prove them to be genuine."

"How did you come by that?" Simon asked.

"Later, Simon," Rule said. "But I'll tell you now, these records also include the personal files of Majorov himself, and they are very revealing."

Simon came off the wall. "Kate, this is neither the time nor the place."

"On the contrary, Simon," she replied, "this is both the time and the place. Now shut up until I have finished." She was trying hard to keep her temper in check.

"Go on, Mrs. Rule," the director said.

"These personal files of Majorov's," Rule continued, "reveal that his plans for invading Sweden were greatly assisted by a mole in the Swedish Ministry of Defense, known as Seal. Seal's name is Sven Carlsson; he was Head of Chancery in the ministry until his arrest yesterday. I'm told he has been talking ever since."

Rule shifted her weight. A part of her was gloating, but she dreaded what had to come now. "The files also reveal that Majorov had a mole in the Central Intelligence Agency," she said, and paused. Her audience sat, frozen. "He was known as Ferret, and his name is not mentioned in the files. However, the files do give something of his history. He was a field agent in Stockholm in nineteen seventy and 'seventy-one, and there he met Majorov, who was serving as Head of Station in the Soviet Embassy, under the name of Firsov. There, he was suborned by Majorov—how, I don't quite know, yet. Considering who the man is and his record in the Agency, it is hard to fathom." She turned slightly and addressed Ed Rawls. "What was it, Ed, a woman? Blackmail? Certainly not ideology."

The whole room turned to look at Rawls, who was pale, but said nothing.

"To continue," Rule said, "Rawls also met Malakhov in Stockholm, only briefly, he contends, but two years ago, when Malakhov suddenly decides to turn in New York, who does he demand to debrief and run him? Ed Rawls, of course, whose career during the previous ten years, aided by feeds of information from Majorov, has been a shining one. It was all abroad, though, and Majorov wanted a mole at Langley, so he fed us Malakhov, and Ed Rawls held the spoon."

Simon had taken a seat and was holding his head in his hands.

Rule took a deep breath and continued. "Then, Ed, because of his spectacular career and great work with Malakhov, gets appointed deputy to Deputy Director for Operations, and he is poised to empty the Agency's files into Majorov's in-basket. Then, he makes two discoveries. First, an extremely stupid disinformation operation called Snowflower, which was designed to make the Soviets think the Swedes were going to join NATO, and which was all too successful, since it gave Majorov the initial impetus for his invasion plan. Second, he discovered that I was onto Majorov, and that nobody believed me. Then he really got clever."

"Are you guessing at all of this, Rule?" the director suddenly asked. "Or is this more of your theories?"

Suddenly, Ed Rawls came alive. "Shut up and listen, you great fucking oaf," he said to the director. "There's a pro talking. You might learn something."

"Thank you, Ed," Rule said. "Rawls saw what a time bomb Snowflower was, since he knew about Majorov's invasion plans, and when he heard about my theories at the meeting in your office, Simon, he knew he had found the fuse. Ed began encouraging me, while, no doubt, bad-mouthing me to you lot behind my back. He fed me Malakhov, who whetted my appetite. He sent me an old military journal in the interoffice mail, which had Majorov's appointment announcement; he really kept me going. Of course, he planned to see to it that I would fail, but after the invasion of Sweden had come off, he would have seen that the press got wind of Snowflower and of my valiant, but failed, attempt to get somebody to warn the Swedes. The Agency would have been skewered both ways—the Agency, arguably, had caused the Soviets to take steps to defend their Baltic flank in the first place, and the Agency also would have failed to warn the Swedes of what was about to descend upon them."

Now the director was looking pale. He motioned Alan Nixon to pour him a glass of water from the flask on the table.

"So," Rule continued, "had the invasion come off, the press would have conducted the largest roasting of a government agency in the history of the nation. Simon, of course, would be out on his ass for dreaming up Snowflower, and who would his replacement be? Why, his deputy, Ed Rawls, of course, who was in Eastern Europe when Snowflower was born, and whose hands would, therefore, be clean. Then, Mr. Director, assuming you survived until the president's term expired—which would be doubtful—a new president might be leary of appointing another political crony and, instead, opt for a professional. Who would then be in line for the job of Director of Central Intelligence? Ed Rawls, of glowing repute, hero of the Malakhov defection." Rule stopped and poured herself some water. "Everybody got the picture, now?"

Everybody was staring at the table, except Ed Rawls, who was staring at the FBI men.

Rule looked over her shoulder. "All right, Agent Madison," she said, "you can arrest Mr. Rawls, now." She took a Xerox copy of Majorov's files from her briefcase and thumped it onto the table. "That will be everything you'll need to back the complaint. I'll give you a corroborating statement later. You'll need to make an immediate arrest of Malakhov, too, before he has time to bolt. Ed, you'll give them Malakhov's new address, won't you?"

Rawls nodded. He seemed unable to speak.

"Mr. Rawls?" Madison said.

Ed Rawls stood up slowly. Madison and Ward put him against the wall and began searching him.

"Look for a pill or a needle," Rule said. "I want him alive to stand trial."

The agents continued their search for another three minutes. "He's clean," Madison said finally, pulling Rawls's hands behind his back and snapping on handcuffs. "Let's go, Mr. Rawls."

As they started out of the room, Rawls stopped where Rule was sitting. "Katie," he said, "I'm sorry about that business at Stockholm airport. I had no idea, I swear."

Rule stood up, drew back, and hit him as hard as she could with her open hand. Rawls, in spite of his bulk, was knocked reeling into Agent Ward.

"Now get him out of here," Rule said, her voice shaking with anger. The others were on their feet. "Sit down, all of you," she barked. "I'm not through, yet." They shuffled back to their seats.

"Now, gentlemen, we get down to how much of this becomes public."

"Katharine," Simon broke in, "you can't still be serious about going to the press."

"You're goddamned right, I am," Rule said. "The only thing open to discussion, now, is how much the press gets. This is what I propose. Mr. Director, when we leave this room, you make a short statement, to the gathered press outside, that a high official of the Central Intelligence Agency has been arrested and will be charged with spying for the Soviet Union. There'll be a firestorm of press coverage and congressional investigation, of course, but the Agency can weather that in time. What the Agency can't weather is the continuing presence of any of you three gentlemen."

"*What?*" Alan Nixon almost screamed. "You expect us to leave?"

"I don't see how any of you can possibly stay, Alan. I not only expect you to leave," Rule said. "I insist. You, Simon"—she pointed a finger—"have hatched, without congressional approval, a harebrained operation that nearly resulted in the Soviet conquest of eight and a half million Swedes; and of all the thousands of personnel of the CIA, you chose the biggest traitor since Benedict Arnold as your deputy. That won't stand scrutiny in the Congress or in the press."

She pointed at Nixon. "You, Alan, colluded with the Deputy Director for Operations to conceal the existence of Snowflower and to thwart my efforts to expose the

Soviets' plans, even to the extent of threatening me with transfer or internal investigation. After a congressional investigation, you'd go on the same day as Simon."

She pointed at the director. "You, sir, approved and encouraged the Snowflower operation, and since the day you were appointed, you have consistently moved to cripple the acquisition of human intelligence, as opposed to the use of high technology. You're a walking hazard to the American intelligence services you direct. If any of this airs, your friend, the president, will fire you out of hand."

Rule stopped talking, and nobody else seemed to want to talk. The director had turned an ashen color, and Rule thought he might be genuinely ill until he spoke.

"You will accept nothing else but our resignations, Mrs. Rule?" he asked, and she was touched by the pleading in his voice.

"I'm offering you your reputations, all of you," Rule said, "and your pensions. Get out within thirty days—on any excuse you like—or everything goes to the press. And I hope you will believe me when I tell you that I have taken all the necessary steps for this to be made public if, for any reason at all, I should be unable to do it myself."

"I believe you, Katharine," Simon said quietly.

"I want your answers now, before you meet the press," Rule said.

One by one, the three men nodded. "All right, Mrs. Rule," the director said. "You've won. You have my word. I'll go within a month."

"So will I," Nixon said.

446 / Stuart Woods

"All right, Katharine," Simon sighed. "But what about you? You don't really believe you have a career left, do you? Nobody likes a whistle-blower but the press. Nobody in the Agency will ever trust you again."

"Maybe, maybe not, Simon," she replied. "In any case, I'll be resigning, myself, when I've seen the three of you go."

The director stood up. "Unless you have anything else, let's get this over with."

"I've nothing else," Rule replied. "I'll leave you to deal with the press."

She waited for the three men to precede her, then walked into the lounge. "Come on, Peter," she called to the boy. "Let's go meet Will."

"Is Will here, too? Oh, boy!"

"Yes, and we've got to catch the shuttle home."

"Well, it won't be as much fun as the helicopter," Peter replied.

On the nearly empty shuttle to Washington, while Peter slept in her lap, Rule told Will about the meeting she had just left.

"You know," she said, "sometimes winning isn't all that much fun. Careers destroyed, a monumental shake-up at the Agency in the wake of Ed Rawls's arrest—it's going to be a god-awful mess."

"I like you for not gloating," Lee said, "but maybe the Agency needed something like this. It's bound to be a better place when the dust has settled. And you'll have done it."

"Thanks," she said. "And listen, when the Swedes are

through talking to the press, and when you've kept your promise to talk to that reporter, it's going to make a lot of noise, you know. It's just the sort of thing that might make a candidate for the Senate race in Georgia stand out from the pack."

"That's a thought," Will said. "Let's see how it goes. How would you feel about being a Senator's wife?"

"Let's see how it goes," Rule replied, squeezing his hand.

"Kate," Will said, "you told them you were going to resign from the Agency. Are you really going to do that?"

Katharine Rule smiled broadly. "Let's see how it goes," she said.

ACKNOWLEDGMENTS

In roughly chronological order of their contributions, the author wishes to express his great gratitude to: **Richard Cohen**, for thinking of me when he had an idea and for his efforts on behalf of this project; **Ebbe Carlsson**, for his friendship, his enthusiasm, his warm hospitality in Stockholm, and his many introductions to invaluable contacts (and my apologies for naming two such unfortunate characters after him); **Admiral Sir Ian Easton**, Royal Navy (ret.), for his insight into strategic considerations and his good company; **Richard Clurman**, for unearthing vital information with such blinding speed, and for his friendship; **Stafan Skott** for background and for introducing me to my first Russian; **Clive Egleton** for introductions; **Colonel Jonathan Alford**, Royal Army (ret.), of the Institute of Strategic Studies in London, for listening to me without laughing and helping me bolster my theories; **Captain John Coote**, Royal Navy (ret.), for technical advice, useful chats about submarines and introductions; **Jan Henrik and Babro Schauman** for my first close look at the Baltic and for generous hospitality in Helsinki; **Ewan Hedman**, for his contacts and kindness in Stockholm; **Raymond Benson**, Counselor for Public Affairs at the U.S. Embassy in Moscow, for invaluable background, contacts, and experiences in that city, and **Shirley Benson**, for her kind hospitality and for all the caviar I could eat; **Lyndon Allin** and **Nicholas Burakow** of the American Consulate in Leningrad, for introductions and hours of fascinating conversation, and **Mary Ann Allin** for her warm hospitality and equally good conversation; **Anne Eaton** for her kind introductions in the Soviet Union; **Tom Susman**, for sharing his intimate knowledge of Washington; **John Packs** of Senator Edward Kennedy's office, for his help with arrangements in the Soviet Union; **Commander Richard Compton-Hall**, Royal Navy (ret.), director of the Submarine Museum at Portsmouth Naval Station, for sharing his intimate knowledge of submarines in general and minisubs in particular; **Wendell Rawls, Jr.**, for introductions and encouragement; **Bo Erikson** of the Swedish Ministry of Defense, for nonclassified information on Swedish defenses; **David Binder** of the Washington Bureau of the *New York Times*, for sharing his knowledge of American intelligence institutions and for introductions; **Eric Swenson**, my editor, for his continuing interest and support of my work, and for his patience, good humor, and warm friendship; **Judy Tabb Woods**, who married me in the middle of all this, and who nurtured and protected my peace of mind while I finished it. And to anyone whom I may have stupidly forgotten.

Finally, I must give my greatest thanks to those people I cannot name for fear of causing them embarrassment or worse: in Sweden, members of parliament, of the foreign ministry, of the defense ministry, of naval intelligence, of the counterintelligence department of the State Security Police, and of the executive branch of the Swedish government; in the Soviet Union, those refuseniks, ordinary citizens, and high officials who, no doubt without realizing it, gave a writer background, color, and a taste of real life in their country—and especially those who were reputed to be and might even have been KGB; in the United States, to those CIA contacts, loyalists all, who gave me a peek at practice and procedure and let me know what about their organization they love and what makes them angry.

All of the above people share whatever success this book may achieve, but none of the responsibility for the manner in which I may have distorted, ignored, or disagreed with their views in order to tell a story.

AUTHOR'S NOTES

For the purposes of this book, I have driven from office the President of the United States, the Director of Central Intelligence and all his employees, the representatives from Georgia in the United States Senate, the Prime Minister of Sweden, his Minister of Defense and other employees of that ministry. In their places I have substituted persons of my own choosing, which is the constitutional prerogative of novelists. Names of characters were chosen from the ranks of friends and scrambled, or simply made up, and are not intended to represent any real person. Anybody who thinks he is characterized in this book is wrong, guilty of wishful thinking, or crazy.

This manuscript was written on two personal computers, an AT&T 6300 with a Peachtree Peripherals hard disk (using WordStar software, which I do not recommend to anyone), and a PolyMorphic 8813, an ancient, but honorable, machine with its own proprietary word processing software. Frank Stearns Associates of Vancouver, Washington, transferred the material on PolyMorphic disks to IBM-compatible disks. The copyeditor's corrections were entered on the computer, and the finished manuscript was supplied on disk to the typesetters.

Also Available from
New York Times Bestselling Author

STUART WOODS

The Will Lee Novels

Chiefs

Woods' Edgar® Award-winning novel spans fifty
years of racial tension, politics, and murder in the
small Southern town of Delano, Georgia—where a
depraved killer claims his innocent victims even as
three very different generations of policemen
seek to stop him.

Run Before the Wind

Restless and dissatisfied, Will Lee dreams of
shipbuilding and sailing on crystal-blue waters. Then
an explosion of senseless violence drags the young
American drifter into a lethal game of terror and
revenge. Now Will must run for his life from a
bloody past that is not his own.

Capital Crimes

When a prominent conservative politician is killed
inside his lakeside cabin, authorities have no suspect
in sight. And two more seemingly different deaths
might be linked to the same murderer. From a quiet
D.C. suburb to the corridors of power to a deserted
island hideaway in Maine, Will Lee, his CIA director
wife, Kate, and the FBI will track their man, set a
trap—and await the most dangerous kind of quarry,
a killer with a cause to die for...

Also Available from
New York Times Bestselling Author

STUART WOODS

The Stone Barrington Novels

L.A. Dead

Cold Paradise

The Short Forever

Dirty Work

Reckless Abandon

Two Dollar Bill

Dark Harbor

Fresh Disasters

Shoot Him If He Runs

Hot Mahogany

Available wherever books are sold or at penguin.com